THE KING'S SHADOW

M. L. FARB

Carry on.

M L Farb

*For Kezia. May the heroes in these pages
have even a shadow of your courage.*

CONTENTS

PART I

1

HALAVANT

Palace, Fairhaven, Lansimetsa
Janúar 13th
Three months after the Slave War

Snik. Metal sliding against metal pulled me from a shallow sleep. Another *snik*. The window latch clicked, and the night air pushed in, along with a weak moonlight.

Should I call for my guards?

A dark form slipped in the window.

No. It would pinpoint my position.

I tensed my body and waited.

He padded across the room to the king's canopied bed and pushed aside one heavy curtain. His back was to me.

Now! I sprang from my low cot beside the king's bed, wrapping my arms around his neck. Foolish choice; my crippled hands were useless to grip his throat.

The assassin drew a knife and slashed. His blade bounced along my hand brace toward my unprotected arm.

"Cat's claws!" I yelped, leaping off his back before the tip broke skin.

The assassin spun, his knife creating a deadly arc.

I rolled to the floor, my dark nightclothes hopefully making me less visible.

He lunged.

No, the clothes weren't helping. I thrust one hand into the path of the knife. The blade skipped off my hand brace and buried itself in the oak floor.

He slipped out a second knife.

This assassin came better prepared than the one in the throne room. I kicked his hand. The knife spun over my head and thunked against the wall. I'd need to have the floor and wall attended to in the morning. Couldn't they leave less damage?

He backed up, and his hand flickered to his belt.

Not a third one! I lunged to my feet and tackled him as the third knife left his hand. The blade scored my left shoulder, and he went down gasping. I'd imprinted my head in his stomach. Didn't feel great for my head, either. I slashed my right hand sideways at his throat, my brace catching him across the windpipe.

His gasping changed to a high-pitched wheeze. He couldn't die, not before questioning.

"Guards!"

My door rattled with repeated thumps—noises I'd ignored in my wrestle with the assassin.

"Sir! Open the door!" My night-guard boomed.

I'd locked it. Like always. The assassin lay under me, stunned for the moment. I rolled to my feet and gave him a swift kick to the side. That would stun him for a moment more. I'd been on the receiving end of that move more than once.

A solid thunk shook the door. They were trying to batter it down? Ridiculous men. It would take more than a man's bulk to break the bar lock. I placed my braced hands on either side of a metal rod and slid the bar sideways, just before another thunk shook the door. Turning the doorknob was another question. I couldn't grasp it well with paralyzed hands.

"It's unlocked! Open the door!"

The assassin rose to his feet, one hand clutching at his throat and the other wrapped around his midsection.

The door vibrated with another thunk. Didn't they hear me? "Use the doorknob!" I pressed my braced hands around the doorknob and rotated my whole upper body sideways to get enough twisting motion. What I'd pay to have wrist movement again.

The door crashed open, spilling lamplight and two guards into the room. I tumbled to the floor as the assassin flew over me and into the two armed men. Swords made short work of the assassin. I looked away as my stomach rebelled.

"Sir. Sir." A deep voice penetrated my nausea. Gent, my giant-blooded guard, kneeled beside me.

He placed a hand on my stinging shoulder, then jerked away. "Get the king's physician now!" he bellowed.

"No!" I held my arm out to stop him and hissed at the movement. "Get my brother. It's only a scratch."

"But, Sir?"

"Do as your king commands." I hated using that line. But it worked.

Hoft, my other guard, charged away to get Yosyph.

Gent pulled a clean handkerchief from my bedside drawer and pressed it to my shoulder. "Sir, you must stop locking your door. How are we to guard you if you won't let us in?"

"I'll do what I feel is best," I muttered.

"You trusted me to stand watch over you when we marched against the queen. You slept under the trees with no locked door between us or the thousands of other men who followed you. Why don't you trust us now?"

Why? Who could I trust other than a handful: Yosyph, Galliard, the Poet, Katrin, Elise? I needed those men to help rebuild the kingdom instead of standing guard over me. And the women? They weren't warriors. Everyone else was suspect. Anyone else could try to stab me in the back. Or poison me, like that demon-spawn Fredrick.

My half-brother slipped into my room. His gray clothes, dark skin, and black hair made him a blur in the dim room. At least I had Yosyph to share the burden.

I half-grinned a greeting.

He returned a slight frown. "Gent, light the lamps." The room brightened as Yosyph untied the lacing of my nightshirt and pulled it from my left shoulder.

I sucked in my breath as he fingered the split flesh, then gritted my teeth as he dabbed astringent alcohol on it. But when he pulled out a needle and thread, I had to speak. "It's not that bad. Just paste it together like you did last time."

"If you don't want me tending it, I'll call the physician or Elise." He spoke softly and with level emotion. If I didn't know better, I'd have tried to argue.

"At least." I gritted my teeth. "We can—" I moaned, "talk about." I bellowed and pulled away as the needle pierced the skin close to my neck.

"Gent, hold him."

Gent gripped my arms.

I could have moved easier, and been more comfortable, if they'd chained me to the floor. I should have let them get Elise. She'd have been gentler. But then she'd worry and get a royal physician to tend to me. Yosyph understood my reluctance to trust the physicians.

Yosyph snipped the thread and dabbed my wound with a numbing salve.

"Why didn't you numb it before sewing me together?"

"It causes increased bleeding."

"I think you like to see me squirm in pain."

"Little brother, I don't have to do anything to see you in pain. You bring it upon yourself. Why did you lock the guards out?"

"I just need a better lock on the window."

"Or a room with no windows." A smile hinted on his grim face. "Maybe a tight cell in the dungeon. Just reverse the lock."

I whacked his arm with one of my braced hands. "Why does your humor only come out when you mock me?"

His face smoothed back to an emotionless mask. "I'm not mocking. If you can't even trust your personal guards, then you might as well imprison yourself in a cell."

"Do *you* trust anyone? You disappear into a shadow-walk whenever others are around."

Yosyph grasped me under the right forearm and pulled me to standing. "I am not the king, but his shadow. My role is to watch, listen, and protect. Yours is to lead, trust, and rule." Yoseph looked up and quoted me verbatim from three months previous—before multiple assassins tried to take my life. "You told me, '*The people can do great things, noble things. Can't we trust them? Can't we teach them? If they learn to govern themselves, to choose their own leaders—good leaders—to help us make decisions, then our land shouldn't fall again.*'"

I sat on the edge of my canopied bed. "I still want that. I want to trust the people. I want to create a ruling where I lead while being supported by leaders chosen by the people—both common and noble. But—"

That was impossible. I was too radical for the noble class and too cautious for the commoners. Crops rotted in the fields because of the Slave War and early rains. Children and families

7

were starving because I couldn't get grain reserves to them. The royal granaries were already near empty, sold off previous to the war by my reckless mother to purchase the men and means to enslave a third of my people. We'd stopped the enslavement, but how would we keep the people alive until the next harvest?

Yosyph watched as I struggled through the problem, again. I'd argued it over with him at least once a day for the last week, ever since we received the first reports of children dying of empty stomachs. He wanted us to demand the grain from those noblemen who had reserves, stating the common people grew the grain and they should have it. I wanted less drastic measures. I'd offered to pay them from the royal treasury and have them sell me the grain. Delays and grumbles later, still nothing.

Even before changing laws, I had to get food to my people. Did it mean marching against my noblemen and taking their barns of plenty?

Yosyph touched my non-wounded shoulder. "Halavant, you should sleep."

"And you should be king. Wed Katrin, for she rightly prefers you, and rule this people."

Yosyph sucked in his breath as if I'd punched him. He flickered out and into sight three times, his face etched with pain. I winced along with him. At the end of the Slave War, his god blessed him so when he buried his emotions too deeply, he was pulled into the shadow-realm and experienced intense pain. It seemed more a curse than a blessing. But there were many things I didn't understand about Yosyph's god.

Yosyph solidified and gripped the bedpost. "I'll not marry her. And I'll not rule."

I jumped to my feet. "But you've courted her for three months, and she lights up every time she sees you. Why, if you're not going to marry her?"

"Things have changed. I'll tell her in the morning, she

8

should marry you, and soon—" a wry smile hinted at the corner of his mouth, "—so she can keep watch over you at nighttime when you won't let the guards."

Things had changed? Why? A warmth bloomed over the question. Katrin would marry me.

Yosyph pushed me back to sit on the bed. "Rest. We'll talk in the morning and figure out how to get food to our people." He turned to leave and stopped. "How did you defeat the assassin?"

My grin spread. "I used your lessons in Lausatök. He didn't expect the commoner's wrestling skills from a king. Though I gave him an illegal blow to the windpipe."

He nodded, "Good. In self-defense nothing is illegal. I'll practice with you more, when your shoulder has healed."

I locked my window, left my door unlocked, and lay under my heavy down comforter, trusting my guards wouldn't knife me in the night. Tomorrow, I'd again ask Katrin's hand in marriage.

2

YOSYPH

Palace, Fairhaven, Lansimetsa
Janúar 13th

I SLIPPED OUT of Halavant's room and *quawlaared,* becoming invisible. Coldness embraced me as I shed my emotions and entered the realm of shadow-walking. The shed emotions glowed in inky ribbons of color—colors that only another in the shadow realm could see.

The hall ended at the library. I stumbled against the low threshold and caught myself against the library door frame. The numbness was worse, though still just in my feet. How quickly would it progress to my hands, legs, arms, and finally my lungs? After a week of stumbles, I'd recognized it for what it was. Another five years before I joined my father? Did shadow-walking exacerbate the situation?

Interesting questions to ponder in the shadow state. I avoided them when open to emotion.

Tomorrow, I'd release Katrin from my offer of marriage. It was only right. I'd keep Halavant safe and help him establish a kingdom ruled by law and not whim. Then, come what may, my people would be safe, and I could rest.

I lit a lamp and scanned the book-stuffed room. I must study —learn everything about the ruling of the desert council. They'd lived in peace for a thousand years, long before my father's kingdom formed.

Leather-bound tomes lined the walls to my right. I pulled out *Kings of Lansimetsa* and tucked it under one arm. Stacks of loosely bound papers sat on a high table where I'd left them from the night before. I plopped the leather tome next to them and opened it to the front. A long line of dates ran inside the cover: births, coronations, marriages, deaths. At the bottom a neat hand inked:

Luukas, 12th king of Lansimetsa.
Born: 295th year of Lansimetsa's rising from the sea.
Crowned: 311th year. Defended country against Carani invasion.
Married: 315th year. To Tanyeshna, princess of the Kishkarish. She
was lost to the sea, 319th year.
Married: 320th year. To Analiese, baroness of Conborner.
Died: 321st year. Died of slow wasting in his twenty-fifth year. His
reign was glorious.

I dipped my quill in the desk's inkwell and inked in a new set of lines.

Halavant, 13th king of Lansimetsa
Born: 321st year of Lansimetsa's rising from the sea, and the 1036th
year of the Kishkarish peace.
Crowned: 338th year. Saved his people from slavery.
Married:

Ink dripped from the quill as I paused. Katrin would marry

him. The official chronicler could ink in that line, when we found one again.

I set down the quill and thumbed through the loosely bound papers until I found the feather. Swirls of yellowed words flowed across the page. Desert script. Mother's hand.

My only-heart-song grows worse. I must support him when he comes to bed, for his legs won't bear his weight. I am still barren. We must pass the power of the king to the people before he becomes too weak to rule. If the people would accept the laws of the desert, then we could establish a council. Luukas still hopes for a child, and that hope keeps him from considering my plea.

I record my hopes on these pages for a peaceful, people-led government. And when he is ready, I will share it with him. In a month, when the summer storms die down, I will visit the Sage of Truven. Perhaps he can lift this curse on my womb.

Even if we have a child, I would not burden him with ruling Lansimetsa by himself. Too many wars, too many deaths come from this ill-conceived ruling. Not that it is Luukas' fault. It is the way of most kingdoms to rule such. I miss my land, my people. Yet I would die without my king.

The pages were filled with her words of the council that ruled by a set code of laws rather than whims.

The library door swung open and a tall, slender figure entered with a second lamp—Elise. She was Halavant's only trusted healer, aside from me, though I was a novice compared to her. She reminded me of my mother. Although one came from a moist island and the other from the dry desert, they were similar in their long black hair, quiet demeanor, and sharp mind. She scanned the room, her eyes passing over the table where I stood, then headed to a wall of books behind me.

It would startle her to see moving pages. When she was behind me, I pulled in my emotions. Reds, blues, greens and other colors slipped from the surrounding shadows and grated into place under my skin like sandpaper. I clenched my jaw as the emotions settled. *Please God,* I signed, *help me carry the weight of these new emotions. It is becoming too much again.*

A balm of peace flowed over me, and the pain eased slightly. I couldn't expect more for ignoring His direction to be honest with my emotions and not carry so many alone. But I couldn't tell Halavant yet. And Katrin? It would be best if I faded from her life.

Elise gasped. She clutched a medical tome and stared at me.

"Good morning, Elise."

She pressed a hand to her chest. "Yosyph, you have a twisted sense of humor to greet me so."

"I can't feel humor while *quawlaared*."

"You can feel it now you are visible. And I don't enjoy the scare. What are you doing here in the middle of the night?"

"Same as you—studying."

"So you are the reason Halavant has stacks of books in his rooms. Every time I go to treat his hands, he's reading some dense tome or another. You should let him rest. He can't change a nation over one winter, let alone one year."

His lack of sleep was due more to worry and watchfulness than reading. I'd study elsewhere.

I signed a prayer heavenward, *Please God, help me let go of Katrin and bless my efforts to create a stable government.*

3

ELISE

I DIDN'T MIND when Yosyph appeared in a lighted room. But in the flickering library lamplight at night? I shivered as he gathered a bundle of papers. He was the fabled Yorel and the shadow demon who'd saved Halavant's life at the end of the Slave War. His appearance in the library left me recalling bedtime tales of less kindly shadow demons.

He was a tall, leanly muscled man. His black hair curled across his forehead and at his neck. Lamplight flickered over his tattooed left hand. Bards sang of his tattoo and how it showed his adventure through the King's Trial, but his gray, long-sleeved tunic covered the rest of the inked story. His skin was desert-toned. Only his green eyes and his square jaw showed his shared heritage with his brother, the king.

He strode from the room, his movements off. How? What was different? He reached the door and stumbled, catching the door frame. The Yorel, stumbling? Why?

A large tome lay open on the table. Fresh ink gleamed near the bottom of the left page.

Halavant, 13th king of Lansimetsa

Above it stretched the line of the kings back to the first.

Kamal, 1st king, died at the ripe age of seventy-eight
— 2nd king, died at eighty

All old ages until the sixth king, then the words slow wasting appeared.

— 7th king, died at fifty-six of battle wounds and slow wasting
— 8th king, fifty-two of slow wasting
— 9th king, twenty-seven, in battle with the Carani
— 10th king, forty-seven of slow wasting
— 11th king, thirty-four of slow wasting
Luukas, 12th king, died at age twenty-five of slow wasting

The stumble. Yosyph. And then Halavant? When would their death dates be inked into this book? Mother told of the slow wasting taking King Luukas. She never said it took the previous kings.

I ran after Yosyph. *Please don't let him disappear again.*

The palace echoed like a maze of caves. Long halls branched into cavernous rooms. Tall ceilings echoed my pattering footsteps. My lamp lit a small circle around me.

His room was near Halavant's. A single guard stood in front of his door.

"Please," I panted, "has the Yorel returned to his room?"

The guard smiled. "Have you joined him in his night roaming? He's just returned with an arm full of papers. I doubt he'd want a visitor."

"Please, I must speak with him."

The door opened, and Yosyph stepped out. "What is it, Elise?" His deep voice rumbled against me, even in its quietness.

"The tome, the dates, slow wasting."

Yosyph nodded and motioned for me to enter his room. When he'd shut the door, he moved his hands in some language I had yet to learn.

"I saw you stumble. You have the slow wasting."

Yosyph nodded again.

"I can help. I'll find a cure."

Yosyph motioned for me to take a seat. "After six generations of this plaguing my father's line, they haven't found a cure. There isn't one."

"It comes earlier and earlier each time. What will you do?"

"Help create a rule of law before the line of kings dies. We need a law that will hold future rulers accountable."

"When will you tell Halavant?"

Yosyph flickered out of and into sight once. "Maybe he won't develop it."

"Fool." I clapped my hand over my mouth as soon as the words slipped out.

"I am, and many worse things. You may speak openly with me."

I gathered my thoughts. "I will search for a cure, and you must tell Halavant."

"He carries enough weight. I'll not add this."

"And when you can't hide the fact of your illness?"

"I still have time. My father was seeking a cure in the desert when he met my mother. And he still lived five years after. It gives us enough time to create a new government and see it settled. I'll tell Halavant when necessary."

Stubborn as his brother. I'd start my research that night. I stood to leave.

Yosyph reached out his hands and clasped one of mine in his two. "Don't speak of this to anyone. The nobles need no more reason to rebel."

I shook my head and sniffed. I'd give him a week before I told Halavant. He needed to know. Why did this illness come to the line of the kings, to the Yorel, and someday to Halavant? I sniffed again. "May the gods bless your effort to make a stable government."

Yosyph fixed his gaze on me. "And may God bless you in your search."

~

I STEPPED onto a west-facing balcony and gazed over the three-walled city as the rising sun lit the snow-dusted farmland beyond the cliff's shadow, then the outer wall. It would be hours before the cliff's shadow allowed the sun's warmth on this balcony. The cliff protected the palace, but I'd rather be back on my father's farm where I felt the first rays of light. Especially after last night's discovery.

I took one more breath of brisk air and shook off the weariness of a short night, then returned to my room to prepare for the day. I packed herbs and bandages into my woven satchel and ventured into the halls. Halavant would be waiting for me to attend to his hands.

As I approached Halavant's chambers, Yosyph fell into step beside me. His tread was even and firm, as if his weakness of last night was only a nightmare.

Two guards stood outside the king's chambers. One watched us approach while the other kept scanning the halls. Both were new.

"Permission to tend to the king's hands," I said.

The one watching us held out his hand. "I'll search your bag first."

This was also new. He pawed through my healer's bag, unrolling my bandages and sniffing at my ointments. I'd have to sanitize everything. He handed back my bag and stepped aside. He didn't ask Yosyph to hand over the sword tucked in his belt. Why hadn't I earned that trust?

"His Majesty is waiting for you, honored Yorel." The guard bowed, and Yosyph cringed.

Served him right for scaring me in the library.

We entered a room bright with yellows and whites. Halavant sat at a desk spread with parchments. The light reflected off his short golden hair, the tips still bleached from the time before he'd left the palace. It had grown long enough to cover the scar from his head injury. His face had filled out since I helped tend him at our farmhouse, when I thought him crazy. Maybe he still was. He was trying to change the entire system of ruling the kingdom.

Halavant stood and extended one braced hand toward Yosyph. "Good. You are here. Now we just need Katrin and we can start." The light and his green leather jerkin highlighted his green eyes, filled with weariness, determination, and more than a hint of stubbornness. I missed his laughing eyes. They'd been rare since the war.

I unbuckled his right hand brace. "Start what?" I'd never been part of their meetings.

Halavant winced as I slipped off the brace. His fingers curled into rigid claws. Feeling had returned to his hands, but not motion.

He looked away from his hands. "You can leave as soon as you've tended to my hands." He paused and smiled. "Or you can stay. I doubt you'd find the conversation pleasant. We are trying to decide what to do about Duke Pulska, and how to persuade him to sell some of his grain reserves to feed the people of his dukedom."

I rubbed salve into his palm, the thick muscles already atrophying. "And why is Katrin part of it?"

Halavant laughed tightly. "She's persuasive with men."

"And you let her?" After everything he went through for her, he was letting her ply her charms on other men?

"It wasn't my choice. She'd have tried on her own to persuade every nobleman to accept our changes to the government. This is the only way to at least know what she is doing and keep her safe, short of locking her in the palace."

Yosyph's bass voice startled me. "She never goes alone."

I'd forgotten Yosyph was here with us. He was so silent he disappeared even when he wasn't shadow-walking. *So he shadowed her.*

The door opened, and in breezed Katrin. If Yosyph was a shadow and Halavant sunlight, then she was fire. Her hair curled about her face in tight ringlets and cascaded down her back in a red contrast to her blue, embroidered dress. I'd once seen her hair wet as she'd come from the women's baths—it stretched to her knees.

She plopped onto a couch. "Sorry to be late. Sir Egvar caught me in the hall. He could out-talk a crow. He blabbed that several of the nobles are going hunting this afternoon. They include the six hotheads we've been worried about. They'll have a few lady friends along for the ride."

Halavant scowled. "And you suggested you join them?"

"I am accurate with the throwing knife."

"How is Yosyph to follow you, if you are galloping around on horses?" Halavant yanked his hand from my grip and slapped the desk. It thudded like a dead weight. Papers scattered.

"He can ride my spare horse, the one to carry back my kills."

I took Halavant's right hand and re-braced it. Tending to him would be difficult today.

"Is Duke Pulska part of the party?" Yosyph asked.

Katrin giggled. "Amazingly so, though I don't know how they'll get his mountainous form onto a horse. You could follow us on foot at the speed we'll be going."

I pulled off Halavant's left hand brace and stopped. A ragged line split the leather, and the whalebone had a deep groove across it.

"Your Majesty." I held up the brace. "What did you do?"

Halavant looked at the brace and coughed. "You said you'd call me by my name."

"Halavant, what happened to your brace?" I enunciated each word.

Halavant coughed again and studied the floor. "I was practicing blocking weapons with my braces. They're like shields, and since I haven't figured out how to attach a sword at a moment's notice, I thought it a good skill to learn."

He was lying. I didn't like the emotion of worry, and it transformed to heat in my chest. "In your *practice*, did you take injury elsewhere?"

Halavant turned slightly to his left.

"Show me your left arm." I caught at it, but he backed toward Katrin.

Katrin jumped up from the couch and caught his left arm.

Halavant sucked in a breath through clenched teeth.

She pushed up his sleeve. Nothing. She released his arm. "Halavant, what happened last night?"

Halavant backed away from both Katrin and me. "Yosyph, help."

The corners of Yosyph's lips twitched. "You should tell them."

Halavant glared at him.

A hint of a smile broke through Yosyph's sternness. "A man climbed three stories to Halavant's window, picked the lock, and decided to practice knife fighting with a sleeping cripple. What he didn't expect was a quick-witted warrior. Halavant is an astute study in the art of Lausatök."

Lausatök? My uncles often competed in the town festival competitions of wrestling. It was a confusing combination of kicks, open palm strikes, choke holds, and throws—an ideal fighting style for Halavant. Who'd taught him?

Katrin eyes sparked. "You wrestled an armed man?"

Halavant stepped back. "He wasn't armed for long. I'm not hurt. And we have more important things to talk about."

I picked up the scored hand brace. "Like getting you stronger shields."

Katrin sat down with a laugh. "Very well, I'll let it go. Please let your guards fight the next nighttime petitioner."

Halavant let out a held breath. "You make sure Yosyph is with you before you meet Duke Pulska this morning."

Katrin turned to Yosyph. "What do I need to know?"

Yosyph stepped forward and stood stiff, his eyes not meeting hers. "Duke Pulska has recruited more men for his men-at-arms. He refuses to sell us his grain, even for royal coin. He's reinforcing the walls of his estate. None of this is against the law, but—"

Katrin finished. "He needs someone to reassure him he'll not lose his land and power to changes in the government."

"At least not all," Yosyph said.

Katrin snorted. "That is why I'll talk with him. You'd make him defensive and unreasonable with your blunt honesty."

Wasn't honesty the best way to win another's trust? I finished rubbing the herbal paste into Halavant's fingers, re-buckled his scored hand brace, and excused myself from the room. Thankfully, my place wasn't to rule. I'd make a mess. Besides, I had a work as important to do.

4

KATRIN

PALACE, Fairhaven, Lansimetsa
    Janúar 13th

YOSYPH WALKED beside me down a palace corridor, his face as impassive as a statue.

I hated to act like I didn't care for Yosyph, just so the nobles would trust me. It was all part of bringing a lasting peace to Lansimetsa. I wanted to openly hold Yosyph's hand when we walked, to whisper sweet nothings in view of everyone and let them gossip on what we said. Lasting peace better come soon, because, though I told Halavant and Yosyph they'd have to wait a year for me to decide, I already knew.

I knew the night he'd led me from the New Year's ball into the empty council room and sang *Dancing on the Docks* while he spun me in a slow dance. The night he first kissed me. We'd talked until dawn about us, our future. How much longer must I hide my feelings in public? At least I'd tell Yosyph and stop his anxious wait of not knowing whom I'd choose.

The hall was empty. I'd chance it. I reached out my hand and slipped my fingers through Yosyph's. A shiver of delight ran up my arm as my hand pressed against his cool palm. "Yosyph, I love you. I want to m—"

He jerked away from me, flickered into the shadow, out, and back into invisibility.

I reached into the space beside me to grab his hand or tunic. I found nothing. "Yosyph!"

"Katrin," this time his voice came from the air in front of me and was flatly emotionless. I hated that voice. "Things have changed. I cannot marry you. You should accept Halavant's proposal."

"Oooo!" I balled my fists. "No—you—don't. I don't know what happened, but we'll figure it out together. Come out of the shadow-walk."

"It wouldn't be wise." More of his flat tone.

I reached toward his voice.

The soft sound of leather retreated over stone. "Halavant is the best choice for you."

I leaped forward and again caught emptiness. "That's my choice to make!"

Silence.

What did he think when my words couldn't impact his emotions? He was beyond reasoning, hiding in the shadow-walk. "I'm not talking to you until you are ready to listen." I turned away.

"That is wise," he said.

"At least come out of the shadow."

"Duke Pulska will be at the fountain soon."

Impossible man. Duke Pulska could wait. I'd see him at the hunt this afternoon, and I was in no mood to *persuade* him with my charms. I liked using knives as weapons better. Less treacherous. Also less effective, unless I wanted to kill off every hesitant or rebellious nobleman. Considering I'd not even killed one man, it was better to use my charms. Of course, I couldn't use either on Yosyph. *Oooo! Impossible man. Why must he twist my heart into a knot?*

I stomped away from the fountain and Yosyph.

"Katrin." A stone could have spoken my name with more emotion.

"I'm not talking to you."

~

I COULDN'T EAT the midday meal. Bread stuck in my throat, and the wine soured on my tongue. I shoved the tray aside. Let my maid enjoy the food and add roundness to her bones.

She rushed forward to take the tray. "My lady, if you are not well enough to eat, I'll send a message that you'll not join the hunt."

I started unlacing my morning dress to change into my riding clothes. "I'm well enough now," I lied. "Plait my hair quickly. I shall not be late."

~

MY HORSE GLEAMED WITH SWEAT, even in the cold winter day, as I reined in beside the twin oaks that marked the entrance to the royal hunting grounds. Snow dusted the bare branches. It was mid-winter, and a hard one for hunger. Behind me, my *riderless* horse heaved in breaths. Yosyph was already shadow-walking when we mounted our horses half an hour before, and he'd only greeted me with a single word before we'd raced through Fairhaven to get to the hunt on time. Sometime, he'd have to come out of the shadow, and then he'd get a tongue lashing.

Ten mounted nobles, seven men and three ladies, turned their heads, their faces a mixture of amusement and disdain. A houndmaster stood next to his horse while twelve hounds played in the snow around him.

A nobleman dressed in dark furs pulled away from the group toward me. His face was classic Lansimetsian beauty: long nose, acorn-brown hair, piercing blue eyes. "Lady Katrin, we are so happy you made it. Duke Pulska said you were ill." He motioned to a man who dwarfed his knight's charger, his form sagging over and around the sides of the saddle. Poor horse.

So that is how the duke interpreted my apology note. "Sir Egvar, I am well enough. I needed to get out of the drafty castle and into the fresh openness. Shall we hunt? The sun will not walk backward for us."

Laughter tinkled from behind a slender hand. A woman my age raised her eyebrows, then turned to her companion.

Egvar nodded to the houndmaster.

The houndmaster lifted a small metal whistle. Two short notes pierced the air.

I half-raised my hands to cover my ears, and the woman laughed again. I forced my hands back to the reins. So what if I hadn't gone on hunts with hounds and whistles? She'd cower before what I'd been through.

The hounds stopped romping and gathered around him.

He blew a high note and a low note.

The hounds stiffened on the high note, and on the low note they scattered like children released from school. Most headed north into the royal forest, while some curved to the east and west. We trotted after the main group. If the others scented something, their baying would call us.

I pulled up near Duke Pulska. "I sincerely apologize for not meeting you this morning."

He frowned at me. "I doubt there is anything sincere about you."

I flashed him a teasing smile. "I'm a flighty young lady. Would you expect anything else?"

"No, but I dislike being left waiting. Don't do it again." He shifted in his saddle as the trotting jiggled him like the gel on cold meat.

"We have time now, and I'm a good listener, if you have something to say."

He looked off into the trees. "Just stay away from the imposter king. You broke off your engagement, so now break off your association. You are too lovely a prize to get ruined in what is coming."

Though his words were not a surprise, I still sucked in my breath. How soon? Would he trust me to slip more information? Not likely. I'd work on Egvar. He acted as if he had a chance of winning my affections. But first, to persuade the duke.

"Dear Duke Pulska." I coated my words in sweetness and swallowed my gag. "In all your greatness, will you spare a little wheat for those who lost their crops in the war?"

He grunted. "That's the imposter king's fault. Let the temple priests take care of them. I contribute my share to the gods' upkeep."

"The temple priests don't pay you for your contributions. Surely you could use more money in your coffers. Coin from the royal treasury is respected even as far as the Truvian Island and the Kishkarish desert. Think—fruit fresh off the ships in the middle of winter, a horse fine enough to match your commanding stature, jewelry for an adoring young woman."

A deep cough sounded behind me. I hid a smile. Even when he couldn't feel emotion, Yosyph loved and protected me.

Duke Pulska jerked his head around at the sound and scanned the snow-dusted trees.

"Bear?" I offered.

"The dogs should have scented him." He brought his horse to a stop and continued to scan the trees. We fell further behind.

"They would have scented any other danger, too."

He grunted and kicked his horse back to a trot. "I'll think about it. I have enough grain for my own purposes and enough extra to sell for gold."

I reached out and laid my hand on his arm. "You're a good man."

"No, but I will be a great one."

Baying split the air from in front of us and to our left.

Egvar turned in his saddle to face the rest of us. "We'll split up. I like the sound of the baying to the west. Go where you will." He turned his steed to the left and galloped away.

I followed. The pounding of many hooves over frozen ground died away while the rest continued northward. Soon, it was just the squeaking thud of four horses: Egvar's, mine, and our two kill carriers. The baying continued to draw us west. The trees thinned, and the snow thickened.

Ahead, three hounds snarled at a stag pinned against a steep hillside.

The stag leaped onto the slope and slid down. Its repeated attempts left a muddy trail through white.

A hound darted forward, snapping at the stag's rear leg.

The trapped animal whipped around, lowered its antlers, caught the dog under his belly, and threw him back.

The hound landed, whimpering. Red stained the surrounding snow.

Egvar drew his bow.

I removed a thin knife from my belt. Six other knives sat equal distance along my right side.

The other two hounds bayed and snarled but kept their distance.

The stag leaped up the hill again. It slid as an arrow slipped by its shoulder.

I flicked my knife. It sliced through the air and into the soft flesh behind the stag's forequarters.

"Well thrown." Egvar's voice came out in surprise and admiration.

The stag crumbled and slid down the slope as Egvar called back the hounds.

Egvar dismounted and ended the beast's struggle for life. "It's your kill. However, your extra horse looks weary. Shall I have mine carry it back for you?"

"No, my horse is plenty strong for it." Yosyph would have to walk home.

"Then your horse is like you. Stronger than it looks. Though you are much more beautiful and dangerous. Where did you learn to wield a knife?"

"Growing up near the desert had its own dangers."

He gutted the stag, then hefted it onto his shoulders, turning his dark furs darker with blood, and slung it over my spare horse, then lifted the wounded hound, draping it across his own spare horse.

The hound whimpered then growled, snapping his head around at the space behind him.

Yosyph, you didn't!

The hound snapped again and something dropped to the ground, indenting the already trampled snow.

The other two hounds sniffed, went rigid, then raised their baying cry as footprints appeared in the snow. They bounded off in pursuit.

If Egvar saw the appearing prints, I'd lose all his trust. *Yosyph, why did you mount the other horse? You could have come up behind me.*

But Egvar didn't watch the snow. Instead, he looked into the distance after the hounds. "Another prize. This is turning into a fine hunt."

My hands flickered in the few words of prayer I'd learned in the King's Trial. *Please God, protect him.*

"Lady Katrin, it's getting away."

I bit the inside of my cheek and mounted. I'd just urged my horse into a gallop when I had to rein in. The two hounds stood with their forepaws against the trunk of a pine, their baying cry tolling death. Snow fell from flexible branches as someone climbed higher.

Egvar nocked an arrow in his bow.

"Oh, let it go," I called out, trying to keep my voice light. "Squirrels aren't good eating and don't have enough fur to make a mitten."

"Too big to be a squirrel." He squinted into the dappled light and thick-needled branches.

"But we left behind my kill. Why waste time on something small enough to climb a tree? Let's seek better hunting." *Please God,* I signed.

The branches stilled above us.

Egvar squinted...

He's shooting blind. He wouldn't hit Yosyph.

... and released his arrow.

Snow showered as something large tumbled through the branches. The hounds scrambled at the trunk.

No!

I kicked my heels in the tenderest parts of my horse's flanks.

He reared on his hind legs with a neigh of pain.

I tumbled to the snow with my own, only partly feigned, scream.

The hounds turned, their mouths open and teeth slathered.

I screamed again. What had I done? They were in a blood lust of the hunt.

In a bound they were on me. I thrust out my arms to shield my face and neck.

Two low notes vibrated, and the hounds stilled.

"Lady Katrin!" Egvar kneeled in the snow next to me.

"Get them away from me! Get them away!"

He grabbed the leather collars of the hounds and pulled them away from me, then again trilled the whistle in the two low notes, and the hounds sat in the snow. He kneeled by me. "Are you hurt?"

He's dead. For once I understood Yosyph's state of no emotion. I felt nothing. Empty and cold as the surrounding snow. He was dead, and it was my fault. "Dead," I mumbled, and the spoken word opened the gates for searing pain. "Dead!" I screamed.

A goose honked from the tree, and I burst into tears and shaking laughter. He was still alive. And he mocked me for being such a goose. But he was alive.

"Katrin," Egvar's voice edged on panic. "Where are you hurt?"

"I'm not." I hiccuped. "Please, let's return to the city."

Please let Yosyph be unhurt and make it back safe. I didn't want to leave Yosyph, yet Egvar would as likely kill him as help him.

Egvar helped me to my feet and lifted me to his horse, then mounted behind me.

I signed slowly in front of me. *You. Safe. Promise.*

Yosyph honked one last time.

Egvar looked up the tree as another fit of trembling attacked my limbs. "I must get you home. I'll send the houndmaster to get our other horses." He turned, and we rode away from Yosyph.

5

YOSYPH

A forest outside of Fairhaven, Lansimetsa
   Janúar 13th

I CLUTCHED my upper arm where the arrow scored through leather coat, linen shirt, and enough skin for blood to soak between my fingers.

Katrin disappeared into the forest, riding in front of Sir Egvar. The hounds ran behind them, and Katrin's horse followed meekly, now that it didn't have a kicking woman on its back. She'd saved my life.

Stay safe yourself.

I lay, stomach draped across the lowest branch, my legs well within reach of the hounds if they'd remained. My body stung and ached with the fall through the branches and the final impact on this lowest limb. My lungs began to pull in regular breaths. The two goose calls took most of my gasped-in air. Thankfully, Katrin's screams and the hounds' scrambling covered my ragged breathing. My right arm throbbed.

I needed to stop the blood loss first. No. First, get out of this tree.

I slid off the branch, stumbled, and pitched forward into the snow. My feet were numb. The slow wasting was worse again. It would ease if I came out of the shadow-walk, as it had before. But in a forest of hunters who hated me, that wasn't a wise choice.

Stop the bleeding.

I removed my leather coat, finished tearing off the linen sleeve, and, using one hand and my teeth, tied the sleeve around my upper arm. The throbbing eased slightly, and the bleeding stopped.

Next, get to a horse.

I stumbled toward the stag kill site and fell to my face again. *I was shot in the arm, not the leg.* Irony floated in an orange emotion beyond my grasp.

A distant hunting horn echoed through the air. Had Egvar remembered the horses?

I pushed to stand and staggered forward. My feet acted like wooden, wobbly stilts beneath me. I fell again and crawled forward, my arm throbbing with the weight of my body.

There. Two horses stood patiently. One with a hound whimpering on its back, the other with a silent stag.

The hound weighed less but it could still bite. I crawled to Katrin's horse.

The horse danced sideways at my crunching movements through the snow.

I stood and flung myself forward at the horse's side, wrapping my arms around the stag.

The horse lunged and kicked out. The air whooshed as hooves flew by my head.

I stumbled backwards with my arms still wrapped around the stag. The carcass fell on top of me in the snow.

The horse shied away.

I pushed the stag off and rolled. "Easy boy," I murmured.

The horse pricked his ears towards me, eyes wide. I'd ridden him many times in the shadow-walk state. But then, I'd been able to mount quietly without scaring him.

Approaching hooves squeaked through the snow.

"Easy boy." I stood.

Katrin's horse stood trembling, his eyes looking toward my voice.

I reached out and stroked his neck.

He exploded into a series of bucks and kicks, turning in circles.

I threw myself backwards and scrambled in the snow, increasing the distance between his hooves and my head.

The houndmaster mounted on a horse trotted into the clearing. A hound tagged along, tied by a long rope to the saddle.

I'd have to stumble the miles back to Fairhaven, or out to the closest village. I'd make it, eventually. It was only my feet not working. The rest of me was only an achy mass of non-vital injuries.

The houndmaster swept his gaze over the horses, the fallen stag, and the snow. "Yorel, if you are still here, I am a loyal follower of the king. Egvar," he spat the name out, "said he shot something large in a tree, something he couldn't see through the thick branches. He sent me to retrieve it and the horses. Let me help you."

He carried a broad hunting knife and a heavy bow. If I came out of the shadow, he could end my life before I took two breaths. Or he could release the hound, and it would end the same.

My arm throbbed as blood soaked through the linen bandage. My knots had loosened. Flecks of light flashed as my head lightened.

The houndmaster dismounted and walked about the snow, touching the blood-spotted snow in one spot and the pile of stag entrails in another. He drew closer, his feet squeaking in the snow. A stride, half a stride.

I drew back as his foot fell where my leg had been.

He turned.

Metal sang softly as I pulled my knife from its leather sheath.

He stepped back. "Yorel. You can trust me. If you need help, let me help. If you don't, I will take these horses and return." He took another step back.

Could I trust him? *Please God, I need your guidance.* It was harder to hear Him when in the shadow state, as He often spoke through my emotions. Could I trust the houndmaster? Could I make it to safety on my own, with my blood loss? It wasn't much, yet I already felt weaker than I should. Which way?

The houndmaster turned from me and soothed Katrin's horse. "There now. The Yorel meant no harm. Nor do I."

He speaks the truth. A thought whispered through my mind.

Then I'll let him help. I responded, pushing away my caution. I'd not listened to God often enough to prove I should. *Thank you.*

I pulled my emotions back into me. Fear, anger, pain, and worry dominated the colors. "Please, God, help me. I am too weak today." I'd not meant to speak out loud.

"Amen," the houndmaster murmured as he aided me to a sitting position. He pulled the cloth away from my shoulder, then wrapped a clean one over my wound. "Are you hurt elsewhere?"

I shook my head. The motion caused spots to swim before my eyes. I slumped back to the snow.

His face whitened. "You've lost too much blood. Can you

ride?" He pulled my good arm over his shoulders and half carried, half dragged me to his horse.

I tried to walk, but my feet would not respond. They left long trails through the trampled snow. The Yorel, the mighty shadow-walker, helpless as an old man. I laughed, finally able to feel the irony.

6

HALAVANT

THE SUNLIT THRONE room echoed with angry noblemen. Ten of them huddled like grouchy sheep at the bottom of my dais, an impromptu committee to help me mend my ways. Two guards stood on either side of me, and eight more spread throughout the room. None, guards or noblemen, had drawn weapons—yet.

I hid my smile at the ridiculous scene. In the day, fear didn't lay so heavy, as if the sun provided a layer of safety the dark could not.

"You want to add another foreign-blooded commoner to your royal council!" shouted a man, sweating in his winter furs.

I pulled my mouth out of the quick grin and back into solemness. I must act much older than my seventeen years. Tomorrow, I'd turn eighteen, and they'd respect me more, or at least shout less.

"You've already soiled the council with four foreign-blooded advisers." This nobleman didn't shout. His voice dripped with condescension. "You need those who were raised to guide this country, just as you were raised to lead it."

I stood from my throne and descended one step. My guards kept pace and within arm's reach of me. "I don't just *want* to include another *commoner*. As of this morning, I *have* added three of them to the royal council. I welcome any who show they think more of the vast, diverse people of this land than they do of their childish prejudices. You may want to rethink your priorities if you want to remain on the council."

The words still felt awkward, even after practicing them any spare moment this morning. The previous day, Yosyph and I had worked on what to say when the noblemen approached me with their demands. These words would force them one way or the other instead of having them sit grumbling on the fence.

"You mean to throw us from the council," blustered the winter-furred noble.

"No." I descended another step until my head was just above theirs. "I want to keep each of you on the council. You are good men and have served our country loyally. However, our people are starving, and you still delay sending them aid. If you desire to remain my counselors and advisors, then send your fastest riders to your estates and distribute a winter's worth of grain to every family within your stewardships."

The condescending noble lifted his head. "It was their own fault for not preparing for winter better. Why should I pay for their idleness?"

"War destroyed the fruits of their industry."

"And that was your fault."

It was my fault, but they'd be slaves by now without the war. How often we'd danced this conversation over the last several months.

"I've offered you gold for your grain."

"We've yet to see a coin."

I nodded to one guard standing alongside the room. He opened a side door, and men carried in ten sacks.

I motioned to the sacks as they were dropped at my feet. "Each sack contains enough gold to buy a winter's worth of grain for five hundred people. The one who responds fastest to supply grain to five hundred gets two sacks. I will send a recorder with each of you to tally your work. Anyone who can convince a fellow nobleman to sell a part of their grain to help the people will also receive two sacks of gold. The rest will receive one sack, which is a fair price for what I'm asking of you."

The expressions of my ten noblemen changed from disgruntled contempt to gleams of avarice. Yosyph would reprimand me for paying so much when he felt we should just take it from the nobility and give it to those who grew it.

A slightly built nobleman, old enough to be my grandfather, nodded. "Quite fair. I'll be on my way. The poor and starving need *my* grain."

The other nine watched a moment as he hobbled from the room, then took off in hot pursuit. With their backs turned, I let my grin spread again. Today would be a good day. This would break the delays and feed the people. I wouldn't have to face another report tallying how many died of hunger. In the spring, we'd change the government.

Next order of business, better locks on my rooms—especially the windows. Maybe metal bars installed over them. I didn't need a balcony.

I descended the last step of my dais when the herald opened the main throne room door and announced, "Sir Jonas of Gatchenbrat."

A tall man with wild, sandy hair stepped into the room. He wore travel-stained clothes, and his sun-baked face shined with what must have been a quick scrub at the castle gates.

"Galliard!" I dashed across the long room, my guards shadowing me.

"Well met." He clapped me on the back. "I see you've upgraded your hand braces to engraved metal. A fine accessory for a king."

I glanced at the lines of gold and silver scrolling over my light steel braces. Two smiths worked all morning to make them. They'd deflect a sword or arrow, if I was quick enough.

Galliard lay a hand on my shoulder, and I sucked in my breath. He removed his hand and lifted an eyebrow. "That gasp starts a story. I would hear the rest."

"Just a little nighttime knife fighting."

His other eyebrow rose. "And where were your guards?"

"You too? I'll tell you the story after you report, as long as you don't add to the lectures I've already borne."

He chuckled. "You probably deserved each word." He swung into step beside me as we headed to my rooms. "How are things with your red-haired maiden?"

The sunlight from a window fell in warm bands across my face. "My brother has relinquished his pursuit of her. At dinner tonight, I will ask her again to marry me."

"I am happy for you. Didn't seem fair for her to choose otherwise after everything you went through for her. Though you are a handful to watch over. Maybe that's why she hesitated."

I'd have slapped him on the back for his teasing, but with the hand braces, it would be more of a clubbing. Instead, I tapped the back of Galliard's calf with my boot.

He danced away sideways and chuckled.

Once we were in my rooms, Galliard's face turned grim. "They said no."

"Blast the Mountain Clans! We've provided food to supplement their poor soil crops for years. And they refuse to aid us in our year of need? Our walls and streets are a crumbled mess from the war. Many people of my city are freezing because they have no homes. We need the clan's skill in wood and stone work. They have to come. We have a treaty!"

"A treaty our nation broke when the former queen ordered the enslavement of all their people in our lands."

"I've not broken the treaty. I stopped the enslavement."

Galliard held up a calming hand. "They wait and watch to see if you remain king before they send their people. I've traveled to each of their isolated clans, and none will come, yet. Give them time. Lansimetsa holds its own builders and craftsmen. Turn the work to them."

He was right. I'd already hired men to build shelters for those whose homes were destroyed. We were making progress. I just wished I hadn't lost three months of Galliard's counsel and companionship to a fruitless mission. "Blast them anyway. At least I have better news. I've convinced some nobles to help with the famine."

"You didn't order them, as their king?"

"I'm trying to win their loyalty by giving them right over what they own, despite how it was gained. I wish now I'd not promised them this before the coronation."

Galliard shrugged. "It was a way to end the war."

"Not a good one. They are pliable as donkeys and many murmur things were better under my mother. Though under her, none could keep a guard or weapons for more than fifty men, and a third of their increase went into the royal treasury."

Galliard nodded. "Men reminisce with blind eyes and act with about as much vision. You should keep a stronger command over them; not as much as the old queen, but more than this."

I laughed through my nose. "More this, less that. I walk a rope stretched over a river, and one of these days I'll fall in and get a dunking. I'm seeing more how Fredrick could influence my mother through fears. His poisonous words crippled her mind as much as his poisonous herbs crippled my hands."

"She remains difficult?"

"Spiteful, vindictive, secretive, foul-mouthed as a sailor, and boastful she will regain her power soon. The remnants of her spies and murderers have already tried to carry out her promise." I swallowed and then forced a half smile. "I don't visit her often."

"I don't plan on making a house-arrest call. Now that red-haired maiden is another story. When will I meet her?"

"At dinner toni—"

Katrin's shrill voice carried through the door, "I must see the king."

My guard's deep voice responded, "He's occupied. But you are welcome to wait."

"I must see him now!"

Galliard tilted his head towards the door.

I smiled. Katrin was excitable, and this was surely one of those times. It would be good to introduce her to Galliard. He'd left on his assignment before she'd returned from the desert.

Dratted door knob. My braced hands slipped on its polished surface.

Galliard grinned and turned the knob. Beyond the open door, Katrin struggled against Gent's hold on her wrists.

She turned to me. "Yosyph's hurt!"

"Let her go," I ordered. "Katrin, come in."

She shoved the door shut. "Sir Egvar shot him. I don't know how bad. He was still in the shadow. He's in the southwest reaches of the forest."

I thumped into a chair. "When?"

"Three hours ago. I couldn't get Sir Egvar to let me go."

"He held you prisoner?"

"No, he worried because I'd fallen from my horse. Stop asking me questions. We must help Yosyph."

"Gent!"

Gent entered the room. "Yes, your Majesty."

"The Yorel's been injured in the royal forest. Have a dozen guards, plus Elise, be ready to ride in the next quarter hour."

"Immediately, your Majesty."

Hoft took up the main guard position outside my door as Gent jogged down the hall. Couldn't he move faster?

I closed the door. I needed nondescript winter clothes and someone to wrap the reins around my hands. "Galliard?"

He saluted me, with a touch to his forehead. "I'm coming with you. Just like old times."

"Except this time I'm not seeking my bride."

Katrin's blanched face didn't even hint a blush.

Tonight was the wrong time to renew my proposal. I brushed my arm against hers. "We'll find him. No one could kill the mighty Shadow-Walker."

7

ELISE

P<small>ALACE</small>, Fairhaven, Lansimetsa
Janúar 13th

S<small>TACKS OF TOMES</small> and papers spread across my table, bed, and floor. Histories, herbologies, medical logs. All said the same. *We searched for a cure and found none.*

I picked up *The Herbs of the Mountain Clans* and opened to the index of ailments. *Colds, Crushed thumb, Cuts... Lice, Love ill... Paralysis...*

The slow wasting was a type of paralysis. I turned to that page. *Paralysis: due to fall, due to old age, due to poison.*

Poison?

If a child eats the sweet Stilling Death Berry, you must immediately get him to empty his stomach (I prefer Toad's Foot Leaf, but for other options see the section on expectorants). Then dose him hourly with a tea of dried June's Blossom (or fresh if in season), Rabbit's Root, and Crawling Tree Bark, all in equal parts. When his movements cease to be sluggish, dose him three times a day for four days. Imme-

diacy of treatment is vital. If you wait even an hour, the effects become irreversible.

Not for the slow wasting. However, if those three herbs didn't have ill side effects, I could try them on Halavant's hands and see if they had a positive effect. It would only be a temporary reprieve. Without a cure for the slow wasting, it wouldn't matter if I cured Halavant's hands.

Nothing else in this tome. I hefted *The Strange and Magical History of Lansimetsa*. Some old kook surely wrote it. But even craziness had elements of truth.

Merpeople, their habitations and ancient ruins
Dragons and the valiant war to end their menace
The god kings and where they got their strength

I closed the tome and lay my head on the cover. It was hogwash and craziness. My thoughts swam with words, shouting *this way, listen to me, I have the answer.* "Will you please be quiet," I whispered.

Two sharp knocks echoed through my door.

"What is it!"

"Elise. The king needs you."

I sighed. Why now? I had to find the answer. "Coming." I opened the door to find one of Halavant's guards.

He glanced at the thick robe over my dress. "The Yorel is hurt. Get into winter riding clothes. And bring your healer's bag."

"Oh." My annoyance evaporated. "How soon?"

"Be at the stables in ten minutes."

~

WE GALLOPED through the last gate of Fairhaven. I rode a short distance behind Halavant and Galliard, with Katrin next to me.

45

Halavant wore plain clothes, but the entourage of a dozen uniformed guards shouted his station.

A man galloped along the road toward the gate and us.

The guards pulled in closer, their height and bulk cutting off our view of the approaching rider.

A hurried voice carried past them. "I have an important message for the king."

"You can give it to us," said the front guard, "or take it to the palace."

"Is he not with..." the rider stopped. "My message is, I've found a wounded black bear, the kind that passes like a shadow through the forest."

Halavant stood in his stirrups. "Lead us to him."

"As you will, Sire."

We spread slightly as we trotted, and I glimpsed him. He wore a hunter's brown leather, and a thick bow was slung across his back.

Katrin gasped beside me and whispered. "It's the houndmaster."

Halavant turned in his saddle. "Who?"

"The houndmaster. Sir Egvar sent him back to collect our other animals."

"Do you trust him?"

"I... I don't know. I'd not met him before today, and I've not spoken with him."

Halavant's guards pulled in tighter as the words slipped between Katrin and Halavant.

The houndmaster turned south away from the royal forest into a tangled, unkept mass of trees—the commoners' forest.

The front guard halted. My horse bumped into Halavant's and then pranced backwards.

"Sir." The guard turned in his saddle. "I'll go ahead with him and come back to report."

Halavant leaned forward. "We go together."

The houndmaster called back. "Your brother is with a healer. You can trust me, but your guard is wise. If you will, send him with me. We'd be back within a quarter hour."

Halavant repeated, "We go together."

We ducked into the commoners' forest. There was no path. I bent my head as we rode under a low branch. The guards tucked their bodies next to their horses' necks. Our horses high stepped through brambles. The vines, even in their winter deadness, snagged my clothes.

After long minutes of weaving through the trees, the forest opened up to a small clearing and a brambled hill. Smoke wisped from a lightning-blackened stump at the top of the hill. A raven cawed as the late afternoon sun slanted through the trees.

Our guide dismounted near the hill, pushed aside brambles, and knocked.

A reedy voice carried across the clearing. "Come in if you are here to help; otherwise go away."

The houndmaster motioned with his head for us to follow and disappeared into the hill.

Halavant turned to the closest guard. "Unwrap my reins."

The guard put his hand on his sword. "Sir, one of us should go first."

Before either of them could argue further, Katrin bounded off her horse and pushed her way into the dwelling. Her worried voice carried out the open door. "Yosyph!"

He was there. I dismounted and slipped under the brambles to enter a whitewashed room with a table, shelves and a glowing fire. The Yorel lay stretched out on a bed, his skin almost as gray as his clothes, with white bandages wrapped around his right arm. Katrin kneeled at his side, holding his left hand.

A slight man with a storm cloud of hair bent over the bed,

trying to spoon some liquid into Yosyph's mouth as the hound-master held Yosyph's head. Yosyph's pinched lips caused most of it to dribble down his chin.

"Stubborn mule," the reedy-voiced man said. "I've tended to enough of your friends for you to trust me."

Yosyph pinched his lips tighter.

I stepped forward. "Sir. I'm a healer. How may I help?"

The old man appraised me. "See if you can talk some sense into him. His heart is beating far too fast, but he won't take the calming tea." The healer stepped back.

I moved to the bedside, "Yosyph. Do you trust him?"

He nodded.

"Then why won't you let him help you?"

He glanced at the healer, then back at me. "It will make it worse." His voice came out in a low and dry croak.

Katrin squeezed his hand. "What worse?"

He whispered something.

I leaned my ear near his mouth.

"The slow wasting. I used Gaven's calming tea last week when I couldn't sleep, and in the morning my feet were worse."

"You haven't told him." My voice rose above a whisper, and Gaven's gray brows formed a solid line above his eyes.

"Tell us what?" Katrin pushed me aside and leaned close to Yosyph. "What haven't you told us?"

"Don't, Elise." Yosyph's plea came out weak.

"Do you trust the healer?" I asked.

He glanced from Gaven, to Katrin, and back to me. "I trust him with my life. Yet to save my life, he'll keep me from doing what I must. I cannot be trapped here because of his care."

Katrin touched Yosyph's cheek, turning his face back to her. "Yosyph, please tell me. I need to know. I want to help you. Let the healer help you." She glanced up at me with a fierce gaze. "Elise, tell me."

The door swung open, and two guards ducked in.

"It's safe," I called.

Halavant entered the room with four more guards, and the room grew cramped.

Gaven's brows drew lower over his eyes. "Come in, if you're here to help; otherwise go away. And that means all you meaty-headed oxen, and the chattering red squirrel. Out!"

Katrin crossed her arms and planted herself on the bed next to Yosyph. Halavant crossed the room and planted himself on the floor next to her. I shook my head with a smile. Yosyph thought he could fade away? Not with those two around.

Galliard poked his head in the door, then backed out again. Wise man.

"He's safe." Yosyph's voice cracked. "The guards don't have to stay."

After a brief argument between Halavant and his guards, all but one retreated outside, and that one guard hunched over along the curved ceiling edge.

"You said you'd bring someone to make him behave," Gaven muttered to the houndmaster, "not the whole traveling circus." He turned to Yosyph. "What aren't you telling me?"

Yosyph pinched his lips again.

Gaven pressed his fingers to Yosyph's neck and counted. "It's faster now than before. You must take the tea."

I pulled a packet of herbs from my healer's pouch. "Yosyph, will you drink chamomile?"

He nodded, and Gaven harrumphed.

While the chamomile steeped, Katrin stroked Yosyph's brow and Halavant paced. Each time either tried to speak, Gaven shot them a warning look.

I chanced the question neither of them could ask. "What happened, Sir Houndmaster?"

He glanced to Gaven, and when he didn't get a stormy warning, he said, "I found the Yorel lying in the snow, with an arrow wound scored across his upper arm. The wound itself was not dangerous, but he'd lost so much blood he couldn't walk. He directed me to this healer. By—"

Gaven interrupted. "He shouldn't have lost that much blood. Something else is ailing him. He's too weak for the effects of just a surface wound. But he won't tell me. And so I bound up the more apparent problem."

An echoing silence settled on the room. Yosyph needed to tell them. He wasn't helping Halavant nor Lansimetsa by hiding it. Plea or no plea. "He has the slow wasting."

Katrin cocked her head in confusion. Halavant and the houndmaster blanched, and Gaven looked to the ceiling, "I see." He pulled a large volume from a shelf.

Katrin kissed Yosyph's forehead. "What is the slow wasting?"

Gaven answered as he flipped through pages. "Finally, an intelligent question. The slow wasting is a weakness of the kings, passed from father to son. It was worse for the daughters. None lived to adulthood. It starts with a weakening and numbness in the feet and progresses up the legs and along the other extremities until the person can only move their head. Then it moves into the core, attacking the lungs. The person has to fight to breathe. And when they can't fight any longer, they die."

Katrin stifled a cry.

Gaven glanced up at her, then went back to flipping pages. "It won't happen today or tomorrow. He still has years, and I know some herbs to lengthen his life—ah, here it is. You, healer girl, do you know how to make the base paste for an herbal rub?"

"Which one? I know five kinds."

He glanced at me and a twinkle entered his gray eyes. "Five? Prepare the one that will absorb fastest. And you, red squirrel girl, get him to drink the chamomile. The slow wasting is worse with injuries and weariness. He'll heal up quicker if he rests in an unworried state." He lowered his brows at Katrin. "So don't worry him."

Halavant stepped forward. "And me?"

"You can be a better king so he stops fretting about it every blasted minute."

Halavant winced.

Gaven waved towards the door. "Now get along home before something happens and Yosyph tries to save the kingdom again."

I winced along with Halavant.

Gaven glanced at my scrunched face, and his clenched jaw softened. He turned to Halavant. "When I have time, I'll look at those hands. There may still be something we can do about them. Though you should have come when Yosyph first told you. Didn't he tell you? I don't make house calls. Not even for a king."

～

HALAVANT LEFT with his guards after the biting comments, but he'd been far from cowed. He walked with a determined step and a straight back. Hopefully, he'd do nothing rash to prove himself a *better king*. The houndmaster left with them.

I created pastes, counted out drops of tincture, and cooked up a hot stew to feed the three of us. Katrin spooned thin broth into Yosyph's mouth, and he slept.

Working beside Gaven was similar to working beside my mother, as long as he wasn't criticizing someone.

Long after the sun retired, I sank into a chair, my arms limp from pounding bark to a pulp.

Gaven added the pulp to an infusion for Yosyph to drink

when he woke. Gaven assured me that would be soon, since the Yorel never slept more than a few hours at a time.

Katrin dozed in another chair, her hair frizzed out from her braids and her face pinched even in sleep.

"Gaven?"

He nodded to my question, without looking up from the large volume. Strips of old bandages stuck out from several pages he'd marked.

"How long have you studied the slow wasting?"

"Longer than you've been alive, ever since the time Yosyph's grandfather lay dying of it."

"Did you know Yosyph would develop it?"

"They all do. Though I'd hoped his desert heritage would spare him."

"So Halavant will too?" A band tightened around my lungs.

He nodded.

"Is there no cure?"

He paused in his reading and closed his eyes.

"Not even a hope of a cure?"

He walked over and stood beside my chair, laying his hand along the chair back. He stared into the fire. "Only a wild guess."

A guess? Then there was a chance. I bunched my skirts in my fists as I waited for him to speak.

He patted one of my fisted hands. "Where have you been all these years? I need a quiet apprentice with a solid-thinking head. I always thought it would be a man. Although with a man's clothes and your hair cut short, you could pass yourself off as a boy easy enough. Maybe I'll apprentice you. I'm getting old, and I thought my knowledge would die with me."

I frowned. I wasn't here for an apprenticeship, unless it meant finding a cure for the slow wasting. "The guess?"

"A wild guess. One I cannot study because of the travel."

"I'll travel. Where?"

"Carani."

Carani! The people who'd attacked Lansimetsa every generation. The stories of them were even worse than the fireside tales of the shadow demons. Father didn't tell his battle stories until the little ones were asleep. And I'd often wished after a telling he'd waited for me to be asleep, too. His words haunted my dreams. Screams as the Carani peeled skin from prisoners. The Carani's trained creatures that slipped into nighttime tents, silently killed, and left the mauled bodies to be discovered in the morning.

Gaven touched my shoulder. "Do you know where the first Lansimetsian king came from?"

"On a silver ship, sailing from the sky land of the gods." I grimaced as I repeated the lines from my childhood history lesson. The kings descended from the gods, the end. Not a satisfying answer.

Gaven chuckled. "You believe it as much as you believe you can draw a net of fish from the sky. No. The first king was a Carani, fleeing his own blood-thirsty people, seeking a land to live in peace. He was a shipbuilder, a leader, and a man with vision. Over the years, he brought other peace-seeking Carani here. He became a smuggler of people and goods between the two lands. For years, the kings kept Lansimetsa a secret from their homeland. Then in the seventh's king's reign, the Carani discovered them and came to battle to claim this rich land. That war ended the connection between the two lands, and it started the incidents of slow wasting."

He paused and let the words sink in.

Did the Carani poison the seventh king? Could a poison pass from father to child? If it could, why was it worse for each new generation?

Gaven continued. "What happens if you try to feed an infant meat or greens? Will he survive?"

"No. An infant needs his mother's milk, or at least milk from an animal—though the animal milk will not be as healthy."

"What if the Carani need a specific food to survive, something that only grows there?"

Ah, I was starting to see. "Shouldn't all of Carani descent suffer the slow wasting?"

"Some do. But, like the infant that can survive off of other animal's milk, so it seems with many of those of Carani decent. However, certain infants must have their mother's milk or they die. I believe the line of the kings has a weakness that has passed down the generations, something that requires them to have a specific nutrient from Carani or their bodies waste away. And the further down the generations, the sooner the deficiency appears."

"What's the nutrient?"

Gaven shook his head. "It's not in any book I can find."

I shivered. The Carani. I would go there. I couldn't not seek a cure. Why must it be the Carani?

Gaven patted my hand again, his papery palms rustling over mine. "I've seen many a man die. It's part of being a healer. Yet I do not want to see this nation fall to endless war between bickering nobles because the line of the kings ceased. Perhaps it is time I took that journey."

I glanced at Yosyph's grayed face, and for a moment it was as if Halavant's face overlaid it. "Would you allow an apprentice healer to join you?"

8

KATRIN

A FOREST OUTSIDE OF FAIRHAVEN, Lansimetsa
Janúar 14th

THE ROOM GLOWED with a low fire. Dawn's sunlight struggled through the forest and vine-covered windows. And Yosyph lay breathing deeply and evenly in sleep. The lines of his tattoo lay dark red and black against his illness-blanched arm.

I laid my hand against his neck, like I'd seen the old healer do. His heart beat in a steady march, nothing like the fluttered bird wing beats of last night.

Why didn't you tell me? I swiped a tear away from my cheek before it could fall on his face.

He'd said he couldn't marry me because of the slow wasting. He'd have to do more than develop a deadly illness to frighten me away.

I missed the next tear, and it dropped onto one of his eyelids.

He took a deeper breath and rolled his head sideways. My tear slid down his cheek. He turned back, blinked, and looked into my face. His lips curved into a soft smile as his eyes focused. He reached up and stroked my face. "Katrin."

"Yosyph. We'll find a cure."

He closed his eyes again and sighed, his chin falling toward his chest. "You're going to be difficult."

"Yes! I'll be more stubborn than you, which is a difficult thing. And you won't die." My voice rose above the whisper I'd started at. "I almost got you killed. You can't die."

"Katrin." Yosyph stroked my face again as he whispered my name. "I'm not dying yet. I'll be back to shadowing Halavant and you by tomorrow."

"No, you won't! You will rest, you will get better, and I'll make sure you never put yourself in harm's way again."

Yosyph chuckled. "You plan on becoming the shadow's keeper?"

"No, I plan on becoming Yosyph's wife."

The chuckles died in his throat, and his eyes widened like a spooked animal. "No, you can't—I won't—you deserve more than early widowhood."

"You keep thinking you can make my choices for me. *Marry Halavant*, you say, but he'll develop the slow wasting too. How is that any better? If I'm going to be a young widow, I'll spend my years before it with you. But you won't die. I won't let you."

Yosyph started to fade with my words, a sign he was pushing his emotions down deep and getting pulled into the shadow state without him trying.

A cold breeze washed across the room, and a reedy voice called from the open doorway, "Red squirrel girl, stop agitating the patient." The old healer trotted over to Yosyph, poured a thick liquid into a spoon, and shoved it into Yosyph's mouth before he could close his lips. "Now rest, or I'll give you something that will make you sleep for a week, and then we all can get some rest. And you, red squirrel girl, get out. You won't come back until after the sun rises tomorrow."

"He needs me."

"As much as he needs a toothache. Go. Or I'll have that oaf of a guard, who is camped outside, carry you out. You can stay out there with him or go home."

I glared at Gaven. "I'm not going."

Yosyph whispered. "Please, go, Katrin."

Serious Elise entered the room with a basket brimming with herbs and branches.

I nodded to her. "Take care of him until I can." And I strode from the room, only partially resisting the urge to slam the door behind me.

9

HALAVANT

PALACE, Fairhaven, Lansimetsa
Janúar 14th

MY SPARRING PARTNER rolled away from me in the dust of the sparring yard. Gent was a good head taller than me, several stones heavier, and an awful pretender. The chill morning did little to cool my emotions. But the exercise worked the emotions out better than the sleepless night had.

I shifted to a defensive position as Gent stood. "I didn't put much force behind the kick. You shouldn't have moved."

"Sir, your shoulder."

"Blast my shoulder. I'm using my legs. Now give me something to fight, or I'll call in the guard you said I should imprison for his muttering words."

"Injuring yourself won't solve any problems."

"I'm not hurting myself, and sparring will clear my mind so I can be a *better king*. I only have a short time this morning before I must attend to my kingly duties. Now, fight."

Gent stepped out of a soft-dusted corner of the sparring

yard, the section created for my Lausatök practice. "Sir, the old healer was worried about the Yorel. He said things he shouldn't have. Go back. Be with your brother. The meetings can wait. You'll be a better king for tending to him than fighting me."

My defensive position slumped. "I can't do anything for him. I'll just be in the way. And someday, too soon, he'll go where I can't follow, and I'll be left alone to rule this people."

"Go. He needs you. I've watched him. When he's around you, he brightens from his sternness."

I smiled and shook my head. "Gent, you should be a king's councilor, not a guard."

He guffawed. His laughter startled several birds roosting in the trees around the sparring yard, and they rose into the air with indignant squawks.

I stepped from the Lausatök practice dust. "I'll go."

～

MORNING SUN WARMED the small clearing in front of the healer's hill. The guard I'd left behind sat by a fire in the clearing, and beside him hunkered Katrin. She jumped up as I rode in with my retinue of guards and Galliard. "You're back. Good. I don't like the healer. He won't listen. Yosyph needs someone else."

She didn't say Yosyph was worse. I let go of a held breath. "How is he?"

"Elise says he's doing better, and she has something she needs to tell you. She won't tell me what it is. Why can't people just talk?"

Elise stepped outside as she dried her hands on a towel. "We think we've found a cure."

"A cure!" Katrin's voice overlapped mine.

I tried to unwrap the reins from my hands, and my horse whinnied in complaint at my tugging. "What is it?"

Galliard reached over and unwrapped the reins. His grin matched mine.

Elise bit her lower lip. "It's some plant in Carani."

"Carani?" I shook my head as I dismounted. I'd misheard.

She looked down at the towel in her hand. "The healer Gaven and I will sail as soon as we can get our supplies together and Yosyph heals enough."

She *had* said Carani. I gritted my teeth. "Then I'm going with you."

The chorus of no's filled the air.

Galliard dismounted beside me. "Impetuous as ever. I'd heard you'd become overly cautious this last month. I guess I heard wrong."

It didn't matter what he thought. "I'm going."

Galliard raised his eyebrows. "So, you're going. Who will rule while you gallivant to a foreign land, peopled by those who would peel your skin from your back as soon as say hello?"

"I know the stories," I grumbled. "But Yosyph saved my life. Besides, one person has already tried to peel off my skin in my bedchamber. Can the Carani be any worse?"

Galliard humphed. His single syllable said what my overactive caution was telling me, too. They could be a lot worse.

Elise stepped forward. "Galliard brings up an important point. Who will rule if you voyage with us?"

Who? My nation was already unstable. Could I pass the responsibility to another and not have it fall apart? Who would a greater portion of the people respect enough to keep the country from breaking into factions following different nobles? "You said you'd leave in a couple days. I'll find someone."

Galliard and Elise exchanged glances.

I tensed as I waited for one of them to pounce on me.

Galliard patted my shoulder. I winced, and he dropped his hand with a sheepish smile. "You're the king. We'll not stop you like you were a crazy, head-injured patient. Let's sit and discuss it over breakfast."

A reedy voice called from the door, "Elise, come. We have much to do before we leave, plus Yosyph is awake and as ornery as ever."

I followed Elise in, returned the glare of the old healer, and planted myself on a stool next to Yosyph's bed. Yosyph lay, half propped up on pillows. His face had regained its rich-brown tone and cool, impassive features. He nodded a greeting to me.

I nodded back and grinned. "You look better today. And Elise said they've found a cure."

"Perhaps, but—" He stopped as angry whispers rasped through the air.

Katrin stood at the threshold, and the healer blocked her entry.

"I'm quiet," Katrin whispered. "I'll not talk. Just let me enter."

"No." The healer shifted his feet to a stronger stance.

Yosyph sat up further. "Let her enter."

The old healer grumbled. "... Force their ways into my space, mess with my methods... I didn't dig out this hill just to turn it into a market's gossip spot." He raised his voice. "Elise, shake the tinctures. We'll need six months of them prepared to leave with Yosyph, if one of these *concerned* intruders will take care to shake them daily while we are gone. And may six months be enough time to find it."

"What tinctures?" I let the question slip out and earned myself a scowl from the old man.

Elise picked up two jars of liquid packed full of herbs. She handed one to Galliard and another to Katrin, then picked up a third jar. A strong odor of alcohol wafted through the corked tops.

I glanced down at my braced hands. Useless. The jar would slip through them.

Elise spoke in a quiet voice as she shook the jar. "One tincture is to slow the progress of the slow wasting. The second eases the muscle cramping caused by the first tincture. And the third helps him sleep despite the stimulating effect of the other two, so he is strong enough to continue to fight the slow wasting. It's what the healer Gaven used to help King Luukas, and it prolonged the king's life long enough for Halavant to be born."

Yosyph spoke, his voice neutral. "All those tinctures are pointless. Besides, they won't be effective for another month, until the alcohol absorbs the properties of the herbs. The slow wasting is only in its beginnings. I have years before I'll need to resort to such measures or medicines. I have my duty. You've tended to my arm, I'm regaining my energy, I'll be leaving by tomorrow. And you can all go back to your duties instead of worrying about me."

Gaven finished steeping herbs in hot water and brought a cup of tea to Yosyph. "My duty is to worry about you, because you won't, you thick-headed mule. You'll drink this tea morning and night until the tinctures are ready. The slow wasting is progressing too fast as it is. You should not have lost the use of your feet."

Yosyph pushed the cup away. The blankets shifted as he wiggled his feet. "I can move them again. It's only when I'm shadow-walking that they grow worse. I'll only enter that state when necessary. If I take your tinctures, I'll be useless to do anything more than sit and observe."

A thought niggled. I needed someone to rule while I sought a cure. Yosyph couldn't travel, yet he could sit on the throne. He'd already helped me draft declarations and issue edicts. He'd counseled me in each of the major issues troubling our kingdom. And perhaps if he were ruling, he'd be more careful with his own health. "I know who will rule while I seek the cure."

Everyone turned to look at me.

"Yosyph."

That broke through his impassive mask. He shot to a sitting position. "No!" After a deep breath, he settled back on the pillow. His face drained of the emotional burst, but it didn't return to the mask. Instead, his jaw set in hard lines. "It wouldn't work. The nobility don't trust me. I'm the Yorel, the hunted criminal from the time of the queen. I don't know how to lead. I've planned, I've created armies, but I've never stood in front of them. That place is for you. God knew you were the one to lead the armies I'd formed and the one to rule the country after overthrowing the tyrant. You shouldn't go seek the cure. Your duty is here. If there is a cure, then Gaven and Elise will find it."

I set my jaw to mirror his. "I will go. I had to learn to speak Carani. I've endured lessons on their practices and ways of life. My mother had planned I marry some Carani princess and open trade between us. Though the ambassador she sent never came back."

I glanced at Katrin. She didn't move her gaze from Yosyph's face. That was a lost battle. Maybe I would still marry a Carani princess, if that would get us a cure.

Gaven raised his eyebrows. "You speak Carani? Yes, that would be useful. Though your knowledge of their customs would be obsolete and your wording archaic, it still would be better than what I know. We'll see if you can be a better translator and ambassador than king."

Since he welcomed me to come, I'd endure his biting words. The battle was half won. I turned to Galliard. "Will you help Yosyph rule while we are gone? You've worked with him before, haven't you?"

Galliard glanced at Yosyph. "Not directly. Only through messages, detailing how to create the quiet gathering of a rebellion. He has a brilliant mind for strategy. He'd make a fine regent."

Yosyph's jaw stiffened. "It wouldn't be wise. The nobility will revolt."

Katrin set down the tincture jar and took one of Yosyph's hands. "No, they won't. You've listened in on my many conversations with them. Only some fear you. Many respect you and some even think," she paused, glanced at me and shrugged, "you'd be a better king than Halavant."

"See," I said, trying to ignore the sting of Katrin's comment. "You rule, for a time. I'll find the cure. And we'll both live to an old age."

The argument continued through a lunch of root-vegetable soup and a dinner of stewed rabbit, compliments of my bored and frozen guards.

Elise's quiet voice cut through Yosyph's argument against me leaving. "Yosyph is only a few years older than Halavant. That means Halavant may develop the slow wasting soon. Neither brother has an heir. And even if one were to marry and have a child, that child won't be able to rule until long after the father has died." She closed her eyes for a moment. "We need to find a cure, or Lansimetsa will fall to bickering nobles. If Carani holds a cure, we must have someone who speaks the language. Halavant knows the language. Few others do. Could we find another trustworthy translator? If Halavant comes, we need to leave behind a regent. Yosyph is the obvious choice. He won't be corrupted by bribes or offers of power. He cares for the people. He's level-headed. He'll keep the nobles from revolting." She turned to Yosyph. "Help us save Lansimetsa by watching over her while we find the cure."

Yosyph's fingers flickered in agitated signs, while his face pinched. Was he praying or cursing? He stilled his hands and nodded. "I'll take on the regency."

Gaven scowled at us. "You've worn out my patient, condemned him to the full weight of a kingdom, and overstayed your welcome. Go home or camp outside. I'll see you again in the morning. We have plans to make, now that we're done arguing."

We needed to plan. One of the biggest hurdles was how to let my royal council know I'd be leaving and Yosyph was regent, but not give them the reason why. If they knew Yosyph had the slow wasting, some nobles would revolt that day.

I stepped onto Hoft's hand to mount my horse.

I could tell the council I was seeking a cure for my hands. And I had to go so we could test the cures on my hands instead of having a bunch of things brought back and none of them work. Yes, that would be a good tale, one they'd believe. I wouldn't tell them it was in Carani. If they knew that, they'd bid me farewell and never expect to see me again, and my kingdom would fall into chaos.

Why did it have to be the Carani?

PART II

10

YOSYPH

PALACE, Fairhaven, Lansimetsa
    Febrúar 4th

WITH THREE WEEKS OF HEALING, my arm no longer stung with movement. Gaven's tea helped my feet regain their movement and feeling, though the cramping muscles were bothersome and I was becoming useless to run or even walk far. Worse, it left me in a constant fog. How to rule when I couldn't think? So I stopped drinking the teas and let the numbness creep back into my feet.

It had been fourteen nights since Halavant sailed with Gaven and Elise and I'd been ordained as regent of Lansimetsa. I'd been given all the rights and powers as if I were the king, except the power to bereft a noble of his title or his power. Every minute upon the throne crushed me under the weight of counsels and decisions.

I paced along the top of the dais. My heavy, unbalanced tread echoed in the empty throne room. Four guards kept their eyes averted.

Useless. I was useless to do what I needed to do. Why had God blessed me with the ability to spy and garner information, to only take it away when I needed it most?

A clear bell carried from outside the throne room. The time of the petitioners. I seated myself on the throne, drew my royal robes about me, and braced my arms against the armrests. I let emotion fall away from my face but didn't bury it so deeply I'd flicker into the shadow.

A guard looked to me, waited for my nod, and opened the grand entrance doors. The people washed in like waves eating away the seashore. How different it was to be the center of their attention instead of a shadow along the edge.

The herald leaned in to hear the first petitioner's name, then announced for the whole throne room to hear, "Brennan, farmer of Hothwell, with a complaint against his neighbor."

A voice further back yelped, "And I have a complaint against him. He's a silver-tongued liar."

The herald's clear voice carried. "All who will not abide by the rules of the petitioner, namely waiting until their turn to speak, will be escorted out."

I motioned to the farmer Brennan to proceed.

"Sir, we've had a thin winter of it. Just enough food to line the bottom of my family's bellies. My neighbor promised to trade a cow for two sacks of wheat. A little milk would go a long way for my small ones. He gave me an almost-carcass. It died two days after our trade and he won't give the wheat back."

"T'wasn't my fault she died," piped the other voice. "And you could still eat 'er."

"She was diseased. I'll not kill my wife and children on poisoned meat."

It wasn't either of their faults. They probably had both lined their soup pots with the under-bark of trees, pine needles, and frozen bulbs. Some poor even ground dry bark to make flour for bread, though it led to bloated bellies and the runs, worsening their plight.

"Hey!" the piping voice yelled. "I get to petition." Two guards held a patched, threadbare man by the elbows.

"Wait." I stood. "You both need food for your families. How many are in each?"

Brennan looked at me with open mouth, "My wife and I and seven—no, six—children."

The neighbor kept his head bowed and ducked it further at that news.

"And you?" I prompted.

He kept his head down. "Five children. Wife's dead this winter."

I nodded. "Follow the page to the royal granary. Farmer Brennen, you may take three sacks and one for your neighbor, which he may earn from you by labor. And Brennen's neighbor—"

The shaking man wrung his hands.

"—do not cheat your neighbor, even to fill your stomach."

Most of the other petitioners held similar complaints: empty larders, empty bellies, ill children. Pleas for help. Pages directed them one by one to the granary, which had been near empty when we first overthrew the queen. Another month of this and we'd be handing out potatoes and barley instead. And when that was gone?

I was acting like Halavant, making decisions without having a plan for the consequences. Was he impetuous because if he thought over the matter too much, he'd go crazy? When I organized the rebellion, it was just numbers and locations. Now I had faces, ones that looked me in the eyes and pleaded for help.

When the time of petitioners ended, I sagged on the throne.

The herald re-entered the room. "Lord Makkara."

A tall, middle-aged nobleman strode forward. His winter

clothes still bore the remnants of melting snow, and his eyes were shadowed with sleepless bags.

He bowed in sweeping elegance, born of a lifetime of practice. "Sir Yorel, mouth-piece of King Halavant, I have distributed grain to five hundred of the starving commoners around my estate. I hope I am the first to return. The king's recorder has verified my work." He held out a folded parchment, sealed with a blot of red wax.

I motioned for one of my guards to bring it to me. Lord Makkara *was* the first to return. I broke the seal and scanned the numbers down to the recorder's stamp at the bottom. One sack of grain per adult, half a sack per child. Enough to sustain them through the time of early spring greens, and perhaps to the first fruits of summer. Five hundred people. It was good.

When I glanced up, Makkara opened his mouth, then closed it and waited.

Ah yes, he waited for payment. Halavant made that decision without me, and it looked to be a good one, though he'd promised more gold than the grain was worth. Yet, the lives saved were worth much more than the gold. Another reason Halavant should rule and not me.

I nodded. "You are the first." I wrote the order for gold on the outside of the parchment and stamped it with my seal. "I hope you will not be the last."

"I may be. The price of grain is six times what it was. The other nobles can get more than the king's offered price by selling to those who can afford it. Yet I feel the king's compassion for those who have not the means to buy, and I chose to ignore the opportunity the others are taking."

True, the price of grain had shot up, however, by the morning's report, it was only triple the usual price. Halavant's offer was still generous. Three weeks was plenty of time for the lords of closer manors to return. Where were they? Why the delay? Had this lord given out the grain recorded on the parchment?

If I didn't have the slow wasting, I'd have found the answers already. I was making decisions blindly.

I gripped the parchment. "Where is the man who recorded this?"

Lord Makkara lifted his hands in apology. "He went home to sleep. I pushed him hard to follow as I distributed the grain."

"I will speak with him before I give you the gold."

"Do you renege on the king's word?"

"No. I will keep his promise as soon as I verify this paper."

He bowed acknowledgement and left.

I *quawlaared.*

My guards gasped. They'd have to get used to me disappearing.

I stumbled down the dais to follow Lord Makkara. Hopefully, he'd keep to noisy streets and taverns, where my footfall would be blend in. I would sit blind no longer.

11

KATRIN

TODAY'S INVITATION was to enjoy the talents of *three fine Trou-veres, noble born and divinely taught in their music,* or so Sir Egvar promised me. I'd wanted to spit in the messenger's face for the offer. Egvar lived under the mistaken impression that I favored him, an impression I'd nurtured but didn't want to maintain after he shot Yosyph. Yet, he'd hinted at movements among the nobility that could mean trouble. And until I knew more, I'd put the craftiest actor to shame.

My maid wove jeweled pins through my hair, sweeping locks away from my face and keeping the main mass trailing down my back over my three sheathed throwing knives.

"Hurry, Maggie."

She wove another jeweled pin into my hair with trembling fingers. "My lady, you shouldn't go if you feel you must bring those awful things."

"That's not your worry. Just finish, or I'll go with my hair half-hiding my face."

"If you don't come back breathing, I'll tell all the other maids your secrets."

I half smiled at her threat. "You already do; that's why I don't tell you any."

She probably didn't tell them anything. She was an orphaned commoner, bird-boned and mannered, though she was growing bolder around me. Her quaint mannerisms isolated her among the other servants. That was why I chose her, someone I could trust to not add to the gossip chain, at least not much.

She tucked my last piece of hair into place. "Be careful. I want you to live long enough that I can learn your secrets to tell."

I turned and grinned at her. Yes, she was growing bolder. "I'll be careful. If anyone discovers the knives, then they'll be getting too close and deserve me using them. Be worried for them, not me."

~

WARM AIR PUSHED against my chilled face as I entered Lord Makkara's mansion. It was even larger than Egvar's. A servant took my furs and directed me through the vast entry to a cozy sitting-room. Three musicians sat along one edge and filled the air with the gentle tones of the viol, pipes, and harp. Women, each trying to outshine the next with jewels and embroidered dresses, lounged next to men in equal peacock attire. Duke Pulska glowered alone, filling a divan with his mass.

"Lady Katrin." Sir Egvar separated himself from a flock of women and took my elbow. "Come sit. Are you healed from your fall at the hunt? I've worried about you, especially since you haven't answered my other invitations."

I fluttered my eyes in coy embarrassment. "I'm sorry, Egvar, that I didn't answer earlier. The fall gave me headaches for weeks." I tottered, pulling myself away from him, and sank to the divan. "I'm well now. Thank you for inviting me. This music is lovely on the ears."

He sat next to me, his leg touching mine.

I tightened my fingers and then relaxed them, but didn't shift away.

He leaned closer. "Did the houndmaster ever bring you your stag? I wonder what kind of animal was in that tree? If only it had climbed a bare-branched oak instead of into a curtain of pine boughs."

I pressed my hand to my forehead. The headache wasn't all an act. I'd had one since the fall, but not due to it.

Egvar stopped. "I'm sorry. The memory of the hounds pains you. Let us talk of other things." He motioned over a wine-bearing servant and handed me a goblet.

The door to the sitting-room slammed open, the music stopped, and a snow-dusted man entered.

Egvar stood. "My dear Makkara. We've been waiting for you. What in the world is wrong?"

Makkara, master of the house, gripped the door frame. His face was a purplish red. "That imposter won't fulfill the pup king's promise."

Egvar put his arm around Makkara's shoulder. "I told you he wouldn't. He doesn't care for the long line of nobility and pure blood. He'll get rid of us as soon as he has gathered enough of a foreign-blooded army to mob us from our homes."

"I gave away that wheat. I spent three weeks doing every-thing the king had asked. I'm getting the money."

Egvar stepped back. "You gave it away? You promised us to not add any strength to the commoners. How could you?"

Makkara grabbed Egvar's arm. "You are a pup yourself. Don't you counsel me in what to do. I would have gotten the gold if I hadn't told that lie you urged of me. He grew suspicious when I told him the other nobles were selling their grain at the market instead. Besides, the king was right in this one thing. There are many starving women and children. I didn't give a single sack to a man. And the gold will help us maintain our power."

"Do you believe the husbands won't force their wives to share?"

"It was to widows and orphans."

The quiet room dropped into silence. Makkara was turning out to be one of the honorable ones. I'd tell Yosyph to pay him for the wheat. But Egvar dropped below my opinion of a pig. He and the others had promised each other to keep the food from the commoners just so they'd stay weak and unable to form an army? Starve those they feared? Even if these nobles weren't planning a rebellion, they were killing the people.

Still, they had rumors to fuel their fear. It was the common people, and a few nobles, who took Fairhaven, overthrew the queen, and put Halavant into power. And the rumors of Yosyph's desired changes had grown into tales of turning the nobility into slaves.

We had to build trust. Where to start?

Duke Pulska belched. "Still a waste of grain. And you'll never see the gold. The shadow demon hates us. He'll take everything from us. And you'll be wishing you were childless like me, rather than see them dead and frozen on the streets."

Makkara shuddered at the words. "He can't. He swore upon his ordination to not touch our power and authority."

A small voice called from the sitting-room door. "Papa, why aren't the musicians playing? I so like to fall asleep to them."

Makkara turned and scooped a little nightgown-clad girl into his arms.

She wrapped her arms around his neck and laid her dark head on his shoulder.

"Shylie, sweetheart." His voice caught in his throat. "Go back to your sister, and I'll tell the musicians to play again."

The little girl scampered off, and the musicians resumed.

I stepped forward. "Lord Makkara. No harm will come to you or your little ones."

He narrowed his eyes. "How could you make that promise? Who are you?" His face paled. "You're that red-headed consort to the pup king."

I lifted my chin. "I'm Lady Katrin, once betrothed to King Halavant. I can still influence him and his brother. I will make sure you get paid for the grain you gave away, and your family will be safe."

"If you are part of their circle, then why are you here?" He looked at Egvar as he asked the question.

Egvar lay his arm around my shoulders. "She has influence on them, but is not influenced by them. She's sympathetic to our plight since the war and has given us bits of helpful information."

A chill ran down my back. What information had I given them? These nobles trusted me enough to include me in these social gatherings, but at what cost? Had I betrayed my trust to Yosyph and Halavant by some thoughtless word?

Makkara leaned over me, and I shrank back. He was broad-shouldered, and his face held an intensity that made me tremble. "Do you know how the king's brother plans to take away our power?"

I straightened and looked into his searching eyes. "He doesn't—"

"Then you know nothing." And he turned from me.

"Wait!" How much could I tell him, to win his trust and still maintain my somewhat thoughtless act? "The king and his brother sometimes talked about making a council equally composed of the nobility and the commoners, yet they didn't say they'd take away your power."

He lowered his face toward mine. "The king already has added enough mixed blooded commoners to the royal council to muddy any chance of civil communication. And you say they aren't taking away our power?"

Egvar pulled me closer to his side and faced Makkara. "You are too hard on her. She doesn't make the decisions, but she's trying to help us."

Makkara nodded curtly. "Then she'd better tell that shadow-king he needs to denounce and imprison all who tout the overthrow of the noble class. I don't feel it safe for my wife or children to leave my home."

Had it gone that far? I'd heard the rumors of attacks targeting the nobility. I'd assumed it was rumors and criminals, not reality and the common people. *Oh, Yosyph. We have to do something.*

The vicious barking of dogs, followed by the long bay of a hunting hound, pushed past the closed windows.

Makkara called in a servant. "Go see to them. And bring back, alive, if possible this time, the person they've cornered."

My knees wobbled beneath me, and I would have plopped to the floor if Egvar hadn't steadied me.

"Lady Katrin." He put his other hand at the small of my back, just below my hidden knives. "You are still not well. I'll take you home."

"No." I braced my knees. "I want to see the intruder."

12

YOSYPH

M<small>AKKARA</small>'<small>S</small> <small>MANSION IN</small> F<small>AIRHAVEN</small>, Lansimetsa
   Febrúar 4th

I <small>WAS BEGINNING</small> to dislike dogs. My shadow-walk meant little when they could hear my heavy tread and heavy breathing and smell my sweat-soaked body.

I pulled myself back onto the top of the wall that surrounded Lord Makkara's mansion. The dogs scrambled at the wall's base and filled my ears with aching explosions of sound.

My horse sat on the other side of the wall. I'd leave without having entered the mansion. So be it. I would find some other way to discover Makkara's secrets.

I lowered myself to my horse and pulled my emotions back in. A riderless horse trotting through the evening streets was worse than a dark-clad rider. My useless feet were the only part of me that didn't zing with the onrush of emotions.

Thank you, God, I signed after the emotions settled, *for protecting me from the dogs. Please help me know what to do next.*

Nothing. No impression. Only my tired body pleading to go home and rest. How could I rule blind?

I signed again, *Should I try to enter visible as a servant? I'm still unnoticed by most, if they aren't looking for me. Or should I find the Makkara's recorder?*

No feeling, not a thought outside my own. My mother's journals had said God didn't want us to idly wait on him for direction. We had to make decisions and move forward, listening for his guidance along the way. But I was so tired. Why couldn't He tell me this time?

A voice carried over the wall. "Quiet! Down!" and the dogs quieted. And a moment later, "He got away. Lord Makkara won't be pleased."

I would seek out the recorder. But, first I'd have to find where he lived. A long night lay ahead.

13

HALAVANT

O<small>FF THE COAST</small> of Carani
   Febrúar 5th

O<small>UR BOAT ROCKED</small> in a small green inlet as the sun rose behind us. Instead of pines and oaks lining its hills, palms waved over a sandy beach before the land rose into deep green jungles and distant cliffs. No docks or houses marred the birdsong-filled land. My stomach unclenched from the rolling surf we'd just crossed only to re-clench with nervousness. "I'm sorry to say, there's no welcome committee," I tried to joke.

The grizzled sea captain stepped next to me and gazed at the land. "Be glad there ain't any. My old man got butchered by them when I was a cabin boy. I only escaped because one of the women thought I had a beautiful voice. Not sure how she figured that from a screaming, weeping child. She let me steal a small fisherman's skiff and be on my way. Your gold better be worth it for me to return here." He glanced at my hands. "You certain you want to risk your life for those?"

"Yes."

"Well, you should be safe until you make your way to the highland. The Carani despise the jungle. Only reason I'd land here. I'll let you off and come back in sixty days. If you're not here, I'll assume you're dead. Half the gold alive is better than all the gold dead, so I won't risk more than one return." His lips had thinned to a tight line as he looked toward the shore.

"You promised to come back three times, at two-month intervals."

"I've changed my mind. I'll come back once, and if you're not here, you'll have to find some Carani fisherman to sail you home."

"I'm your king!"

"You ain't nobody's king in this land. I'll take you back now, and you can continue your charade in Lansimetsa. I don't care. I'm sailing away with the next tide, and you'd better get off if you're staying here."

~

I SWATTED A WHINING BUG. My face was already an itchy mess from their bites and bruised from my braced hands hitting at the biters. Jungle spread about us as we trod along a well-beaten path away from the beach. Surely, it led to some village.

I rubbed my cheek on my coarse-woven sleeve. It did little to alleviate the itch. "Elise, I don't think your ointment is keeping them away."

She swatted her neck. One of her eyes was puffy and half closed.

The healer, Gaven, looked at the two of us, drew in a ragged breath, and then sniffed. He didn't have any bites. "You should have listened to the captain and washed yourselves with those stinking herbs and sea water. Serves you right for marching off at such a pace. I'm an old man, not made for running through the jungle."

Elise laid her hand on his arm. "I'm sorry. We can rest. And I'll see if I can boil up some salt and bitter herbs for Halavant and me."

Gaven leaned on his walking stick and sank to the ground. "Sensible girl."

I shrugged my neck and face as deep as I could into my shirt collar, trying to cover my skin. "Tell me again what to say when we meet someone."

Gaven leaned against a tree and sighed. "Tell them you are my inept translator who can't remember a simple thing, traveling with a healer and his granddaughter. We offer our services in exchange for food and lodging."

"I don't know the Carani words for *inept* nor *pompous healer*."

"Oh, they'll figure that part out without you saying it. Every village has need of a healer's help, even the pompous kind." A smile crept along one corner of his mouth.

I pulled out the book of Carani words. It slipped from my braced hands to the ground. Its pages were bent and crinkled with my frequent and clumsy turning of them. My old tutor was always appalled at my slaughtering of the accent and my sloppy enunciation of the clipped language, even after five years of study. The written language was similar to Lansimetsian, however, when spoken, each word was bitten off before half-finished. Maybe the people here spoke slower than my tutor.

Elise dipped a cloth into an acerbic scented liquid. "May I?"

I nodded, and she dabbed the cloth over all my exposed skin. It stung and stunk. She dipped a longer strip of cloth and wrapped it around my neck. The scent tickled up into the space above my eyes and the whining bugs distanced themselves. *Finally.* I settled against the roots of a large tree. Only then did she tend to herself.

"Thank you."

She shrugged and smiled as she tied a second soaked cloth around her neck, then stiffened as she stared off to my side and behind me.

I turned and jumped to my feet. Two men pointed spears at us. Brown-patterned wraps extended from their waist to their knees. Deep brown hair waved around square faces and long noses, and even though their skin was a golden caramel, it was not much darker than mine grew in the summer.

One pointed at me. "*The——stares like—foreigner. But he ——like—son.*"

I closed my eyes, trying to pick out the missing words.

A point prodded my chest.

I jumped back, tripped over a root, and tumbled to the ground.

The two men shook with laughter.

"*Please,*" I stuttered in Carani, both in anger and fear. "*Old man, girl, healers. Give service.*" I motioned to Gaven and Elise. "*Food, shelter.*"

The second man stopped laughing and slapped the first. He spoke slowly to me. "*You speak like a foreigner, but have a familiar face. We don't need healers, but we welcome family.*"

He grasped me around my wrists and helped me to my feet. His gaze shifted from my face to my braced hands. He was taller than his companion, with a long scar running along his jawline, and looked a little older than Yosyph.

"*My friends, too.*" I could speak smoother now I didn't have a spear waving in my face.

"*Brother, your friends are welcome, too.*"

Brother? Did my Carani blood come through so strong in my features? Gaven told how the first Lansimetsian king fled from Carani. That was generations ago.

He waited for me to walk next to him and then set down the path at a rapid pace.

"*I am Halavant,*" I said.

The first man burst into laughter, then slowly said, "*We should call you Odion. Your hair is yellow as daffodils.*"

The second man cuffed the first again. "*Forgive his impudence. I am Jabare. And you, Ha-a-fant, must take a new name, Moswen, for your light skin. We must hurry. I'll tell you more when you meet my uncle.*"

The first man's eyes grew wide "*The Moswen? That cripple, the Moswen?*"

"*Hush.*" Jabare cuffed his companion so hard he fell backward.

Elise touched the back of my boot with the toe of her shoe. "What are they saying?"

"They think I'm a relative and welcome me as family. You and Gaven are allowed to come, too, since you are with me."

Her sigh of relief was buried by Gaven's snort.

He leaned on his walking stick and gasped a few breaths. "I guess it's a good thing I let you come along. Could you use your family influence to stop this blistering pace?"

We slowed to a snail's pace through the jungle, enjoying the birdsong, and the distant whine of bugs, and no conversation, until the scent of roasting meat announced the village. The jungle opened into a clearing spotted with rounded dwellings made of woven lattice and leaves. Children ran about in states of half to full undress. Women wore wraps similar to Jabare, but covered themselves from just under the arms to the knees. They tended fires and scolded children. A girl turned the spit of meat over a fire. There were no men.

Jabare stepped from the trees while we remained in the shadows.

"*Uncle Jabare!*" The girl at the spit dashed to him and threw her arms around him. Then she noticed us, and clung tighter to him, hiding her face in his chest. Her whisper slipped past his shoulder. "*Foreigners?*"

"*Family.*" He turned to us, motioned us forward, and pointed, starting with me. "*Moswen, old uncle, and cousin.*"

"*The Moswen? The one that——*"

Jabare gave a quick shake of the head, and she stopped.

What was the *Moswen,* other than light-skinned?

Jabare patted the girl on her back. "*Go turn the meat before my sister scolds you. Have they returned?*"

She called back as she ran to the roasting meat, "*You are the first—*"

A nasal, trumpeting note echoed from the other side of the village.

"*—and the luckiest, because you found the Moswen.*"

Was I hearing the words right? These people were easier to understand than my tutor, or I'd inadvertently learned more than I'd intended in my studies with him.

Men strode into the far end of the village. All were armed with spears. Pairs of them carried long branches, from which swung carcasses of more deer-like animals, though their horns spiraled instead of branched.

At the front of the group, a man with a black staff and gold encircling his head walked apart. He held up his hand. The men halted, dropped their hunting kills to the ground and pulled back spears in readiness for distant throws.

Jabare's companion flattened to the ground. I considered joining him, or running. Elise could have kept up with me, but Gaven would be skewered.

Jabare stepped forward, placing himself between us and the spears. "*Honored Uncle,*" he yelled across the village, his tenor voice sending birds screaming from the surrounding trees. When they quieted he continued. "*The ancestor tree walks.*"

Ancestor tree walks? The Carani lore was never part of my lessons.

The gold-crowned man stared at me. His stance was as rigid as a wildcat ready to pounce.

Jabare, grabbed my arm and dragged me forward a step. "*The ancestor tree walks.*"

A high trilling cry split the air. One of the women raised her arms into the air and let out another trilling note. Another woman joined the cry. And soon all the women of the village were tearing the air with sounds more shrill than a metal flute.

The gold-crowned man flicked his hand. The spears lowered, and the men joined in the trilling call, adding their deep voices, till the huts should have shaken apart.

That was a good thing, hopefully.

"*Come.*" Jabare dragged me into the village. "*You are our honored guest.*"

I jogged after him. "*What is the ancestor tree walks?*"

He grinned. "*When lost family returns, it is as if the ancestor tree carried them home.*"

I drew close enough to see the gold-crowned man clearly and stopped. He had my father's face, and my grandfather's. The jaw, lips, nose, and brow that passed down so closely in the generations it seemed minted in a coin—the features my child-hood roundness melted into—the features of the king of Lansimetsa.

14

ELISE

Jungle, Lower Carani
Február 5th

I'd hoped to be welcomed as a healer, but they welcomed us, or rather, Halavant, like a god.

The chief, his three wives—one of them much younger and hugely pregnant—and their two half-grown daughters sat on woven mats near a stinking fire. A second fire burned near us. It stunk, but it kept the evening bugs away, and the salve a village woman gave me numbed the itching.

I had much to learn from these people.

The rest of the village sat in a half circle of families and fires, facing the chief and us. There were about a hundred of them, including the children.

I nibbled at the meat. Its coating of bitter herbs was worse than the stinking fires. The people looked healthy enough it couldn't be poisonous. My stomach disagreed. I set the meat on the bark platter and bit into a thick-skinned purple fruit. Tartness burst in my mouth, and I dropped the fruit.

The woman serving us laughed as she picked it up. She chattered like a squirrel as she peeled away the skin, revealing clusters of bright, translucent seeds. She separate one cluster and handed it to me.

This time sweetness accompanied the tartness, and the bitter taste washed away.

The chief watched us with a joyful face that was an aged version of Halavant's. How had the family resemblance survived so many generations in two lands? Was that same strength of family line the one that caused the slow wasting? If so, I'd watch what the chief ate and drank, and we'd find the cure. He was much older than any of the kings in recent generations.

The gods were favoring us.

Halavant grinned around a bit of food a lovely young lady had placed in his mouth. His braced hands were not a hindrance in this meal. He was enjoying this a little too much. He'd been raised a prince and treated with respect. Yet the vibrating, trilling welcome, and the villagers' adoration was something more than he'd enjoyed as king.

The chief stood and the murmur of voices fell away.

His rapid words poured over the clearing.

"Halavant," I hissed. "What's he saying?"

He tilted his head and closed his eyes.

The chief paused, then continued slower, pausing as Halavant translated.

"Many years, I have," Halavant paused searching for a word. "Wanted a son. For longer than my sister's son has been alive. But even with my three choice wives, I have only daughters."

The chief continued, and Halavant blanched.

The chief lifted his hand and motioned to Halavant, and the people's voices rose in another village-shuddering trill.

I touched Halavant's shoulder. "What happened?"

"He thinks I am his son sent from the golden gods. The promised Moswen. To renew the line of the chiefs. I don't believe we'll leave easily."

15

YOSYPH

Palace, Fairhaven, Lansimetsa
Februar 6th

I HALF-DOZED on the throne as the counselor of agriculture
outlined plans to help the people harvest early crops. I should
have been listening better. This was vital to our kingdom's
survival. Yet after the last two nights of shadow-walking, weariness grasped me as if I'd climbed the Devil's Teeth.

And for what? The recorder who'd gone with Lord Makkara
verified the records and added details that meant he was either
telling the full truth or was an artist of lying. I'd attempted to
enter another of the gatherings of my not-so-loyal nobles. Dogs
chased me away, again.

The counselor's voice rose. "If they build bins of soil to plant
cabbages and other cold weather crops in their huts, then they
will have something to eat this spring."

I nodded. "This could help. However, we must consider,
where will they get the wood to build these boxes? Where will
they sleep once the bins take up what little floor space they

have? And will the seeds even sprout in the short winter daylight?"

The counselor blinked, then stuttered. "Ah, yes, good questions. Please forgive me for presenting such an ill-conceived plan, honored Yorel." He bowed and backed from the room.

"Wait," I called out. "It's a good idea. We must address the particulars. Please look into those questions and return with further ideas."

"I'll see to them and return tomorrow." He scurried off.

I hadn't meant to demean his ideas. I wasn't good with people. Logistics was where my strength lay. I'd find a way for the people to build the boxes to grow winter food. Yet, I'd rather the nobles sell—even at an inflated price—the grain the people needed. Why wouldn't they?

Katrin stood waiting in the corner of the room, her forehead creased.

Once the agriculture counselor exited, Katrin strode forward, stopping at the foot of the dais. "Honored Yorel, I have a boon to beg."

She'd not approached me in the throne room before. It was part of our charade to not interact much in public, especially since I became Regent. What brought her here? I motioned for her to continue speaking.

She stepped up one step and stopped as two of my guards lowered their spears. Her eyes flashed before she bowed her head and stepped back down. "One of my desert-blooded servants has fallen ill. I ask for your help with your desert herb knowledge."

Ah, I see. I signed. *I'm the desert-blooded servant, and she wants me to rest. But I can't yet.* I folded my hands in my lap. "I'll go when I've listened to the petitioners."

She lifted her chin. Her jaw hardened. Her eyes burned with a fierceness. If the guards noticed, they might throw her from the room. And if they didn't notice, they surely thought her naïve to ask this of the regent. She clenched her fists, then relaxed them and dropped to her knees, bowing her head in apparent humility and pleading. "It can't wait. He's growing weaker as I speak. Please come. The petitioners can ask the priests at the temples, or wait until tomorrow. He may not last until then. The physician said he can't do anything else. Only you can help."

I shrugged inwardly. Weariness sat in a fog on me. I'd judge better if I had a little rest.

My chamberlain stood at ready attention at the edge of the room.

I nodded to him. "I will see Lady Katrin's servant, and I do not know how long I will be gone. Please tell the petitioners I will see them on the morrow."

The chamberlain bowed. "I will inform them, my lord."

I pushed against the throne armrests and came to a wobbling stand. Numbness reached halfway up my calves.

My closest two guards, the two who knew my weakness, took up a stance on either side of me and marched in slow steadiness to my stilted steps down the dais and out of the throne room, following Katrin. Thankfully, the king's chambers were a short walk from the throne room.

Katrin gripped my arm as I stumbled into my room. "You're wasting too quickly. Have you taken your teas as you promised?"

I hadn't in several weeks. I could move with numbness. But the foggy thoughts caused by the tea was a luxury I couldn't afford. I let my steps fall to a shuffle now that others couldn't see me.

She gripped my arm tighter. "You didn't answer."

"I'll drink them tomorrow."

"Yosyph, you can't help the people if you kill yourself."

I stumbled again, and this time she couldn't rebalance me. I took her down with me to the floor, her gown poofing out as I fell on her.

My guards lifted my arms over their shoulders and carried me to my bed.

Katrin followed muttering, "Too weak, too stubborn."

∼

THE TEAS TURNED my weariness into a warm and soft drowsiness. As I lay in bed, the world faded in and out around me.

Katrin sat beside me, holding my hand. "If you can stay awake a little longer, I must tell you something. If not, I'll tell you when you wake."

I forced my eyes to focus on her.

"Lord Makkara gave the grain to the people. He's been honorable to his word and is one of the few of the fence-sitters you can still trust. Yet, he may not stay that way. Sir Egvar and Duke Pulska both are urging him and the other nobles to not give grain to the people, because they fear the common people, given enough power or even food, will rise and overthrow the noble-blooded just as they overthrew the queen."

"I've ordered Makkara's gold delivered. And the others need not fear. Halavant and I've both promised to let them retain their powers."

Her brow pinched. "Many of them don't trust you to keep that promise, and the rising threats of the commoners to the nobility is giving them reason to distrust you. You must do something about it."

"The common people have reason for their discontent. They are starving. If those who have grain would sell it, then the people wouldn't rise against them."

"Yosyph." She caressed my cheek. "The nobility have families, too. They fear for their wives and little ones. They are scared. Help them have reason to trust you."

"I'll not imprison a man for seeking a loaf of bread for his family."

"And the man who attacks like a highway robber?"

I pushed against my rising emotions: fear, worry, helplessness. As I did so, the shadow-realm pulled me in and spat me back out. Pain scraped the underside of my skin like glass shards.

Katrin kissed my cheek. "I'm sorry. I shouldn't worry you about this now. Sleep, then we'll figure this out together."

~

I woke to the chill of a bedded fire and low lamps.

Katrin dozed in the corner.

I sat up in bed.

The guard at the door shifted. "Honored Yorel. It's the middle of the night. Please sleep more. I may speak out of turn, but I—"

"You speak out of turn. Take me to the queen's prison. I must speak with her." If I couldn't gather knowledge outside the palace, I'd gather it from her.

"But—"

"Then I'll go myself. I know the way." I set aside my emotions and *quawlaared*.

"Wait." He hurried to where I'd been and still was. "I'll go with you; please stay out of the shadow-walk. I fear it makes things worse."

I pulled my emotions back in and leaned on his arm as the emotions settled. "Let's go."

A long walk later, I entered a guarded room that had no window but was richly furnished with rugs, chairs, table, and a

large poster bed. Two guards stood in the hall and two within the room. A curtained corner for the queen's privacy and personal needs was the only place I couldn't see. A fire glowed along one wall, and beside it the queen's maid slept on a pallet. The queen sat at a glass table, scribbling away at papers. Lamps glowed around her—on the floor and even under the table—lighting her face in upside-down shadows.

She glanced at me as I entered, then turned her gaze back to the papers. Her shoulder-length yellow hair was plaited and curled, her dressing gown tailored to a slim body, and her face a crazed mask of flinching muscles. Her muttering drifted over the scratch of the pen. "I must make plans. Fredrick will free me. He loves me. He didn't mean to hurt me. It was a mistake. I didn't listen. I will now."

"Your highness." The words came easier than before. It was the only address she'd respond to.

She looked at me closer and the crazed look changed to surprise. "Luukas, what have you done to your skin and hair? You are so dark now. Will it help? Our son is still a babe. He needs his father."

I startled and caught at the wall. This was the first time she'd mistaken me for my father. It must have been my voice. And her mind was going fast. "Your highness."

"Analiese, my dear Luukas, I'm your Analiese."

"Analiese." I shielded the word from the disgust welling up.

She reached out to me. "Luukas, I'm so scared. What if they don't find a cure?"

I let her hands curl around mine. Her hands had written out the orders for so many deaths, paid for the enslavement of a third of her people, and now were plotting against her son, Halavant. If she thought I was Luukas, then she might tell me what I needed to learn.

I sat on a chair next to hers and let her caress my hands. "Analiese, who are loyal to you?"

"To us. They are all loyal to us. They love you. They will love our son."

"Who protects you from those you fear?"

Her face shifted, and she dropped my hands. "Traitor!" she screamed and pushed against me.

I stood and backed away.

"You destroyed him. You turned my son against me. You," she stopped as I stumbled backward against the edge of a rug and fell to the floor. "And you are fading, just as my husband did." A sneer hardened on her face. "You are fading faster than him. Fredrick will free me. Halavant will love me again. And you will die."

That didn't go well. I'd hoped she'd finally tell me who'd worked under her. Who to watch for. Even if she had told me names, could I have trusted it in the state of her mind?

I leaned heavily on my guard as I passed one of her prison guards. "Her papers."

He handed a loose stack of parchment. The top page was a jumble of shapes, ink blots, and images. The drawings were more confused than ever. She was fully crazy. I'd not visit her again.

16

KATRIN

Palace, Fairhaven, Lansimetsa
Februar 7th

I spun about mid-pace as the door clicked open and Yosyph stumbled in, supported by his guard. "You left!"

Yosyph sank into a chair, his head hung forward. "I did."

I turned to the guard. "And you! How could you aid him in his midnight wanderings?"

The guard fixed his gaze to the floor. "He shadow-walked."

"You could have stopped him."

The guard met my eyes. "The Yorel is my liege until King Halavant returns. I will treat him with such respect."

I threw my hands in the air and plopped into the chair next to Yosyph. "You have to rest. If I could learn to shadow-walk, I'd do it for you. Maybe I will learn."

A deep laughter broke from Yosyph. "Katrin," he gasped, "it isn't something you can learn. Only those with the inborn ability can. Besides, your emotions show clearer than most; you'd never be able to set them aside to *quawlaar*."

"How can I help you then? You won't rest. You keep shadow-walking. You're killing yourself." My voice dropped to a whisper. "Yosyph, let me help you. Let me take some of this weight."

He closed his eyes. "Katrin, I'll rest."

"The remainder of the night?"

He stood, and I rushed to his side, steadying him. He shuffled toward his bed. "I'll stay here the remainder of the night. Tomorrow, I must be back to my duties. I can't rule from a bed."

"Yes, you can. Your father did. And he was the best king we've ever had, except for one. You are the most honorable leader this land ever had."

YOSYPH SNORED avalanches while he slept. This was a new development of the slow wasting, another part of his body not working as it should.

I chanted in my mind again. *Stop feeling the emotions. Stop feeling the emotions.* I breathed deep and pushed at the worry that clutched behind my stomach like a terrified child clinging to the skirts of her mother. *Stop feeling emotions.* Fear joined worry. Helplessness piled on top.

One of Yosyph's snores turned to a whistle, almost like a bird. Would he honk like a goose next? I giggled. *Stop feeling the emotions?* If anything, the emotions glowed fiercer. I must do it someplace away from Yosyph, where I could still my emotions. Would he behave if I left?

"Guard. If the Yorel tries to leave the room, please do all you can to convince him to stay."

"I will try."

I stood to leave. "That's all I can ask. Thank you—what is your name?"

The guard bowed. "Hoft, at your service. At least he lets us watch over him in his room. That's more than King Halavant allowed."

"A bother of brothers."

Hoft stifled a chuckle, then straightened. "Take care, Lady Katrin. And please don't do anything foolish."

"I won't." I looked out the window, to where the morning sun first kissed the distant farm land. I would learn to shadow-walk. I'd watched Farid teach Yosyph. I knew the steps. I had to learn, otherwise he'd shadow-walk one time too many and not come out of it because he was too weak. But to learn, I needed a calming place.

17

ELISE

The village was primitive, the dwellings lattice domes of flexible branches and woven leaves, and the people—they wove charms into their hair, the fringes of their wraps, and along the door holes of their huts. Everything was superstition.

Gaven bent over a boy whose leg swelled with days-old broken bones, never set. He fingered the bulge where the bones pressed against the skin and untied the poultice of herbs wrapped around it. He muttered under his breath, "Blithering idiots. Don't need healers? Clearly they don't care for their children to grow up, or their women to survive breech births."

I bathed the boy's sweating head and shot a tight smile to his mother, who stood hovering.

Gaven turned to me. "Elise, get that poor excuse for a translator in here. And have him bring two strong men."

I ran from the hut.

Halavant knelt in a circle of young men, including the two

who first found us. One man threw striped sticks into the middle of the circle. Some sticks landed crosswise and some parallel. A mixture of cheers and groans rose, and flecks of gold passed hands.

Gambling? What a waste of human intelligence. "Halavant."

He glanced from the sticks to me and grinned. The man next to him put a gold fleck into the sack at Halavant's knees.

"We need you and two strong men."

"What happened?"

"Broken bone. It needs setting."

Halavant spoke, no longer halting, and two of the men jumped up to follow us.

We entered to find Gaven spooning a thick liquid into the boy's mouth, something to dull the pain.

"You there," he pointed to the larger of the two men, "hold the boy's upper leg, and don't let it shift. And you," he pointed to the other, "when I say go, pull on his lower leg while I set the bone."

Both men turned seawater green as Halavant translated.

A boy's scream and a mother's weeping later, the boy's leg lay straight on the mat. The boy lay in a faint as we splinted the leg.

The mother looked at us with tears as she spoke. Halavant translated, "Will he travel to the lands of the gods? I will submit, but I'd hoped to keep my precious child for longer."

I glanced at the red, hopefully not infected leg. We'd have to watch him carefully. "If you let us tend to him, you may keep him even till the time of grandchildren."

Both she and the two men who helped shuddered the hut with their trills of joy. I wish they'd find some quieter way to express their emotions.

Halavant knelt down next to me. "They should worship you and Gaven, not me. Thank you for helping him." He gave me a quick side squeeze.

I leaned into him momentarily, then pulled back. He was still king, and I was just a healer. "Please ask who else needs help."

Halavant glanced at the boy, now sleeping with less of a pained crease in his forehead. "They'll trust you more after this. I never knew a people who didn't trust healers."

I nudged him with my elbow. "You don't trust your royal physicians."

"That's different. Bribery and noble blood bought their position, not ability. I trust you, and I suppose I trust Gaven. He'd never put on a show of liking me to just poison me. He'd tell me first and give the reasons why."

I chuckled. He joked about it now, when he was tight-mouthed about it before.

We went from hut to hut. Sometimes we found a wound that needed stitching or a deep sliver to dig out. We gathered a trailing of children and even some mothers. They stood outside the hut, waited for the trilling of joy as we finished tending to a person, and joined in with their own.

The one thing we didn't see was malnutrition. These people were healthy, and they rivaled Gaven in herb knowledge. They knew how to drive off the bugs, they'd created ointments to kill infection, yet when we stitched an open wound or splinted bones they watched with a mixture of fear and awe. Did they believe the inner body untouchable?

I asked Halavant my question, and he gave me their answer with an incredulous look. "We are all from the gods, from the oldest man to the newest baby. Some, like the Moswen are half god, but we each have a sliver of divinity. And we each return to the gods when our journey is through. Our blood and our bones are sacred. To touch them brings the wrath of the gods on us. We must only wash them with sacred water and bind them with holy herbs. Only in the birth of a child is this ban lifted; it is when another brother journeys from the heavens to us. The old man and girl are messengers from the gods and heralds for the Moswen. The gods do not ban them, and they bless us."

"They said all that?"

"Actually more. That is the best I can translate. How do they believe this?"

It was a poetic view on life, but dangerous for those who needed help. Perhaps we'd add to their superstition in a healthy way. Something else to do in addition to finding the cure for the slow wasting. Hopefully, the chief would allow us to question him about what he ate and drank, now that we'd earned the respect of the people.

18

HALAVANT

Village, Lower Carani
  Februar 7th

Being the Moswen rivaled and surpassed being a king. I had the undeviating adoration of the villagers without the responsibilities. No one asked me to rule or judge betwixt them and another. No one tried to kill me in my sleep. We'd find a way to leave, when we found the cure. Why not enjoy this now?

I leaned back against a tree trunk as seven children performed an intricate dance to the thumping of their older sisters' drums. They were delightful people, sweet and childlike in their simplicity.

"*Moswen.*" One of the chief's wives, the youngest one, knelt down next to me. "*My husband seeks your holy presence.*"

I followed her to mats set outside the chief's hut.

The chief rose to greet me and waited until I sat before sitting again. "*Moswen. Do you remember the house of the gods?*"

My throat tightened. What was I supposed to say? Should I pretend to remember and know things of myths and legends I'd never heard? No, I'd speak as little as I could and hopefully they didn't kill me for impersonating a divinity. *"No."*

He nodded grimly. *"Do you remember your father?"*

"No."

He nodded again. *"Have your hands always been crippled?"*

"No. I was poisoned."

He glanced at his pregnant wife, and she nodded, her face glowing with hope.

His face softened, and he raised his eyes to the sky. *"We thank each of you for sending the true Moswen."* He looked into my face and smiled. *"You do not remember, as you could not, to be the true Moswen. I will teach you of your prophecy."*

I leaned forward.

"Before the golden gods planted the ancestor tree in this blessed land, our ancestors lived in a desert land. Then one goddess grew to love our father chief, enough to take up the lowly place of the second wife, the servant-wife."

"Servant-wife?"

"First wife is ruler of the home and bearer of chiefs. Second wife is servant to the first and bearer of warriors to protect. Third wife," he smiled at his pregnant wife, *"is beloved in old age to bring forth new seed.*

"The goddess, golden as the sun, lowered herself to be the servant-wife. The chief loved her more than his first wife. And poison grew in the first wife's heart. When the goddess gave birth to a golden babe, half god, half man, the first wife cried her poison into a striped orchid and gave it to the goddess as a gift. The goddess died and returned to the bright realm of the gods. The first wife took the child as her own. As the years passed, the child grew powerful in goodness and likeness to his mother, and the chief loved his son more than his first wife. The first wife again grew poisonous with jealousy. One night she cried poison onto his head, stealing his memories, and onto his hands to stop

him from creating beauty. The half-grown boy no longer remembered his father."

How strange his three questions would match me. I leaned back, not sure if I was ready to hear more.

The chief continued. *"The chief, who had already lost his wife, pled with the gods to heal his son. His golden wife came and carried off the child, saying when the people no longer were filled with jealousy, then her son would return and his memories would be restored. But his hands would forever remain crippled as a reminder against that hateful first wife. And you are he. We have waited long for you. Do you remember now?"*

How had I become the center of a myth? Should I point out that if I'd forgotten everything then I wouldn't remember my hands being poisoned? A fatal fallacy to bring to light. *"I don't yet."*

The chief's shoulders slumped forward.

His wife patted his hand. *"Give him time. He's wandered the world and the heavens without memories since the beginning of the ancestor tree."*

"What is the ancestor tree?"

The chief removed his crown and laid it in my lap. He pointed to an engraving on the inside that would have sat over his forehead—a tree in full bloom with roots reaching deep into the earth. *"When your mother took you, she led your father to a new land, more dry than where they'd lived before. There she planted a tree which spread into this vast jungle. Each of our ancestors are buried at the roots, and it carries them up to the heavens. Now it has walked from the heavens and carried you back to us. You sat at its roots when Jabare and Donkor found you."*

Jabare's friend was named Donkor? I laughed, and my next question slipped out before I could think better of it. *"But, Donkor thought I couldn't be the Moswen because of my crippled hands."*

The chief slapped his leg. "*Donkor is a fool. He never listened to the histories around the fire. He thought the Moswen would come as tall as two men and strong enough to tear up the leg-thick tree. His is tales. Mine is truths.*"

If only I could pinch myself to wake up. I dug one of my hand braces into my leg. I didn't wake. "*What is the Moswen supposed to do when he returns?*"

"*You will renew the line of the chiefs. You will take to wife three women of our village, and I hope you will choose from my daughters. The gods did not bless me with sons, so I could provide you with worthy wives.*"

I didn't want many wives, even worthy ones of my Carani kin. Besides, we weren't staying here. *Elise and Gaven, you better find the cure soon. I don't know how long I can keep up this facade.*

19

YOSYPH

PALACE, Fairhaven, Lansimetsa
Februar 8th

GALLIARD WROTE as I dictated from my bed. Two days of rest, and I felt strong enough to sit on the throne again, but the royal physician, who'd finally realized I had the slow wasting, wouldn't let me from my bed until 'I was stronger than a new calf.' Where Katrin pled, the physician ordered.

Galliard was a competent and quiet aid. I'd chosen him years ago to help raise the revolution. An honest man with a solid head. It was good to converse with him. Before the war, I'd always kept my identity secret from him.

He stopped writing. "Honored Yorel, if you set up spies and secret police, you will be re-instituting and entrenching what evil is already in the land."

A good head, except for that. My hands muttered signs. *I need information. I can't gather that myself.*

As if he'd understand my signing, he said, "The spies could be useful, within certain bounds. But the soldiers taking those you suspect prisoner in the nighttime? You will turn the people against you."

"I could choose spies that could also act as assassins." I was only half joking.

Galliard laughed darkly. "Not all have your honor and restraint. You could have killed Lord Fredrick, General Jonstone, and many others. You imprisoned them instead. I doubt if you gave another man a knife and permission to kill as needed, you'd get many prisoners to question. And what if the spies were wrong in their estimate? My brothers were part of the queen's elite and did many things under their captain's direction, not knowing it was wrong," he clenched his hands, "until too late. No. Do not institute that dark organization again."

I tried to think through the tea-induced fog. "How would you suggest we root out the existing corruption?"

"Keep your guards close, arrest openly those who break the law, and be impartial to noble and commoner."

"That is simpler said than done. I don't know enough."

"You never will. You're not a god."

I smiled wryly. "Too true. Yet, I can rule more justly by knowing more. I need spies to see for me."

"Then send them under strict command to only gather information and not injure."

"Some will slip away if I don't have a means to take them in the night."

"Aye, some will. But you'll retain the trust of the people, and the honest outnumber the dishonest."

"Why is it, as a ruler, I have less power and freedom than I did as the silent servant spy?"

Galliard just laughed.

I laid my head back against the pillows. Even half-sitting in bed was tiring. "New proclamation: Let it be known, any man who attacks another, even for a loaf of bread, will be whipped with five stripes and put in the stocks for a day. If the attacked person is injured, the attacker shall work off the debt with a month's labor. If the attacked person dies, then the attacker will become a servant to the dead person's family or die themselves. Those who need food must come to the temples or the palace, and work will be found for them to earn their sustenance."

Galliard tilted his head as he wrote the last line. "A wise addendum. I've worried some were taking advantage of your benevolence of giving away wheat."

"Only partially wise. Some have grown too weak to work. And there are still too many who live far from the palace, and the temples have not been honoring my orders to help feed them."

"Then send some of your *spies* to help keep them in line."

"No. They need giant-blooded soldiers to put some shiver into their obedience."

Galliard laughed again. "I was wrong to think you were an emotionless shadow, full of honor and intelligent but not much else."

Honor, yes. Intelligence? I was far beneath where I needed to be.

~

A DEEP SNORE WOKE ME. It came from a slumped figure against the wall. A second figure sagged over a chair. My guards were asleep. The fire had burned down to a soft glow.

I tensed.

The door swung open on well-oiled hinges. A dark figure slipped in, swung his head from side to side, then walked towards me without even padding his footsteps.

I sat up.

He laughed in a harsh whisper. "So it's true. You can't even rise from your bed." He slipped his hand to a knife at his hip. "I'll take my time with you. The guards won't wake to your cries."

I pulled a knife from under my pillow. Katrin had been teaching me, but I hadn't practiced enough to be more than a fair toss. Foolish oversight.

He drew closer. How much closer to be sure I hit him? Another step. Close enough. The assassin could also throw his knife.

I flicked the blade. It arched in a shallow path and slipped by his arm.

He flinched back a step, his intake of breath sharp in the silence. Then he raced forward.

I gripped the edge of my wool blanket and waited until he was a leap away.

As he dove, knife drawn, I rolled off the bed, pulling the blanket with me.

He landed face down on my bed as I thumped to the floor on my knees.

I flicked the wool blanket over him.

He rose to his hands and knees under the heavy covering.

I lunged, teetering on near-useless legs, wrapped my arms around him, pinning his arms against his sides, and pulled him from the bed. We rolled once, and I landed on top of him.

He squirmed under the wool like a weasel under a chicken coop fence. He bucked and twisted. My arms weren't impacted yet by the slow wasting but the teas weakened my whole body. I trembled as I fought to maintain my hold, the wool giving me additional grip.

"Guards!" I bellowed.

Nothing.

He tried to roll.

I threw my weight the other direction. Too much. We both

rolled across the floor and smacked into the wall, me first, with him landing on and against me. The blanket had tangled around me in the roll.

He slipped free of my grip.

I pushed the blanket away to arms' length as a blade ripped through it. Gripping the blanket, I pulled it tight around the blade, then yanked the blanket sideways, pulling the blade with it.

The man kicked one of my numbed calves. I spun on the polished floor, curling sideways to increase my momentum, then released the blanket as his feet came within reach to pull one of his legs from under him.

His elbows cracked against the floor moments before his head.

I rolled onto him and pinned his hands against the ground.

He spat in my face. "I heard you were as weak as a newborn calf."

"You heard wrong."

"You tremble like one. I'll outlast you. And then I'll kill you." He shifted his weight, a tiny movement, then stilled.

I loosened my taut muscles. I needed to respond to whatever direction he threw himself next. If he got on top of me again, without the blanket to shield me, he'd use one of the three knives that still sat in his belt.

His face settled from anger to watchfulness. His legs tightened under me.

I gripped his wrists more firmly as he brought his knees, then legs up, pitching me over his head. I pulled my knees to my stomach and tucked in my head, increasing my rotation. My feet did their first useful thing and caught him under his chin.

The clack of his teeth was followed by a curse.

I hit the floor on my back and *quawlaared*. I gave each of his wrists a quick twist. And in the noise of his bellow I rolled toward the door. If I could get into the hall, he'd have a harder time finding me.

The man jumped to his feet and ran to the door, then stood listening.

I froze. My breath rasped against the silence.

He stepped forward. "You're as loud as a winded horse. I'll soon silence you."

The door pushed open, and the man yelped.

Katrin's voice came from behind him. "Hold your hands above your head, or I'll prick you to your heart."

His hands rose into the air.

"Maggie," Katrin called. "Get some guards, now!"

A second woman's voice protested, "I can't leave. He could hurt you."

"Now!"

The assassin spun on her word and screamed, toppling backwards, a knife buried in his chest.

Katrin stood, her form outlined in the back glow of the hall. "Yosyph?" her voice came out shaky.

"I'm unhurt."

"Thank Providence!"

A small woman stepped into the room and wrapped her arms about Katrin. "My lady, are you hurt?"

Katrin pushed away from her. "Get guards or someone now!"

The woman scampered off.

Katrin scanned the room. "Are you shadow-walking?"

"Yes."

She took a step towards my voice.

"Don't turn your back on him."

She knelt and pressed her fingers to the side of his neck. "He's dead."

I pulled out of the shadow-walk and cringed. Another potential source of information silenced.

Katrin rushed to where I lay on the floor. "I'm setting up a bed in your room, propriety be tossed to the hogs." She glanced at my sleeping guards. "And I'll prepare my own food. The guards must eat at different times from different cooks, so they can't be drugged again at the same time. And you need more guards. And..." She burst into tears as she put a pillow under my head and draped a blanket over me.

"What brought you here in the middle of the night?"

"I had a nightmare about you, and I couldn't sleep until I made sure it wasn't real. But it almost was. Oh, Yosyph, I'm going crazy with worry over you. Can't we just go back to the desert, traverse the *king's trial*, and live a life where you are healthy and no one is trying to kill you? I'll dance for you every night, and you can tell me dry jokes until I ache with laughter."

Many bare feet slapped down the hall.

If I could return to the desert with her and have all that she wished for, would I do it? Could I forget the people I'd served? Could I forget the kingdom I was first born to serve? If I didn't have the slow wasting, would I fly away to freedom?

My room filled with lamplight and men, not guards, but servants in their nightshirts, who lifted me into my bed, hauled off the dead assassin, and dragged out the drugged guards.

"We'll keep watch over you until the guards get here," an elderly servant said.

Katrin muttered, "Need separate eating times, separate cooks. Foolish uniformity!"

I laughed. "Shall I appoint you general, so you can keep them in order?" She'd keep them in line, and she'd be too busy to spy on the rebellious nobles.

20

KATRIN

PALACE, Fairhaven, Lansimetsa
Febrúar 9th

WITH YOSYPH SITUATED with conscious guards and the royal physician's assurance that he was uninjured, I retreated to my quiet place. Dawn crept across the palace grounds, shooing shadows before it. I entered a small alcove in the gardens. Bricked walls smothered in winter-brown rose vines, surrounding a space about twenty paces by twenty paces. A single bench sat under an arbor. Snow-dusted beds of dead flowers sat in squares between paths.

Since the queen no longer visited here, the gardeners ignored this place. It was dreary and cold, so no one would bother me.

"Don't feel, don't feel," I chanted under my white-misting breath. My emotions sat squarely in my chest and stomach.

Why couldn't I recreate the numbness that happened in the forest when Yosyph was shot?

How did Yosyph do this? What had Farid said? Set the emotions down, like a heavy pack. But how?

"Go away emotions. Be gone." Oh drat! I'd clutched a rose vine in my frustration and pricked my palm.

I sucked at the stinging wound. I wasn't getting anywhere, even after days of trying. I wanted to tantrum like a toddling child, but that would only add emotion instead of removing it. I breathed until I'd achieved calm and tried again and again.

Each attempt to remove emotion made me even more aware of it.

Maybe Yosyph was right. Only those who had an inborn ability could learn it.

The sun was halfway across the sky. I would have to hurry to be ready for the dinner party and dance. Why was I even trying to shadow-walk? Yosyph couldn't walk much, even out of the shadow. He had no choice but to behave. I would do better to spy in the way I had, as a thoughtless belle amongst the nobles.

I wrapped my hand in a handkerchief and headed off.

～

"WE'VE MISSED YOUR LOVELY COMPANY." Sir Egvar waltzed me around the marble floor to vigorous strains of strings and flutes. "*I've* missed you."

He spun me away from him, my dress twirling out in a bell, and pulled me in so my back was tight against him. Would he feel the knife tucked into my boned corset? I must have blanched, because when we faced each other again his brows pinched and he took my hand. "Come. Sit down."

"But the music, the dance."

He led me from the twirling couples to a padded bench along the edge of the room. "You are too fragile since your fall. Have you seen a physician?"

I looked down. "I didn't want to bother you with my little worries. I can't stop thinking about what Lord Makkara said about the commoners attacking the nobility. It keeps me taut with anxiety."

Please let him tell me their plans for what they intend to do. I sent my prayer heavenward to Yosyph's god.

Sir Egvar cupped my chin in his hand and lifted my face to look at him. "Dear, sweet Katrin, I would never let anything happen to you. Someday soon, you won't act as my delicate spy into the heart of that cold palace, nor shiver by the side of that shadow demon. I will marry you in the bright flowers of spring. We'll honeymoon on the Truvian Islands and enjoy long lives along the lush ocean-front of my estate."

If I had been the fainting type, I might have become a heap upon the floor. Instead, my blood raged to my head, and my face tightened. *Faint, swoon, something!* I couldn't show him my anger.

I buried my face in his chest and let him interpret my shaking as trembles of joy.

He stroked his hand through my curls. "My beloved Katrin, if I could send anyone else in your place, I would take you away now so you'd never bear that burden again."

I swallowed my anger and smoothed my face down to just worry, then looked into his eyes. "Please tell me what will happen, so I'm not so anxious. I don't know if I'll wake in the middle of the night to an army attacking the palace or be shot down because I'm beside the Shadow Demon in public."

Uncertainty flickered across his face. His fingers curled into my hair and tugged for a breath. Then he relaxed his fingers and held me by the shoulders. "I'll send for you the night before it is to happen. I cannot tell you more. It will come sooner, depending on what you can tell me. How is the *honored Yorel*?"

He knew, as did everyone else, that Yosyph had not sat at council or on the throne for three days. Did he know why? How much tale could I mix into the truth to delay the coming revolt? "Someone must have poisoned his food, for he fell to a violent sickness. But he's recovering and will soon lead again."

Sir Egvar touched my cheek. "It's a pity. That would have made things easier." He stood and offered his hand. "You are tired. I shall have my servants take you back to the palace. Keep safe. Wait for my message. Soon this will be but a nightmare, fading into memory."

Minutes later, I was wrapped in fire-warmed furs and nestled in a carriage. I leaned my head back against the cushions. What would I do?

21

ELISE

Village, Lower Carani
    Febrúar 10th

I SAT NEXT to the chief's three wives as they mashed a root into a yellow paste, cut blue star-shaped tree fruits, and tore several varieties of green leaves into small pieces. A tang of sharp-scented herbs tickled my nose with flavors I'd not yet grown to appreciate.

I'd yet to find a consistent food. Depending on the meal, we prepared roasted meat from the hunters, fresh fruits and greens, or pasty roots mixed with savory herbs. Their drinks came in the same confusing variety: fresh pounded fruits, creamy milks from a nut the size of my head, spring water, and occasionally a fermented drink that left me fuzzy-minded.

Each of these foods needed this climate. Could we plant them on the Truvian islands between Carani and Lansimetsa, and if so, which plants? Which one or ones held back the slow wasting? What if an animal was the cure?

"Ma'at E'ese." The oldest wife handed me a bowl with the

121

mashed root. She scooped the root with two fingers and ate, then nodded at me to do the same. Spoons were an exotic notion. They either picked up, scooped with their fingers, or drank their food.

I took a one-finger taste. The bland, starchy substance coated my tongue with a hint of sweetness.

If only Halavant could translate as we prepared. But it was unbecoming for a man to sit at the preparation of foods, and he was not just a man but the Moswen. So, instead, Halavant asked about each new food at the meals. The chief never wearied of telling stories of each food and its history. It was yet another way to help the Moswen *regain his memory.*

The youngest wife stopped tearing leaves and pressed one hand to her baby-full middle. Her face creased with lines of pain. A soft moan escaped. She'd cringed many times through the food preparation; now her whole body tensed.

"Nono," the first wife cried, her face brightening with a smile. She sent the second wife running while she heated water.

I ran for Halavant and Gaven.

Gaven sat on a mat next to Halavant as they listened to Lapis, the village healer woman. She was aged and smile-creased and surrounded by various native herbs. Gaven sniffed and tasted the herbs, while Halavant translated his questions.

Halavant looked up with a smile of amusement as I skidded to a stop next to them.

"The chief's youngest wife will have a baby soon."

"I wish her well, and may it be a son," Halavant said.

"I need you to come."

Halavant blanched. "They've had babies for generations before we came. They can keep on having them without our interference."

"She lost her first baby in childbirth. We'll help her not lose this one."

Gaven grunted in agreement as he packed his satchel and added a few of the native herbs. "Don't watch if you think you'll faint. Just listen and translate."

Halavant turned a deeper shade of green. "I won't faint." He added under his breath, "and I won't watch."

~

I UNLOOPED the cord from around the baby boy's neck. He was blueish and not breathing. Gaven tended to the mother, who had lost much blood and lay in a half faint, her body too tired to even shudder.

Lapis, the village healer, snatched the baby from me and thrust him into a basin of warm water, then cold and warm again.

Please let it work. It had for so many other babies I'd helped birth. But the baby lay unmoving in the Lapis's arms.

"Halavant! Tell her I must have the baby."

Lapis handed the child to me, tears streaming down her cheeks. She rent the air with a wail, and the chief's two other wives joined in the keening.

We'd not lose this child. We couldn't. I lay him face down on my arm and rubbed his back briskly with a cloth. Fluid flowed from his mouth. His body lay limp in my arms.

I lay him on the blanketed ground and blew into his mouth and nose. His chest rose and fell. Again and again I pushed my air into his lungs. He coughed and shuddered and cried, a thin wail, covered by the women's voices.

"He lives," I whispered, then cried. "Gaven, Halavant, he's breathing!"

"Good." Gaven kept his hands busy with the birth mother. "Get him warm and get him a wet nurse."

I looked at the mother. "Is she?"

"She'll live."

Halavant must have translated both my cry and Gaven's declaration. The keening turned to trilling of joy.

I rubbed the baby until his skin glowed and his thin wail turned to a frantic cry, then wrapped him tight. He quieted and opened his eyes, dark gray framed by thick black lashes. He'd have rich brown eyes when he grew older, like his mother and father. He turned his face into me and nuzzled.

Oh sweet child, I cannot give what you seek.

A full-bosomed woman entered the chief's hut and took the child from my arms. Before she nursed him, she unwrapped his blankets and saw he was a boy. She clasped him to herself and spoke with a radiant face.

Halavant translated. "She's honored to nurse her future chief." He added, with a watery smile. "Perhaps I'm free from the obligations of the prophecy, now he has his own son."

When both mother and child lay resting and Gaven settled down to watch over them, I stepped into the starlit night with Halavant by my side. My legs ached from the long hours of kneeling.

The chief stood outside the door, not yet having entered to see his son. He took my hands into his and wept into my palms.

Halavant gave me his words. "You allowed my son to stay with us, instead of returning him to walk the heavens. You shall have the choicest husband." Halavant stopped and blushed.

I nudged him to tell me the rest.

He stared at the ground. "... even the Moswen, if he will have you as his first and honored wife."

I blushed, too, and studied the ground beside him.

The chief laughed and patted Halavant on the shoulder, then entered his dwelling to see his son. Soft murmurs reached us through the woven walls.

Halavant scuffed at the dirt. "I'm sorry, Elise. I wouldn't force you into any arranged marriage. Though I'd prefer you to any of the village women."

I blushed deeper. "That's because you need someone to take care of your hands, who speaks your native tongue."

He laughed and looked past the star-studded sky to the dawn-brightening horizon. "Exactly. I'm weary from a night-long vigil. So, until further awkward translations or discovery of the cure, I bid you goodnight."

22

HALAVANT

THE WHOLE VILLAGE gathered to celebrate the birth of the chief's son. Even the mother and day-old-baby lay near the door of their hut where everyone could see them and were tended by the chief's other two wives. Elise and I sat next to the chief on his woven mat. Gaven declined the honor and enjoyed a quieter corner of the open air meal. I'd have joined Gaven if it didn't smack of discourtesy.

The chief stood. *"When the Moswen first came, I thought my joy could grow no fuller, but now I have a son to watch over our people when I return to the heavens. May my son grow in honor and valor. Now that the line of the chiefs is renewed, the Moswen will take his other prophesied role."*

The people responded with their joyous trill and tore into the feast.

Good. They didn't expect me to marry three women and bring many sons into their village. The other role had to be

126

better, maybe sitting as a figure to be honored, served, and released to go his way when he decided it was time.

Wide leaves of roasted deer, bowls of puddings, soups, fire-blackened vegetables, and fruits piled in front of me. It was as if they'd prepared all the foods of the previous weeks into one meal. One woman set a cork-stoppered gourd by the chief. He unstoppered it with reverence.

A rotten, foul scent overpowered the other foods before me. It was like a barn, a latrine, and skunk blended together. And something dead. I put one braced hand to my mouth and the other to my stomach.

He poured a gloppy yellowish substance into an egg-sized cup. He pinched his nose and swallowed the mouthful. He poured again and held the cup towards me.

The scent hit my face with a slap. I gasped, taking in a mouthful of the scent, and gagged.

He pulled the cup back and chuckled. *"The fruit of the gods is not for the weak. I am sorry I cannot offer it fresh so you may have its sweet scent of roasted sugar cane and almonds. Come spring, men will bring the first of the duri and you may enjoy it as it is meant to be. You must drink. It will give you strength for the trial ahead."*

Which was more alarming? I must drink the fetid substance or the trial ahead? I didn't like either.

"I'll embarrass myself in front of your village if I try."

"You had it many times before you lost your memory. You stomach will remember what your mind does not."

He held the small cup toward me again, bringing it closer to my face.

I scooted back, bumping into Elise.

She shifted forward so she sat between the chief and me. "What is that awful stuff and why is the chief giving it to you?"

The chief paused and waited for me to translate.

Instead, I answered her. "He says it the fruit of the gods and it will give me strength for a trial ahead."

Elise's mouth opened as she studied the small cup. "The fruit of the gods? Perhaps that is the cure. Gaven!"

The cure? I'd die quicker by drinking that than by the slow wasting.

The chief set the cup down. "*What does the heaven's gate woman say?*"

The cup and the unstoppered gourd stifled the air with noxious fumes, and my stomach rebelled. I ran for the edge of the village where I emptied my stomach. The chattering voices hushed, as I'm sure all the villagers watched my hunched form foul the vegetation.

A hand settled on my shoulder. Jabare, the man who had first welcomed us to the village, stood next to me with a smile twitching on his face. "*I also emptied myself when I first ate the gods' fruit, and I had it fresh. It gets easier. My uncle sometimes forgets.*" He glanced at my hands. "*Someone should have plugged your nose for you.*"

I wiped my mouth on my sleeve. "*I didn't drink it. The smell alone was strong enough to cause this.*"

He chuckled. "*The smell is worse. The taste is... less strong.*"

"*Why must I drink it?*"

"*It is a gift from the gods to keep us strong. Those who will not eat the gods' fruit grow old before their time. Once a child is no longer a child, they must eat it often when in season and drink the preserved fruit monthly when out of season. It is the full moon and the time of drinking the duri. The chief always drinks first. He gave you the honor of the second drink.*" Jabare chuckled again, "*I will hold your nose so you can receive this honor.*"

It kept them strong, or they'd grow old before their time? It was the cure. Probably. Hopefully not. Why did the gods punish me?

Elise stood with Gaven a short distance away. Her eyebrows rose in a question as she caught my gaze.

Should I tell her?

Her forehead wrinkled as her eyebrows rose higher.

I gave in. "It keeps the people from growing old before their time."

She whooped, and her cry echoed through the air. And even Gaven relaxed into a smile.

She could be excited; she didn't have to drink the stuff.

"Jabare, I'm ready, if you'll hold my nose. Though you may end up with it all over your front."

He grasped my elbow and pulled me toward the waiting chief. *"It will be over soon, and you can forget until the next full moon. The bitter herbs and vinegar will remove most of the flavor from your mouth and nose. Eat those as soon as you swallow the duri."*

The scent assaulted us when we came within ten paces. *"Can you pinch my nose now?"*

He did, and I walked, nose held, accompanied by the quiet chuckles of several villagers.

The chief brought the cup to my lips.

I opened my mouth, tilted my head, and swallowed. And swallowed and swallowed. The thick substance slid slowly over my tongue like rancid deer fat, sweet and sickly. Not as horrible as the smell, but almost.

Jabare shoved a two-finger scoop of bitter herbs into my mouth, and the tightness in my throat eased as the slimy texture was replaced with leafy astringents.

The chief patted me on the back, then turned to the people. *"Now the Moswen is ready. Tomorrow he will start the journey to take his place as the mouth of the gods."*

The village split the air with their trilling.

Why couldn't he tell me these things beforehand, instead of

announcing to all the people and explaining to me afterwards, if at all? Did he think I'd run away? True, I probably would have fled from the duri. *"What is the journey?"*

The chief turned to me and smiled warmly. It did not dispel the chill that ran down my back. *"This one time, you will take a gift from us to the gods, to show our gratitude to them for trusting us again. Afterwards, you will be their messenger by the dreams you bear back to us. Too long have we been without a prophet."*

Prophet! I glanced at Elise and Gaven. We had to leave tonight. We knew the name of the fruit. I shuddered. Hopefully, the fresh fruit was less putrid. We could gather it from some other part of Carani. I couldn't travel to the heavens and return. And I was no prophet.

23

YOSYPH

PALACE, Fairhaven, Lansimetsa
Februar 12th

ANOTHER DAY OF ENFORCED REST. The physician wouldn't even allow the servants to bring the desk next to the bed so I could respond to reports from my newly founded spy network, not that their reports had anything new to tell me—the nobles were uneasy, the commoners starving, hate between races cankered, and nothing I did helped. After my fight with the assassin, the physician had me drinking the mind-numbing teas every couple of hours to help me regain my strength. True, I regained a small bit of movement in my lower legs, yet that meant little if I couldn't think clearly.

The physician bent over me and checked my pulse. "I'm leaving for the night. Rest. You'll heal faster if you do." He left.

I couldn't heal from the slow wasting, and I'd rested more than I needed. I pulled papers from under the covers and set them to either side of me, one stack of pages to my right and a single creased page to my left. The stack was from the queen's room, and the single page had been found on the body of the assassin. Her pages were filled with a jumble of shapes and overlapping scribbles. The assassin's page held a similar jumble of shapes and ink blots, scattered across the page like rain drops, front and back.

I rubbed my forehead. The fog over my brain was too dense for this puzzle.

A knock sounded from the door.

My guard, Hoft, opened it a crack, and a whispered conversation ensued. Hoft opened the door and Galliard entered.

Galliard pulled a chair next to my bed and glanced at the pages scattered around me. "So, you pass your time by studying the queen's craziness? I can find you better reading material, or better yet, bring in a minstrel so you can rest your eyes."

I slid the creased assassin's page toward him. "She may have reason behind her madness. This was on the man who tried to kill me."

"Still looks like madness. What does it say?"

"If I knew..." I began and blew out my breath. There was no reason to vent my frustration on him, but neither should I hide it, or I'd flicker into the shadow. I blew out another breath and started again, "I'm trying to figure that out."

"I see." He picked up the page and a lamp. He peered at it, turning it sideways and upside down. The light from the lamp glowed against the page. The ink from the front showed through like a window, merging with shapes on the back.

I grabbed the page. "Hold the lamp behind the page, a hand span away."

Galliard raised an eyebrow and held the lamp.

I turned the page over and then back. Shapes from both sides merged through the page into letters. Ink blots obscured spots and made spaces between groups of letters. Words formed, running vertically. Every other line swapped sides of the page. "Write this down."

The light shifted as Galliard set down the lamp. "Hoft, help me for a moment. The Yorel has discovered a light key." He sat at the desk with a pen and paper while Hoft held the lamp aloft again.

I spelled out:

SLEEPING HE

I flipped over the page.

RB ENCLOS

Turned the page.

ED. KI

Turned the page over and upside down.

LL SHADOW HOUR AF

Rotated the page.

TER MIDNIGHT WATCH.

Galliard whistled as I finished. "She's not crazy, well at least not in the toddler gibberish sense."

The letters spun in my head. "Read it back to me."

He read, "Sleeping herb enclosed. Kill shadow, hour after midnight watch."

"Someone is helping her, getting messages from her and to others."

Hoft grunted. "Not likely. I know the guards assigned to guard her quarters. They are loyal. And the writing is different on the assassin's page than her's.

I fixed my eyes on him. "They may be loyal to her."

Galliard's face tightened. "Let's read what's on her pages before we rush to conclusions. What servants do you trust to hear what may be on them? They'd be useful to hold the lamps and write."

I leaned my head back against the headboard. Who did I

trust? About as many people as Halavant trusted. And half of them were in Carani.

Galliard nodded to my silence. "We'll take it slow. Hoft, lock the door. We don't want any surprise visitors."

I decoded the first page. The letters began to float apart, even with a steady light behind the parchment. At that point, Galliard and Hoft set a lamp on the table, and one decoded while the other wrote. I closed my eyes and tried to listen as they spoke. Their voices mingled with written words of madness:

Fredrick, forgive me. Save me. The Shadow says you are dead. He lies...

Halavant, where are you? A monster has taken your place. A monster with broken hands and a heart like stone. Even he no longer visits...

Luukas. I'm a prisoner to a shadow and a monster. Both have your face. Have they torn you apart, taking your voice and your eyes, your lips and your jaw. I long for death and freedom...

Too long I've wandered this room like a soul bereft of its restful grave.

I sank deeper into the pillows. Weariness muffled my hearing. The messages repeated themes of Halavant, Fredrick, Luukas, monster, and shadow. No plans, nothing that could impact us. Just the ramblings of a woman falling further and further into madness, yet intelligent enough to write complex code. If she had been the impetus behind the nobles' unrest, we could stop it. Instead, she was another path ending in a cliff.

Hoft's sharp intake of breath slapped me out of a half sleep.

Galliard leaned next to him and read, "*Word comes. My Elite will free me. I will be ready. They need me. I must free this nation of the monster and the shadow. Ten long days.*" He looked up from the page. "When was this collected?"

Finally, something. Ten days?

I opened my eyes. "The guard marked the date of writing in the bottom corner of each page."

Galliard jumped up from the desk. "We have two days left. We must set up defenses. You need to be moved to a safer place."

"And then what? Wait? They'll not attack if they see us prepare. If we can draw them into an attack, we'll know who is part of this and end it." When they gathered an army, I'd slip into their camp and remove the leaders. It was risky. I'd drink Gaven's teas for one more day so I regained more of my movement, then stop for the day of attack so I had my full mental capacity. Galliard didn't need to know this part. It had to work. *Please God,* I signed, *I need this to work. I need to unite our land, and I can't if I have rebellion boiling. Please help me.*

A coldness shivered down my spine.

Is this not right?

More coldness.

What should I do?

The thought whispered through my core. *You're not listening. I'll send you a guide.*

Who?

Watch tomorrow. Do nothing until then.

"Honored Yorel?" Galliard's voice cut through my inward thoughts.

"We'll make plans, but not act yet. Give me one day."

"Aye. I wish I could give you a month. It is strange to be this side of the rebellion. Not a pleasant place to be."

It wasn't. I should sleep if possible. Tomorrow, I'd meet my guide, and things would be clearer.

24

KATRIN

PALACE, Fairhaven, Lansimetsa
Februar 12th

I SAT on the cold marble bench in the garden alcove. Galliard should have been here half an hour ago. The cold seeped through my furs. New snow covered the ground past my ankles, and the sun sharpened the sparkling white into knives to prick skin and eyes.

"Empty myself of emotion, set it down." My mumbling chant had become a tumbling stream of words. There wasn't much chance I'd learn to shadow-walk. However, if I could, it would make my decision easier.

I was getting better at hiding my emotions. But every time I hid them, they burrowed deeper into my core. If I brought them to the surface, would they flow off?

Where to start? No one was around. Galliard probably wasn't coming. Anger? Joy? Fear? Love? Too big. What small emotion could I set on my surface and let go? This was ridiculous.

That was it. I'd pull to my skin the emotion of absurdness.

There was little to laugh over in our current condition. I searched my memories of silliness, of things that brought laughter to my soul. Pictures painted across my closed eyes.

Yosyph's face when I, a pampered young lady, set up camp.

I giggled.

Yosyph mounting his horse in desert robes and getting tangled.

I snorted.

Images and scenes rolled over each other. Some from my childhood with Halavant, some from my journey with Yosyph. One pushed itself to the forefront—from our courtship in the last three months, before everything fell apart.

Yosyph walks beside me through the gardens after the first snow-fall. Pines bend under the winter weight. I dash ahead of him, under a low branch. He ducks to follow me, but not enough, and a pile of snow whitens his head and shoulders. His face morphs from shock to disgust and, at my laughter, to rolling chuckles. He bends down to kiss my cheek and showers me with snow.

I shook with laughter. Tears ran down my cheeks. Humor and love glowed across my skin. I didn't want to let them go, yet if I could let these emotions that sat on the surface slide off, I could pick them up again later.

"Set it down. Come back for it later," I murmured around gasps of laughter. I calmed. The humor still bubbled across my surface, a delightful blend of memories and joys.

Snow squeaked under a firm step. Galliard stood at the alcove opening, watching me with a bemused smile. "You are in good spirits. What news brings us to meet out in the icy gardens?"

My humor sank back beneath my skin. The news was anything but good. "Galliard, I need your counsel." I walked towards him. "Sir Egvar has planned a rebellion. He won't tell me how or what or when, yet he said he would send for me the night before it will happen."

Instead of exclaiming in surprise, Galliard paced. "We know when: two days. If Egvar calls for you, it would be tonight or tomorrow night. At least we'll have that warning. We are preparing now."

I jumped to my feet. "How did you find this out?"

"The Yorel decoded the queen's writings. The Elite will come for her. It probably won't be an attack, rather a slipping into the castle in few numbers and quietly killing. There are likely already some loyal to the queen working within the palace. We are preparing for that."

A series of assassins? I shivered. How to protect against them? We had to stop the leaders before it happened.

Galliard stopped pacing. "You need to tell the Yorel."

My shoulders tightened. "If Yosyph knows, he'll stop me from going."

"The Yorel would be right to stop you. If Egvar finds out you've betrayed him, he'll kill you."

"He's trying to kill Yosyph," I cried in frustration. "If I go, I can stop Egvar." I finger the hilt of the knife I carried. Egvar let me get close to him. Could I act the assassin to protect Lansimetsa? Could I to save Yosyph? If I hurt Egvar, I'd die. His guards would make sure of that. Maybe I could continue as a spy. Would Egvar trust me with any more information than he'd already given?

Galliard sat down next to me. "You should still tell the Yorel."

Dead rose vines clung to the walls like so many dashed dreams and hopes. I gave a tight nod. I'd tell him as soon as I figured out a good argument for him to let me go. As soon as I had an argument strong enough to convince myself.

25

HALAVANT

Village, Lower Carani
Februar 12th

THE WHOLE VILLAGE stood in two lines and sang as we started our journey to the gods. Elise walked to my right and Gaven to my left. Jabare walked ahead, carrying a small bundle on his back—the gift for the gods. At some point, Jabare would bind it onto my back to carry up to the heavens. The village song flowed around me in many dissimilar voices, making the words hard to catch. *Climb Heaven's Wall... flowered stairway... gifts... blessings... life follows death.*

I stumbled as I understood the last phrase. I wouldn't be their messenger. We'd learned what we needed. We'd find this duri fruit and meet the sea captain back at the bay. Their village would prosper along its simple ways without me. They had their future chief, and they had their stories to tell him of the great Moswen's visit. They would be fine.

Donkor, the man who'd been with Jabare when they first

found us, slipped next to Jabare and spoke near his ear. His rough whisper carried back to me. "*Friend. I don't trust the foreigners. The one you call the Moswen—*"

Elise grabbed my arm as we passed the old healer woman. "Halavant, please translate."

I cast my eyes skyward. What was Donkor saying to Jabare? They'd moved beyond hearing. How many more times would she stop to give advice to someone before we left?

Elise took the old woman's hands in her own. "Lapis, as the gods' messenger, I give you permission to touch blood and bone as I have taught you. Teach others. The gods want their children to care for each other when injured."

As I translated, Lapis's face glowed into a smile, and her thin chest puffed.

Elise pulled a necklace from around her own neck—an oak pendant carved into a lily, hung on a leather strip—and placed it into Lapis's hand. "This is the mark of one of the gods' appointed healer."

Lapis closed her fingers over the pendant. "*May you journey safely and return swiftly. I have much to learn from you and the frown-slanted man.*"

I snorted as I translated that last bit. Gaven would have his own place in their myths—the grumpy harbinger of health.

Elise didn't smile at the jest, but nodded gravely at Lapis.

I tapped the back of her boot with my toe. "Any other words of advice, or can we finally go?"

"Yes, I think I'll have a long chat with—" She stopped as a smile crept into the corners of her mouth. "No, Halavant. That's it. We can go."

I rolled my eyes heavenward. She wasn't funny. "When did you become the king's fool?"

Elise's shoulders slumped.

"Elise?"

She turned and hurried down the remaining line of villagers.

I'd have to make it up to her. I lengthened my step and ran into the back of Jabare. He kneeled before the chief and bowed his head.

The chief dropped a necklace of yellow and purple flowers around his neck. *"My beloved sister's-son, may you journey safely and return swiftly. Care for the Moswen as you would a child. He is not fully healed. I have hopes when he comes into the gods' presence, he will remember. We have not yet paid for the First Wife's jealousy. May our gift be enough. Even if it is not, bring the Moswen back. I would rather be blessed by his presence, even if he doesn't become our prophet, than lose him again."*

This was the painful part of my deceit. What would the chief do when we never returned? What would I tell Jabare? Both had treated me as a deity, and also as family. After I'd restored order to my kingdom, I'd send great gifts *from the gods* to this village for their kindness. I'd explain somehow.

Jabare rose and embraced his uncle. *"We will return."*

The chief turned from Jabare to me and dropped a necklace of orange and red flowers around my neck. The fragrance was as sweet as a summer breeze through the palace rose gardens. *"Thank you, Moswen, for braving this journey. May you find what you've lost. Our whole people travel with you in spirit."* He pulled me close, crushing the blossoms between us. Tears from his cheeks ran against mine. *"Our first father's son, you are now as a son to me. When you return, I will make you chief, and my infant son will grow to serve you."*

A son to him, more so than his own? A father's love I'd never known? Why did the gods torment me—and him? I'd explain, somehow.

Gaven grumbled. "We better go while we still have light. Kiss his cheek or whatever is the proper thing for a chief and be done with it. Foolish, emotional people."

I pulled out of the chief's arms and kneeled as Jabare had. "*I am honored by your love. However, your son is the next chief. Raise him to be a man like you, and your village will be blessed.*"

The chief raised his hand, and the village stopped in their singing. "*The Moswen shows humility and wisdom. When he returns, he shall be your next chief and our prophet. May our village grow into a peace as is only known in the heavens.*"

That was not what I planned. I rose and strode from the village before I could say something to make it worse. The silence after the chief's pronouncement rose into trills and chased after me into the dense jungle. They'd never forgive me. And their legends would become one of the false Moswen who stole away with the gods' gift and never returned.

After we'd gone enough steps that the village sounds disappeared behind us, Jabare placed a hand on my shoulder. "*You look as though you swallowed a gourd full of duri. Don't worry, we'll help you learn. You'll be a good chief.*"

"*That's not what I'm worried about.*"

"*The gods will help you when you reach the Heaven's Wall.*"

"*Jabare, I'll lose last night's feast on your feet if you don't let me be.*"

He stepped back from me, then leaned forward. "*Moswen?*"

I put one hand to my churning stomach. My head lightened above my shoulders. The world narrowed and tilted sideways.

"*Moswen,*" Jabare's voice cut across a dark distance and hands caught my shoulders.

"Halavant!" Elise's cry came from a greater distance and faded away.

～

A WET CLOTH brushed against my face. My head pounded like an army marching.

"Halavant." Elise's gentle voice drifted over the pounding.

I forced one eye open. Blurry faces bent over me, surrounded by streams of light. I squinted my eyes shut and turned my head away from the light. "Go away." My words came out thick, like I'd been drinking.

Something sulfurish was thrust under my nose. My eyes flew open, and I scrambled backwards.

One of the blurry shapes formed into a chuckling Gaven. "Should have used that first. He's fine. Just too much emotion all at once. Never thought the king was the fainting type."

Jabare also came into focus. He kneeled beside me and held a gourd of water. His face was scrunched with concern. "*Moswen, did you have a vision? I've never seen a man fall into sleep like that.*"

"*No vision. But if that is the gods knocking on my head to tell me something, I wish they'd stop.*"

Jabare frowned.

"*I'm sorry. I shouldn't joke about them.*"

"*You joke?*" He frowned deeper, then shrugged. "*Your mother is a goddess. So you are close family with the gods. That means you can joke with them. But,*" he shivered, "*I shall not.*" He looked at me and the concern returned. "*You are too pale, even for your fair skin. We should have brought duri with us.*"

That meant he hadn't. I let out a sigh of relief. Until I started having the symptoms of the slow wasting, I never wanted to taste duri again.

Elise helped me to sit and held a cup to my lips. Vinegar wafted.

I turned my head away. I was done with stomach-upsetting things being thrust into my face.

Elise followed my lips with the cup. "Please drink. It will help. Is anything hurt?"

"My head and my pride. Nothing else."

"Your head? Where? Is it where you were wounded?" She fingered my head where her mother had drilled and drained a swelling wound months before. It was now a small soft spot, no longer tender.

"Mostly the front. Give me a moment. Gaven's right, it was what the chief said."

"What did he say?" Elise continued to finger my head.

I explained and Gaven burst into laughter. "If you stayed there much longer, they'd set up a temple and start worshiping you as a god. Not that you need any more inflated head. You already had to get it drilled to deflate it before."

Elise shot Gaven a withering look, and Gaven stopped mid laugh. She turned to me. "We are only a short distance from the village. Shall we return so you can rest easier and set off tomorrow?"

"No!" I lunged my feet. "I'm good. Let's keep going. I can't return there." I swayed and hooked my arm around a branch to steady myself.

It took a sitting rest, water—with the vinegar, and almost losing what churned in my stomach, before I was ready to go. It was still morning when we started down the narrow path after Jabare. He was content to quietly lead. Gaven brought up the back with his grumblings. And Elise walked beside me, with her hand touching my arm as if to steady me. *How would I tell Jabare we wouldn't climb to the gods or return to his village? And what would the chief do?*

∾

ELISE SAT DOWN NEXT to me at the campfire. "I'm sorry for teasing you when we were leaving the village," she said. "You were so tight with the expectations, I thought I could lighten it with humor. It didn't work. I'm not witty like Katrin. I'll never be, no matter how much I try. I'll always be the solemn fool to the king."

"Why are you trying to be like Katrin? You're nothing like her."

Elise poked at the fire with a stick. "I know. I thought..."

"Elise." I put my braced hand under her chin and lifted her face. "I don't want you any different. You are my friend. I trust you. You are a peaceful calm in this crazy world. And you are no king's fool. I'm sorry I ever let those words slip from my mouth. You are wiser than me, and more thoughtful and kind."

Elise's brown eyes shimmered with tears that leaked down the corners of her eyes.

"I'm sorry, Elise," I stammered. "Don't cry. I—"

She leaned forward and kissed me on the cheek, then walked across the camp and rummaged through her herb bags which hung from a branch.

She had a way of doing that. A gentle caress on my cheek and on to her quiet duties. Like a sister.

I was still staring after her, when Gaven sat down next to me. He whispered, "Don't play with her, young man. Tell her yes, she has a chance or no, she doesn't. Tell her, so she doesn't waste her health by not knowing."

"A chance? For what?"

Gaven gripped my forearm. "You are the king of fools. She —" He stopped as Elise came over and rubbed herbs into a skinned animal, hopefully rabbit, and set it to roast over the fire.

Whatever Gaven had to say was left to my imagination. Chance for what? If it was a chance to rise to palace physician, I'd give her the position as soon as we returned. If it was something else—but what? Gaven acted like it was something she'd already told me, yet she'd not mentioned wanting anything. She'd refused most of the many gifts I'd already offered her, though she willingly told me anything her family could use. I'd ask her again once I figured out how to tell Jabare I wasn't the Moswen.

26

ELISE

Jungle, Lower Carani
Februar 13th

The Carani jungle was abundant with bugs and trees, and sparse with trails. Jabare created our path as much as followed it, whacking at the giant-leafed plants with a long, wide knife. We didn't see any wildlife. They probably all ran away at our noise. That didn't stop Jabare from catching us four rabbit-sized rodents. Another man would be impatient at our pace, set by Gaven's age, yet Jabare sedately marched along. Halavant, on the other hand, flinched with tension as we walked. Even in his sleep, he twitched and moaned.

Jabare said, one more day to Heaven's Wall. Sometime between now and then, we must convince him either that Halavant was not the Moswen but to help us anyway, or that the Moswen had another duty to perform. Either way, Jabare could prove an honorable difficulty. It would have been far easier if we'd happened upon a different village and been simply accepted as healers. This whole prophecy and Halavant's likeness in face was... straining.

Halavant's words before dinner were even more so. I was his friend. He trusted me. And I'd kissed his cheek again. I had to stop doing that. He was a king. I was a healer. He'd marry for alliance and power. He needed to, with Lansimetsa so shaky. I'd end up a spinster herb woman. I needed to keep to compassionate service with him, nothing more.

Jabare sat across the fire from me, whittling arrow points onto sticks.

Gaven settled down next to me with a blanket wrapped around his shoulders. "I see why the first Carani king left this climate. The air is so thick, it is like breathing underwater. It's worse here than it was near the village."

"How is the village peaceful when all stories of the Carani are of bloodthirsty warriors?"

"Maybe they would have been bloodthirsty for us if Halavant hadn't looked like a washed-out painting of their chief. Or maybe they are a backwoods village that separated themselves from the main people because of their strange traditions about blood and bone."

"They are a good people."

Gaven nodded. "Aye, they are. A sweet, childlike people. Hmph, if it wasn't for this soupy air, I'd join their village and not spend another worried night over thick-headed heroes and a land falling apart."

"You'd give up your soft bed and home for sleeping on the ground in a hut?"

"Oh, I'd make more comforts here. I haven't lived as a hermit for half a century by trusting someone else to take care of my needs. Though they'll never force that horrid drink down my throat."

I looked into the fire. "Do you think the duri is the cure for the slow wasting?"

"Won't know until we try it. But it fits."

"How will we get a steady supply?"

"Don't know. Hoping that fanatical fellow will help us."

"His name is Jabare."

Jabare looked up from his arrows and tilted his head sideways.

I shook my head and motioned for him to continue whittling.

Gaven snorted. "That's why I gave him a nickname. This whole 'translate everything through Halavant' is a bother, but it helps when we need something not overheard. Though I suppose it goes both ways. Good thing Halavant is so open in his translations. He's an honest boy." Gaven glanced at Halavant moaning in his sleep, and his face softened. "And his honesty is making this charade a heavy burden."

I dug the toe of my boot in the soil. "I wish I could help him carry it."

"He's a king. He'll always carry a heavy burden. You already help him with your calmness and sweetness. I do, too, in my caustic way. Every time I make him defend himself to me, I give him strength to fight for what he's striving for. At least, I hope so. I'm not the best with people."

"You often go too far."

"That's why I need you to shoot me warning looks. Now, I'll go rest these tired bones on an all too thin pile of leaves. Don't wake me until breakfast is hot and ready to eat."

I answered with my own grunt. How much longer before I became as salty as he? Better question, how could I help Halavant carry this burden? I wished we dared tell Jabare the truth, and that we spoke the same language so I could.

~

I SAT DOWN NEXT to Halavant as we rested for a mid-day meal. Jabare promised we'd be to the Heaven's Wall before the sun set. We had to decide soon.

"Halavant?"

He didn't lift his head from his slumped position.

"Halavant, can't we just tell him?"

His shoulders slumped further.

I touched his knee. "He's a good man. He'll listen."

He jerked away. "What will I say? He can't hear me past the holy, ridiculous traditions of his village. If I say I'm not the Moswen, he'll say I don't remember yet that I am. And if I convince him, he'll likely run me through with his spear for deceiving him and his uncle and their whole village. I might as well climb this 'flowered stairway to heaven and die to be alive again' as get him to understand."

"Is that what they expect?"

"I don't *know* what they expect! That is part of the song the village sang when we left. It would be easier if they were my enemies and I could fight them, but to be their long-foretold half-divine kin—how do I fight that?"

The weight of his worry pressed onto my shoulders. We'd find a way.

~

THE SUN SAT low in the sky behind us, and before us, vine-covered cliffs rose into the sky. *Heaven's Wall.* It wasn't sheer. Still, even if steps were carved into it, I'd never brave the climb. How did they expect Halavant to?

Jabare pulled vines away from the cliff, revealing a dark opening. Was the way up the cliff through a cave?

I kneeled and lit a torch. If Halavant went that way, I would, too. We could disappear into the cave and lose Jabare. Convincing him would be better, but this provided another option. I stepped into the cave. It was empty and small. A blackened spot marked the floor where a fire once burned. Torchlight flickered off the gray walls. Gray except at the back. Red and black lines filled the far wall.

Halavant brushed against my side as I stepped closer. Painted words, some in Carani's dotted and slashed language, and—I moved the torch to light the left corner, disbelief buzzing in my ears—some in the rigid block letters of Lansi. "Halavant, what does the Carani say?"

Halavant squinched his eyes and spoke Carani, his eyes scanning over the text. Jabare bowed his head, his face glowing with a solemn radiance, like the zealous worshipers in the Lansi temples.

Halavant then translated:

Dearest Husband. I fled because of your first wife's venom but left behind our son because he was too little to make the dangerous trek. I knew you loved him enough to protect him even among your warlike kin. I'd hoped when your first wife claimed him, she would also love him.

But a mother's heart always longs for that which is born of her. I came back to bear whatever grief your first wife would pour on me, and found our son, my son, ill with her witchery. I loved you, but I cannot leave my son with you. Someday, when he is grown, I will tell him of his father's land, and he may return if he will. If you love me enough to follow me and find my words in this place of our first meeting, then create a new village in this green lower-land, near our tree. Create a people of peace, then our son may return, if he so chooses. Even now, he cries out for you, though his hands are crippled, and his mind wanders in fever.

Jabare nodded when Halavant finished speaking. It was the myth the chief had told us, or bits and pieces of it.

I stepped to the left, peering closely at the small square print of Lansi words and read out loud:

I, Anneli, paint this with my own hand, deep with my grief. If one of my native land should find it, I desire you to know my story, lest my son and I do not survive the sea voyage.

I am a daughter of a Lansi fisherman. His abuse drove me to the sea, and I crashed upon the Carani coast. I wandered until I came to this cliff and cave, where I lived as a hungry and bug-bitten hermit until a young Carani man found me while exploring this dense jungle.

My pale skin and yellow hair saved my life. He saw me as a goddess and took me up the cliff to his dry grassland, where he was chief of a small village, and took me to be his second wife.

He was a good man. He protected his people with honor and loved me with a zeal. But his first wife, though in word and face she gave me every kindness, hated me. She left a scorpion on my sleeping mat and wood splinters in my food. I could never prove it was her. My husband, with the same honor he protected his village, defended his first wife's name. He loved me, but he didn't believe me.

When I bore my first son, the first wife coveted him—lavishing him with all the real love her barren womb held unspent. Her attempts on my life increased, and I fled, believing our son would be safer in the village than in the jungle with me. I was wrong.

I didn't return to my homeland. Instead, I spent seven years living in the lower-land and hiding from my husband's repeated attempts to find me, before my desire to see my child drove me back to the village. I returned to find the first wife with a toddling son, and my son lying sick with a fever. Once she had her own child, her love for mine turned to hate. I walked into the village, lifted my son to my back, and left. My husband watched as if I were a ghost, and only as I left did he call for me. I did not answer.

Half a year I've dwelt in this cave with my son, helping him

regain his strength and lashing together a sailed raft for our journey.
My husband hasn't sought me in this time. He may yet. I've painted a
message for him in his language. If he will leave his dry grasslands,
warlike kin, and wicked first wife, I may one day return with our son.
Now I must protect my child. His mind and hands are whole again.
Soon we sail. May we find our way through the watery deep and to
my cool, green lands of childhood.

The myth was based in reality. The goddess was a Lansi fisherwoman, the Moswen a half-blooded Lansi child.

The painted writing changed in style, but still in Lansi:

I, Kamal...

Halavant stopped me. "Kamal? Founder of Lansimetsa? First
King?" He nudged me aside and read:

I, Kamal, son of Cheres and Annali, returned to my father's land
to find a village of peace, and my father an old man of wisdom. I
cannot reveal myself or remain. I have a duty to my mother's people,
and a promise to fulfill to my dead mother. Lansi is at war with itself,
each clan claiming the right to rule the rest. I must gather the horrid
fruit to still my tremblings, then return to Lansi and continue my
work. If I can bring peace between the clans, I will come to Carani
and never leave again.

Halavant leaned his forehead against the wall.

The line of the kings came from Annali and Cheres, from
Lansimetsa and Carani. And Halavant stood where the first king
had painted these words. A shiver ran along my arms.

27

HALAVANT

I was a descendant of the Moswen. Moswen and Kamal. Two myths merged in this cave. Both were said to come from the heavens. Both were a man born of two nations. And they thought I was he. Laughter trembled up my core. The royal blood ran from a fisherwoman and a small village chief. No wonder Kamal chose to say he came from the heavens. Who would choose a king of that lineage? Still, he brought peace to the land. He unified the people. And now I must return with the duri so we could re-unify the people.

"Jabare."

He bowed. "*Moswen, you remember and laugh with joy. Now you may take our gift to the gods and return whole.*"

"*Jabare, do you know what these other words say?*"

"*It is the language of the heavens, and I am not worthy to know their meanings.*"

"*It is time you knew.*"

Jabare stepped away, his face blanching.

"Do not fear. It is about my father, many, many generations back. About the Moswen. I am his grandchild, three hundred years later. I did not know this when I came, but as I read this, I understand now. And like him, I must return to my native land. First, I must gather duri to take with me. I have a brother who is dying."

Jabare mouthed several words and finally spoke. *"You are the descendant of the Moswen? We are not yet worthy to have him return. Someday, we shall be."* He laid a hand on my arm. *"I shall help you. Duri is not in season for several more weeks. When we return to the village, we will give you our winter supply."*

"Thank you, my friend. I—"

Jabare collapsed with a grunt at my feet.

A spear stuck out his back.

Donkor stepped into the cave, gripping a knife.

Traitorous scum! He'd just killed his friend.

Jabare moaned.

Not dead. I let out a breath and stepped towards Donkor. "Elise! Gaven! Help Jabare!"

Donkor sneered. *"I heard. You are not the Moswen. You are a foreign leech, come to steal my people's secrets. Jabare was ready to betray our people with you. I'll send you swiftly to the dark world where all liars and cowards go."*

No he wouldn't. I leaped forward, holding my braced hands like shields.

He stepped back half a step and swung the knife in a wide arc.

The metal blade screamed against my metal brace. My arms vibrated from wrist to shoulder with the impact. *He'll kill us all if I don't stop him.* I kicked, catching him under the ribs with my boot.

He grunted and slashed the knife downward.

I spun sideways, out of the blade's path, and kicked the side of his head. My leg didn't like the stretch, but the contact was solid.

He stumbled drunkenly.

I hooked my foot around one leg, and he tumbled to the ground.

He rolled away from me and back to his feet, then lunged at me.

Why couldn't he stay down?

A stone whistled through the air and struck his cheek with a crack.

He grabbed his face with a cry.

Another stone struck his shoulder.

"*Demons and spirits!*" He stumbled into the jungle.

"Halavant!" Elise's voice stopped me before I'd made two strides after him. "Let him go. We need to stay together if we are to make it back to the village."

She stood with a stone-loaded sling, its swinging motion slowing to a gentle sway.

Gaven knelt by Jabare.

The spear stuck from his bare back just below the pack he'd been carrying, and near the left edge. Why did Donkor have to be an accurate hunter as well as a coward?

Elise dropped the sling and pressed cloth around the spear handle as Gaven pulled at the weapon.

Gaven grunted. "Blood and bone! His muscles won't let it go."

If my hands worked, I could pull the spear free. But they were useless.

Elise strained next to Gaven, tears running down her cheeks.

My arms still worked. "Tie a rope around the spear and the other end around my forearms."

Gaven looked at me with surprise and then nodded. He

worked quickly, and soon I had my forearms bound to either side of the spear shaft.

"Steady. Pull. Steady." He guided the base of the spear as I heaved upward.

The ropes cut into my arms, but the spear slowly moved. A ripping sound of flesh made me light-headed. I couldn't faint here, not like the last time I helped remove a weapon from a friend. I gulped in air and pulled. Another inch, and the spear ripped out. I tumbled to the ground and lay with the spear tied to my arms while Gaven and Elise bound up Jabare's wound. I closed my eyes and sent up prayers to any god who would listen. *Don't let Jabare die. He believes in you, all of you. Help him!*

Gaven and Elise's quiet words whispered from their work. "Hold it firmer... he's losing too much blood... yarrow... raise his legs..."

My stomach lurched at the iron scent that pushed aside the jungle's perfumes. *God of Yosyph's people, I know Jabare isn't of your land, and I don't even know if you can hear us in Carani, but please help him.*

Time continued in snail movements. Gaven and Elise worked until the last colors of the sun drained from the sky and Elise lit a fire. As long as they kept working, that meant he still lived.

Gaven's voice bit through my prayers. "That's all we can do for him. We'll see if he makes it through the night. Go unbind Halavant from the spear."

Elise kneeled beside me. "Thank you for protecting us. You were amazing."

"You're just trying to distract me. And he ran away because of you, not me."

"Yes. But, I'm telling the truth, too. I'd not have had time to get the sling from my pack if you hadn't fought him. And you figured a way to pull the spear out, something neither Gaven nor I had the strength to do."

"Will he live?"

She finished untying the rope. Her face sat in the shadows. "We'll see."

"When Donkor tells the village about my deceit, at least they'll come to capture us and carry Jabare back to safety. Maybe they'll even listen."

28

YOSYPH

PALACE, Fairhaven, Lansimetsa
Februar 14th

TWO DAYS PASSED, and no guide came. I sat upon the throne and made myself available to petitioners, though my guards had to support me there and away. Who came? Hungry peasants and worried nobles, all asking or demanding I solve their woes. Not one offered me sound advice or thoughtful guidance. Oh, they offered many opinions, but none helped.

At the end of the second long day, Lord Makkara strode to the foot of my dais, his back straight and his face set with determination. He'd delivered grain to peasants, yet he also consorted with those who would overthrow the government. I'd ordered the royal treasurer to give him his gold. What did he want now? My limbs trembled with exhaustion.

Two guards stood on either side of him, their swords half drawn.

Makkara glanced at them and sniffed, then addressed me.

"Regent Yosyph. The nobles have every right to revolt against your meddling of their powers."

"Lord Makkara, I have not meddled with their powers. They retain their lands, their incomes, and their slaves. I only seek to bring Lansimetsa to a balanced rule, where all have a voice in the law, from the pig slopper to the king."

"We hold no slaves, only servants who are cared for with better shelter and food than they would get on the streets."

"And your serfs?"

"My serfs are better than most. Not all hold to honor in their stewardships over the simple-minded and barn born."

My spies had confirmed his words. He was good to his serfs and servants. Still, he treated them as animals to be taken care of and used as needed. I leaned forward. "They are not simple-minded. Given education, they'd join in making this land stronger and more prosperous than it ever has been. And more at peace. I want to give them opportunities to learn: set up schools, give those indentured shorter hours of work so they can study, and..."

Makkara took a step up the dais and stopped as two swords crossed in front of him. He stepped back but straightened his back another inch. "Then it is true. You would bereave us of our power, which is in the strength of those who serve us. You would reduce us to the status of merchant or craftsman."

Why had I spouted off? It must have been the new tea the physician gave me this morning, the one to help clear my mind of the fog created by the other teas. Along with clearing some fog, it loosened my tongue. Was that a bad thing? No. I'd always been too tight-lipped. I let more words pour out despite my clenched stomach. "This land has always been ruled by kings. I want it ruled by a council like the desert people. I want everyone to have a chance to join the council by passing both scholarly and honor tests. I want to set up schools to prepare any willing to learn about justice, order, laws of peace, and protecting armies. If the nobles lose their power, it will be because they didn't deserve to keep it by the voice of the council."

Makkara paled. "You speak madness. I came to warn you, to help turn aside what others set in motion. I do not want this fair city ravished again by war. Lay down your right to rule. Appoint another, one the nobles trust. He will hold the power until King Halavant returns. And if you would keep peace in this land, do not influence the king to these rash notions."

I pushed against the throne to stand, gripping the golden arm rest to bear my weight as my legs wobbled beneath me. "I never wanted this power. If I could trust another to protect the people and the peace of the land, I'd give it this moment. But I cannot. There is none. You don't see those below you as people. And until you do, you'll never rule. Get out!"

Makkara raised an eyebrow. "I have warned you. You'll not get a second chance. May your soul rest in misery for the deaths you bring upon this people." He turned to leave when Hoft grabbed his arm. "Unhand me." Makkara ordered.

Hoft glanced at me and then nodded to the other guard, not waiting for my orders. "You have spoken treason. You will wait your trial in the dungeon."

Makkara looked to me. "Regent Yosyph, would you imprison me for warning you? Where is your justice and honor? I came unarmed and uncompelled. If you believe even a small part of what you said, then I shall leave unharmed and free."

He was right. "Release him."

"But—"

"I said, release him."

Makkara shook off Hoft's grip.

"Lord Makkara," I called out as he trod across the throne room. "What will they do? When will they attack?"

"I've told you all I know. I go to take my family to safety far from here. We shall not meet again in this life."

A guard stood firmly in front of the door when Makkara approached.

"Let him go," I ordered.

The guard stepped aside, and Makkara exited.

I slumped back to the throne. "Get a spy, now! I want him followed until he's left the city and is several days from here."

The guide hadn't come. I'd spoken rash words. I'd never drink that tea again. Makkara was right. My words had been madness to share with him. Now I'd lost any chance to convince the nobles to a peaceful resolution.

I must act. All we'd fought for, all a thousand died for, could be undone in a day. I could halt no longer between decisions. My hands stuttered my prayer. *I'm sorry, God, I did everything I could to find the guide. I tried. My mind is thick and slow, my words unguarded. Please help me, despite my faults. Protect this kingdom. Show me what to do to protect this people. I do not want another war. If I can stop this before it becomes war, please show me how.*

Rebuke washed through me, and the thought: *You spoke rash words, but I will work with them. He will be back. Listen better the next time.*

Makkara is the guide? I signed.

An imperfect one, but so are you. Between your two opposing minds and united hearts for the people, you may find peace.

I bowed my head at the truth. I'd driven away my chance for peace. If God would give me another chance, I would work beside Makkara. *Please forgive me. I will listen.*

Your heart is in the right place. Be at peace.

Do I call him back?

No. Much will happen before he returns. Do not lose hope, despite how dark the night becomes. Prepare to defend the people. If you listen, I will send those to carry you back to the day.

Carried back by another? My shoulders tightened with shame at my weakness. Why was I given charge over this people, when I had so little power to help them? Why could I converse with God and yet could not do what He needed me to do? My responsibility far exceeded my capacity. *I am not strong enough. What I once could do, I cannot now.*

Peace gently caressed me. *I gave you these weaknesses so you'd turn to me. I will make you stronger than you have ever been. Be at peace.*

I sat trembling on the throne, my whole body shaking with the touch of the divine.

"Honored Yorel?" Hoft kneeled before me and looked into my down-turned face. "We must prepare for an attack."

"Yes. Call Galliard and all my generals." I'd listen as I prepared, even if I must prepare from a cot in the council room.

29

KATRIN

Palace, Fairhaven, Lansimetsa
     Februar 14th

Two days and no word from Sir Egvar. Someone could have strung a lute with my nerves. The whole palace was in a flurry of preparations for a battle. Lord Makkara's visit an hour before had turned foreboding to frantic action.

Yosyph planned in the council room, no longer hiding his weakness nor yet telling why he was weak. How many already knew? Galliard, his guards, the physician. As the number of those who knew grew, so did the chance others would find out. Did it really matter now? The nobles would attack.

I hadn't told Yosyph yet of Egvar's plans to get me. I should have told him days before. What would I say? Egvar hadn't sent for me. He must have decided I had no more use. I shifted my feet as I stood outside the council room, preparing myself. I needed to tell Yosyph.

A man in messenger red strode down the hall, his gaze fixed on me.

Whatever his message, he'd have to wait. I took another deep breath and opened the council room door.

Words poured out. "We should attack them—no, we must prepare the palace for siege—the honored Yorel must be removed to a safer location."

"No." This last word was in Yosyph's strong command. "I will stay. I can no longer lead from the shadows."

Yosyph sat in a well-padded chair at the head of the room, and his generals sat in a half circle around him. Yosyph glanced at me, then turned back to the men. "We will triple the guard."

I stepped into the council room.

Yosyph's guard, Hoft, lowered his spear in front of me and raised his eyebrows in a question.

I leaned toward him. "I need to talk with the Yorel."

Hoft glanced behind me. "You should take care of him first."

I turned to find the messenger in a low bow and holding out a gold filigree envelope. "Lady Katrin."

I snatched it from his hand. The rose of Sir Egvar was pressed into the wax seal. Tightness squeezed around my ribs. Would I still go? Could I do what I needed?

The messenger came out of his bow, tilting his head as if he expected a response, and when I gave none, strode away.

The envelope crinkled in my fists. What if this told when and where they'd attack? I peeled back the seal and pulled out a thick card written on with looped writing, almost making the Lansi letters elegant.

My sweet Katrin,

It would be my greatest pleasure if you joined me at a winter ball this evening. I will send the servants to bring you an hour before sunset. They will meet you by the west gate.

Yours in heart and soul, and soon in marriage,

Egvar

My stomach rebelled, and acid climbed my throat. I was

useless with Egvar, just another pretty face. Egvar never told me anything, why would he start now? I touched the hilt of my hidden knife and shuddered. It was one thing to kill Yosyph's assassin in self-defense. Could I assassinate Egvar? Acid burned at the base of my tongue.

I slipped the card into the folds of my dress. No one else needed to see Egvar's seal.

"Lady Katrin." Yosyph studied me from his seat.

The room silenced.

"Yes, honored Yorel?"

"Let me see the card." It was a command, though gentle, and left no room for argument.

I walked towards him like a child caught snitching tarts from the windowsill. Why did I feel guilty? He knew I worked as a spy among the nobles. This card was one of many invitations. Yet, I'd not told him Egvar's plans to send for me, nor his plans to marry me. I could cast the card into the fire. And lose all his trust? No, I must bear the shame of him reading these words. I handed him the card.

As he read, his face stilled into stone, then he flickered into the shadow. The gaze of the ten other men in the room moved from his seemingly empty chair to me.

"Honored Yorel." I stumbled on the cold title. "It's not what it seems. I'd never marry Egvar. I hate him. I've led him on so I could find out his plans. You know this."

Silence.

Please listen. My throat tightened around my next words. "I've told you everything he's told me, except this last part. He said he'd send for me the night before the attack. I told Galliard, and I was going to tell you."

Galliard glanced at me with pained eyes. "It's true. She told me."

Yosyph's chair remained silent and empty. Was he still there?

"Yosyph." I kneeled before him and whispered. "I can remove Egvar from power, because he trusts me. Forgive me for not telling you his plans."

Yosyph clasped my hand and pulled so I leaned forward. His flat whisper brushed against my cheek. "Listen. Get ready, dress yourself in your finest gown, draw all eyes to you. You will go, but only as a distraction. I'll do the rest. The servants will come soon, and I have much to do before we go."

He'd come with me? How? What insanity had he planned when his heart couldn't temper his thoughts?

Yosyph emerged from the shadow, sitting hunched over on the chair. He cringed and then spoke, loud enough for all to hear. "Lady Katrin has been a useful spy in finding out the workings of the rebellious nobles. She will continue her work tonight. None will hinder her. Do you understand?"

Ten men nodded.

Yosyph leaned back in the chair. "I must rest. Come get me after I've had a few hours sleep, or when the attack comes." He motioned for his guards help him stand. "Galliard, please come with me. I'd have a few words with you before I rest."

I rose from my knees and fled to my rooms to get ready. My blood pulsed in time to my rapid steps.

30

YOSYPH

Palace, Fairhaven, Lansimetsa
   Februar 14th

I SAT in my bed and drank a third cup of coffee. I needed all the temporary energy I could muster. My head buzzed with the stimulant which helped drown out my fear for Katrin. When I read the note, emotions of doubt and betrayal rushed over me. *Irrational emotions. I must think logically. Galliard vouched for her. She doesn't care for power, otherwise she'd have chosen Halavant from the start. She loves me.* I trembled. *She loves me, despite my illness, and enough to help save Lansimetsa. She was ready to sacrifice her life to get rid of Egvar.* I shuddered again. I'd not let her. That was my responsibility.

Galliard took the cup from me and opened his mouth, then shut it.

"What is it, Galliard?"

"May I speak freely?"

I nodded.

"If you go, you may die."

I looked up, surprised at his honesty, but not his doubts. "If I can incapacitate the rebellion's leaders, I can stop this war from starting and prevent thousands of deaths. It is worth risking my single life. I unwittingly provoked the nobles to rebel against us, and now I must stop it. I believe the leaders will gather to Sir Egvar's. This may be our only chance to remove all the leaders at once."

Galliard kneeled next to me. "Then send someone else to take them out. Someone stronger."

I shook my head. "I'm strong enough. I'll be invisible. No one else would get close enough." Katrin could, I added silently. She'd kill Egvar and die. I had to go, to save Lansimetsa and her.

"Don't go. We need you to lead our people."

"I'm a strategist. They need a leader, like you." I handed him a sealed document. "This gives the rights of regent to you until I or Halavant return."

He stared at the document. "No. This isn't right."

"Galliard. I command you."

He bowed his head. "And I will obey, honored Yorel. Please be careful. You are more of a leader than you realize."

I turned to Hoft. "Put the leg braces on me."

Hoft buckled two long padded strips of metal to either side of my left leg. The pieces ran from ankle to upper thigh, and the buckles crossed at the ankle, below knee, above knee, and upper thigh. A leather piece looped under my soft-soled shoe. My leg stuck out in a rigid line. Hoft repeated the process with my right leg. He handed me two padded canes and pulled me to my feet.

I stiff-leg-walked across the room and back. My feet and the canes whispered across the floor. I nodded. It was much better than my stumbling.

Galliard lay his hand on my shoulder. "You don't have to go."

"But I will."

"I know." He stepped aside.

Hoft kneeled down with his back to me.

I sent a quick prayer heavenward—a wordless plea for God's blessing—then *quawlaared* into the shadow and wrapped my arms about Hoft's shoulders.

It was a good he was giant-blooded. He barely leaned forward as he carried me and my canes through the palace where servants ran and worried voices carried out of lit rooms, past the barracks of soldiers honing their swords and fletching arrows, past the pounding smithery, out the west gate. Only one servant stopped to give Hoft's slightly stooped walk a second glance.

Katrin stood by the gate in a gown of cream and gold, shadowed by her maid. "Yosyph?"

"I'm here."

She bit her lip. "We shouldn't do this. It feels wrong."

I didn't feel anything, which made the decision easier. I patted the poison pouch on my belt and sent another prayer heavenward. *I can't listen well with this coffee buzzing through my head and the quawlaar stopping my emotions. I don't know what else to do. Bless this endeavor. Protect this people. Help us stop this war.*

Hoft lowered me to the ground.

I set my canes to steady myself, then whispered to him. "Get back to the palace. Obey Galliard as you would me."

Minutes later, long enough that the metal of my braces turned an aching cold against my legs, the clopping of horse hooves and the rumble of wheels over cobble came from around the corner.

"Yosyph." Katrin's quiet voice rose in pitch. "This is wrong. We shouldn't do this."

"Katrin. We can stop the war before it starts. You just draw attention. I'll do the rest. Stay safe, and get out as soon as you can."

A carriage rumbled to a stop before us.

Katrin glanced at it and hesitated, her eyebrows drawn into a line of fear, then she lifted her chin.

A servant jumped from the carriage ledge and opened the door.

Katrin gathered her skirts as she approached a dirty, thinly iced puddle of water and leaped over. Her shoe cracked through the ice, and water splashed, coating the edge of her skirts and the white pants of the servant.

"Oh dear," she simpered, shaking water from her skirts. "I had hoped to show dear Egvar this lovely little thing, but it's ruined."

As she fussed over her dress, I walked stiffly to the carriage and, using my canes, climbed into the padded interior. A moment later she entered, followed by her serving maid. She reached out and patted the seats until she touched one of my legs and sighed. The worried line creased her brows again.

I leaned back and closed my eyes. Under the buzz of stimulant, my bones ached and my muscles trembled. I'd follow Katrin into the ball, watch for a gathering of noblemen, and follow. No dogs would menace me this time. I should have followed her this way before. So much had changed in the last month. I'd been slow to change my tactics as my abilities decreased. I was finally learning.

Katrin sat stiffly across from me.

Her maid patted her hand. "My lady, don't do anything foolish. He's with us this time, and he'll keep us safe."

Katrin pulled her hand away from the maid's. "That's what I worry about."

The carriage stopped outside a brightly lit mansion. Patches of red plaster covered war-damaged walls, and the colors didn't quite match. Music poured from the open doors as couple after couple climbed the stairs. Stairs would take time to maneuver.

The carriage door opened, and a servant stood, hand outstretched to help Katrin.

Katrin stayed seated, fussing with her skirts. "Oh, I don't know if I can enter like this. What an embarrassment...."

I slid to the carriage door as she fussed and simpered, set both canes into the floor rug and swung my legs over the edge, barely missing the hand of the servant. My feet came down on the cobble with a muffled, jarring thud. I swayed forward and pushed the canes to steady myself, then stepped to the side.

The servant stood with his hand raised and a long-suffering, half-listening look on his face.

Katrin wrapped up her words. "... Could I sneak in the servants' door and go change? I'm sure dear Egvar has something I could wear. He'd hinted at having a dress made for me. Oh, what if it isn't finished? I suppose I must go as I am. It isn't so bad. No one will be looking at my hem." And she descended from the carriage, followed by her serving maid.

I fell behind as I ascended the twenty steps after her, keeping to the side as other couples or singles promenaded up the center. I set my canes on a step, pushed my body upward, swung my legs forward, set legs, steadied myself, took quiet-deep breaths, and repeated.

Four stairs from the top, rapid footsteps closed in behind me. A young nobleman, carrying a lace shawl, dashed up the stairs two at a time, and headed into my space. I threw myself sideways and rolled three stairs downward. Several people turned, then returned to what they were doing with confused shakes of their heads.

The young shawl-carrying man stopped beside a lady and draped the shawl over her shoulders.

"Oh, Hans." Her high voice skipped over the air. "You are so quick. I shall drop my shawl more often."

My shoulders throbbed where the corners of the steps met

them in my roll. I pushed to my unsteady feet and ascended the last seven stairs.

The grand entry and ballroom glittered with crystal and hundreds of candles. Katrin was doing what I'd asked—drawing eyes to her. Her long red hair shone like fire among the other more muted tresses. She spun into the arms of Egvar, and her cream-and-gold gown belled out. I settled onto a nearly empty bench close to an elderly nobleman who smelled strongly of alcohol and rotten teeth. I watched dance after dance. The stately ganger and the energetic springar, the free form lausdans and the close-held samdans.

Egvar led Katrin to a group of other women clustered around a table of card-playing men. Katrin slipped in with the chattering women, while several men excused themselves from the table. Egvar glanced around the room and nodded to several others. Men passed off their dancing partners, and others grabbed a last pastry from the refreshment table. In ones and twos, they left.

I followed, dodging feet stretched out from the benches on one side and twirling skirts on the other, and into a side room where a fire burned hot enough to make my stomach turn. Fourteen men sat around a large table, Egvar sat at the head, and Duke Pulska sat to his right. Six more men followed after me and took their seats. No servant entered with refreshments, though goblets sat at each place, along with several bottles of wine.

Egvar motioned for the last who entered to close and lock the door. "Makkara has fled. He was never reliable. Too much sympathy for the dung born. A few others now lie chained in my cellar for their hesitancy. Any others who have second thoughts may join them."

"Who were they?" a graying man asked with a tremor.

Egvar shook his head and tsked. "Oh, Karhu. You should have taught your son better."

Karhu put his head in his hands, and his gulp echoed across the room.

Egvar looked at the others. "If no one else desires a damp week's stay in my cellar, let us proceed. Ten allies have infiltrated the castle, as pages, lamplighters, and even a coal bin girl. Tonight, they will free the true queen, and, if possible, kill the shadow demon. We must be ready to place her on her throne and hold against the Shadow Demon's supporters. Many common folk are already dissatisfied with how the usurper Halavant and the Shadow rule. We will make it easier for them to go back to the proper rule and order."

If these *allies* did manage to free the queen, they'd have a figurehead for others to follow. It wasn't a battle, but rather like strategies I'd so often created. Take out the leader, and the rest will fall. Put in a leader, and the rest will follow. I'd make these men unable to plot, at least for a few days.

Murmured conversation passed around the table as Egvar let them absorb his words. Egvar opened a corked wine bottle and poured himself a goblet before passing it to Pulska. Others followed example. I used the noise of conversation and imbibing to cover my rigid walk towards Egvar. He and Pulska were the most important to remove. I placed my weight on the cane to swing my right leg forward, and my wrist shot through with fire. Teeth gritted, I brought the other cane forward, and then my left leg. The shadow-walking was making my weakness worse again.

Egvar continued. "Each of you will gather at least a hundred folk, common and otherwise, to meet by the palace gates in the morning. I want a mob demanding the queen be placed on the throne. Give them gold or food or violence to convince them. If some get hurt by the Shadow's response, then all the better for us. We must show we are not starting the war. We are defenseless and innocent people, only seeking to voice our opinion. We will make the Shadow show us the demon that he is."

I stopped beside Egvar's chair, leaned my canes against my legs, reached into my belt pouch, and fingered the three narrow-necked poisons. One ridge on the vial meant debilitating stomach cramps. Two ridges—muteness for a day. Three ridges —death-like sleep that could lead to never waking. Muteness meant nothing because he could write. Sleep or cramps?

My legs cramped from balancing on useless feet, and my arms trembled. The buzz of the coffee was fading away into a headache. Sleep. I'd make them sleep. If I could continue through pain, so could they. However, if they slept, they could give no orders or organize no rebellion. Once they slept, I'd get Katrin, and we'd leave. I'd send an army to carry the men to prison.

I unstoppered the three-ridge vial and reached over the goblet beside Egvar. Plunk. One drop, two. The wine in his goblet rippled. A drop for a day of sleep. Maybe three, but that could send him into an endless sleep. No, just two. I tilted the vial upright.

Egvar shot out his hand, sweeping it through the air, and caught my wrist.

I tried to jerk away and dropped the vial. As it left my hand, it became visible and rolled across the table.

Egvar twisted my wrist.

I lost my balance and sprawled backwards to the floor.

Egvar kept hold of my wrist and called out. "Quick, bind him or something."

"Who?" several surprised voices asked.

"The shadow demon."

Duke Pulska lumbered from his chair, "Where is he? I'll sit on him!"

Egvar pointed in my general direction.

I tried to twist away as Pulska lowered himself onto my legs. At least it wasn't my chest. I'd not have been able to breathe.

Egvar released my wrist. "So you came to us. I wondered when you would. But I've heard you've fallen to the slow wasting much faster than a normal man would. It must be your demon blood weakening you." He kneeled and felt around until he touched my cheek, then pulled back his hand and slapped me three times.

My teeth clacked.

Egvar grabbed the goblet from the table. "Did you think you could drop poison into my cup and I not see the splash? I don't know how I missed your heavy breathing. It must have been Pulska's own loud breath that covered you. Come into the light, or you'll die a slow and painful death in the shadow."

I'd be more susceptible to his torture if I had my emotions to battle. I stayed *quawlaared* and silent.

He brought back a foot to kick me, glanced at the goblet, and lowered his foot. "It would be fitting for you to drink your own poison. And I need you dead more than I need you for entertainment. Virtanen, hold his mouth open for me."

A full-muscled man kneeled next to Pulska.

I threw a punch at him, catching him in the shoulder.

He backed up and spat. The mucus sprayed over my face. "If he's going to make me fight blind, I'll share the fun with others. Who wants a piece of the mighty shadow demon?"

Half the men at the table surrounded Pulska and me. Grumbles and jabs became shouts and rib-crunching kicks.

"Hold back, men," Egvar said when I couldn't stifle my moans. "I don't want him dead before he drinks this. Hold him."

Hands fumbled and grasped my torso, arms, and head. Thick fingers shoved into my mouth, jamming my jaw open.

"He's been drinking coffee," the thick-fingered man snickered. "It's as strong on his breath as on my dame's after she's been up all night planning a party."

Another man chuckled. "To think, the shadow demon needs coffee like the rest of us. It almost makes him human."

Egvar kneeled by my head. "Pinch his nose."

The thick-fingered man crushed my nose between thumb and forefinger.

Then Egvar poured the poison-tinted wine into my mouth. I couldn't eat or drink in the shadow state. I'd vomit the poison, as with anything else I tried to consume while *quawlaared*.

I coughed, gagged, and swallowed.

A minute later, my throat tightened, but before my body could eject the poison, a paralysis stilled all my movements. Darkness closed over my eyes, and my hearing grew muffled. Even my thumping heart slowed. *I cannot sleep in the shadow state. The poison has sent me into a frozen awareness, and I won't be able to move until it wears off.*

31

HALAVANT

Heaven's Wall, Lower Carani
  Febrúar 15th

I PACED the thirty steps between the back of the cave and the jungle, then back. Morning sun heated the thick air. Jabare lay sleeping on his side after moaning through the night. He'd not yet come out of his faint.

Elise stepped beside me. "You should eat."

Strips of rabbit-rodent sizzled on rocks set in the fire, the last of the animals Jabare caught. "No. I'm still not hungry."

"Do you want to help our friend?"

I nodded.

"Then eat so you can help drag him back to the village."

I stopped pacing.

Elise stopped, too, and faced me. "Donkor may not tell them. No one may be coming. And even if they come, it will take two days for Donkor to tell them and two more for them to get here. Jabare needs more help than Gaven or I can give him. He needs herbs we don't have, but they do. We need to get him back."

"We don't know the way."

Elise raised an eyebrow and pointed to the slashed foliage going into the jungle.

"Oh." This jungle wasn't a forest where paths ran in a hundred directions through widely spaced trees. We'd follow the slash marks to return.

I forced down sharp-flavored strips of meat, then paced again while Gaven and Elise made a sledge of branches and vines.

Gaven grumbled as he worked. "Agitation and irritations. Couldn't he stop pacing long enough to lend a hand—" he glanced at my braced hands, "—or a foot?"

I gritted my teeth. "What can I do?"

He pointed to the branches he was weaving with vines. "Hold these in place while we bind them together."

I leaned on them with my forearms.

By noon, we'd made a bed of branches, bound with vines and padded with leaves. Along the bottom ran two narrow branches, acting as runners. We dragged the sledge next to where Jabare lay on his side.

Gaven glared at me. "Halavant, you will lift under his shoulder and hip. You will not roll him or touch anywhere near his wound. I will take his head, and Elise, you carry his legs. On the count of three. One."

I crouched next to Jabare.

"Two."

I slipped my braced hands under his shoulder and hip.

"Three."

I hefted. His body lay limp and heavy as a speared deer.

"Careful!" Gaven shouted as Jabare began to slip from my hands.

I shoved my arms over the sledge, and he rolled onto his back, despite Gaven and Elise holding his head and legs.

"I told you—"

Elise cut him off. "Let's get him back on his side and get going."

Jabare moaned, "*Moswen.*"

I leaned over as his eyes fluttered open. "*I'm here.*"

He reached out to touch my face and winced, dropping his arm back to his side. "*You are alive. Thanks be to the gods.*"

"*Be still. We are taking you back to the village.*"

"*The gift to the gods. You must take it.*"

"*I'm not the Moswen. I'm his great-grandchild.*"

Jabare's eyes opened wider, and he nodded. "*The dream was true. We are not yet worthy for the Moswen to return. You are still his family, as is your brother. I will get the duri for you.*"

"*That will be wonderful—when we get to the village. Rest now.*"

Gaven pressed his fingers to Jabare's neck. "Pulse is better than yesterday. He needs to stop talking. Tell him."

"*The healer man says you must not talk, or he'll whip you with words.*"

Jabare grimaced. "*He whips many with words. You most of all. I can bear him. I must ask, was it Donkor who speared me?*"

"*Yes.*"

Jabare closed his eyes and cried out, "*Oh, Donkor, my friend, why? I heard your voice and prayed I heard wrong.*"

Gaven touched his forehead. "Talkative thing—when injured —no fever. Is he delirious? Can't you get him to stop talking?"

"I'll try." I kneeled back by Jabare. "*You must be still and rest.*"

He grabbed my forearm. "*Who defended you against him?*"

"*Donkor? He was a coward. I wrestled with him, Elise slung a stone at him, and he fled.*"

Jabare looked at my hands and a reverent awe softened his distressed features. "*Even with those broken hands... We are protected and blessed. Thank you.*"

The thanks seemed heaven-directed, as it should be. Donkor

was a coward, but he could have killed me if he'd stayed or if Elise hadn't clobbered him with a stone. "*Will you be quiet now? Otherwise the healer man will force you to drink something even more nasty than duri.*"

He smiled weakly and nodded.

Elise checked his bandages then tucked our blankets around him.

Gaven tied a harness of vines over my shoulders and bound it across my chest.

We plodded into the jungle, with me pulling like a peasant who plowed his own field. They were made of hardy stuff. Even Gaven picked up his pace, and soon I sweated with exhaustion. But we'd make it. Two days, and we'd be back.

32

KATRIN

How could the sun still rise? Yosyph lay dying of poison some-where in this mansion—Egvar boasted of that at a breakfast for two. He'd freed the queen and brought her here. Mobs surrounded the palace walls, demanding the queen be rein-stated. Everything was falling apart.

A honey-and-plum-tapestried room surrounded me. Dried roses filled vases in every corner. A fire burned near the deep basin where I sat in bath water as icy as my fear. The rapping at the door became more insistent.

"Lady Katrin," a female voice called with subservient respect and a hint of exasperation, "Sir Egvar awaits, as does Queen Analiese."

I waved over my serving maid, Maggie. "Remind her I have a cold and would not jeopardize the queen's health."

Maggie delivered my message through the closed door.

The female voice called loudly, and her highlander brogue slipped through. "He don't care. You can present yourself at a distance."

I didn't care anymore, either. I didn't want to keep up this pretense. Cold water dripped from me as I stood and slipped into a fire-warmed bathrobe. "Maggie, I'll have to wear that dress Egvar had made for me."

Maggie touched my hand and muffled a cry. "My lady, you are chilled. You should not have sat so long in cold water."

"It numbs the pain."

"You can't help him if you catch your death of stubbornness."

I dropped my voice. "Take extra care with my hair, I don't want my daggers to show."

"You can't," she whispered back, as she loosed my hair from the pins that held it dry above the water, "They'll kill you for an attempt on the queen's life."

"If Yosyph is dead, I can respect his memory by doing what must be done."

~

I PASSED under the stare of four guards and entered a small sitting room. A fireplace took up one full wall. Guards stood at watchful attention in each corner. Two divans and a thickly padded chair sat in a close grouping.

A woman who'd filled my earliest memories—who'd laughed beside my mother, who'd ordered my death so I wouldn't marry her son—sat in the padded chair and watched me approach with a disdaining tilt of her head. "The dead continue to haunt me. What do you seek?"

Egvar kneeled at her side. "Your majesty, your mind still is ill from imprisonment. No dead haunt you. Though she seems a heavenly being, she is flesh and blood. Without her help, we could not have freed you."

How? I swayed on my feet.

Egvar was at my side in a moment, catching my arm. "I'm sorry to call you out when you suffer from a cold. But I had to introduce you to the queen and let her thank you." He turned to the queen. "Lady Katrin was the key to everything, always staying close to the false king and the shadow, sharing with me what happened in the palace, the little routines. Lady Katrin even insisted one of our people get hired to work in the palace, the one who freed you."

I was a fool. When I spoke of little things, I didn't think they mattered. I'd gotten a traitor hired at the palace. Which of the many I'd spoken for? I'd let Yosyph come along with me, and Egvar caught him.

I reached out to a divan and sat before my legs gave out beneath me. "Oh, Egvar, you praise too highly. Yet, before I can feel safe, you must show me the Shadow Demon. I must know you've caught him, for he's followed me so often I can still feel him in my waking hours."

The queen took a crustless sandwich from a tray beside her and muttered, "Beware the viper."

Egvar shrugged his shoulders at the comment and whispered to me. "I'm sorry for her incivility. She lost a portion of her sanity while imprisoned. I hope my doctors can cure her soon, so we can restore her to her rightful place upon the throne."

"Is the Shadow Demon dead?" I let my fear tremble through.

"No, but he is not entirely alive either. If it will give you peace, I will bring you to him. You won't be able to see him. He refused to come out of the shadow state before I gave him the poison he intended for me, and even now he remains invisible."

I shuddered. They'd caught him last night, and now evening

fell. He'd been a full day in the shadow. Even a little time made the slow wasting worse. Would it travel to his lungs? "Please, bring me to him. Then I'll be able to sleep at night."

He put his arm around my shoulders. "Soon you'll not sleep alone, and you'll never fear again."

I clenched my fists in my skirts to hold the anger from my face. "Can we see him now? I'm so tired, and this will allow me to rest."

Egvar stood and bowed to the queen. "If you will excuse us."

He led me from the room. We climbed a narrow staircase to a single, well-lit room. A planked table stood in the middle and chains ran from bolted floor to four suspended points slightly above the table. A guard sat in the corner.

Egvar pointed. "He's chained to the table. If he heals from the poison, then I'll try one of the others he carried." He pulled three ridged bottles from his pocket. "Maybe demons don't die of poison."

"Then what will you do?"

"Kill him in the proper way—beheading." He chuckled. "Not even a demon can haunt without his head."

I gritted my teeth to hold in a scream. If he killed Yosyph, Egvar wouldn't live to see dawn. "Can I touch him? To assure myself he's really there?"

Egvar strode to the table, pressed his hand against the empty space near the head of the table and counted. "His pulse is still slower than that of one in a deep sleep. He's safe to touch, if you must."

I found Yosyph's face. His lips lay parted and let out the slightest breath against my fingertips. His pulse beat thump, wait, wait, wait, thump.

Yosyph, Yosyph. I will get you out, I vowed. *I will learn to shadow-walk. I'll drag you down those steps one by one. Don't you dare die on me.*

I turned to Egvar. "I am satisfied. Thank you."

∽

"MAGGIE, you will sleep in the servant's quarters off of my room tonight. I need to be completely alone."

Maggie stopped plaiting my hair into a bedtime braid and stared at me in the mirror. "I'll be listening if you need me."

"Thank you."

She finished plaiting my hair and left.

I locked the door after her and kneeled on the floor. Once, before Galliard had interrupted, I'd pulled the emotion of humor to my skin. Humor was an especially small emotion now. I pulled the ragged bits and pieces to my skin and let it sit there. Underneath the giggling surface sat deep fear, anger, and distress, mixed with everything else. Humor sat on the surface, but how to get it to wash off my skin? Wash off!

I ran to the washbasin and poured a pitcher of water over my hands, imagining the flow of water took the emotion with it. Sparkles of light flickered off with the water and floated like dust motes around my hands. A chill settled where humor once sat.

I squealed and covered my mouth.

Could I draw the emotion back?

I reached into the sparkles and rubbed my hands through them. They scattered and re-gathered around my hands. I tried to catch them in my cupped hands and they flitted out the sides. I swatted at them, like pesky bugs. What if I never learned to come out of the shadow? I'd worry about that later.

I washed worry off next. A coldness replaced it.

I gathered emotion after emotion onto my skin and learned to mentally wash them away. Anger came off in layer after layer. Fear took even more skins to peel away. Each left me chilled. I saved love and joy for last. I needed those emotions to stabilize me.

Morning sun glowed through my hands while sparkles glittered around me. How many more emotions to wash away before I became invisible?

Maggie knocked for the fifth time that morning.

"Go away, Maggie," I said, my voice coming out in a slight monotone. I wasn't annoyed with her, but I needed her to let me be.

"My lady, if you won't let me in, I'll get the housekeeper to unlock your door."

The housekeeper would complicate things. I unlocked the door and backed into a dark corner before calling out, "You may come in."

Maggie glanced around the room, her gaze passed over me once then came back with a gasp. "Oh, my Lady. You shouldn't. It's dark magic."

"It's not dark magic. It's a skill, like spinning thread or knife throwing. I must continue to practice it until I've become fully invisible. You will not speak a word of this to anyone. Tell any who asks that I am sleeping, finally at peace enough to do so."

"You speak strangely, like you are under a spell or speaking in your sleep."

"I am under no spell, but my emotions are partly gone."

"You've given up your emotions? You will cease to be a woman without your heart."

"Only for a short time. I will take them back once I've done what I need to do." If I learned how to take them back.

Maggie crossed the room till she stood a hand's reach away and studied me with wary eyes. "Do you still feel what is right and wrong, or have you become a wild creature, or worse yet, a slave to a demon?"

"I've not given up my thoughts, only my emotions. I am still in command of myself."

She studied me several moments longer, then reached out and touched one hand. "The Yorel was honorable even as the shadow. How can I help?"

"I'm hungry, though I don't know if I can eat in this half-shadow state."

33

YOSYPH

I LAY TRAPPED INSIDE A MOTIONLESS, sightless body. Only muffled sounds, slight pressure around my wrists, and a growing stink reminded me I existed. A story Farid told in my training called to my sluggish thoughts.

Pride breaks peace. It sets man in enmity with man.

Before the sage Akram founded the great council, the people were divided not by tribe but by pride. Some dug in the earth and found precious metals and gems. These set themselves above the others, claiming by their labor and wisdom, they were better. Classes formed, with walls as strong as stone. Those born to wealth continued in wealth. Those born to daily labor became slaves and servants to the others. Shepherds, wandering the grasslands, were mocked as less than a servant. All divided themselves against another. The years cemented the division into hate.

The people began to justify breaking the law. Pillage turned a

189

servant into a thief. Hunters became killers of men for a price. The rich abused the poor. The judge let the evil man go free for a bribe.

Both low- and high-born thought their cause was just. The high-born saw the low as lazy thieves and robbers. The low-born saw the high as oppressors. Both were right, in part. Their blind rightness led them to forget to plant, or fish, or harvest. Instead, they formed armies to destroy their enemies—their neighbors. The low-born army was larger than the high-born army by ten times. But the high-born had horses and well-made weapons.

War grew in the place of crops. Blood watered the ground. Bones were buried in the soil instead of seeds. Our people would have killed each other to the last child, if two leaders did not open their eyes to see. One was a shepherd man, old enough to remember before the pride poisoned the people. The other was a boy, born to luxury, and not yet old enough to know the ways of man.

Something pressed against my throat. Voices slipped through the fog, "His heart is quickening, yet still too slow to be anything but asleep."

"Tell me as soon as he wakes."

The voices slipped away, and the story called again.

The shepherd led his flocks far from the wars, seeking peace in the sparse desert grasses and rare rains. One day, a boy stumbled into his camp, famished and shaking with fear. His father, the leader of the high-born army, had taken him into battle beside his mother and older sister. He'd fled. The old man fed and sheltered the boy and listened to his nightmares. A month passed. The old man fell into a new content-edness with the boy's company.

The boy could not forget. He crept away one night to stop the fighting.

When the old man discovered him gone, he followed, leading his flocks into the stinking land of death, where two armies camped across a plain from each other, each preparing for a final battle. He did not find the boy, but he did find the low-born army without a leader, the most recent one having died. One man, in more dark mirth than meaning, said since the old man had shepherded sheep through a land of battle, he could lead men to victory. The word spread through the ranks, and soon the shepherd found himself responsible for a war and an army ready to follow him to death.

In the high-born army another leader also rose. The young boy had returned to find his father dying of wounds. His father bestowed on him all honor and rights of leadership. That night, the boy took the red banner of his family, the gold banner of the high-born, and the yellow banner of surrender, and marched across to the low-born camp. He was beaten, bound, and brought before the shepherd leader.

In tearful reunion, the two embraced, and together they plotted peace. Many words and weeks later, the two armies, what was left of a once prosperous people, agreed to a treaty. Swords were beaten back into plows, crops grew again from the ground, and step by step, the walls of pride fell. The people learned to see each other for who they were, rather than how they were born or what they owned. And it was possible because the boy was willing to surrender to his enemy.

The story silenced, and questions filled the emptiness. What if the shepherd hadn't been the low-born leader? They'd have killed the boy, and the war would have continued. But if the boy hadn't taken those steps, the whole nation would have died. His actions allowed a space for peace to grow up. Was surrender ever the honorable way? Or working with your enemies?

My body began to tingle. Darkness drew back. I forced my eyes open. A wood-beamed ceiling formed out of blurriness. Ribbons of pain shot up my side with my increased breath. A broken rib or two? They gave me sufficient beating before Egvar forced the poison into me. Cold bands encircled my wrists. I shifted, and metal clanked.

A deep voice chuckled. "Oh, ho, now for the fun."

I didn't have the energy to lift my head.

A key turned in a lock and a door opened. "Get Egvar. The demon is waking!"

Thumping boots faded downward.

What shall I do now? I sent my question into the heavens. *Do I offer to work with Egvar? It isn't logical, but I'll do as you direct.*

A memory from before my capture whispered through my head. *Do not lose hope, despite how dark the night becomes. If you listen, I will send those to carry you back to the day.*

Who would carry me back?

I slipped back into a fog. Light and sound muffled around me. Then a rap, rattling, and voices. I forced myself to listen again.

"—release him? My lord, why?" It was the guard's voice.

"I said release him!" Egvar's voice came high and strained.

Was he the one to carry me to safety? How strange.

Someone yanked one hand-shackle upward, and then, with a grating click, the metal fell from my wrist, then the other wrist and ankles. I should have jumped to my feet and fought my way free, but I couldn't even open my eyes.

"Lift him onto your shoulders," Egvar ordered.

"He could slit my throat."

Silence for a moment and a slight sound, a whisper, floated through the air.

Egvar gasped, then commanded, "I'll slit your throat for him, if you don't obey."

Someone was controlling Egvar, someone the guard couldn't see. The pieces came together. God had sent my mentor, Farid.

The guard patted around on me until he found my arms, then with a yank, he pulled my arms over his shoulders.

Fire shot up and down my side. I cried in gasping whimpers as I hung down the guard's back and my feet dragged on the ground.

Egvar's hurried voice cut through my agony. "Be careful with him."

"If you want the demon carried like a baby, get someone else." The guard's bristly chin rubbed against my arms as he spoke.

"Don't injure him any further and follow me."

The guard grumbled as he carried me. "High-handed nobleman, making me carry the demon up the stairs and now back down. Should have locked him in the dungeon in the first place."

My feet clunked against each step, shooting more fire up my side. When we reached a level, I strained my eyes open. Polished wood and bright plaster walls passed by with the occasional vase of dried flowers and framed paintings. Then into a bustling kitchen.

Muffled exclamations blended together.

"What's the lord doing in here?"

"Blimey, the guard's like an old man, hunched over and clutching at his chest."

The guard halted. "My lord, where are you taking him?"

Egvar walked a short distance ahead. Sparkles of light flickered behind him. Farid's floating emotions had changed form. They'd once been like fireflies but now glittered like diamonds in sunlight.

Egvar ducked under a low-hanging soup pot, spun about, smacked his hands into the glittering light.

The light fell. A knife skittered away. The light form sprang towards the knife.

"Kill the shadow demons!" Egvar roared as he ducked under a table against the wall. He pulled a stock pot in front of him. "Kill both of them."

The knife disappeared.

The kitchen exploded in confusion. Some ran for the doors as others grabbed cast-iron pans and cleavers.

The guard dropped me to the ground. I landed face upward. The guard stood over me with drawn sword, then fell. His blade skipped off the stones to my right, and his body crushed over me.

"Kill the she-demon first!" Egvar shouted. "She won't leave without her mate."

She?

Egvar squealed like a kicked dog. "Stop! Everyone stop!"

Katrin's flat-toned voice came from beside Egvar. "You, in the butcher's smock, move the guard's body off the Yorel. Be careful."

"Do as the she-demon says," whimpered Egvar.

Katrin was shadow-walking.

34

KATRIN

The butcher lifted the guard's body. Yosyph's form glowed with streamers that flowed outward like the ribbons of traveling jugglers, loosely outlining his limbs, torso, and head. He'd not glow if he were dead.

I kept my knife pressed against Egvar's throat. No knife prodding his side this time. "Call for a carriage to carry Yosyph, you, and me back to the palace."

"You promised I'd be free once I released the Yorel."

"You broke your part, so the cost has gone up."

"Cold demon, you might as well kill me here."

"I could, but I won't unless it becomes necessary. Is it necessary?" I pressed the edge of the knife more firmly against him.

He shrank back against the wall. Anger fought with fear in his face. "How could I miss you being shadow spawn?"

"Call for the carriage."

"Get me a carriage now!"

The remaining kitchen staff scattered.

"Wait," I called out. "I want the butcher, the man in the red-striped breeches, the ash-faced boy, and the fat cook."

They shuffled forward.

"You will carry the Yorel. And someone get Katrin's serving maid."

A short time later, a carriage rumbled to the kitchen door. I guided Egvar to the door, and the four men carried Yosyph behind us. It was awkward getting into the carriage while still keeping proper pressure on my blade. Egvar let out a few choice curses as I drew a thin line of blood. Maggie sat across from us, and her eyes grew wide at the sight of Egvar.

"I'm here, and the Yorel is coming."

She relaxed slightly.

Yosyph's glowing form joined us along the floor of the carriage.

I nudged Egvar's foot with mine. "Pull your boots under the seat."

His leg stiffened as if preparing to kick. After a pause, he pulled his feet under the seat.

A short ride later, we pulled through a shouting angry crowd to the gates of the palace.

"Maggie, you will find someone to let us in. Tell them whatever you need, the truth, or if they won't believe the truth, lie through your teeth."

She was efficient in her words. Minutes later, the gates opened and a regiment of soldiers poured out. They surrounded the carriage and escorted us through. The gates shut behind us, and the door to the carriage opened.

A soldier thrust his spear in, skimming it by me as the point settled against Egvar's chest. "Come out slowly, with your arms held away from you."

"Careful," I cautioned. "The Yorel lies on the floor."

The soldier shuddered, knocking his spear against my shoulder. "Another shadow demon? Is that you, Lady Katrin?"

"Careful with that spear. You should remove the Yorel first. Yosyph, if you can hear me, come out of the shadow so the soldiers can care for you."

The ribbons of light shrank back into Yosyph until he lay shuddering on the floor of the carriage. His eyes rolled back, and he went limp.

They'd tend to him. I had to keep watch on Egvar.

When they'd carried Yosyph off, the soldier poked his spear in again. "Your turn, traitor."

I prodded Egvar out with a second knife at his back. Once he was gone, I lay back against the seat and breathed. Exhaustion lay heavy on my sleepless eyes; hunger gnawed at my stomach.

The soldier poked his head back into the carriage. "Are you still there, lady-shadow?"

"I'll be going now. Move."

He scuttled away from the door.

I trudged to my room. Maggie met me there. "Lady, will you come out of the shadow now?"

"I will as soon as I learn how."

35

ELISE

JUNGLE, Lower Carani
   Febrúar 16th

THE VILLAGE HAD to be close. We'd followed a slashed trail, and we'd dragged Jabare for two days. We'd be there soon.

I brushed against dripping leaves and got a pitcher's worth of water down the neck of my dress. It didn't increase the moisture of my clothes. Halavant stopped ahead of me and leaned his braced hands on his knees, taking in deep breaths. He'd stripped down to just leggings and boots.

"Halavant. I'll take a turn now."

He turned and shook his head, still gulping in air. "Too muddy. You can't."

I hated to admit he was right. I'd barely pulled the litter on dry ground. Now in the rain, mud coated the runners.

"At least let me help pull."

Halavant sat and rolled his shoulders. "Wish you could. The path is too narrow, and we'll trip each other. Give me a moment and more of that nasty drink Gavin concocted, and I'll be good to go."

Gaven kneeled next to Jabare, checking his bandages as we talked. Gaven's storm-cloud eyebrows pulled down against his eyes. Jabare moaned as Gaven shifted the blood- and rain-soaked bandages.

I touched Jabare's forehead. It burned with fever.

Gaven moved my hand. "I'll take care of him. You tend to Halavant. If any of those blisters get infected, we'll be stuck here."

I slipped past Jabare's litter to Halavant and held the water bag to his mouth.

He took a swallow and scrunched up his face.

"Is it really that bad?"

He grinned. "It's nasty."

"As much as the duri?"

His grin widened. "Nothing is bad as duri. That is the king of nasty. This is everyday nursery medicine nasty."

"How are your shoulders?"

"Them? They grumble as much as Gaven. I've stopped paying attention."

I slipped the vine harness from his shoulders and chest, then gently tugged at the folded cloth that provided padding between the vines and his skin.

Halavant sucked through gritted teeth. "Just take the cloth and not my skin."

The cloth pulled away, leaving lines of burst blisters. I opened a jar of salve and dabbed it on the largest blister.

"Ouch!" he hollered.

He was making such a fuss. I touched his brow. He wasn't fevered, and the corners of his mouth turned up. I glared at him.

"No sympathy," Halavant muttered. "I'd find more compassion from my skin-peeling Carani kin."

I grimaced. The Carani we'd met were as far from skin-peeling, heartless barbarians as I was from an elegant lady.

"How is my esteemed kin, the one reclining on the moving divan?" Halavant kept his words light, yet, his voice caught between words.

I bit my lip. "We need to get him proper food and out of this rain."

"Something more than soggy biscuits and rain-washed jerky?"

I pulled the mentioned food from my side pouch. "You might as well eat while I tend to the rest of the blisters."

Halavant clasped the damp jerky between his hand braces and chomped off a piece. Between chewing, he said, "I'll have you know I prefer my meat piping hot, with crispy edges and juicy middle—not this rubbery, soggy substance."

My mouth twitched. He was such a clown. "I'll see what the cook can do."

Halavant laughed "Hah! I knew you still had humor in you. I expect to see more."

"But—"

"Look, Elise. I never apologized for my words when we left the village. I don't expect you to be witty—though you are. But you've been all too serious since then, and I can't pull Jabare another inch through the mud with your cloud hanging over me, too."

I dabbed ointment on the last of his blisters. "I'll work on it."

"Thank you." He bent forward and brushed his lips on my cheek.

Heat rose to my face as fast as a candle taking flame.

He blushed, too, and mumbled, "Just a brotherly kiss. Smile or something."

Gaven drew in his breath, and I braced myself for a caustic comment. He stared past us, his face blanched white.

I unlooped the sling from my belt as I turned. Ten men emerged from the jungle. Three held spears in ready position, a couple trained arrows on Halavant, and five carried drawn swords. Each wore striped and spotted skins over every inch of their body, including animal-skin masks with just eyeholes cut out. In the middle of them stood Donkor, his face a mask of horror.

36

HALAVANT

Jungle, Lower Carani
   Februar 16th

Donkor stood bound in the middle of the animal skin-masked warriors.

Smugness at his discomfort fought with fear at our potential place beside him. "*Donkor, who are these men?*"

His gaze darted at the man holding his ropes, then he stared at the ground. Angry red bruises welted on his face, and only one of them was from Elise's sling days before.

A warrior with a necklace of red and crystal stones stepped towards me. His words came muffled through his orange striped mask. "*You speak our tongue. Where came you? Speak quick or die slow.*"

He spoke like my tutor had. The clipped words and missing niceties of helper words. Should I chance the gamble? "*I am the Moswen.*"

The necklaced warrior burst into laughter, and his comrades

joined him. "*Moswen? Lowlander's godling? You'll make great sport in king's court. And bring in ransom from lowland village.*"

Donkor looked up, weaselly hope playing in his face. "*He's an impostor. He may still bring a ransom from his pale-face land. Take him, ransom him or skin him and sell his lily skin, but leave our village be. We have nothing but death for you if you cross into our lands.*"

One of the other warriors grunted, his black-spotted mask puffed out with the air. "*Nkosi. The king wanted foreign sport. These three are more foreign and less dangerous than lowlander fanatics. Let's kill the two lowlanders and take these three. One lowlander looks most dead. And the other is a coward. No sport in that.*"

Nkosi, the necklaced warrior, stepped towards us. "*Thabit, you are coward.*" He lifted his mask enough to spit into the mud at his feet. A flash of purple skin showed.

Purple? Where these not men, but creatures that spoke?

"*No,*" Thabit, the black-spot-masked man, said, "*I give my skin for the king. I let him carve off a patch each year of my service—more years than you've lived. I am no coward. But what good servant kills himself when he has a way to fulfill his duties? Take foreigners, kill lowlanders, return with required sport.*"

Nkosi lifted his sword over the closed-eyed Jabare.

Elise threw herself in front of Jabare and held out one hand. "Stop, you can't kill him!"

My voice overlapped hers. "*I will provide sport, here and now. I'll fight your strongest man, without weapons. If I win, we go free. And if I lose, I go with you without a struggle.*"

Nkosi laughed. "*If you lose, you'll be dead. If you win, you can pick one lowlander not to die.*"

I'd take him out quickly. I'd—

Nkosi dropped his sword to the ground and charged at me.

"Cat's claws!" I jumped to the side, drawing the vines taut between me and the litter.

He slipped in the mud as he followed and barreled into the vines.

We both rolled into the mud, him face down and me on my back beside him. I lunged upward. The vine harness yanked me back. How to fight bound to a sledge? Nkosi scrambled in the mud. I drove my elbow into his back as he came up on his hands and knees.

He flattened face downward.

I drove my elbow down again, but before I struck him, he rolled and caught my arm. He pushed against me and stood. Mud sludged his striped skins.

I rolled to my hands and knees, my vines free of Nkosi's weight.

Nkosi's soft shoe caught me in the ribs.

I gasped, sucking in air against the pain.

His fist struck me across my bare shoulders and a line of blisters.

I flattened to the ground. A whip would have hurt less. I rolled again, and the vines bound around me.

Laughter burst around me. "*He'll tie himself up prisoner.*"

"*Stop her!*" shouted a different voice.

Nkosi stumbled away from me with a grunt.

Elise screamed.

I rolled to unwrap the vines and pushed to my feet as Nkosi's punch landed beside my eye. Lights danced. I kicked, and my metal-toed boot connected solidly with his knee. A crack.

He bellowed and toppled.

I leaped on him and swung my elbow into the spot between his ribs and stomach.

Short, small gasps sucked at his mask.

I raised my braced hand to chop across his throat.

Hands grabbed my arm. *"Enough!"* He yanked me upward, then spun me around so I stared into the spotted mask of Thabit. *"If he were anyone but the king's spoiled son, I'd let you finish him."*

Elise struggled in the arms of a leopard-skin warrior. A sling hung from her fist.

Gaven kneeled next to the overturned litter. He held Jabare's face from the mud.

Nkosi shuddered on the ground.

"Then let us free. I've given you your sport."

Thabit shook my arm. *"The girl interfered."*

"And the king's spoiled son charged without warning." I should have held my tongue.

He toed the shuddering Nkosi, then stared into my eyes. *"You held your own well. I give you one lowlander."*

Jabare, of course. Could he make his way into the village on his own? *"Both. The injured can't live without the other one."*

"One."

"Halavant?" Elise asked.

"Silence, girl." The warrior holding her, squeezed tighter.

"Stop it!" I tried to pull away from Thabit. *"Don't harm her. She's a healer, as is the old man. They can cure the king of old age. They can—"* I paused, *"make skin young again."*

A bird trilled its notes in the silence.

Nkosi pushed up on one elbow and gasped, *"Can they remove scars?"*

"Yes. If you hurt them, or the lowlanders, they won't."

Nkosi lifted his mask just enough to spit. Again a flash of purple skin. *"I'll make them. What do I care for lowlanders? Bind coward to tree and let them starve. Foreigners come with us."*

Donkor quavered as silent as a deer as they bound him to a tree.

"Gaven, Elise—" I began.

"Quiet. No foreign talk," Nkosi wheezed.

I bowed. *"I must tell them what you expect, honored prince."*

"Then be quick."

I turned to Elise and Gaven. "They let us live because I told them you could make skin young again and remove scars."

Gaven harrumphed. "We are no gods. Why couldn't you lie closer to the truth?"

"Any closer and Jabare's head would be severed. They leave him to starve. Unbind him from the—"

"You talked enough." Nkosi cut in.

Gaven nodded, unbound Jabare from the litter, and rolled him onto blankets.

Rain mixed with tears and ran down Elise's cheeks. Her jaw hardened. "Donkor, how could you betray us? How could you betray your friend?" she screamed.

The fur-covered men laughed, and the one holding her shoved her forward.

She stumbled, looked about, then fixed her gaze on Donkor. She shook her fist as she stalked toward him. "You are nothing but a bug. I'd squash you with my foot, except I wouldn't want to soil myself with you." She came within inches of him, yanked his head forward, and slapped him.

The Carani howled with laughter. Nkosi pulled out a knife. *"Tell her to kill him. I'll enjoy this sport."*

She'd snapped. Would she kill Donkor if given a knife? "Elise. Stop it. Please."

She kept her back to me as she answered, her voice trembling with anger. "I've given Donkor my healer's knife. He can cut himself free and help Jabare."

Oh! What could I do about Nkosi's order? "They want to watch you kill him."

"Tell them I'd do so, except I've made a vow to never kill, and if I broke the vow, I'd lose my power to make skin young." She slapped Donkor again, hard enough his head knocked against the tree.

I told Nkosi.

He spat, then cursed. The spotted-faced warrior cut the vine harness from my back. The Carani bound Gaven, Elise, and my arms, and marched us off into the jungle, perpendicular to where we'd been heading.

I raised my face to the dripping heavens and sent a silent plea. *Please, whoever can hear me, please let Donkor be honorable enough to help Jabare—and if we can't figure a way out of this mess, please help us, too.*

PART III

37

KATRIN

PALACE, Fairhaven, Lansimetsa
  Február 17th

MAGGIE REPLACED the midnight candles with the early morning ones as I lay on my bed.

Sleep wouldn't come, though my eyelids rubbed like sandpaper against my eyes. The sparkles of my emotions flitted like a cloud of gnats, brushing against me, but never letting me catch them, never coming back to be a part of me. Yosyph was right. I couldn't properly shadow-walk. I'd forced the emotions from me. Perhaps the talent to shadow-walk was more the ability to take them back. How long could I function without sleep or food?

Maggie opened the door to gentle tapping.

A man's voice carried through the opening. "General Galliard would see Lady Katrin."

He'd wanted to see me as soon as Yosyph and I arrived back yesterday. I'd requested time to pull out of the shadow-walk. He'd given me that time. And I'd not figured it out, nor would I.

Maggie shook her head. "She cannot come yet."

I sat up and moved to the door. "I will. Give me ten minutes. Where shall I meet the General?"

The servant startled, then bowed. "At the council room."

Maggie reached out to me and grasped one of my hands. "You must try to eat first."

"It will end in a bucket again."

"Please, lady, you'll die if you don't."

"Maggie, many have died. I'll do something good before I do. I don't feel fear or worry, so it will be easier for me than most."

"Call for a doctor. Someone to help you."

"No doctor can help me. Not even Yosyph could push my emotions back into me, if I cannot pull them in myself. I made a choice. Do not cry for me."

Maggie sobbed out soft words. "The shadow makes her as cold as blind Justice in judgment. I would see her again."

She was right. I was cold. There was one for whom I must leave words. I sat at my writing desk.

Yosyph, I am unable to come out of the shadow-walk. I know this will hurt you. And I would take that hurt from you, if I could. I love you. Even though I cannot feel it, I remember it, I know it, and I choose it. I will do all I can while in the shadow to stop this war from happening. And if your God will allow it, we will meet in the afterlife. Katrin.

I blotted the ink, folded the parchment, and sealed it. "Take this to the Yorel's room."

Maggie took the note with a sniff.

I slung a cloak over my shivering body. The material disappeared as I bound it to me. I slipped three knives into my belt and turned toward the council room.

Yelling tumbled down the long halls, words too muffled to understand.

I ran toward the commotion, trying to lighten my tread so

my wool slippers only rustled along the floor, but they still fell in a steady patter against the stone. It would be interesting to learn to move quietly as Yosyph did. I loped into the grand entry.

A few strides from me, a side door stood open, and just inside stood Lord Makkara, surrounded by soldiers. His arms were bound, his clothes rumpled and travel-stained, and his feathered hat lay on the ground. He held his head high and stared over the shoulder of the soldier in front of him.

A captain sat on the ground with a bloody lip, and a common soldier struggled in the grasp of his fellows.

The struggling soldier yelled, "He's a traitor. He deserves no trial."

The captain wiped his hand across his face, leaving a streak of red. "Mikael, you are relieved of duty. Go muck the stable."

The soldier looked to the men on either side of him. "You can't let him. We have to kill the traitors before they kill us. Do you want Oskari to have died for nothing?"

Indecision fought on the faces of the men holding him.

Mikael broke free and drew his sword.

Not Makkara. Not today.

I drew a knife, then slipped it back. Mikael wasn't a criminal. I dashed forward and caught Mikael's sword arm as the captain leaped to his feet.

Mikael spun towards me. His eyes widened as he looked through where I stood. Then he went slack as the hilt of the captain's sword knocked against his head.

I backed away as the other soldiers bound the fallen man.

What was Makkara doing here? He'd warned Yosyph and then left to keep his family safe. Why would he come back? Or had he? Had someone else gone after him and brought him back?

The captain spat blood onto the flagstones. "Get General Galliard. Even if he's asleep."

I followed as the captain led the bound Lord Makkara toward the council room.

Galliard met them in the hall and stepped towards Lord Makkara. "Have you come of your own free will?"

Makkara lifted his chin. "I've come through necessity. When I returned to put my home in order, after taking my family to safety, I heard rumors you've captured Egvar."

"Yes." Galliard nodded for Makkara to continue.

"His plans were to place the queen back on the throne. With him gone, many others will vie for that honor. Anarchy sits ready to topple our nation."

"And what would you have me do?"

"Send a flag of peace. Speak with them. Listen to their demands."

"Both King Halavant and the Yorel have sought this and been rejected."

"Neither listened," Makkara said. "But you are wiser in years. You can stop this from becoming a blood bath."

I called out from a safe distance. "I will help."

Galliard jumped, Makkara wobbled, and the room filled with the slither of swords drawn from sheaths.

I backed up another step. "I'm Katrin. I'm still shadow-walking. I will help."

Makkara's face lost the last of its color, and he sagged against the ropes a soldier held. "Another shadow demon? How many now haunt our land?"

"Don't hurt her," Galliard called as one soldier took a step towards my voice. "Katrin, I greatly appreciate your help. Come out of the shadow so we can talk face to face."

"I can't."

Galliard rubbed his forehead. "You can't, or you won't."

"I can't. I've tried. Now let me be of use while I still may be."

"He didn't teach you, did he?"

"Galliard, you are wasting minutes of the day or two I have left. Makkara, what can I do? Who is the most dangerous? Who needs to be removed so he cannot cause war?"

Makkara straightened. "You are worse than the other. He didn't go about *removing* people. You'll just stir them up worse. Now go off to some dark corner and die as you've hinted."

Galliard placed a hand on Makkara's shoulder. "That was uncivil." He turned toward me. "You will not go off and die. As soon as the Yorel is awake, you will learn how to come out of the shadow. And in the meantime, you will rest outside of his room —I know you cannot sleep or eat, but you can rest. And if any assassin comes for him, you can put your skills to use."

Protecting him from assassins was a worthy use of my abilities. "I will protect him."

Galliard rubbed his forehead again. "Good. Captain, go with her to the Yorel's room and explain her role to his guards. She is to see the Yorel as soon as he wakes." He turned to Makkara. "We have much to discuss."

I followed the captain from the council chamber. A yawn slipped out my mouth and bounced off the walls.

The captain turned. "Can you truly not sleep or eat while a shadow demon?"

"No."

"What a hellish state."

In some ways it was. My stomach added its gurgling noise to another yawn. I'd not be sneaking, yet my noise could scare off an assassin.

38

YOSYPH

PALACE, Fairhaven, Lansimetsa
Febrúar 17th

TWO VOICES CUT through a fog of pain.

A deeper one whispered, "He has broken ribs and bruising that could be internal. He's worn his heart to a weak and rapid pulse. His slow wasting has probably progressed much further than it had before he left on that fool's errand. I would send him into a week-long half-slumber, allowing him only enough wakeful time to drink teas and broth. He cannot exert himself or his heart could stop. He needs time to heal."

A tenor voice responded. "She's stuck as a shadow demon. I wouldn't ask this if there was anyone else who could help her. She will die if she remains in the shadow."

Who? I wondered.

"She can last another day without water or sleep. I will re-evaluate your request at that time. She saved the Yorel, but her life is less important than his, and I will not chance trading the one for the other."

Katrin? She was stuck in the shadow? "Katrin." My word came out thick from a cottony throat.

The deeper voice growled, "Look what you've done. Get out."

A hand lifted my head and pressed a cup to my lips.

I compressed my lips and turned my head.

"Drink and then sleep." This time the deep voice was gentle.

I swiped my hand and knocked the cup away from me, then forced my eyes open. The room filled with blurs. Out of the blurs formed a knit-browed face. My ever-loyal physician. "Get Katrin, now. I'll not eat or sleep until she can."

He opened his mouth, then shook his head and turned to the man next to him. "The damage is done. Get the shadow girl in here." He kneeled next to me. "You must not exert yourself. If you heard our conversation, you know your life is teetering on the edge. Do not push yourself over."

I nodded. Pain wove its fingers over and through me. Fear raced through my heart.

The door opened, and the man re-entered.

Katrin's disembodied and emotionless voice came from behind him. "Yosyph."

"Katrin, you need to pull your emotions back in."

"I've tried."

"What have you tried?"

"I've tried to capture the sparkles that float around me with my hands, but they slip through. I've tried to breathe them in but they remain a handspan from my face. I've tried thinking *let the emotions back*. I've tried—" She continued with a long list of what she'd done.

How did I pull my emotions back? The first time, I'd envisioned pouring the liquid ink of my emotion over myself. Hers seemed more ethereal.

I *quawlaar'd*.

My physician sank to a chair with a groan. "Why do I even try to save his life?"

The sparkles of Katrin stood at the foot of my bed. They shimmered much brighter than sunlight through crystal.

"Come here."

Her form approached until she stood next to my elbow.

I picked up one of my strands of emotion, an orange blended with rose. I reached out and wrapped the strand around her wrist.

The strand flashed, Katrin gasped, and the strand flew off her.

"I felt that." Her voice was still emotionless. "For a moment, I was warm."

I reached out and ran my hand through her sparkles. They slid over my skin like sun-warmed sand. I grasped a handful. "Katrin, kneel."

Her form shortened. I pressed my fist to her chest, then opened my hand, pushing the sand against her. The sand slipped out between my fingers and back into the air.

Why did her emotions repel from her? How could we get them to re-enter her? My emotions had for a moment entered her.

I took the same orange-rose strand. It shimmered with heat. I wrapped it around a handful of Katrin's crystal sand and pressed it against her chest.

The ribbon dissolved into her with the handful of sand. The other sand swirled like water going down a hole and pulled into the place where the ribbon had disappeared. Katrin flashed into sight and crumpled to the floor. Her screams rent the air.

A tattered orange-rose strand flew back from her toward me.

My guards rushed into the room.

Katrin's screams turned to gasping laughter. She pressed a hand to her stomach. "I was falling. Fear and excitement and joy and anger and… and everything rushed into me like the wind. I've flown apart into a thousand pieces, and now I'm not certain if I'm together right. Yosyph, come out of the shadow. Please. I must see you again."

I un-*quawlaar'd*.

"Yosyph? Yosyph!"

A tightness clutched my chest. I gasped for air that wouldn't fill my lungs. Blackness tunneled my vision.

A cool hand pressed to my neck and another to my chest. "Take slow breaths. Breathe. In. Out."

I coughed and breathed and coughed again. The band around my chest loosened slightly.

"Drink this." He lifted my head and pressed the cup to my lips.

This time, I didn't turn away. I coughed around swallowing, focusing on each breath.

My physician tsked. "You've pushed too far. Now it will be up to the gods if I can save you."

Katrin wove her fingers around mine, and at her touch, a tranquility entered me. "Sleep, Yosyph. I'm here for you."

"What did you do?" my physician asked. "His heart is settling to a steady rate."

She smiled at me. "I gave him part of my calm. Like he gave me part of his love."

"How?" I mouthed.

"Sleep."

I let the questions settle under the warmth that infused my being. *Thank you, God, for sending Katrin.*

39

ELISE

Jungle, Lower Carani
    Februar 18th

The fur-faced Carani lounged around a campfire while I turned the spit roasting their meal. I'd be lucky if I got a bone to chew. Not that they'd shared on previous days. We'd subsisted on our own supplies of soggy biscuits and jerky. Why hadn't we packed our food in waterproof satchels like our herbs? It didn't matter now; we'd eaten the last of our food early that day.

One warrior—the one plastered with mud and wearing a red necklace—prodded me with a stick and said something.

The others laughed.

I hid my discomfort with silent questions. *Why did they wear the masks of skins? What did they hide?*

A cliff loomed before us. Not the one Jabare had led us to, but a shorter one with a narrow path criss-crossing its face. Tomorrow, we'd ascend the cliff to the land of the skin-peeling Carani.

Jabare. Did he still live? We'd left him two days earlier, wounded and fevered but still alive. Did Donkor still have a thread of honor or friendship running through his cowardice? If he did, and Jabare survived, the village would rescue us. I held onto the thin strand of hope, wrapping it around the nightmares that haunted my waking thoughts and overwhelmed my dreams.

Gaven tended to the blisters Halavant had earned from pulling Jabare through the mud. Most had scabbed over, but a few had taken infection. We'd been allowed to keep our packs of food and medicines, though they'd taken my sling and Halavant's metal-toed boots and hand braces. Halavant's fingers curled rigidly at the ends of his arms. His face took on a perpetually pinched look of pain. Without the bracing, his hands and wrist must have ached with each motion. They wouldn't even allow us to splint them with wood. His stockings had long since worn to holes. The jungle floor had lacerated his feet.

A bug whined a short distance from my ear. The potent herbs Gaven soaked my neckerchief in three times a day still kept them at bay. There was one blessing. I wasn't ready to search for others. "Halavant?"

A stick slapped me on the legs. A growled word must have meant quiet. I could only speak if Halavant had something to translate and it was addressed to me. Halavant used those times to say much more. He'd lied between his teeth, explaining Lansi took many more words to say the same thing.

The old-voiced warrior, the one with black-spotted animal skins, moved to Halavant. He touched Halavant's feet and shook his head. He drew out a pair of leather shoes and handed them to Gaven.

The necklaced warrior yelled at him, and the spotted warrior responded with a word. They stared at each other, only their eyes showing the intensity of their power.

The necklaced warrior broke the stare first. He riffled through the bundle in his lap. It was the village's gift to the gods

—golden polished wood, carved with the faces of five villagers: chief, old man, young woman, child, and babe; long leaves from the ancestor tree that were twisted and woven into a crown and dotted with dried flowers still strong with their perfume; and stone etched with words—probably a poem of praise. The necklaced warrior placed the crown on Halavant's head and read the etched rock.

The other warriors rocked with laughter and bowed to Halavant.

Halavant stared off into the distance. His jaw worked in and out.

The necklaced warrior threw the crown on the ground and crushed it under his foot, then slapped Halavant, once on each cheek and then on each hand.

Halavant bit his lip.

I reached for my sling and found the empty space at my belt.

Please let Jabare be alive, and please let the village come after us.

40

HALAVANT

Cliff to Upper Carani
Februar 19th

I jogged up the narrow path. The front of my leather shoes, gifted me by Old Spotted Face Thabit, slapped and curled under my toes. The tall trees of the jungle stretched below me, and the sounds of the long-tailed howlers—cat sized creatures that swung from tree to tree—rang upward in fading volume. Above me, the cliff stretched in an unending wall.

The leather toe of the shoe curled under as I stepped on a patch of shale. I skittered.

Old Spotted Face's big feet could be my undoing. Choice: keep the shoes on and risk tripping and falling to a quick end, or take them off and shove pieces of stone inside my split feet. I stopped to consider.

Nkosi, the necklaced coward, lashed a stick against the back of my legs, across the same line he'd hit repeatedly over the last hour. He had an accurate aim.

I started jogging again.

Elise jogged ahead of me, a shadow in the fog. And some-
where behind, Gaven brought up a shuffling rear. The line of
Carani warriors stretched thinner as we spread out. We each
had at least three focused captors. I had four, including Nkosi.

To escape, we'd have to get them to relax their watch. How?
Win their trust? That was as simple as leaping off the path and
flying the rest of the way to the top.

I stumbled over the leather toes again.

Old Spotted Face respected me enough to give me the
shoes.

I fell to my knees, and laughter rang out behind me.

Or he'd given the shoes to provide amusement for his
fellows.

The stick slapped against my back as I rose to my feet, then
slapped against my legs. "*Faster clumsy.*"

Elise turned.

I waved her forward and pushed into the jog again. Another
hour, and I could rest. We'd have to wait for Gaven when we got
to the top, and they couldn't do much to hurry him, other than
carry him.

~

"It's beautiful!" Elise's words tumbled down the path.

I braced for the follow up of '*quiet girl*' and the slap of a stick
against skin. Instead, a sigh drifted. "*Home. Blessed, bug-free home.
Get moving, girl.*"

A few steps later, I rose above the edge of the cliff. A band of
white rock, shot through with green, sat at the edge, and beyond,
the land rolled away in gentle hills of spring grass. No trees, just
vast variegations of green lying under an eye-aching blue sky. A
small collection of tents in bright reds, oranges, and yellows sat
in the grass. To my side, the jungle hid under clouds that sat

below the cliff edge. Wind blew first behind me, then in my face, like the tide.

Elise jumped up from sitting in the grass. "Your arms are scraped." She pulled me toward the grass and urged me to sit.

"Water first." My tongue stuck to the roof of my mouth. I'd not taken a drink the whole climb.

Elise tipped the water as I glanced around for someone to yell at us for talking.

They were all too busy stripping off their fur coverings. First came off the full-headed animal-skin masks to reveal blotchy brown skin and short black hair pasted to scalps. Then the gloves, long-sleeved shirts, boots, and pants. A bunch of sweaty, blotchy skinned men in loincloths surrounded us, laughing, stretching, scratching, rolling in the grass. They were men, not creatures, though they stank like polecats.

Nkosi disappeared into a tent.

"*Water*," he bellowed.

Two of his men grabbed collapsed leather buckets from the grass and ran off.

Another man pulled a narrow wooden tube from his tent. He blew into it, and a whistle like a squeal of rusty hinges, and tenfold louder, split the air. I brought my arms to my ears as he blew again.

A whinny answered on the wind. A tall horse with braided mane and tail loped into camp, leading a herd of twenty more. The whistler greeted the horses one by one, pressing his face to their muzzles and offering treats in opened hands.

A short time after the horses arrived, the two men trudged back with dripping buckets and handed them into Nkosi's tent. Then, by turns, they each disappeared into tents with their own bucket of water. When the first one re-appeared, he'd scrubbed his beardless face to a glow, and his short hair stood on end. His white breeches came to just below the knees. He also wore light brown shoes and a white, sleeveless, open-neck shirt. He sniffed under one arm and grinned. *"I smell like man again."*

"You'll smell like dung," called my guard, *"if you don't come take my place and let me strip my jungle sweat."*

"You always smell. Water can't change that."

My guard swung his fist at the cleaned-up warrior.

The other dodged. *"Don't get your stink on me. I'll watch him."* He settled next to me as Elise applied salves to my scrapes. *"She'll clean up pretty. Even with the bug scars."*

They were in an expansive mood, and I'd talk as long as they allowed. *"Bug scars?"*

"You think we wore those accursed furs for fun? They repel the bugs, protecting us from the bugs marring our skin."

I glanced at my arms. The bites had turned to little white spots. They'd fade with time. If not, then it was a little thing—to me. They'd suffocated under furs rather than get scarred by bugs.

"What happens if you do get a bug scar?"

"Any scar not won in battle, or in subservience to our king, is a scar of cowardice and sloppiness. I could lose my rank."

I whistled.

He nodded. *"Our king must have angered our gods. Why else would they send him an ill-luck child?"*

"Ill-luck?"

"His face, it's pur—" He bit off his word as Nkosi emerged from his tent, dressed in similar short breeches, sleeveless shirt, leather shoes, except each was embroidery-edged.

His damp, burnt-brown hair was pulled into tight rows of braids that ran from purpled forehead to purpled neck. Lumpy skin streaked across his face like someone had taken a loaded paintbrush and swiped from his forehead above his right golden eye, across the bridge of his long nose and left eye, over his left cheek, and curled around to finish at the back of his neck.

He raised his eyebrows as our gazes met, and the motion puckered the purple skin around them. "*Your healer friends will cure this. Or they'll look much worse before they die. And you will watch their deaths before experiencing it yourself.*"

He spoke less clipped without the mask. The words cut sharper than the ones he'd spoken before.

"Plague and famine!" Gaven stood at the top of the cliff with Old Spotted Face and stared at Nkosi. "That's what you promised we'd fix? Black fleas, scurvy rats, and slow wasting!"

"Amen." Elise murmured.

I motioned Gaven over. "If we want to get free, we must befriend them. They already think we're harmless." I glanced at Nkosi to see if he would stop my chatter, but for once, he didn't care. He stretched out in the grass and soon fell asleep. If only the others would follow suit, we could escape down the cliff and back into the jungle. But three kept watch over us, and in our state of weariness, three were sufficient.

"That's your plan?" Gaven groaned as he lowered himself to the ground. "Chummy up to these skin peelers and hope they'll just let us walk away free?"

"No. I want them to get lax in guarding us. They like to be entertained. Elise, you're good with that sling; we can have a slinging contest. I'll do leg wrestling and other tests of strength. Gaven, mix up drinks that actually taste good, and we'll share it with those who will share food with us—we'll need that, too. And when they get to trust us enough that they all want to drink your concoctions, *then* add something to the drinks to make them sleep longer than usual, and we escape. Simple."

Elise giggled, a tight sound bordering on hysteria.

"It will be all right Elise. We'll get out of here."

"How can you be so confident now?"

"They don't expect me to be a god, or even a prophesied

hero. They think I'm a helpless cripple. And that is something I can meet and exceed. Plus, I don't mind lying to them."

She swallowed. "I know some songs. I'll sing one tonight."

My stomach pinched. I turned to my guard, the one who'd spoken with me. "*How do we earn food? Do you let the girl hunt with her sling? Give me back my hand braces, and I can show you how I can club a* rabbit."

"*What is* irhabbit?"

"Rabbit *is a large beast with fangs as long as my fingers.*" I brought one rigid hand next to my mouth so my fingers curled like teeth. "*Its favorite food is green grass and flowers.*"

He slapped me on the back. "*You are a jester. Our king may keep you for your tongue.*"

"*My jest holds more laughter when my stomach isn't empty.*"

"*Do you know stories too?*"

"*Ballads to bring tears to your eyes, love stories, ghost tales to keep you awake all—*"

"*Songs?*"

I pointed to Elise. "*She has the voice to soothe away worry or bring you dancing to your feet.*"

He grinned. "*Our return trip will be much better. Wait here. I'll get you food.*"

"*There's no place I'd go, if you are getting food.*"

A white-haired man emerged from his tent. "*Stay guarding until another has taken your place.*"

It was a quiet order, but the food proffering boy-warrior dropped back beside me. "*Yes, Thabit.*"

So this was Old Spotted Face. His face was lined with age but no spots. Shiny patches of scars ran down both arms, coin-sized and white on his dark skin like scales from shoulders to the backs of his hands. Is this what he meant when he said he'd given skin to the king for each year of his service? None of the other men sported such scars. He'd been kind before with the shoes. Would he be so again with the food?

"Thabit, please may we have food?"

"When Nkosi eats and has finished, then you will."

I pushed against my complaining stomach. We could wait, though we hadn't eaten since the previous night's gnawed bones. We'd be compliant. We'd be entertaining. Then we'd escape.

41

KATRIN

I LAY on a cot an arm's reach from Yosyph's bed. Dehydration and exhaustion, plus the physician's herbs, had kept my waking moments brief the last two days. I turned on my side and snuggled deeper under the down comforter, its softness beckoning me to close my eyes and return to sleep.

A snore rumbled. Yosyph lay on his back with the cover pulled under his chin. A beard framed grayish sunken cheeks. Though not as sunken as they'd been when he'd come out of the shadow and his heart almost stopped.

I shivered under the comforter enough to rattle the legs of my cot.

Maggie laid a heavy wool blanket over me.

"Maggie. How is he today?"

"Sleeping, as you should be."

"You are getting entirely too bossy."

"I learned it from my mistress. Now sleep."

The royal physician came over and took my pulse. "Healthy beat and good color today. You've recovered quickly, but you appear to regress each time you wake. Rest."

"If I'm asleep when he wakes, wake me. I haven't spoken to him since I came out of the shadow."

"That is why I don't wake you. He should only wake enough to take nourishment, then sleep again. If I need you to do your calming trick, I'll wake you. Now quiet."

"Bossy, bossy. Get me something to read if you won't let me talk."

A smile flickered around the physician's stern lips. He picked up a thick volume and laid it on the bed next to me. *Herbs and tonics for the weak constitution.*

I'd just watch Yosyph. Even sleeping, he proved a more interesting study.

Someone closed the curtains and turned down the lamps. Tricksters. I reached out and found Yosyph's hand beneath his covers, pushed a smidgen of my love to my skin, and squeezed it into Yosyph's palm. He twitched, and a sigh interrupted his snores. He took my hand in his and relaxed into sleep.

Love dripped in to slowly replace what I'd given. What other emotion could I give to help him? No, I'd wait until I woke next. I sagged from giving that bit as if I'd climbed the wilderland hills.

~

"KATRIN." The whisper was rough from a little-used voice. Yosyph squeezed my hand.

"I'm here," I whispered back, pulling my thoughts from the sluggish mud of sleep.

"Thank you for saving me."

"I'd do it again."

"Even though I will die?"

"You're too stubborn to die."

He snorted. "Kettle calling the pot black."

"No, the shadow calling the shadow dark."

"How did you learn?"

"Pure stubbornness."

He caressed the back of my hand. "Only God could take your flame and shadow you. I am grateful you are a flame again."

"You and your faith. Can't you ask your God to make you well again?"

He fell silent, then said, "I've asked. He's answered: wait and be patient."

That wasn't helpful. I cast my own unspoken prayer upward. *Please send Halavant with the cure—soon. And I know Yosyph said you won't force anyone to your will, but can you do something more to stop us from falling into another war? Maybe a plague on the rebellious nobles?* I stopped, then added, *Thank you for helping me learn to shadow-walk. You made the impossible possible.*

"Are you praying?"

"Yes."

"That is good. Though don't be demanding. He doesn't answer those types of prayers."

"Speaking from experience?"

"All too much."

I stifled a laugh. "I like you, Sir Yorel."

"I like you too."

Someone shifted in a chair and took a deep breath of interrupted sleep.

I held my breath as I wrapped Yosyph's words around me. I didn't want to lose this time to speak with him. The breathing across the room settled.

"Katrin," Yosyph whispered.

"Yes."

"I need to talk to Galliard, but the physician won't let me. Are you well enough to get him?"

"Can't we wait a couple more days?" A couple days to whisper words and draw closer to him before the world intruded.

"No. I must speak to him now."

"Only if you behave."

"I cannot rise from my bed. All I'll do is speak."

I grasped his hand tighter.

He added. "I give you my oath."

"You better keep it." I slipped from my bed, kissed Yosyph, then headed to the door. The physician slept nodding in a chair to one side of the door, and Maggie slumped in sleep on the other side.

I pulled the door open and shut it softly behind me.

A guard put out his hand as I wobbled. "Lady Katrin?"

"The Yorel has requested General Galliard."

"Right away." He paused and looked into my face. "I am glad to *see* you again. I didn't know being a shadow demon could kill you."

"I don't plan on being one again unless necessary."

He nodded. "You better lie down before the physician has my head for talking with his patient." He motioned for one of the other guards. "Get General Galliard. I don't care if you wake him. The Yorel wants him."

I returned to the room.

The physician still slept, but Maggie caught my arm. "My Lady, you shouldn't be up."

"I won't be, if you let me return to bed. Please prepare for General Galliard's arrival."

"You didn't."

"I did what the Yorel asked."

A laugh slipped through Maggie's tight lips. "You two together are as difficult as catching muddy piglets."

I'd settled into a half-sleep state when Galliard arrived, his firm knock waking everyone.

Our physician stood and blocked the door. "You can't come in."

"Enter." Yosyph pushed himself to half sit.

Galliard slid past the physician. "I came on your command. I will leave if you distress yourself. What can I do for you?"

Yosyph lay back down, his face blanched.

Had I done the right thing in sending for Galliard? I reached out to take Yosyph's hand, but he'd turned on his side to face Galliard. I'd give him as much of my calm, peace, and love, as I could when Galliard left. Whatever it took to help him recover from this meeting.

42

YOSYPH

PALACE, Fairhaven, Lansimetsa
Februar 20th

GALLIARD KNEELED NEXT to me so his face was level with mine, his quick-to-humor mouth drawn into a taut line.

I would add to his burden. "I need Lord Makkara."

His eyes widened. "Lord Makkara?"

"Yes. He may be the key to stopping this rebellion of the nobility."

"What do you want done to him?"

"You will bring him here, and I will learn from him."

Galliard laid a hand on the bed and bent his head forward. His shoulders shook.

"Galliard?"

He lifted his head, and silent laughter softened his face. "I expected torture, bribery, or some other coercion to bend him to your will. Yet, you ask to learn from him. Humility befitting a leader."

"Not humble by choice. I'd lick the dust from Makkara's shoes if it would help us unify our people."

Galliard turned serious. "I will bring him now, if you so wish."

"He's here?"

"He came the night after Katrin rescued you."

How? Why would he come back? "Yes, bring him... what time is it?"

"You've beaten the sun to rising by hours."

"How long has Makkara been in the dungeon? How many days have I been ill?"

"Katrin returned you to us four days ago. He's not in the dungeon. We've given him a guarded room, and he's helping temper the mobs."

God's blessings poured upon us. Thank you for preparing the way, I prayed. "And what of Egvar?"

Katrin's hand squeezed my shoulder. "We captured him. I hope he's in the darkest, dankest cell in the dungeon."

Galliard nodded. "He's safely behind bars, and he's locked his mouth as tight. At least he can't rile the people now. The other nobles scattered before our troops could take them. We cannot find the old queen, but she was near-crazy. I doubt she'll do much. For now, things are quiet."

"The quiet before the storm."

"The quiet is the best time to store up our strength. So sleep. I'll bring Lord Makkara—"

The physician cut in, "In three days, if the Yorel does exactly as I say."

Despite the physician's concern for my health, I would meet with Lord Makkara. "This morning."

"Three days, or your death be upon your own head."

"It always has been."

The physician shook his head and muttered.

He was a good man. He'd saved my life several times. My heart still ached in my chest, and I caught at my breath even with this little talking. The rest of my body was a mass of merging pains in greater or lesser degrees. Only my legs lacked feeling, a benefit of the slow wasting.

Galliard watched me. "I'll bring him this evening, after I've heard you've slept a good portion of the day."

"Very well."

As Galliard walked out, I rolled to my back, and Katrin sought my hand.

I pulled away. "No, Katrin, you can't anymore."

"Can't what?" she said with sweet insincerity.

"You'll fade, giving me parts of your emotions."

The physician came over. "Is that what you've been doing? No wonder he improves when you wake, but you decline. I thought you just comforted him when you reached across to his bed."

She thumped the side of the bed. "We are all doing what we can to keep him alive. Let me do my part. Besides, I only give a little, and that little replenishes. I'm not fading." She held up one hand to the lamplight. "See, I am solid."

I caught her hand. "You are as dense as stone and as hard-headed."

"No comments on my intelligence. I'm not the one seeking to rule a country. You should do as our good physician advises."

The physician chuckled as he brought over hot broth and a sleeping draught. That pattern I remembered through the fog. I accepted both and slipped towards sleep. Katrin's fingers wrapped around mine and peace washed into me. She shouldn't. I'd have our beds moved further apart.

GALLIARD AND LORD MAKKARA entered the room in the glow of sunset. Two guards followed.

I lay with a second pillow behind my head. "Welcome, Makkara. I was foolish in my words to you. I am ready to listen now."

Makkara sat several yards from my bed while the guards stood to his sides and slightly between us. Makkara sneered. "Are you? That would be a first."

I had no energy to banter words. "How can we stop the people from civil war?"

"You won't like it."

"I'm sure I won't."

He leaned forward. "We should send a flag of peace to the rebellious nobles. Speak with them. Listen to their demands. Many are vying for power and gathering followers. If we can pull enough to unite under one good leader, whoever that leader is, then we may avoid anarchy."

I closed my eyes. *Should we send a flag of peace? What leader could we entrust with power to rule, who would not abuse it and would hand it to Halavant when he returned? Makkara? One of the nobles who remained loyal to Halavant? Who would the rebellious nobles accept—other than themselves?*

Instead, could we gather all loyal into one place and defend? How many of the common people already gave allegiance to one of the rebellious nobles? How, who, when? Ah, when was another piece. When would they attack? With Egvar in prison and the other scattered, they would be delayed. And they could hinder each other in their seeking their own power.

A scrape of a chair brought me out of my questions. Makkara was halfway to the door, Galliard beside him.

"Wait."

Galliard turned. "We've overstayed our time. We'll return tomorrow."

"Have you tried to talk with the rebellious nobles?"

Galliard glanced at Makkara, then bowed his head. "I've prepared invitations for every noble, including those fighting against us, for a council in three week's time to decide who will rule until King Halavant returns. We hope this promised council will keep them from attacking. I'm sorry, Yorel, this is what we felt was best, and they may still choose you. I would have sent it out by our fastest messengers today, if you'd not requested Lord Makkara's presence."

Tell them to wait, an impression whispered. *Meet again tomorrow.*

"Don't send them yet."

Makkara stiffened. "Have you not listened?"

"Don't send them until we can plan together—tomorrow. I would talk more now, but I must rest."

43

ELISE

I CROUCHED in the tall grass next to old Thabit. The thumbprint-sized scars ran down his arms and glimmered in the hot sun. A deer-like creature with spiral horns grazed in the distance. I fingered my choice of stones. Yesterday, I'd picked too small of a stone and driven off the game instead of stunning it. Thabit killed another one later. We prisoners didn't get a part of the feast, though the bones still had remnants of meat when tossed to us.

Today would be different. I chose a smooth stone the size of an egg and set it in the sling's pocket, then silently stood. The spiral-horn deer didn't turn. With one end of the sling looped around my middle finger and the knotted end pinched between my fingers, I raised the stone-loaded pocket in line with the deer, then let it drop, starting the swinging rotation. Once around, then on the second rotation, I released the knotted end of the cord, and my stone shot forward. It smacked into the deer's head, and the deer crumpled.

Cheers rose behind us.

Thabit turned to me and nodded.

The two other warriors gutted the deer, lifted it so it swung upside down between them, and carried it back towards camp. As they passed Thabit and me, one reached out and slapped me on the shoulder. He grinned and pointed to the deer and then to my sling, and held up two fingers, then he pointed back to the open grassland. Did he want me to kill another?

I rubbed the spot he'd slapped. These Carani liked physical expressions too much, stick-slapping on the leg for talking and hand-slapping on the back for being a good hunter.

Thabit motioned for me to follow the deer bearers back.

Laughter carried on the constant wind, then died away as the wind shifted direction. A few of the lean-legged horses grazed. Colored tents rose from the waving grass. And in the middle of the tents, Halavant sat, surrounded by six laughing Carani. Halavant's animated face made up for the lack of hand motions.

Gaven kneeled off to the side, next to a bed roll where Nkosi lay, applying strips of cloth to Nkosi's face and neck. Gaven motioned me over with the tilt of his head. "Did you kill this one?"

"Yes."

"Good. Now grind more flaxseeds for the poultice."

"Is it still helping?"

"It's still reducing the inflammation. It won't do much more than we've already achieved. I'd give the skin off my nose to have a bushel of Truvian lemons. I probably will, if I don't find something more effective."

"Maybe they'll have lemons in the city."

"Or something like it. This land is warm enough for it."

I scooped a handful of flax seed from the pouch. We had only enough for one more application for Nkosi, and it also meant we had no more to apply to Halavant's hands. I begrudged the use of the precious seeds. But so far they gave us more freedom. Nkosi let us talk as we worked together to tend to his birthmark.

I finished grinding the seeds when Thabit called, "Barda, tabach." I was Barda, or as Halavant explained, slave, and tabach meant cook. I strode to the dung-fueled fire and turned the spit-speared deer. A slave alive and serving was better than skinned and dead.

Had Donkor helped Jabare? Would the village rescue us? We moved slowly enough, even with horses to ride. Nkosi seemed in no hurry, or perhaps he hoped we'd fade away his birthmark before he returned to his royal father. We traveled in the morning and stopped for the afternoon to hunt. The Carani went through meat like dogs.

Halavant was the only one not made to serve. His crippled hands protected him from the work, but not from Nkosi's mocking. Halavant endured the laughter and created even louder laughter through his own words. He never elaborated on what stories he told. Based on the raucous laughter, I probably didn't want to know.

His plan would work. We were only two days into the grasslands, and already the Carani warriors treated us more as servants than prisoners, though we were still bound at night and kept under one watchful guard.

Halavant finished his tale and one of the men glanced at me. "Barda, ghanna!"

I started a mournful song of lost love.

"La! Barda ghanna hayawi!"

So they didn't want sad today. "Halavant, what is hayawi?"

"Lively. They want something they can dance to."

Lively? My younger siblings loved to run around to a nursery song, dodging and tagging each other. The Carani wouldn't know any better, and I could mock them safely by singing a children's song. With a smile I began.

The peasant in the field,
The peasant in the field,
Work hard, all day and night,
The peasant in the field.

The peasant takes a wife,
The peasant takes a wife,
Work hard, all day and night,
The peasant takes a wife.

The wife takes the child,
The wife takes the child,
Work hard, all day and night,
The wife takes the child.

The child takes a dog,
The child takes a dog,
Work hard, all day and night,
The child takes a dog.

As I sang, the men crouched down in the beaten grass, their thighs parallel to the ground. They held their arms straight out to their sides and kicked out their feet in time to the words. They circled each other and spun as they kicked, raising dust into the air. Two men caught left hands as they continued to kick their legs straight out in front of them. The goateed man yanked the smooth-faced one over, to the laughter of the other dancers. Two more dancers clasped hands and the short tug-of-war repeated, though this time, both fell.

The song ended, and I sang it again. The last two dancers clasped hands and spun into a tugging, high-kicking war. Their legs must have burned with straining muscles. Neither let the other unbalance him. A deeper voice took up a chant, and I slipped into silence. Thabit sat on a canvas stool and thumped out a rhythm on his legs while chanting. The dancers continued. Sweat soaked lines down their white shirts. The fallen dancers took up the thumping rhythm. Even Nkosi thumped the ground from his prone position.

With a triumphant cry, the stouter of the two dancers yanked the other to the ground, then kicked out twice more before sinking to the ground himself.

I clapped and cheered along with the rest.

Then Halavant stood and spoke.

Thabit responded with a few words and moved over next to Halavant. In slow measured motions, Thabit showed the crouching, kicking movements.

Halavant would try the dance. This would prove interesting.

44

HALAVANT

Upper Carani
Februar 21st

I PROBABLY SHOULDN'T HAVE ASKED Thabit to teach me. True, I'd spent several months learning the leg-wrestling techniques of Lausatök, but this was a different athleticism.

The Carani warriors panted on the ground, while Thabit turned the quick-kicking dance into a stately display of strength. He crouched with both feet underneath his straight back, then he kicked one leg out and kept balance on the toes of the other foot. Then he jumped and returned the one leg under while extending the other.

I crouched down and balanced on the toes of both feet, kicked my right leg out, and thumped to the ground on my backside. I crouched again to laughter, some of it my own, and slowly extended my leg. My extended foot wavered inches above the ground.

"*Now jump and change legs.*" Thabit instructed.

245

I jumped and fell, twisting one leg under me. "*I'm not graceful like you.*"

"*You moved with grace when you fought Nkosi.*"

"*I would learn more of your dances, when I have a full stomach.*"

"*That you shall have tonight. The sling girl is a deadly aim. The first choice of meat goes to her.*"

"*Then I'll have a full stomach if she shares with me.*"

A rare smile touched the corners of Thabit's mouth. "*She shares with you, even when it is bones. Now try again.*"

I crouched and extended one leg, balanced. Instead of jumping, I brought the leg back and extended the other. I shook but didn't fall. I repeated the balancing exercises, one leg and then the other, until my whole body shook.

Something shoved into my side and I greeted the packed grass and dirt with my cheek.

Nkosi stood, his half-bandaged face in a malicious grin. "*You are graceful as pig in mud. Why my father want foreign entertainment? You're only good for your skin.*"

"*Maybe he'll adopt me to replace his plum-colored son.*"

Nkosi stomped his soft leather shoe on the inside of my calf. "*The healer man and girl will make my skin new. And I'll allow them to live. But you, I will savor your death and wear your skin.*"

I should have kept my mouth shut. It had felt good to strike back though not enough to offset my aching calf.

Thabit grasped my forearm and pulled me upright. "*Try again.*"

"*My leg?*"

"*Try again.*" He bent close. "*Nkosi fears you. Keep him fearful of your strength.*"

Nkosi lay back down upon his mat and ignored us.

"*Why do you care?*" I whispered back.

"*Because you stand up to him, when the others won't. I serve his father, not him.*"

I crouched back down. My calf knotted as I extended it. I fell to the ground.

"Again."

I pushed my leg out and balanced for a moment, then swapped legs.

"Don't stop between. Jump."

I jumped and swapped legs and stayed upright. Sweat ran down my brow, along the bridge of my nose and salty into my mouth.

"Again."

I swapped again and wavered.

"Again!"

I jumped and crumpled to the ground.

Cheers exploded around me.

As I lay, eyes closed, words overlapped in many voices. *"on first try."*... *"not even Seb did on the first try."*... *"twice, he jumped twice."*... *"even with injured leg."*... *"warrior spirited."*

I grinned and pushed with my elbows to sitting. *"I'll leave the dancing to you graceful-legged men. I'm too much a pig in mud, and as hungry as one."*

Thabit nodded. *"Get our pig some meat."*

The youngest warrior, the one who'd almost given us food the first day on the plain, ran into his tent and came out with a strip of jerky and a hard lump of bread. *"This will hold place in your belly until our deer is roasted."*

He'd said the inclusive 'our' that meant me, too. It was much better than the exclusive 'our' where it meant them and not us. He set the bread and jerky in my lap.

I clasped the jerky between my forearms and took a bite. It provided good exercise for my jaw. It must have sat in his tent since before they left.

I offered a piece to Elise.

She shook her head as she turned the spitted meat. "You need it."

Gaven glanced my way.

I nodded to the hard roll. "I won't be able to manage it."

He kneeled beside me and tore into the roll, then pushed up my leggings. "I'll see to your leg."

"You'll not make me drink something nasty."

"Certainly will. Now your legs, both of them."

If I could, I would have clenched my fists as Gaven kneaded the knotted muscles with an herby smelling oil. "My legs are not loaves of bread."

"Better bread than stone."

I shrugged at his truth and winced at the kneading. "Elise, how close is the meat? I'll die of the scent alone."

"Depends if you like it raw. My mother said many of her people preferred meat that way. Do you?"

"Today, I would."

"I would, too, if they only allowed me a knife to carve off a piece."

I turned to the youngest warrior, who sat by his tent rubbing grease into his leather boots. He'd never told me his name and all the rest called him boy. *"Boy, in exchange for a slice of the roasting meat, I'll tell you a tale of woe to even cause old Thabit to weep."*

"You'd eat it raw?"

"A pig isn't choosey."

"And a pig doesn't move like a lion. You are lion-blooded and fox-tricky, and they eat their meat raw." He sliced a piece of roasting meat and held it out to me on a forked stick.

It dripped red, and one side crackled brown. I blew on it and bit. No royal meal could compete. And like an animal, I ripped off a piece of rare meat with my teeth. The rest pulled from the stick and fell to the ground.

"Don't you dare touch it," I shouted at Gaven. "Your hands are covered in oils. I'll eat it from the ground; it's already dirty."

And I bent over and ate to the amusement of the Carani warriors.

"*Pig, pig, snuffling in the dirt,*" chanted Nkosi, and several other warriors took up the chant.

When I finished, the boy warrior leaned forward. "*Now for the tale.*"

I brushed the dust from my face with my shoulder. "*In a land of cliffs taller than the one we climbed, a queen hated her people. She sat in the shadows planning ways to enslave any not the same blood as her. Her son was as foolish as she was cruel. He spent his days in games and dance, though no dances like you noble Carani do.*"

This brought out several chuckles. A few more of the warriors gathered near me.

"*He loved a fire-haired lady. And when she disappeared, he acted with honor for the first time in his life. He disguised himself as a stablehand to search for her. But dirt and muck could not hide his pride. He earned a beating for his sharp tongue.*"

The boy warrior said, "*He shares that with you.*"

"*Let me tell the story.*" I shifted to a more comfortable position as Gaven finished with my legs and returned to tending Nkosi's face. "*Left for dead, he was saved by a wandering laborer. Still, his foolish pride kept him blind. He demanded.*"

"*As he should,*" said Nkosi. "*A prince should be obeyed.*"

I'd found a story that pulled him in. What would he think of the ending?

"*He demanded what was not his right to demand. The wanderer cared for him despite thinking him crazy. And it was good he did. The beating hurt the prince more than either imagined, and soon the prince could not speak.*"

"*Could not speak?*" said the boy warrior.

"*Not a word. His friend took him to a healer. The healer drilled a hole in his head, about the side of old Thabit's little finger.*"

"*Why would the healer do that? Did he mean to kill the prince?*"

"*No, she meant to save him, and she did. The prince healed from the beating and could speak again.*"

The boy warrior touched his head. "*I'd rather die than let one drill into my head.*"

I mentally fingered the soft spot on the side of my head. I'd have said the same before my injury. "*The healer was different-blooded than the queen, and the prince learned she and her family would be sent to slave in mines along with all other different-blooded people. He could not let that happen. He forsook his search for the fire-haired woman and joined a rebellion against the queen.*"

"*Good for him.*" Nkosi sat up. "*A woman never should rule. The prince should have been ruling since his father died.*"

"*The prince trusted a man of high rank to help them into the city. But as soon as the army entered the city, the man betrayed the prince —poisoning his hands to become like dead at the end of his arms.*"

"*What happened?*" The boy warrior scooted forward another inch.

"*He would have died, save for the help of his common-blooded friends and a shadow demon. They saved his life, and together they overthrew the queen.*"

"*Did his hands ever heal?*"

"*Never.*"

"*So he became a crippled king? Did the people accept him?*"

"*Some of them did. Many did not.*"

Nkosi stepped towards me. "*You tell a weak tale of a weak man. A king would force his will. A king would never allow another to betray him.*"

The boy warrior shook his head. "*I think he was strong to seek his love and then fight against his mother. Did he ever find the fire-haired woman?*"

"Yes, but she'd come to love another."

"So he lost his voice, then his hands, he had a hole drilled in his head, he was poisoned, his people didn't respect him, and even his loved woman turned from him. Was there any happiness in his tale?"

"Yes, but then it wouldn't make Thabit weep. You've interrupted it enough to break the sorrow into little pieces."

"I'll be quieter next time."

He always promised that.

Nkosi shook his head with disgust and returned to his mat to sleep until the meat was ready.

It felt good to tell my own story, even though it was a tall tale to the listeners.

45

YOSYPH

PALACE, Fairhaven, Lansimetsa
Febrúar 21st

THE TIME TO meet with Galliard and Makkara arrived. It was late evening, a day since I last spoke with them, and my thoughts overflowed with the dreams and impressions God gave me between those two times. *Please,* I prayed, *help me speak the words I must, and help Makkara listen.*

My physician checked my pulse. "Your heart is steady and your color good. I'll give you ten minutes." He turned to Katrin before leaving. "If he overexerts himself, call me in. I'll not let this meeting undo the healing he's reached. At least he allows you to stay. Use your calming trick if needed."

I closed my eyes and drew deep breaths, inviting calm. She wouldn't give me more of her emotions. She couldn't fade to help me.

Galliard and Makkara entered, trailed by two guards.

I motioned Galliard over and whispered, "You may stay if you choose, but I will speak with Makkara."

Galliard nodded and took a seat by my bed with his hand resting on his sword. His caution could prove necessary. What would Makkara do when I spoke the words God asked me to, especially the dream? Even unarmed and middle-aged, he was a powerfully built man.

"Lord Makkara, please sit."

He sat, and his guards took up a stance on either side of his chair. Makkara tilted up his chin. "Are you ready to let us gather the nobles and keep a war from starting?"

"Yes. But I have questions first. How are the other nobles? How many do we have loyal, how many undecided, and how many in opposition?"

He rested a finger on his chin. "About a third are loyal to the crown, though some only waver along that line. More than half will not give their strength either way. The remainder are scattered opposition; some gather under the flag of Duke Pulska."

The Duke would provide a formidable foe. "And the Queen?"

"We still don't know where she is hidden. Though most of the voices calling for her reinstatement have silenced with the imprisonment of Sir Egvar. If we gather the nobles who will come, to vote in three weeks' time, we can unite under a leader before any gather sufficient force against us."

"Then we have time." I closed my eyes. *Thank you, God.*

Makkara leaned forward. "Time for what?"

"We'll have the council you've asked for, not to choose a new leader, but to create new laws that will protect all in the land."

Makkara opened his mouth, his face twisting into frustration.

I continued. "Laws to protect all, including the nobles, and give them the right to overturn any laws they feel should not be. I believe granting this power will unite most of the nobility while not leaving to chance them choosing a tyrant."

His face softened. "Your granting of power could unite them."

"There is more. You know the nobles as individuals, perhaps what Duke Virtanen fears or Lord Karhu desires. They won't trust me, but they may trust you. You must convince them to come with all their provisions and arms to prepare for a siege."

"Siege?" Makkara stood from his chair and his guards closed in on either side. "Siege! We're calling this council to stop the war. The opposition is still scattered enough that when we unite, we can crush them."

I shook from speaking and from the grim dreams God had sent. "The coming war is larger than we can imagine. We cannot turn it away, not even with your planned meeting with the nobles. We must gather all the people with their flocks, grains, and anything they need to subsist, to the capital and shore our walls against attack. And we must do it before a month passes. We will be safe if we do this. However, if we are scattered, we'll be destroyed like plants at the bottom of a flooded canyon."

Makkara's eyes widened as I spoke. He plopped back to his chair, gripped both knees, then looked into my face with searching eyes. After a long minute of scrutiny, he said, "You believe this. Yet to gather all the people and their possessions is a task of many months. We could not do it in a month's time, even if it was summer and a time of peace. To do so now would lead to fighting in the streets and banditry. Sickness will spread in the cramped conditions. Every home, mansion, and even the palace, would be filled by the people of our land. They'd fill every alley and square. Call together the nobles as I've counseled, feed the poor as you suggested, but let this ill-founded dream rest."

I had one more way to reason with him, but not one I wished to say. "I had a dream last night, and if it is true, will you aid me in what I ask? Will you help convince the nobles to gather to Fairhaven with all their supplies and help the commoners?"

He shook his head.

"Your wife was expecting and was near due."

He froze, and his shake turned to a slow nod.

"She did not survive the birth, but the child is healthy. News will come today. Your sister wants you to know."

He blanched to a grayish-white. "If what you say is true, then you are either a demon or a prophet of bad news."

"Will you help keep the rest of your family and your new child alive by gathering our people into safety?"

He lunged forward.

Katrin threw herself between him and me, a knife flashing in her hands, Galliard drew his sword, and the two guards caught Makkara by his arms, hauling him back before his hands grasped me.

Makkara turned a fierce face. "I will not listen longer to your talk of visions and foresight. Do not call for me. I'll not offer my aid again." He stumbled out with the guards holding his arms.

I'd destroyed my chance. *What is the next step? I'm walking blind.*

The voice of divinity washed through my mind. *Be patient, my child. You've started him on the path. I will comfort and guide him to where he needs to go. He may help yet again. Be still.*

The strength that had sustained me through the meeting drained away, and I collapsed against my pillows.

"Yosyph!" Katrin grabbed my hand and a mix of calm, love and a hint of anxiety pushed into me. She yelled, "Get the physician!"

The physician rushed in.

Katrin lifted my head while the physician spooned a sweet liquid into my mouth.

Weak. Weak and helpless. Why did God choose to speak to me? I only fell again and again.

Be still.

I slipped back into the fog of drugged sleep.

46

KATRIN

PALACE, Fairhaven, Lansimetsa
Febrúar 21st

YOSYPH SLEPT, his rapid heart calm again.

I shivered with the empty spots where I'd pulled emotions. The more he'd spoken with Lord Makkara, the more emotions I'd pushed to the surface, ready to help Yosyph. I went too far. Emotions trickled into the empty spots, like trying to fill a bath basin with single drips.

I held my hands towards the fire, and they glowed. I'd not be able to eat or sleep at this point. Might as well finish what I started. Makkara needed watching.

I moved to the door. "I'm going for a walk."

Maggie followed me.

"Alone. I will return soon."

She opened her mouth, then closed it. Her eyes filled with worry.

I walked to my suite, put warm clothes over my nightgown,

then sat by the mirror. Pushing my emotions to the surface came more quickly. Once I'd packed them along my skin, I mentally poured a bucket of water over me, sluicing the emotions. They danced around me in bright contrast to my empty coldness, shifting away as I swiped my hand through the cloud. I'd need Yosyph's help again to return from the shadow state. I could wait a couple of days till he was stronger.

For now, where was Makkara? If he waited for a messenger, he'd be by the gates.

I slipped through the palace and into the courtyard. The western sky held the last of the evening glow. Guards manned the walls at regular intervals, more regular than in times of peace. Pits of fire burned along the base of the wall where the light wouldn't outline the wall sentries, make them targets, or destroy their night vision. The off-duty men huddled around the fires. One man stood straight, with only his out-stretched hands to indicate he sought warmth. Two large men stood to either side of him.

It was Makkara with his two guards.

I slipped closer.

"—should have pulled on a second pair of wool socks." One guard shifted his boots on the stone cobble.

The other guard tightened the cloth wrapped around his neck. "And I wish I had that wool scarf my wife has half-knitted. If only the children would let her sit long enough to finish it."

Makkara stayed silent, his eyes fixed on the gates.

The sky grew into cold-cutting dark.

A voice in the guard tower called out. "Halt! State your business."

Makkara stepped toward the gate, but his guards lagged, keeping closer to the fire than him.

A muffled voice spoke on the other side of the gate.

The tower guard called again. "You cannot enter at night. Come back in the morning. Such news is best kept to sunlight."

Makkara called upward, his voice cracking. "Who is it? Is it a messenger for Lord Makkara?"

"Who asks?" replied the tower guard.

"I am Makkara. Is it a message about my wife?"

Silence answered him.

"Please," Makkara called. "Tell me. I must know."

"A messenger is come from Lord Makkara's sister. His wife bore a healthy boy."

"And my wife?"

"Named him after his father."

"Does she live?"

"You should go in. 'Tis too cold a night for such news, my Lord."

Makkara thumped his head against the gate, his fingers clawing against the polished wood. He lifted his head and rent the air with wails.

His guards stood to either side, almost touching him, but pulled back as he thrashed the air with his voice.

The tower guard called down. "Get him away from the gate. A whole army could sneak in under cover of that noise."

His guards took his arms, and he stumbled between them, his voice rasping into sobs.

Yosyph had been right. Would Makkara help now?

I followed them back into the palace and to Makkara's rooms.

He stood head bowed in the center of his room, where his guards released his arms. "That cursed shadow demon knew she died. He killed her!"

I stepped forward and laid a hand on his shoulder.

He jumped away from me with a shout.

"Be still," I said.

259

His two guards shook the floor with their high leaps away from me.

I would need to be more careful in announcing my presence. "Don't fear. I am Lady Katrin."

"Why are you here?" He spat out the words, pushing his hands towards me.

I stepped aside. "Will you help the Yorel now?"

"You shadow demons have no heart. I've lost my wife, and you disturb my grief."

How could I forget? He was in no state to think. If I'd lost Yosyph, I'd be beyond words for days or even months. He didn't need questions. He needed comfort. Could I push my floating emotion into him as I had with Yosyph? Peace shimmered the purest white out of my emotions—I'd seen it often enough as I washed it from me and pressed it into Yosyph. But Makkara wasn't Yosyph, or even a shadow-walker.

His guards squeezed against the wall, far from my voice. They wouldn't interfere.

I cupped my hands around a cluster of white with a bit of gold and blue. Determination wouldn't hurt him. My shared sorrow could also be healing.

I pressed my cupped hands against his forehead.

He jerked away from me.

I followed, flattening my hands until I held his head between them. Bits of the sparkles flitted away between my fingers, but most disappeared, and it wasn't into me.

Makkara fell to his knees. Tears poured down his face. He wept until the clock struck midnight. Then he looked upward. "What have you done?"

"I shared my emotions. I cannot feel grief for you, or your wife and children, while I am in the shadow, but I can give peace to you."

"Thank you. The wolf's maw still clamps my heart but does not consume me."

"Lord Makkara, you carry a burden no husband should carry, but many men will if their families are not safely gathered."

His face hardened. "You still seek to convince me to help that Shadow Demon."

"I am one, too, though not a true shadow-walker. I can only shed my emotions, and I can share them with others, like I did with you, but I cannot take them back myself."

"I would that I could shed my emotions as easily."

"You would die."

"And you do not?"

"I will, too, if the Yorel doesn't help restore them to me."

"So you became a shadow demon again, knowing you'll die if he can't help you."

"Yes."

"You trust him."

"With my life and the safety of Lansimetsa."

He moved to a chair and slumped into it. "Oliana," he murmured, "what shall I do without you? How shall I care for our daughters and son?"

I waited until his murmurs died into silence. "The Yorel seeks to save Lansimetsa from another war. He knows there will be one, and all must be gathered in to survive it. He needs your help with the nobles."

"How does he know this?"

"The same way he knew to seek the prince when Halavant was poisoned. His god speaks to him. Will you help, or will you flee with your family?"

He closed his eyes. The pendulum moved to the swinging of his emotions: fear, grief, disbelief and worry shifted across his face. His brow furrowed. His mouth drew tight. He clenched his hands on his knees; his fingers worked in and out on his wool knickers. The clock struck the first hour of the new day. "I will help, if he will take my family and extended family into the palace and protect them."

"He will. Begin today writing letters to convince the undecided nobles to gather."

"You give me no time to grieve."

"I won't. But I will help comfort you, if you will let me."

He shook his head. "I would have my own emotions, even this grief."

"Then I will leave you to your grief and your work."

∾

AFTER TWO DAYS, I couldn't wait longer to ask for Yosyph's help. I entered his room with Maggie announcing me beforehand.

Yosyph's skin looked gray in the lamplight.

I stood next to Maggie, near the physician. "I need the Yorel's help."

"Why did you become a shadow demon again?" he replied tartly.

"To assist our nation."

"Can't you help another way?"

"I will next time."

He grumbled and waved ill-smelling salts under Yosyph's nose.

Yosyph's eyes flew open, but they didn't focus. He was still in the grasp of a sleep-inducing drug. What was the physician using this time? It was far stronger than he'd used before.

"Yosyph, I need your help to take back my emotions."

"Katrin?"

"Can you wake?"

"Katrin, where are you?"

"I'm in the shadow."

"Where?"

I placed my hands in his.

"Your hands are ice. Where are you?"

I'd have to try later, when he could wake. "I'll rest here until he wakes naturally."

The physician nodded. "If I measured the powders right, it will be a day or two. And then I'll have you to tend again."

I tried to pull away my hands from Yosyph.

He tightened his grip. "Katrin, I need to find you. I can't." He lifted my hands till the backs of them touched his wet cheeks. The tears ran onto my hands.

A sparkle of my emotions drifted closer and stuck to the wetness. Others gathered and clung until my hands glowed. I felt them, like echoes of emotions. Could I pull them back in? I closed my eyes and opened myself. The wave rushed through my hands, up my arms and neck to my head and down my body to my toes. I choked, caught in a whirlpool, then collapsed, pulling my hands free from Yosyph's.

I kneeled next to Yosyph's bed.

Yosyph stared with his unfocused gaze. "Katrin. Don't leave."

"Hush, I'm here." I stroked his face, but he still stared into the space.

"Don't leave. Katrin, I need you."

"I'm here." I kissed his cheek.

He turned his head away from me and wept.

The physician spooned something into his mouth, and Yosyph fell to silence.

Then the physician and Maggie took my arms and helped me to a cot.

"You're a sight to behold." The physician took my hand. "Now rest and let him rest."

I stumbled between them. "Let me help him, like I have before."

"Not this time. Rest."

Only until I could sneak back by him. I'd be more careful to not give too much of myself next time. And now I knew another way to take back my emotions, one where he didn't have to enter the shadow to help me.

47

ELISE

The tall-grass plain surrounded us like a shallow bowl, and the cloudless sky was an upside-down bowl above us. No matter how far we traveled, we stayed in the center of these two bowls. Maybe we'd never reach the capital and instead travel forever as servants to ten Carani warriors. It wouldn't be a bad life: ride horses for half a day, hunt with Thabit for a couple hours, roast the dinner, and enjoy the remnants of the feast—more if I killed an animal—pick up a word or phrase of Carani, and tend to Nkosi's birthmark. He still believed we could remove it, and our daily travel grew shorter, lengthening out the time for us to perform a miracle we had no supplies or knowledge to perform.

Old Gavin fretted each night over ways to reduce the birthmark. His caustic comments fell away to muttering madness. I would brew him a calming tea if we still had any chamomile. But that, like the rest of our supplies, was set aside for Nkosi.

Gavin earned a beating across his shoulders for using the herbal oil on Halavant's legs two days previously.

Halavant fared the best. He brought laughter from his first words in the morning until his parting words as they bound him for the night. He ate from the ground when food fell from his hands; he pulled his face into contortions of emotions as he told stories—he was their fool. They still bound us and kept a guard over us. But one of these nights the guard would nod off, we'd cut our bonds, and ride away on the horses. Soon. Maybe tonight. The sun set, turning the sky bowl into shades of gold and red burning into rich purple.

"Barda, ghanna!" It was the young warrior, the one Halavant said everyone called Boy. He was the friendliest out of them and hungered for music and story.

I started singing one they'd enjoyed three nights previous. It wasn't sad, heroic, or even romantic. It was a song our family would sing in the winter evenings when the sun set early.

The cold wind howls—howls.
The ice frost claws—claws.
But in our home, warmth grows
Bright with family faces.

So hey and ho, dance the floor,
Stomp away the cold.
Winter's joy is with our kin,
Around our glowing hearth.

The field lies in a bed of snow.
The barn is full of harvest.
And our home is filled with song,
Joyful sound, claps and voices.

So hey and ho, dance the floor,
Stomp away the cold.
Winter's joy is with our kin,
Around our glowing hearth.

Pull Pa's beard, hear him roar,
Chase older sister,
Spin mother to the tune,
Tickle little brother.

So hey and ho, dance the floor,
Stomp away the cold.
Winter's joy is with our—

Thabit clamped his hand over my mouth and hissed a single word to be quiet.

One warrior, the one who'd won in the low-kicking dance, galloped into camp. He made three sharp motions with his arms.

The other warriors dashed about the camp in silent haste.

Why the silence and rush?

Thabit released me, pressed a finger to his lips, followed by sticking out his tongue and making a scissors motion with his fingers.

I swallowed.

Men made messy bundles of bedrolls and supplies, strapped them onto their bareback horses, and bound our arms in the same haste, shoving us onto three horses. Ropes connected my horse to Thabit's, Gaven's to the Boy's, and Halavant's to Nkosi's.

We galloped away. The still-standing tents and glowing coals of dinner shrank as grass filled the space between us. Then many figures, tall and dark, ran into the camp, then beyond it, following our trail.

I almost shouted with joy. They'd come!

But the horses gobbled the miles faster than running feet. The figures faded before the sky grew dark. Could they catch us?

The grass flattened in weaving lines behind pounding hooves. We galloped in a group for a distance, then at a command from Thabit, the group split into three. The group with us prisoners veered to the right, another to the left, and the third continued forward. We had only three guards. We could escape. Jabare's kinsmen were a short distance behind us and we had a packed path through the grass to follow.

"Halavant," I cried, "It's time. Convince Thabit and the Boy to help us. Thabit hates Nkosi. And—"

A hand slapped me across my shoulders, and I tumbled from my horse.

Carani curses poured from Nkosi. His horse pranced the earth next to where I lay.

I rolled towards my horse, whose hooves were more still.

Thabit wheeled his horse about. I lay bound, surrounded by three horses. Thabit leaped down, drew his knife left-handed, and with his other hand yanked me upright by my arm bonds. My toes barely touched the ground. He nicked my cheek.

I cried out.

He nicked my other cheek.

Halavant called in a commanding voice, and Thabit pulled back the knife.

Thabit slung me stomach down on his horse, mounted behind me, and we continued on our gallop. My stomach thumped against the horse in rhythm to its strides and I lost my dinner down its foreleg. We galloped onward.

When horse lather had soaked me through, we stopped. I slid from the animal and thumped to the ground with a moan.

Thabit held a flask to my mouth.

I spat as the burning liquid hit my tongue. I'd not be addled by alcohol.

He tsked, then held up a leather water pouch.

I gulped, then looked to Halavant.

He sat astride his horse, a straight-backed shadow in the moonlight. No one tended to him.

"Hala—"

Thabit hissed.

I silenced but motioned to Halavant.

Thabit took water to Halavant, too.

My cheeks stung, and when I rubbed them against my shoulders, my dress took on a dark wet mark. So close. We'd been so close to escape and rescue. We still were. If we camped. If they followed the right path. We only had three Carani uplanders to fight. If I only had my hands free and my sling. Thabit wore it on his belt. So close.

Oh, gods of Halavant's Carani kin, help us, I prayed silently. *And Yosyph's god too, if you can hear us. We don't need much help, just for them to sleep. Please. I'll give you an offering of all my hair if you free us. It isn't much, but it is my most valued possession. Please, just make them sleep.*

Thabit gagged me, then pushed me back onto the horse. I leaned forward against the neck and wrapped my fingers through his mane. We set into a jarring trot.

None of us would sleep for many hours.

48

YOSYPH

THE FOG LIFTED. I lay in my room. How many hours had passed since I'd told Makkara about his wife?

Katrin talked quietly with the physician.

I must have slept for a day or more. Nightmare fragments—pieces of the drugged sleep—whispered lies to me. She'd been stuck in the shadow. I'd held her icy hands and wept into the invisible space.

But she wasn't stuck there.

"Katrin."

She spun about and ran to my side, grasping my hands. "Yosyph! You're awake." She lowered her voice, "I thought you'd sleep away the week."

"Week? How long ago did I speak with Makkara? Did he leave?"

"He's here. He's already drafted letters to at least half of the nobles of Lansimetsa."

"How many days have I slept?"

"Four."

"Four. And Makkara is helping? Did news come about his wife?"

"Yes, his wife died, and his family should arrive sometime tomorrow to be housed in the palace. I promised him protection in exchange for his help. He now believes you know the future."

"It's not me, it's God. And I only know what He tells me."

"It's the same thing to him. He's worked night and day, poor soul. I was in the shadow, and I don't remember how to be delicate when I don't feel my own emotions."

"You entered the shadow-walk again!"

"Yosyph, you lay back down, or I'm done talking with you."

I lay back. "How did you get out?"

"You helped me, though you must not remember it. You were so deeply drugged, you didn't even recognize me when I came out of the shadow."

The nightmares. I almost lost her again. *Thank you, God, for keeping her safe, and please protect her from her own foolishness.*

"I'm good now, and you look almost normal. Four days of sleep was exactly what you needed." She brushed her finger along my cheek and chin.

"I'll feel more normal when I can trim this beard back to a goatee. What do I have now, two weeks of growth?"

"Close enough. It's getting full enough to frame your face."

How had I been sidetracked on something so trivial? I felt more awake and clear-headed than I had in weeks. I needed to call in Galliard and Makkara. We had to gather the people. "Get me clothes and a chair."

"No." Katrin's voice overlapped the physician's.

He continued. "You need to eat, and then you'll sleep again for..." He turned to Katrin. "Do you think three days will be sufficient?"

"Another four," she said.

I lifted my head to look at them better. "You conspire against me. When did you two start agreeing?"

"Only when he makes sense. Galliard, Makkara, and I have talked often over the last several days. They are gathering the people. We'll need your inspiration and help soon enough. For now, you must rest. Not even your god can use you dead."

"I'm not much use to Him, as it is."

Katrin laughed. "He seems to think otherwise. Now if you won't listen to us, ask him, and I'm sure he'll tell you to rest."

Please, I prayed, *I'm rested enough. I need to work, otherwise there won't be enough time. Please give me the strength to do what I must.*

God's reply soothed. *You will have enough time. Your friends will carry the work for now. Be still.*

I whispered. "He just did."

Katrin went somber. "Just like that. He spoke to you?"

I nodded.

She looked upward as if to see a heavenly vision through the vine-painted ceiling. "Then you should listen."

"Could I rest without taking what you gave me last time? I don't know which was a nightmare, but I wish to not see them again."

The physician stopped pouring a powder into a liquid and tilted his head. "I'd rather not give you something so strong. If you will behave, I'll only aid your rest."

"I'll rest, but while I rest, at least tell me what Galliard and Makkara are doing."

"No!" came the duet of voices.

"You are a conspiracy, though God is also sided with you."

"For your good."

As long as it was also for Lansimetsa's good.

49

HALAVANT

Capital City of Upper Carani
Februar 26th

IF I THOUGHT my capital of Fairhaven was grand with tall cliffs backing its three-tiered city, I re-evaluated as we entered Nhiwt, the center of Carani power. The plains stretched behind us. Before us, a wall stretched side to side as far as I could see. It rose into the air like sheer mountains. A chariot cast up dust as it raced along the top, perhaps taking news of our arrival.

We'd galloped and walked and galloped for three days. It was only when the horses couldn't push longer that we rested. Though trying to sleep bound wasn't restful. The other warriors rejoined us yesterday.

How hard we pushed could only be matched by the fear they showed for the shadowing runners who entered our camp three days previously. But we'd left them far behind. Still, we would escape. We had to, for my brother and Elise.

We passed through open gates, under the wall into a wide

tunnel lit with torches. Nkosi veiled his face. Once through, we entered the city.

White clay buildings lined the wide street. Only their solid structure could keep the buildings there in the flow of humanity. Men, women, children and animals all pressed to occupy the same space. Stalls of bright vegetables and fruits lined the street. As we pressed forward, the crowd parted and then closed again behind us.

The market stalls continued, but the contents changed: cages of fowls, cramped pens of pigs, and even a cow added new notes to the tumultuous noise. Further on, fabrics and rugs in gaudy colors were stacked under worn awnings. And beyond those, the crowds thinned, and bulky men that rivaled my giant-blooded Lansimetsians guarded stalls of jewelry.

Nkosi stopped before one of these stalls. How did he have the energy to shop after our endless ride? *"Blue stone. Add to my necklace. It is fitting for my courage in bringing back magicians."*

Claiming we were dangerous magicians? I bit back a laugh.

When we left, Nkosi wore his red stone necklace with a larger blue gem hanging in the center.

We wove through homes the same stucco white as the ones along the market but cleaner and grander, then through a second, smaller city wall. The homes changed out for vine-covered walls. A distant mountain rose behind the city.

Many yellow, heart-shaped fruit hung from a vine to my side, some at face level. I nudged my horse to go sideways, and he sidestepped. As we came close enough that my knee brushed the wall, I leaned over and caught one fruit with my teeth.

Tartness burst in my mouth, and I spat out the fruit. My tongue burned with acid.

The Boy warrior laughed. *"Sun darts are not meant for eating. Rich only grow fruits on their walls they care not if stolen."*

"Poison?"

"*Only an upset stomach.*"

Good. I didn't have much to lose from my stomach. And I didn't have the energy to deal with poison again.

We continued forward through the wall-lined streets and came to a third tall wall with a shining iron gate. In ways, it was like Fairhaven: three parts of a city; common, noble and royal. The palace must lie behind this last wall, near the mountain I'd watched grow on our weary walk through the city.

Thabit pulled a small trumpet from his saddlebag. He blew three brassy notes. Three notes responded from atop the wall. The iron gate swung open, and twenty men in spotless white robes, with swords strapped to their sides, strode out. Each one took the reins of each of the twenty horses, rider-laden or not, then led us forward through the gate.

"Oh!" Elise gasped.

"Poisoned dreams," murmured Gaven.

A courtyard of polished tiles spread from us to a mountain. The mountain didn't sit behind the city, but in the heart—small enough to fit within the palace-protecting walls, a man-created miracle. The top looked to be the height of the walls that protected the whole city. The sides were a mixture of walls, columns and gardens. Water poured from the top and dropped in four terraces of falls. Flowering trees, vines and bushes mixed in with small lawns. Birds twittered in the trees.

Like a dream, though not a poisoned one. Surely a people who created such beauty, who loved song and dance, were not as cruel as our bedtime tales made them out to be.

"*My grandmother's gardens,*" Nkosi said, motioning to the mountain. "*My grandfather created it for her so she'd not miss her mountain home. Before him, his father created our vast city wall. My father does nothing. I will conquer all lands and bring all riches to beautify my kingdom.*"

"*How did he build it?*"

"By his supreme wisdom and with prisoners won in war. I will bring more prisoners than he ever did."

So far, he'd only captured three. Not much of a beginning. I tried not to laugh.

Nkosi swung off his horse, and the other nine followed suit. *"No horse may soil my grandmother's gardens."*

I leaned against my horse's neck and slithered over one side. My legs were rubber from long hours of riding, and I almost slid prone to the ground.

Elise and Gaven fared little better.

The white-robed men led the horses to a stable along the wall while we continued onward on foot. It would have been a pleasant change from riding, if my legs weren't rubbed to sores along the inside. I walked in a spread-leg shuffle, but so did most of the others, even Nkosi. Only Thabit seemed immune. Two of our captors had to carry Gaven.

We skirted around the base of the mountain gardens. Beyond it, a single-level palace sprawled in bland comparison to the garden, a vast, white columned building. We passed through an entrance hall and entered a sunlit courtyard. A fountain sparkled onto blue stones. Large pillows lined the walls, and potted trees added fragrance to the air. A portly man in embroidered white sat on one cushion and smoked a narrow pipe. He wore his hair in rows of braids tight against his head, like Nkosi. Four large servants waved fans above him. They also wore swords at their waists. Did he double his guards as servants or the other way around?

He studied us as we approached. The smoke puffed faster from his pipe.

Nkosi stepped before the rest of us and bowed. *"Honored Father of Great Carani. I bring you two great magicians. They have healed much of my skin, and when they have proper supplies, will make my skin like new."*

The king inclined his head and puffed on his pipe.

"*And also I bring one who will fight like a lion in our arena. Only with great skill did I subdue him.*"

The king pulled his pipe from his mouth. "*How is it I send you to bring back lowland savages and you bring these pasty skinned foreigners?*"

"*He is fiercer than they. And magicians—*"

"*Magicians—bah!—show me your skin before you fill my ears with more lies.*"

Nkosi unveiled his face. The purple glared brighter with his angry blush. Any improvement Gaven and Elise had achieved was undone by the heat, the ride, and Nkosi's emotions.

The king tossed his pipe to the tile floor, stood and circled Nkosi, touching his skin. His frown deepened. "*It is less bumpy. Perhaps your magicians will stay for their paltry tricks. But the other is a cripple. He is only good for his skin. And I am tired of skins. They lack the beauty of fine linen or the softness of cotton. Our fathers destroyed many good slaves for their skins. He'll pull my cart through the gardens. He has strong shoulders.*"

"*No,*" Nkosi sputtered. "*Put him in our arena. I deserve to see him eaten by lions or skewered by lance. At least I deserve his skin. He —*" Nkosi stopped.

The king sneered. "*Did this cripple best you?*"

"*No!*"

"*Then I shall enjoy watching him fight in the arena—against you.*"

"*I'm your son. Prince of Carani. Jewel of your life.*"

"*You are a fool.*"

Nkosi stepped back, head bowed and face bright purple-red. He clenched his fists, and his shoulders stretched his tunic tautly.

The king turned to Thabit. "*What news do you bring?*"

Thabit kneeled before the king. *"My lord and master of my life. The cripple is king of the people across the sea."*

What? How did he know? I spun to stare at him.

Thabit nodded at me. *"His expression tells the truth of my words. I know not why he came to Carani, but he will tell you if you pressure the girl healer."*

I stepped toward the king, holding out my bound arms.

The king's servants stepped between him and me until the king motioned them back.

"Thabit is mistaken," I said. *"I am an interpreter for the old healer and his granddaughter. We came to offer our services in Carani, for we heard of its wealth and sought our fortune here. Your son took us prisoners. Is this how Carani treats its merchants of health?"*

The king motioned Thabit to stand next to me. *"Why do you say he is king?"*

"Because I spied on the across-sea land before you sent me to watch over your son in the underland. The new king of the land is a cripple. And as we traveled from the underland with him, he told stories, including ones of his own life. He speaks and acts as a king when he's not playing the fool."

Thabit spoke our language. I'd been unguarded in my words to Elise. What had he heard? And why had he let us help Donkor and Jabare? He couldn't be all bad for that kindness.

"Do you still suggest we attack them?" asked the Carani king.

"More so than before. Their king is gone. They've suffered a revolution. You will succeed where your fathers repeatedly failed."

"Our ships are too few to attack with much of our armies. We could only send thirty of our two-hundred thousand."

Even that would destroy us.

"Always, your fathers made too little effort to conquer the sea. But now, even the little army your ships can carry will conquer that land."

I kneeled before the king, *"He tells untruths. I am no king, though I am of Lansimetsa. My land is strong in armies and will drive* yours away as it has many times before. Do not waste your armies and your navies. You govern a great people and will be remembered as the king who brought peace and prosperity to her people. Why stain your name with war?"

He picked up his pipe and puffed, then tossed it to the side. "*I am not a king of peace. And neither are my people. Why have you come to Carani?*"

"*To interpret for the healers.*"

"*You are the crippled king. Do not lie more to me.*"

"*I'm not. I'm—*"

The Carani king picked up a bell from a line of bells beside him and rang it.

Feet scurried away at the door.

I tried again, "*I'm an interpreter. I—*"

"*Silence.*"

I bit my lip.

A long time later three men entered. Each dressed in dark red linens and one wore knives of various shapes and sizes along a diagonal chest strap.

The king motioned to Elise. "*Make a chamber servant mark along her right shoulder.*"

"*No!*" I shouted stepping between them and Elise.

Thabit grabbed me, while the two of the three took hold of Elise and the third drew a thin blade.

"Halavant," she whimpered.

I struggled against Thabit. "*Stop! I am the crippled king. I came to find a cure for my hands.*"

The Carani king motioned for the red-clad men to let Elise go. "*And did you find it?*"

"*No.*"

"*Then I hope you are a good fighter with your feet. You will fight my marked son in the arena, and if you win, you will fight another and another, until you die. When you've provided me that sport, I'll sail at the head of my finest armies and take your land for my own."*

Nkosi sprang up. *"I am king after you. You cannot kill me for sport."*

"You only die if you let the crippled king kill you. If you win, you may be worthy to be king after me. But if not, my new wife bore a son. His skin is as clear as the cloudless sky and smooth as water."

50

KATRIN

PALACE, Fairhaven, Lansimetsa
Febrúar 28th

IT HAD BEEN ALMOST a week since Makkara agreed to convince the nobles to gather to Fairhaven and feed the commoners. Galliard and I read over the last of his letters to be sure nothing would betray Yosyph and Lansimetsa before a servant sealed them. Letters to the most distant nobles were sent a week ago.

My dear Karhu,

Egvar betrayed your son, throwing him in his dungeon, and Pulska seeks to put himself on the throne. We must band together with our other noble brothers to keep our land from falling into yet another war. I've convinced the Shadow Demon to grant our right to overturn any laws we as royal council feel should not be, and to meet with us on Marc 12th, where we will make new laws that protect the nobility of the land. In return, he only asks we gather all our people in Fairhaven and shore it up against attack, and we sell him a portion of our grain so he may feed the workers who will do the hard labor of making defenses against Pulska's attack.

Our strongest weapon is a solid defense. Behind strong walls with our food supplies and deep wells, we'll outlast Pulska or any other traitors to our land.

Your brother of the noble-blooded Lansitmetsians,

Makkara

I handed the letter to the servant to be sealed, then turned to Makkara. "You tell the truth without letting him know the royal council is now half non-noble."

Makkara frowned. "Lady Katrin, they are as noble as you. They've been knighted. Though I will use my most rational, yawn-inducing arguments to help the rest see it that way. They'll agree just to get me to stop talking. And with the Galliard's commitment that those who have been in the council longer than a year get a double weight on their vote, I believe many other lifelong nobles will allow for it. Especially when I've schooled the new nobles in proper etiquette and what will happen if we cannot reach a consensus in our meetings."

"Still, I am impressed at your sleight of words."

"I am not. I despise the intrigues of my station."

"Probably the reason Yosyph chose to work with you."

"If you're done reading my personal letters, I have something of importance to discuss."

Galliard leaned forward. "What is it?"

"Is Egvar still in the dungeon?" Makkara raised an eyebrow.

Galliard flinched. "Yes, why wouldn't he be?"

"I received a note this morning inviting me to join Egvar in reinstating the old queen."

"Who brought it?" Galliard said.

"It was slipped under my door and brought to me by my manservant."

"Your guards didn't see the person?"

"They were in the room with me, instead of outside, as

you've ordered. And no, they didn't see the note. My manservant slipped it to me without them seeing."

Galliard lunged to his feet and pointed to one guard. "Get down to the dungeon. Make sure Egvar is still there. And be more aware next time!"

The white-faced guard dashed from the room.

Galliard turned back to Makkara. "Why didn't you tell me when you got the note?"

Makkara studied the table, then looked at Galliard. "I was considering my options."

Galliard gripped Makkara's collar. "You'd betray us after everything?"

"I'm telling you now."

I laid my hand on Galliard's. "If the Yorel trusts him, then so can we. Do we know who freed the queen?"

"No. Though the Yorel said it was through the most invisible of servants—pages, lamplighters, and even a coal bin girl."

I brought my hand to my mouth. "We know one. I obtained a position for a coal bin girl. Her older sister worked for Egvar. She told me her little sister was a simpleton and ill-treated by the upper servants in Egvar's mansion. I should have suspected!"

Galliard leaned forward. "Where is she?"

"Sweeping out a hearth?" There were hundreds of them in the palace.

"What's her name?"

"I don't remember, but I will find her."

"Wait," said Galliard. "Take a guard with you."

"No, she'll suspect if I'm shadowed by a guard."

"And she'll suspect even if you are not. Take one."

～

A THICK-LEGGED guard with a bland expression and hound dog jowls, attired in servant's clothing, followed me to the household mistress's office.

A stately woman blotted ink on a paper as we entered. Neat piles of paper lay in cubbies behind her. "Do you have another poor soul you want to burden me with training?"

She'd lost her polite reserve with me a month ago, after we exchanged somewhat heated words about the suitability of a lame boy as a floor mopper. He had strong arms and back and could scoot along the floor with a bucket and rags faster than most. At least, that is what I argued. I'd won at the cost of her treating me as a lady.

Hopefully, she'd help me. "Do you remember the girl you took on as a fire keeper and coal bin carrier?"

"Small with a sullen expression?"

"Yes, that one."

"She's under the charge of the north wing head maid. Go complain to her if the girl has slighted her duty."

"Thank you." I turned to leave.

She dipped her pen in the inkwell and paused, the ink dripping back into the well. "You don't have rooms in the north wing."

"I don't."

She shrugged and went back to her writing.

I followed a maze of suggestions from many servants until one pointed me to the banquet preparation room, the one that now lay empty for lack of balls. The head maid sat in the back corner of the room on the lap of a coachman, their eyes closed, and her hands twined through his hair.

"Head maid, north wing?"

She jumped like someone had jabbed her with a hot fire iron, then came to a stumbling curtsy. "Yes, my lady."

"I need to find a certain coal bin girl—small, black hair,

sullen..." I searched for a clearer memory of her. "And she's missing her front teeth."

The maid's expression changed from fear to disgust. "The little mouse is always sneaking, never saying a word. She's startled me many times, worse than you just—" She stopped and turned red. "Pardon me, my lady. I'll get her for you." She hurried off in one direction, and the coachman slunk off in the other.

My guard's eyes crinkled while the corners of his mouth twitched.

"You find their situation amusing?" I tried to keep the laughter out of my voice.

"We always have duties and catch our amusement when we can. But she's notorious for it. I'll bet she'll have her fingers through the butcher's hair tomorrow. Good thing I'm a married man, and an ugly one. Keeps me out of trouble with the likes of her."

"Should we follow her?"

"No, she'll find the girl if she can. She'll not lose her position by ignoring your request."

Dust motes danced in the empty room as we waited. A spider strung a new circle on her web. *How long until she found her?* I laid my hand on the door. *I'll find her myself.*

An alarum bell rang from the depths of the palace. Distant and discordant.

"The dungeon!" I dashed through the door.

My guard ran next to me. "I'll gather men to reinforce the dungeon guard. You let General Galliard know."

We didn't have time. I ducked into an empty bedchamber as the guard rushed towards the tolling bell. I shed my emotions and entered the shadow-walk almost as fast as Yosyph could.

The alarum bell tolled again.

I ran along the halls, following the tolling, and fell in with a stream of soldiers. I dodged elbows as I dashed to the front and stumbled when one soldier tread upon the hem of my dress.

We reached an open door and steep descending stairs. I leaped down the stairs two at a time, the stomping of booted feet echoing behind me. At the bottom, a long hall stretched in the flickering gloom of wide-spaced torches. The guard Galliard sent to check on Egvar lay against the wall. A long needle with a feathered end stuck from his neck. He held the rope of the alarum bell and pulled it again. The sound ricocheted around the stone and steel hall and up the stairs.

The head soldier reached the bottom step and jogged down the hall.

A second soldier kneeled by the fallen, bell-ringing guard. "What happened?"

The guard whispered, "Poison d—" He slumped, his hand falling from the bell rope.

A thud echoed down the hall. I raced, jumping over fallen guards as I ran. Metal doors lined both sides of the hall, each of them closed. Which one held the dart blower? I flinched as I passed each cell. Cautious boot treads followed me. Cell doors opened and shut.

The hall ended in a single, grated door. A stink worse than an unmucked stall poured from it. Behind me, boots thudded in slow caution, and doors opened and shut. Beyond the door came scratching. I ducked under the level of the cell grating and pushed against the door.

A feathered dart shot through the grid above me as I darted, crouched over and invisible, through the open door before it was shoved shut again.

A slight figure stood on the other side of the door, grasping a tube. The coal bin girl? The shadows hid her expression.

"Did you get him?" Egvar crouched next to a stinking hole.

"I don't know." It was a girl's voice. She kept her face to the door. "I didn't see him. Must be on the floor. If he tries to push his way in, I'll stop him."

"Stop him better than the man by the bell."

"He's not human to stay awake like that. I'll knife this one."

The room was ripe. I took small breaths. This must be where they dumped all the prisoners' chamber pots. The girl had gotten Egvar to this room, and others must have cleared a path from this cesspool to get him out. How many were in a tunnel? The scratching continued below.

A muffled voice called from the pit. "We're ready. You'll have to crawl, but there is enough room above the sludge to breathe."

Egvar unfolded a strip of cloth, and a strong herbal scent struggled against the stink of human refuse. He tied it around his mouth and nose.

I wouldn't let him escape. I grabbed the dart from the girl's hand and jabbed it into her arm.

She screamed and fell.

Egvar spun about.

I put the tube to my mouth and blew. Good, it was loaded. The dart stuck his shoulder.

"Cursed sha—" and he also fell.

The others below could still carry him off. I searched the girl for more darts.

Her hand shot out, a dart in her fingers, scratched it against my cheek, then fell back limp.

My cheek burned with fire, then numbness. The room turned fuzzy. I dropped to the ground. I couldn't move any more than I could in a nightmare. It wasn't a poison but a sleeping potion, had to be. And I couldn't sleep.

A person covered in sludge emerged from the hole. "Deodor, get up here and help me. That blasted girl betrayed us. Must have had second thoughts. We'll leave her to the demon's justice."

A second person emerged halfway from the hole. Together, they pushed and pulled Egvar into the hole.

Let him drown along the way.

The opening and shutting of cell doors grew closer.

A guard shoved into the cesspool room with a drawn sword. He treaded on my arm and stepped back.

Pain shot up my arm. The sleep poison stilled even my scream.

"A shadow demon?" He scanned the room and dragged the dart-blowing girl into the hall, then felt around for me. "It's the girl shadow demon. She's breathing but seems to be unconscious like the rest. You three—" he pointed to three of the soldiers who stood outside the hall, "get down that hole and bring back the prisoner. I want five more to stand ready to help them. And the rest of you, carry up the fallen guards. We'll need a doctor for this lot. Hopefully, the poison isn't fatal."

The first of the soldiers hesitantly lowered himself into the hole. The floor rumbled, and muck splashed upward, coating the soldier up to his chin. Had the tunnel caved in or had they caused the cave-in after they'd passed a certain point? Probably the latter, though the former would be useful.

～

I LAY in the middle of a line of pallets in the barracks. It was better than being thrust into a cell like the coal bin girl. I was suspect for helping Egvar escape. The guard who'd searched with me for the coal bin girl spoke in my defense, and in compromise, I was lying on the floor, surrounded by sleep-poisoned men. How soon would the guard tell Galliard where I was? Or was the guard suspected, too?

A military doctor moved down the row of men, checking

pulses and lifting eyelids. He stopped at one pallet, lifted the wrist of a soldier, and slapped it.

The man groaned.

The doctor pulled out smelling salts and wafted it under the man's nose.

"I'm awake, I'm awake," the man sputtered.

The captain of the guard strode over. "Tell us what happened. Everything."

The man mumbled, and the doctor passed the salts under his nose again. The man pushed the vial away. "I was guarding the dungeon prisoners. A drudge came down with our breakfast. She was late. We should have had it hours before, but none of us could leave to get it, not without court martial, and you wouldn't court marshal us, because we stayed on duty. We are honorable men—"

The captain grabbed his shirtfront. "Focus, man. What happened?"

"Well, we were hungry and finished the bread and soup before we realized it tasted funny. The room swam, and then I woke up here with those awful smelling salts."

"What did the drudge look like?"

"Small thing, awful mouth, no teeth, black hair."

"That's her. Egvar escaped."

"We didn't do anything wrong. We were poisoned. We—"

"You'll not hang."

"Thank ye, captain."

The doctor called, "Another is waking up. This one got two poisoned darts."

The captain questioned him.

The soldier answered, "The General sent me to check on Egvar. Found the guards all asleep. Voices came from the far end cell. I ran towards it when something stung my calf. It got hard to move, like through water. I fell, but I had to warn the others.

My legs wouldn't work, so I dragged myself back the alarum bell. It felt like hours must have passed, but I made it. When I rang the bell, a dark figure ran out from the end cell and another dart stung me, this time in my neck. She ran back to the cell. But I'm of stubborn constitution. I rang the bell again and again until others came. They'll have to tell you what happened next."

More men woke with similar tales to the first soldier.

I blinked. My emotions sparkled around me. I breathed deeply, opening myself to the emotions. They swirled like a wind stirred them up, but they didn't touch my skin or come in. I'd need another's help again. It wouldn't need to be Yosyph. My maid servant would cry for me. "Br—br—" I tried to speak, but my tongue lay thick in my mouth.

The doctor felt around on my face, then pushed the smelling salts under my nose.

My tongue woke. "Bring my maid, now."

The captain came to my side. "Make yourself visible, demon, and then we'll talk."

"I can't, without her."

Another voice spoke, the guard who Galliard sent to check on Egvar. "She can't come out of the shadow-walk without help. Get her maid. I'll vouch for her."

~

MAGGIE ENTERED the barracks at a run. "My lady. Where are you?"

"I'm here, on the empty pallet in the middle of the others. Rope floating above it. See it?"

She spun about, facing the captain. "Unbind her!"

"We will, when we've determined she didn't help the prisoner escape."

"She wouldn't ever."

"She said you'd help her become visible again. Do it."

"Oh, my lady." She leaned over me and took my hands. "Why do you keep doing this?"

"I was trying to stop Egvar from escaping. And I almost did. I need you to rub your tears on my hands."

"My tears?"

"Your tears."

She pulled my hands to her cheeks and rubbed them until they were salty wet. A few of the sparkles of emotion stuck, and I pulled them into me. The rest followed. The world spun.

"My lady." Maggie cried, wetting my now-visible hands. "There has to be a better way."

I laughed. "This is much better than the first time or even the second. Thank you, my friend." I turned to the captain. "Now that I'm visible, will you listen to what happened? We have much to do, and I'll help wherever I can."

51

ELISE

Capital City of Upper Carani
Februar 30th

I worked at a table in a sunlit courtyard. Around me, potted trees hung thick with lemons and other fruits. A breeze cooled the sweat along my neck. How was a place so beautiful such a nightmare? The Carani king knew Halavant was King of Lansimetsa. He planned to have his own son fight Halavant to the death, just to entertain him before sailing like a plague on my family and people.

I squeezed lemons into a greasy paste. They still expected us to perform the miracle of removing Nkosi's birthmark in the two days before he killed Halavant.

I leaned close to Gaven as he measured out herbs, some familiar and some only guessed at for their properties. One of them might give Nkosi such a rash he couldn't fight Halavant. Such a mistake could cost our skins.

"Gaven, why are we still helping them?"

He looked up with bloodshot eyes. His storm-gray eyebrows had turned pure white over the last several weeks. "Because they'll kill us if we don't."

"They'll kill us when we can't."

"I'll bleach his skin bone-white."

"And then what?"

Gaven grunted and turned back to the herbs. He picked up one, sniffed it, then shook his head, set it aside, and picked up another. He was crazy. And I was close behind him.

I picked up a pouch of powdered nettle. Added to teas, it increased endurance. Halavant jokingly despised that tea. I needed his joking now. I pinched nettle and held it over the lemon paste. If I added it, Nkosi's skin would glow an angry, itching red.

Halavant would say... what would he say? He'd say I was being dramatic and to put it down. That we'd still escape as long as we didn't mess it up by childish revenge. He'd say something like that. No, he'd just shake his head and give me that smile.

I set the nettle back in the pouch.

"E-ise." A whisper.

I must be going crazy. It sounded how the villagers in the lower Carani said my name.

Our two guards stood in the single doorway to the courtyard, and in an opposite corner from them, near to me, sat the old women given to serve us. She sat weaving. Her headscarf shadowed her down-turned face.

"E-ise." The whisper came again.

I excused myself to go to the small closet that served as a private place to use the chamber pot. I passed near the old woman on my way.

She lifted her head. Donkor's face stared from the loose headscarf.

I forced my eyes forward and continued walking to the closet.

I could have kissed Donkor.

They were here.

PART IV

52

YOSYPH

Sun lay across my face, warming it and turning my eyelids red. I blinked and yawned.

Katrin sat at a desk near my bed. She reached over and took my hand, though I couldn't feel her touch. The slow wasting had progressed to the next part of my body.

"Good morning, Yosyph. Or should I say good morning again? You've been in and out of sleep for many hours."

"How many days?"

"This is going on five days. The doctor went back to a strong drug when you wouldn't rest."

"I rested."

"Tossing and muttering about the kingdom isn't resting."

I had no answer for that.

"You are much better now. He stopped giving you the sleep drug three days ago. By then, your body seemed to know it needed to rest, and you slept like a hibernating bear. He says you

297

are healing better than he'd hoped. You'll heal, and Halavant will bring the cure." She kissed my cheek, then laughed. "If you're up to it, I'll try shaving your face. How are you today?"

"Five days. And four before that. We have less than three weeks to gather the people. I need to—."

"They are already coming. You should see the loaded wagons of grain roll in each day. Our granaries will be full soon, and so will the bellies of the people."

Already? I'd told them of God's warning and completed my duties. I could die with a clear conscience. Hopefully, Halavant would still find the cure so he didn't fall to the slow wasting. The bed pressed against my arms, head, and core. My legs and hands had gone numb and immobile.

Please God, is there more for me to do? If so, strengthen me to do what I must. And if not, please take me home. I don't want to be a burden on Katrin or the others. They've taken such care for me, but they will be needed elsewhere soon.

A sharp rebuke poured over me. *I still have much for you to do. You've rested. Now you must work.*

What must I do?

You have a choice. You can continue to influence from the shadow, and I will strengthen you to do that for a short time, then you will die. Or you can openly lead, and I will take away your talent of entering the shadow, so other talents may grow up in its place.

I could never qwaalaar again?

If that is your choice, yes. You would lose even your birth talent of going unnoticed. All would see you as they can see other men.

Which way will help my people the most?

It is your choice. Both could lead to peace, depending on what the people choose. However, if you lead, the people can follow you, which they cannot when you are in the shadow.

God could strengthen me to finish the work using shadow-walking. He could do that miracle. To move freely. To do again, what I once did. Was it the right choice? I wasn't afraid to die. I would soon, either way. But to lead openly? A shiver ran down my spine. To not just be seen and noticed but have all Lansimetsa look to me for guidance and see me clearly for all my faults.

Could God strengthen me to bear that weight? The people needed a leader. Was I willing to lead?

I'll give up my shadow-walking. Please, help me lead. I do not know how.

A calming assurance spread over me. *Go out among the people. Talk with them. Listen to them. Comfort them. Help them work together. They need to be united. Makkara will go with you.*

How can I go?

A rotating image formed in my mind—a chair with large wheels mounted on the sides and bars at the back where someone could push it.

Thank you for directing me. I'll get to work.

Katrin stroked my cheek. "Yosyph?"

"I need a blacksmith and wheelwright."

"Blacksmith? Wheelwright?"

"I have work to do, and I must be about it today."

Katrin stroked my hair back from my forehead. "My sweet Yosyph. You aren't going anywhere."

I nodded to the physician. "I need a chair made with wheels. A servant will push me so I can meet with the people. You've saved my life. Now I must use it to do what God needs me to do. I will return to your care each evening, and I promise to do what you say."

He looked ready to argue.

I continued. "God will strengthen me. I'll not die before I'm finished with His work."

He tilted his head. "And you'll not enter the shadow-walk?"

"My days for shadow-walking are past." I felt different, a solidness. "I'll never *qwaalaar* again."

"You swear it."

"Yes."

He stroked his chin. "You are healed as much as I think you ever will. As long as you don't enter the shadow-walk, then your slow wasting should not increase—much. It will be as its name implies, a slow loss of movement. How much have you lost now?"

"I cannot feel my legs or hands."

"Oh, Yosyph!" Katrin took one of my hands and then walked her fingers up my wrist and lower arm. When she got to midway between wrist and elbow, her fingers tickled my skin.

"I can feel to there."

The physician nodded. "You have a year left, if it progresses like it did for your ancestors."

That was more than I'd expected. "The blacksmith and wheelwright?"

"I've seen your predictions come true. Your desert god must truly speak with you. I'll allow this."

I smiled wryly. "Thank you for your magnanimity."

"You'd find some way to escape that bed, even if I didn't allow for it."

"I would."

Katrin placed her hands on her hips. "Yosyph, you must rest. You have to be strong enough when Halavant comes with the cure."

I shook my head. "I will do what God has asked me to do."

She clenched her fists. "I wish he wouldn't ask *this* of you."

I didn't have the words to comfort her. I'd not lie and say I'd live. "I'd better eat. Get the blacksmith now. I would have the chair finished today."

~

A SERVANT PUSHED me in a jiggling, jolting chair out of the palace and into the courtyard. Two guards walked before me and two flanked me. It was late morning, only a day after I'd asked for the chair made. Early spring softened winter's bite, more than the pillows softened the hastily made chair's movements. I was dressed as a king, my hair and beard trimmed like the painting of my father, though his hair was rich brown and mine black. The full beard itched.

A scribe walked behind holding a roll of parchment and a pen. An inkwell hung from his belt.

Makkara walked at my side. His ever-straight stance and up-tilted chin declared he deserved respect.

I mimicked him, rolling my shoulders back and lifting my head to observe my surroundings. I needed to draw attention, something I'd avoided since I learned to walk.

I grimaced. I could no longer walk, so I no longer needed to hide.

Soldiers practiced in uncertain line maneuvers to my left. A wagon piled high with grain sacks rolled through the gate, and a guard speared several sacks before waving the wagoner forward. Tents lined the walls—new recruits for the army, too many to fit in the barracks. We'd turned some still-ruined buildings from the last war into quarters to house them.

Without dropping his analyzing gaze, Makkara asked, "Where to?"

"I would start where the densest gathering of refugees camp."

"You'll put yourself in harm's way."

"God will protect us."

Makkara shook his head. "I can't believe he'd have you test his protection so foolishly."

A feeling whispered Makkara spoke the truth—as yet I wasn't to go out that far. What then? I was to go among the people. Sitting in the throne room wasn't going out among them. "Where would you suggest?"

"You are the one with a god speaking to you. Didn't he tell you?"

I shook my head. "He expects me to work out the details. He gives me too much trust."

"He does." Makkara glanced down at me. "I suggest you talk with the new recruits within the confines of these walls."

And to the man delivering the grain. It would be a start. "Take me to the granary. I would see how much we've gathered and how it is being distributed."

The granary was made from the quarry pit, where the thin white marble that lined the palace walls had been dug. Under the marble lay the gray granite that formed the strong bones of the palace and city. The vanity to bedeck the palace in the queen's ruling cost the lives of many prisoners. Now the quarry filled with what would preserve the lives of many.

The wagoner bent his back under a sack of grain and trudged to the low open door. He dropped the sack through the opening and plodded back to the wagon. He paled when he saw us waiting there, then bowed, though from his bow, he kept his eyes on me and my chair.

I nodded for him to rise. "What is your name?"

"Ivan." He studied me, his brow creased between his eyes. "So you're the Yorel. I remember you. I often visited your father's —I mean the vintner Hadron's—tavern."

"Remember me?" Few could make that claim from my pre-shadow-walking days. No one noticed me, let alone remembered. How many would now?

"Yes. You were kind to a little girl crying over her crushed kitten. You fashioned a doll from a piece of sacking and grass, and in that moment, you didn't seem the halfwit who served the wine. I didn't know you were the Yorel. Good thing, too, or I might have boasted to my friends in my drunkenness."

Yes, it was a good thing.

"I heard—" He looked down at his own work-roughened hands. "I heard the *kings' death* has taken you. Is it painful?"

"No."

He fisted his hands. "What can I do for you? You saved my brother's life from the noose before the Slave War. I would do anything."

"It is I who should ask. Do you have family or friends in need?"

"We are better off than most. I'm not married, and my grain-hauling is providing well enough for my parents and siblings. We're packed in a single room as tight as pickled fish in a barrel —my oxen have more space in their stalls—but we are healthy and have food to eat."

"And those not as well off?"

"I do what I can for them." He shuffled his feet. "You've decreed the grain to be distributed from the palace granary, and I understand you need to keep records and make sure everything is done in proper order, but the lines to get the allotment of grain are snail-slow, what with all the searching before they can even enter. Some decide to wait until the next day, the next day comes, and they still don't get food. And today they've stopped the lines altogether, what with the Yorel being out of the palace and needing protection from those who might seek his life."

That wouldn't do. "Let the people in."

Makkara shook his head. "Galliard ordered, and I agree, they will be let in *when* you are back inside the palace."

"I am regent until Halavant returns. Let them in."

Ivan coughed. "We should—I mean, may I suggest—store

the grain around the city, so it is easier to distribute. Though we'd need a strong guard at each place. Thieves are making a nuisance of themselves, and some are getting bold enough to rob by violence."

Sound advice. "We'll send a portion of the soldiers to watch the streets and capture these thieves. We'll send the more experienced ones, while the new recruits can train here. They'll have more room this way, and fewer fights."

One of my guards swallowed. He sported a blackened eye.

I continued. "We need a record keeper at each grain distribution site. They must compare records at the end of each day to make sure a single person isn't getting grain from multiple spots. We'll keep a record of work done in exchange for the grain. We need scribes assigned to each work party. We needed parties of soldiers sent out to aid those making their way to Fairhaven."

My scribe scratched his pen across the parchment.

Ivan looked at his partly emptied wagon. "I'll get my wagon refilled. Where do I take it?"

The prison along the walls between the nobles and commoner section of Fairhaven had strong walls and locked doors. And it was mostly empty since we overthrew the queen, though any rooms used to store grain would need a scouring.

Makkara said, "The safest places would be behind the walls of loyal nobles. They would help keep everything organized, while reducing the strain on our preparations and defenses."

"No." I couldn't allow for them, even the loyal ones, to take advantage of the common people. We'd paid for the grain from the royal treasury, and it would stay where I could make sure it was given out fairly.

"The nobles are Lansimetsian too," Makkara said, as if he could read my thoughts. "Many are noble-minded as well as noble-blooded. I will take responsibility that it is fairly distributed."

Ivan looked from me to Makkara and back to me, then cleared his throat. "There is something you can do for me."

"What?"

"Could you talk with my nephew? He's never been the same since his father died in the Slave War. You comforted the little girl. I think you could help him."

He was wrong. I wasn't good with children or adults. I'd made the doll for the girl because I didn't have words. "I'll do my best. Bring him when you can."

"He's here now. Vanya, get on over here, you rascal." He said the teasing words with a sad lilt.

A young man slumped out from the granary and shuffled to stand beside Ivan. He stared vacantly at the ground.

Ivan put his arm around the young man's shoulder. "Vanya, this is the Yorel."

Vanya flickered his gaze up at me and back at the ground. His eyes were the pale blue of a washed-out sky.

Please God. He's hurting. How can I help him?

I felt no direction, only peace that God knew the boy's hurt.

"Vanya, who was your father?"

"An archer in the royal guard."

His father must have died fighting those we'd raised against the queen. "He must have been a fine archer."

"He was. The best."

"Did he teach you?"

Vanya nodded, keeping his eyes downward.

"Will you show me? I've never been good with the bow."

He looked up, disbelief animating his face. "But you're good at everything! You are the Yorel! My father told me everything about you. He said you would change our whole land to one of peace."

I shook my head. "I've never shot a bow, and I'm horrid at knife throwing."

"It's simple. I'll show you." He ran to the wagon and pulled out a bow and a quiver of arrows.

One of my guards stepped between him and me, and another drew his sword.

"Let him be," I said.

Vanya looked at the guards and dropped the quiver. "I'll just show you with the bow." He came back to me. "This is a small hunting bow. Doesn't have much draw weight. But with my father's bow, I could hit that banner." He pointed to a long streamer flapping atop one tower. "You must draw with your shoulder, not your arm." He drew the bowstring back by his cheek in a smooth motion. "More important than draw weight is seeing where the arrow will curve in its flight. It doesn't go straight, but up and then down." He drew a slight curved line in the air as he talked. "Here, you try." He held the bow out to me.

"I can't stand."

"Doesn't matter. This bow is small enough you can shoot sitting. You're the Yorel, and even the *kings' death* can't stop you."

"My hands no longer work."

"Oh." His face fell.

"But I am doing everything I can to bring peace to our land. I won't dishonor your father's name by surrendering."

Vanya stood taller. "And you will succeed. You are the Yorel. I pledge myself to your service."

"I could use a captain of the youth battalion."

"Youth battalion?"

"We need every able-bodied man and youth to stand ready to defend our nation. Will you gather other skilled youth and bring them here for training?"

"Yes, honored Yorel." He kneeled before me and placed his bowed head almost in my lap. "I pledge my life to defend yours."

Ivan mouthed a thank you.

After Ivan and his nephew turned back to loading the wheat, I nodded towards the new recruits. "I'll talk with them now."

Makkara inclined his head. "An unexpected young man. A youth battalion could keep them out of trouble with thieving and vandalism. A clever solution to Fairhaven's bored and crowded youth."

"It wasn't my solution."

"Yours or your god's, I don't care which. If you'll only start trusting the loyal nobles, we could make a united defense against Egvar and Pulska's impending attacks."

I was trying to trust them, while being cautious. It was a fine line of balance. "Take me to the new recruits."

53

HALAVANT

CAPITAL CITY of Upper Carani
  Mars 2nd

I RODE through the streets like a king on a chair born atop the shoulders of four slaves. A king, except chains encircled my ankles.

Men, with voices that carried a block over, cried, "*King of the over-the-sea people will fight scarred son of our great king and god.*"

The streets filled with a shoulder-to-shoulder press of bodies. The curved walls of the colosseum drew closer. It sat in the middle of the outer ring of the city where both rich and poor could gather for deadly entertainment.

We passed through a gate in the colosseum's wall and descended a long tunnel, ending in a torch-lit hall of cells.

A burly man with keys belted at his waist waited for the slaves to set down the chair. He yanked at the chains and unlocked my ankles, then shoved me into an empty cell. A heavy bundle thudded to the floor, and the door clanged shut.

It was my hand braces and boots. Little good they'd do. I couldn't put them on. "*Master Jailer!*"

"*What, sea scum?*"

"*Your god-king will want an exciting fight. And he will not be pleased if I die in the opening seconds.*"

"*Therefore?*"

"*Therefore, help me on with these boots and braces. And a little extra padding around my vitals would help the fight last longer, too.*"

"*Get them on yourself.*"

"*Didn't they tell you, I'm not only sea scum but also crippled?*"

"*I won't see you fight. Why should I care?*"

"*You want the coward scarred son to become your next god-king?*"

The cell door swung open, and the jailer entered. He pulled off the floppy shoes Thabit had given me, then started removing the rest of my clothing.

I blocked him with my forearm. "*I need armor, or at least my clothes.*"

The jailer laughed—a cold, sharp sound. "*Those who fight, do so in this.*" He held out a loincloth.

I gulped. It was better than nothing, but not by much.

After I wore only a loincloth, he shoved the boots onto my bare feet. "*How?*" He motioned to the hand braces.

"*The hard piece goes under the fingers, palm and forearm. Then strap around the back.*"

It took him two tries, but by the end, I had them securely and uncomfortably tight. Now I had a chance against Nkosi.

The jailer glanced at me, then turned to leave the cell.

I called after him. "*Where are my weapons?*"

"*You have your foot and hand weapons. Tale goes you almost killed Nkosi with those.*"

"*He didn't have a weapon then. He will now. Your god-king will have a short and disappointing entertainment.*"

"*What do I care for that?*" And he left.

All that remained were my ever-annoying thoughts. I'd silenced them while talking with the jailer, and before that, with a multitude of mental commentaries on the city through which we traveled. But now, without competition, they nagged and prodded me.

You've failed to get the cure for your brother. Yosyph will die slowly, just like your father. You've failed your country. Lansimetsa will fall to the Carani. And after today, you won't be around to see things fall apart. Because you'll die.

But, I won't die, I argued back. *Nkosi is a fool and a coward. I'll win.*

And after that?

I'll figure out something else, so be quiet!

My thoughts wouldn't be still. *You've failed. You've failed to protect Elise. After all she's done for you, after all she's endured for you, she will become a slave at best, and at worst—*

I hit the wall with a braced hand to silence the thought. My hand zinged with the impact and dulled the tearing in my chest. Yet even dulled, the pain seared in a way unlike anything I'd felt when Katrin disappeared. *I should have kept Elise safe! I should have found a way for us to escape, or at least for her!*

My shoulders shook. How could I be so blind? The gods gave me a second chance to love and I'd treated her like a sister.

"Please," I whispered into the empty cell. "All ye benevolent gods of my Carani kin, and Yosyph's god if you can hear, protect Elise. Help her get free. Help her get back home with the duri. Save her. Save Yosyph. Save my people."

My cell door swung open.

The jailer jerked his thumb.

"*Let me have at least one weapon.*"

He spat.

The glob hit my cheek and ran into my scraggly beard.

I wiped it on my shoulder, then marched ahead of the jailer

through a long hall and up a stairway, my prayer pulsing through my body. *Please save Elise, save Yosyph, save Lansimetsa, save Elise.*

The top of the stairs ended in a metal ceiling. The jailer pushed me aside and lifted the ceiling. Cheering poured down. Then he shoved me up the last few steps.

I climbed into the middle of a flat-bottomed pit. Stone tiles spread out from the trapdoor, making a fighting ground large enough for small armies to compete. At the edge of the tiles, steep terraces rose with every inch of sitting room filled with spectators. They yelled and screamed and cheered. Sections had colored cloths stretched out to shade them. Columns and a tiled roof shaded one section. A fat man with smoke pouring from his mouth lounged under the fanning of servants—the Carani king.

The metal trapdoor clanged shut, and I stood alone in the center of the tiled field.

Where was Nkosi?

Metal clanged against stone, and another trapdoor opened in the field, about twenty feet from me.

Nkosi leaped upward. He'd painted his body in blacks, reds and purples—a swirling mix of color that merged with his scarring, then spun down his chest, across his arms, and over his legs. Only his hair remained its natural burned-brown in tight rows of braids. He wore a simple white cloth like me, and bore a short sword, unlike me.

The crowd's noise changed to mocking laughter. I was more their champion than their own prince. Would they let me go once I bested Nkosi?

Nkosi turned a slow circle, glaring at the crowd. The laughter grew.

An itch of pity grew between my shoulder blades. I hated him. But he didn't deserve this disdain just because of his scarring. If I'd known, I could have shown him respect instead of adding my mocking to a lifetime of others, and maybe we'd not be in this situation.

Nkosi turned to face his father, and his glare softened to a pouting plea.

A drum beat out a steady beat, and the crowd quieted. Then a trumpet bounced its notes into the walls of the colosseum. Once, twice, thrice.

Nkosi rushed at me, swinging his sword in an overhand arch.

It was a short sword. Shorter than my arm length. Maybe the Carani had a sense of justice.

I waited until he was a two-sword distance from me, leaned sideways, and spun, putting all my momentum into the steel heel of my boot. My boot cracked against his ribs.

His sword continued its downward arc and wooshed past my knee, abrading my skin. He sucked in his breath and swung sideways. A sloppy swing.

I dove to the ground and scissored his foot between my boots, then rolled, pulling him off balance.

He stumbled to one knee.

I untangled myself and leaped up behind him. As he spun, still gripping his sword, I chopped my braced hand against the side of his neck.

His sword bit into my hip.

I spun away as a wetness ran down my leg. I could still move it. He'd only cut through skin, not muscle.

He leaned forward, still on one knee, sword drooping and his other hand bracing against the ground. His breath came in wheezing gasps.

I spun into a full-strength kick. His head was my target.

He lunged forward and upward, swinging his sword to block my leg. The blade cut into my boot and stuck in the leather. He ripped it free, pulling me off balance.

I fell to my back.

His sword descended toward my bare chest.

I smacked the blade with my hand brace, knocking it sideways. A shudder ran up my arm to my shoulder as the blade finished its arc against the stone tiles. I kicked Nkosi in the chest.

He fell to his rump.

I leaped to my feet and spun. This time my kick landed against his temple.

He crumpled.

The crowds cheered and yelled, like an ocean surf pounding. Colored ribbons rained down from the stands.

Nkosi lay at my feet.

My leg ached, and a sticky itch of blood crusted it. What would happen now? I glanced at the king.

He drew his finger under his neck.

No. I'd defeated Nkosi. I'd not murder him. I kicked the sword aside and walked away from Nkosi.

The cheering died and hissing replaced it.

I'd provided them with their entertainment. What joy could they take in that final act of taking a life?

Two men carried Nkosi off the field to his father. There, under the royal shade, Nkosi's limp body was hauled up between two of the columns, and the man who'd almost carved a piece of skin from Elise's shoulder moved to Nkosi.

I turned away.

The cheering of the crowd almost drowned out Nkosi's screams.

I defiled the field with my breakfast, and still the noise tore at my ears.

It silenced with the beating of the drum. The trap door opened a stone's throw from me. A man with wavy brown hair and skin in a tone between mine and Nkosi's stepped onto the field. He rushed at me, wielding two daggers.

I crouched, ready to throw myself either way. Two daggers would be harder to defend against than one sword.

"*Moswen.*" It was Donkor. He skidded to a stop and slashed with the left dagger, not the one I'd expected. It skimmed over my chest.

It should have cut deeper. Was he my enemy or not? I kicked his thigh, but only half-force.

"*Softer,*" he groaned, jabbing his right dagger.

I turned it aside with my braced hand.

We circled each other. "*The village is here. Below. And in the crowd.*"

I spun into a slow kick to his side.

He threw himself to the ground as my foot passed over him. "*Follow me.*" He rolled back to his feet and ran.

Laughter and hisses poured from the crowd.

I ran after Donkor.

The trapdoor opened.

I jumped into the darkness and hands grabbed me, pulling me down the stairs.

Voices filled the darkness.

"*Moswen.*"

"*Moswen, we are here.*"

"*He's hurt, get the Heaven's Gate Girl.*"

"*No time. We must leave.*"

My eyes adjusted to the gloom. The chief and many of his warriors surrounded me. I wobbled. "*My friends. We must get Elise and Gaven.*"

The chief pressed fabric to my bleeding hip and pulled me through the tunnel. "*We have them. Hurry.*"

I ran in the middle of my village kin, down the long halls, turning corners.

Guard challenges ended in quick groans and silence.

Then we burst into sunlight.

Before my eyes adjusted again, hands pushed me onto a horse. Someone mounted behind me and grabbed the reins, and we galloped through the city. Shouted challenges and silenced cries preceded us. The same sounds rose in other streets.

How many of my kin were spread through the city causing confusion?

Guards of the massive outer wall lay dead by the open gate.

Our horses thundered under the wall archway, their hoof-beats echoing off the tunnel walls, then into the vast farm and grasslands beyond the Carani city.

Arrows rained from the wall. The man mounted behind me stifled a shout and dropped the reins.

I wrapped my braced hands through the slack reins, leaned forward against my horse's neck and urged him faster.

After an hour, our horses stumbled to a stop.

Elise and Gaven and thirty warriors bunched around me. Five horse stood with empty saddles. Arrows stuck from three other warriors, one who slumped in his saddle. Behind me Donkor grasped his arrow-pierced arm, his face blanched, and his jaw gritted. *"Forgive me. I tried to repay my betrayal."*

He'd taken an arrow for me. *"Someone, help Donkor!"*

The chief frowned. *"First you and the other wounded."* He clasped my arm, helped me dismount and lie on the ground.

My leg throbbed, but the wound wasn't fatal. *"Please help those hurt worse."*

Elise kneeled by me. "Halavant..." Tears trailed her face. She bit her lip and touched my hip where Nkosi cut me. "I wish... I should have..." She stopped and swallowed. "I'll bind your wound."

A thrill ran up my leg at her touch, pulsing in counterpoint to the throbbing pain. "Thank you, Elise. You are my protecting goddess." She was much more, but this wasn't the time to speak such words.

The other warriors tended to their wounded brothers. Donkor kept his gaze downward as a warrior bound his arm.

"*Donkor,*" I asked. "*Does Jabare still live?*"

He wouldn't meet my eyes.

The chief gripped Donkor's shoulder. "*Answer when the Moswen's grandchild speaks to you. He continues to show you mercy when you've betrayed him. You'll never climb the ancestor tree to heaven if you—*"

"*Honored Moswen's grandchild.*" Donkor lifted a sullen face. "*I am not worthy of my Carani kin nor to ascend the ancestor tree. But as you've shown mercy, I plead that you show it again. Forgive me. Let me be your servant through this life so I may dwell with my family in the coming life.*"

"He's dead, isn't he?" My eyes stung. Jabare was the best of my Carani kin.

Donkor shook his head and dropped his gaze to the ground again.

The chief laid a hand on my arm. "*Jabare lay in a fever for five days, and to our shame, Donkor refused to tell us what happened. When Jabare woke, he spoke the truth Donkor hid. Jabare is alive and healing.*"

Relief expanded through my chest. "Elise, Jabare's alive!"

She looked up from cleaning my wound. "We are truly blessed."

I turned back to Donkor. "*Thank you for saving him and me.*"

Donkor's eyebrows pinched in puzzlement. "*You thank me when I tried to kill both him and you?*"

I grimaced. "*Many others have tried to kill me, and none of them helped afterwards. You had better reason than the rest, because I'd deceived your village.*"

The chief gripped my arm. "*You made no deceit. You are of the Moswen's line and goodness. Please, forgive us. We will take you to your home and people. I hope, in time, we may be worthy of our*

Moswen's return." He pulled out a flask. "*This is for your brother and you until we can bring more.*"

He'd brought the duri. I raised my eyes to heaven and mouthed a prayer. *Thank you. I don't know how to pray like my brother does, but thank you.*

The chief thrust the flask in my face. "*Drink, then we must flee. The skin carvers will follow. They expect us to return to our village, but we go to the sea. We set false trails yesterday.*" He poured a small amount in my mouth.

It was as awful as before. I swallowed. I needed the strength.

54

ELISE

Ocean cliff, Upper Carani
Mars 4th

Two day's hard riding brought us to the ocean. Steep cliffs led down to a narrow beach and rolling surf. We'd not seen the Carani, so the false trails must have worked. We were safe. Halavant was alive.

I glanced at Halavant to make sure of the fact.

We'd been too late to rescue him before the fight. We didn't know where he was imprisoned in the maze of cells. We found wild beasts and prisoners bearing scars of many fights. Then he was up on the field fighting Nkosi. Each roar from the crowd left me trembling in a sweat. Would I ever get to hear his voice again or see his mischievous grin? Life would be colorless without him.

I glanced at Halavant again. He dismounted and leaned on two of the village warriors. His leg pained him, but thankfully hadn't caught an infection, because I had no herbs and only boiled water to clean it.

Gaven was useless at this point. Our days in the Carani city had driven him over the edge of sanity. He either mumbled nonsense or fell stone-quiet.

Halavant was still sane, though quieter than he'd ever been. He spoke kindly to me when I tended to him, with few words, and then he turned his thoughts inward. What had he endured when we were separated?

He talked with the village chief, then turned to me. "They'll lower us down the cliff with ropes. Several boats hide in a cave at the bottom. Each is only big enough for four. They'll take Gaven back to the village and send two of their warriors to help us back to Lansimetsa."

"How did they do all this and rescue us?"

Halavant half grinned. "They've always kept boats here for the times they raid their upper-land cousins."

"Oh."

Halavant laughed.

"Will Gaven be all right?"

"You remember him saying he would happily settle with the villagers—"

"—if it wasn't for the bugs," I finished for him.

"Bugs or not, he needs someone to care for him until he regains his right mind."

"And what about you? Who will care for you with Gaven gone?"

"I have my right mind and," he winked, "a goddess watching over me."

My face grew hot. "Halavant. I am nothing of the sort."

Lines of worry creased the chief's face as he urged us to hurry.

We'd found the cure. We needed to get it back to Yosyph. The Carani were pursuing us. I pushed my confused thoughts back behind more urgent ones. I'd have plenty of time on the boat to sort them out.

A towering village warrior bound a rope around my waist and under my rump, then stepped back two strides and wrapped the rope from his hand to his elbow and back. He pulled back so there wasn't any slack between him and me.

Another warrior lifted me under my arms and held me over the edge of the cliff.

I stifled a scream. Wind blew up into my skirts, and the ocean crashed below.

Halavant stood at the edge, facing me. "He said to put your feet against the cliff side, lean back, and walk down. He'll keep the rope taut so you don't fall."

I kicked my feet against the cliff and then pulled them back tight against my stomach.

"Elise. You can do this."

The warrior started to bring me back to solid ground.

I was slowing everyone down. I kicked out my feet and leaned back against the warrior's grip. My feet scrambled for a moment against the stone, then I set them.

The warrior released his grip on me.

I screamed. The rope held taut between me and the bracing warrior. I walked backwards down the cliff. Each step came easier until it was like going down a ladder from my loft bedroom at home. Easier, until I glanced downward—jagged rocks glistened below. My feet slipped out from me. I pushed off with my hands before my face met rock.

Halavant and two others descended. The two warriors stayed right by his side, with one hand each held out to help him if needed. Halavant didn't walk down, but pushed away from the cliff in short bounds. Each time he jumped away from the cliff he fell a couple yards to the right, away from his injured hip. He'd catch up to me soon.

I pushed myself away from the cliff like he did and fell a yard before my feet touched stone again. My ears pounded with my pulse, but I was unharmed. I leaped down the remaining portion of the cliff. At the bottom, I pulled the rope from me and huddled into a ball to let my trembling subside.

Halavant kneeled behind me and wrapped his arms around my shoulders. He whispered, his breath tickling my ear, "You were magnificent."

I shook my head. I wasn't. Still, I snuggled deeper into his embrace as the others descended.

Gaven came down strapped to the back of a warrior.

When all but two warriors reached the bottom, the last two tossed the ropes over the edge of the cliff. The ropes smacked against the stones.

"How will they get down?"

Halavant repeated my question, and the chief smiled and pointed. Two figures climbed down the cliff like spiders on a wall. They came down almost as fast as we had with the ropes.

When they reached the bottom, I look to the sea. Men carried small boats over the stony beach and lay them at the ocean's edge where the surf washed against their sides. Then they carried out bundles from a cave. Supplies? Clothes? Halavant needed something better to protect him from the elements than the wrap-around cloth the chief gave him. We had several weeks of sea voyage ahead of us, if the village warriors knew how to get there. I only knew Lansimetsa was north of Carani, and I didn't know how to sail or navigate on the sea.

Stop it. Halavant hadn't fallen to doubts. Why should I? What would he say? We were together again. We'd made it this far. We'd make it the rest of the way. I looked up into Halavant's face. "Thank you."

He jerked his head up with surprise. "For what?"

"For never losing hope."

He closed his eyes and whispered. "I tried not to, but it was hard when you weren't there."

I had to tell him. Let him think I was a fool to feel so. I touched his cheek. "Halavant, I know you loved Lady Katrin enough to give up everything for her. I know I'm nothing more than a poor farm girl who knows some herb lore. But I am willing to give up everything or become anything for you. If I can just be your healer—"

"Elise, you are much more than my healer. I don't want you any different, but I do want you."

I laughed as tears trickled into my upturned mouth.

He leaned in and kissed me.

A trilling cheer erupted around us. The village warriors stopped where they were working and filled the air with their celebration trills.

I'd thought my first kiss would be more private. I turned to hide my face in Halavant's embrace, and he held me closer. We'd make it back. We had to. I had a lifetime to live with him.

55

KATRIN

IT HAD BEEN MORE than a week since Yosyph woke, ordered a chair made, and started spending his days out amongst the people. They loved him, at least some of them. He seemed to grow stronger with each day, though he regained none of his lost movement. Did his god strengthen him only to wear him thin and let him die as soon as his purpose was supposedly fulfilled?

I plunged my hands deeper in the soapy water of the public washhouse and scrubbed the linen shirt until it should have had a hole. I'd braided my hair into a tight braid and hid it under a washer woman's rags. My shapeless dress stuck to my sweaty back. I'd tinted my skin several shades darker. The dye would fade in a few days. I could have come to this workhouse in the shadow-walk. I could enter the shadow-walk easily and exit it with the help of any human tears—and that I could find in abundance. But I needed information I could only ask as a visible person.

I shifted my feet further from the fire burning beneath the wash trough, leaning forward to scrub the clothes. Every few minutes, I'd shift my feet closer to the fire to ease my back, and away again when they grew too hot.

Where was she? The royal spies reported of a woman who had information on Egvar and his movements that could lead to his capture, but she was a timid creature and would only speak to another woman. No one thought a woman spy was important, so I took on the role. I was safer than most. I could slip into the shadow if trouble appeared. Yosyph only agreed after I promised to take a disguised guard to stand watch outside the washhouse. I had more use than to act as Yosyph's scribe or be his nursemaid, especially since he refused to rest.

Several other women scrubbed at the hot trough of water. None of them wore the token brown-and-red-striped rag bandage on her left arm.

Their chatter was inane.

"Did you see the butcher who arrived yesterday with the other stragglers from the far west?" said a woman, holding aloft a huge dripping shirt. "He makes this look small on him. And he doesn't have a wife to wash it for him."

"Hm-mmm," murmured another woman, "looks like good material. You better snag him up quick."

"No. Not my type. I like the more refined coachman."

"Which one?"

"Any. They all look fine in their tailored clothes."

They talked as empty-headed as any noble lady. Only the objects of their gossip changed.

A pock-marked woman joined in. "I'll take any man who can get me a meal at the end of the day, and I don't have to come scrubbing here."

"That's what Stina did, though all it got her was a child and a missing husband."

"Where is Stina?" asked the first woman. "She's never missed before."

"Who knows? Seeking another husband, one who will stick around?"

"She's too pretty for her own good." The pock-marked woman glanced at me. "All the pretty ones go bad."

I ducked my head and scrubbed harder.

"Ah, Stina," called the first woman, "you finally decided to come. The new lass has taken over your pile; you'll have to split the work and pay with her."

A young woman came to stand beside me. Work hadn't yet destroyed her smooth, oval face or dulled her sea-blue eyes. Her shapeless dress couldn't hide her full, rounded belly. She wore drab, yellowed whites and the only other color was a red and brown cloth around her left arm that matched the red and brown cloth I'd tied about my waist—the fabric she'd given the spy to be a sign I was her contact.

I stepped aside to make room for her by the pile of clothes, and whispered, "Come with me now and—"

She grabbed my hand under the soapy water and squeezed hard. "Not here. The gossips hear everything." Then she placed a hand to her baby-full belly and moaned, then between moans she hissed. "Tell them you will help me lie down somewhere."

"The poor girl can't work today," I announced. "I'll finish her work for her, after I find her a place to rest."

"Better you than me," scoffed the pock-marked woman. "She'll never return the favor."

The other women watched us leave with mixed expressions of disinterest and eagerness for more gossip.

We left the steaming room and entered the alley between the washhouse and the weavers' workhouse. The girl pulled me to sit beside her on a couple of busted barrels against the back wall.

I reached out and patted her hand. "I can take you to safety now. You nor your child will ever want again."

She kept her head down as I spoke. Her fingers knotted into fists as she moaned again.

"Can you walk? You need a midwife. I'll pay for it. I have plenty of coin. Come." I put my arm under hers and tried to lift her.

"Give me a moment," she said through gritted teeth. "I must still tell you my message."

"What is it?"

"Sir Egvar seeks Lady Katrin's life." The girl looked up with unpained amusement.

I shoved my emotions to the surface, clawing them out from the center of me.

Thumping boots came around the corner.

Panic clung to the underside of my skin. I pushed. It grew, spreading under all my skin from my forehead out to my fingers and down my spine to my toes.

Men with drawn swords entered the alley.

I tried to picture water washing off all my emotions. Most of them floated away, leaving panic clinging like a thousand leeches. My world narrowed to a dark tunnel. A fleck of light flickered at the end.

A rich tenor voice chuckled. "So you were trying to become a shadow demon again. You are lovely even in spirit-like transparency. Can a spirit die? I'll enjoy finding out."

The tunnel closed as hands lifted me, and I fell into a stupor.

∾

WATER!
Drowning!
"Help!"

A woman's scoffing voice cut through the darkness. "Aren't you a trembling wisp? Why the lord wants you cleaned up is beyond me."

I had to think. I needed to. I'd die if I didn't. I'd drown. "Help!"

Fingers yanked through my hair, pulling my head under the water, then back out.

I gasped for air. My eyes flew open. I lay in a tub of hot sudsy water. My emotions clung to my skin like a crystal shell. *Please help!* I prayed, teetering on the edge of the black abyss, then fell backwards into the enveloping panic. It tightened around my neck and chest. I'd die. And then my world ripped. Everything poured in: relief, love, hope, joy balanced out the darker emotions and filled me, pushing panic to its minor spot.

The woman cursed and stepped away from me.

How? A full bath of water, maybe some of my own panicked tears, or because I wasn't fully in the shadow-walk—whatever the reason, I was free of that darkness. But not of danger. I laughed and cried as my emotions settled. Then in one mighty shove, I shed my emotions and entered the shadow-walk.

I stepped from the tub.

Curses poured from the woman as thick as the water poured from me. I grabbed the robe that lay over a chair and wrapped it around me. It disappeared against my skin. I'd find better clothes, but for now, I needed to hide before the woman came to her senses. I wrapped a towel around my hair, catching most of it. A wet trail would do little for hiding.

The woman lunged for a bell string and pulled it again and again. The door burst open, and armed men rushed in. I dashed to a corner far from my trailing wet spots. A window sat ajar to let out the steam.

The men spread out, fanning their arms wide to find me.

I rammed the window upward, hopped through the opening, and landed on a small ledge. Another floor of windows sat below me, and below that, shrubbery. I jumped. Hands thrust through the open window grabbing at the space I'd been moments before.

The shrubs caught me with their thorns. I left long snags of my hair in them, a trail of bright red against the green. My pricked skin added dots of blood to the red of the hair. I had to keep moving. My wet body numbed in the spring cold.

"Find her!" Egvar stood at the window, staring down at the battered bushes.

I ran faster, my feet stinging with the sharp, cold pebbles, as armed men poured from the country manor house. Which noble was hiding him on their estate? It couldn't be far from Fairhaven. I couldn't have been in the darkness of panic for more than a day. I still had too much energy to have starved for long.

The long, tree-lined lane stretched westward, toward the evening sky. Less than a day. And a brick archway showed the walled entrance. It would have the name of the manor. I'd be able to tell Galliard and Yosyph where Egvar hid.

Dogs bayed.

I tore down the gravel lane. My invisibility had no defense against their noses.

Hounds bounded across the green. I stretched my stride. My lungs burned. The towel dropped from my hair.

The distance closed between the hounds and me, the gate still many breaths ahead. Too far.

The hounds stopped and tore at the fallen towel.

I stumbled forward again, trying to regain my pace.

Men yelled at the hounds.

The gate loomed ahead. An open working of brass bars and scrolls wide enough for a child to slip between. I shed the bathrobe and shoved it between the bars, then tried to follow.

The bars bit cold against my wet skin. I blew out my breath to make my chest narrower. Still the bars stopped me.

A quick glance back showed men beating the dogs from the towel and urging them toward the gate.

I pulled from the gate, backed away from the brick wall, then ran and leaped against its rough face. My fingers and bare toes scrambled for a hold. Then with more speed than skill, I grabbed the wall above me and pulled. Grab, pull, grab, pull.

The first hounds reached the gate. They howled, scrambling to get to the bathrobe that lay on the other side.

I grasped the top of the wall and rolled on top. A long road led through the just-green fields of winter wheat. I shivered uncontrollably. I had to find clothes, or at least shelter from the cold.

Men opened the gate and sent the hounds bounding down the road.

Escape would not be that way. I walked along the top of the wall, beating my arms against my side to gain warmth. How long before the hounds came back to the wall and picked up my scent? I came to the corner of the estate and turned right. Three thatched huts sat a short run from the wall. The field serfs. I could sneak into a hut and steal some clothes, then make my way back to Fairhaven.

I hung from the top of the wall and dropped to the cold ground. Stubble from last year's crop cut my feet. The first hut glowed through its crooked shuttered window. The other two were dark, their occupants probably fled. Was it better to sneak into an occupied or a deserted one? I needed warmth.

I undid the latch of the glowing hut and entered.

A thin woman hunched beside a bed, looked up with startled eyes. "Blast that latch. The spring wind seems to have fingers to lift it. Johnny, go close it."

A little boy hopped up from beside the fireplace and rushed to close the door.

I stepped to the fire. The warmth sent prickles over my cold skin.

A slack-faced man lay in the bed. His breath came in wheezing coughs.

When they slept, I'd find some covering, and when I returned to Fairhaven, we'd send soldiers to take Egvar—if he stayed at this hiding place.

For now, I must get warm. It would be a long night.

56

YOSYPH

Palace, Fairhaven, Lansimetsa
   Mars 12th

Not even God's peace could touch my consuming worry. Katrin tried to be a spy two days ago, but her guard was found dead, and no one knew where she was.

Please, God. I sent my prayer heavenward yet again. *Help us find her. Protect her. Where is she?*

No answer other than a calming peace.

I shoved away the peace. I didn't want to be comforted. I wanted her safe. If I'd chosen to keep my shadow ability, I could have gone after her.

Just show me where she is, I demanded.

Nothing, and the peace didn't return.

Makkara entered the room. "The nobles have gathered. You shouldn't keep them waiting."

"Have General Galliard speak with them."

"If you desire to retain your power, you must gain their trust and respect."

"I don't want this power. I never did."

"If you want your brother to still be king when he returns, you will go. They are ready to listen. That will change if you don't give them as much attention as you have the common people."

Halavant might never return. Even if he didn't, I wouldn't let my people fall without trying to keep them together. "I'm coming."

Eight guards surrounded me as a servant wheeled my chair to a carriage. A short ride through the noble's part of Fairhaven brought us to the council hall. I'd not met there yet, preferring the smaller rooms in the palace. Today required the vast seating of the hall. Many of Lansimetsa's eight hundred nobles sat in the round, three-tiered chamber. Any of noble blood, whether he'd kept his land through wise enterprise or lost it to gambling, bunched together on the wooden benches. One break in the crowding divided the blooded nobles from the newly knighted commoners. It would take time for that line to disappear. Even time wouldn't erase it if they didn't learn to treat the new nobles with respect.

Or, a divine thought whispered, *if the new nobles don't respect the old ones.*

I've written what you've asked me to speak. And I'll speak it. Do not bother me, unless you show me where Katrin is.

My child. I will. Be patient and trust.

It was more than God shared with me before. I wanted answers, but I would wait. I should not have spoken to my God so. But—no more buts. I took a deep breath and motioned for my servant to wheel me to the throne.

As I was lifted from the chair to the throne, a herald proclaimed, "All rise for his royal highness and regent, Yosyph, eldest son of King Luukas. All hail Regent Yosyph."

Those in the room rose, if only to get a better look at me. Hundreds of voices overlapped. "All hail Regent Yosyph."

As they settled back into their seats, I motioned for the servant to lay the top sheaf of manuscript paper in my lap. The words, formed from lessons taught in dreams and many months of studying histories and other tomes, lay across the page in Katrin's flourished script.

I coughed at the tightness in my throat. *I can't do this. Someone else must read it.*

Read. A gentle command. *I will strengthen you.*

"I am—" My voice came out a low whisper.

The nobles closest to the throne leaned forward, while the rest seemed unaware I'd spoken.

"I am dying." This time my voice carried through the room. "I have the slow wasting that took the life of my father and his father before him. I imagine this pleases some of you. Do you think it is time for a new line of kings?"

The room was a mixture of down-turned faces and approving nodding.

I waited a moment and said, "I agree."

This time, surprise rippled through the gathering.

I leaned forward. "It time for a new line of rule. One I plead with you to help build."

More surprised murmuring.

"You were raised to be leaders, to be overseers of large farms and markets, to organize troops to protect our nation—until the old queen reduced or removed many of these powers from you. Your fathers made decisions that impacted the lives of hundreds underneath their protection. Now you must make decisions that will determine if you retain this powerful stewardship or lose it to a dictator."

"Aye!" shouted out a young man in a blue velvet hat. "You speak like a true king. We've been fooled by Egvar's—"

"Hush, lad." A middle-aged man in subdued grays cuffed the youth across the shoulder.

My servant placed the next sheet of manuscript in my lap.

I glanced at it. The words were burned into my memory. I spoke without reading. These I agreed with. "It is time for a new way of ruling. One by law and not by the whim of a king's indigestion or a queen's spite. I have written a code of laws. Many of them are already in practice, but have been changed from time to time by the current ruler. I would have you help form laws even the king must obey, that will protect you from a ruler taking away your god-given rights."

"Aye!" This time, several others added their enthusiasm to the young man's.

The gray-clothed man stood and inclined his head.

I nodded for him to speak.

He leaned on the half wall that separated him from the lower level seats. "You've mentioned a new line of rule. Who will rule, if not your bloodline? And what will hold him to these laws? Furthermore, what are the laws?"

I nodded. "Sir, what is your name and position?"

"Sir Eemeli. My estate is along the western sea. I am one who did not take part in the Slave War, and I would avoid another if possible."

"Sir Eemeli, I will answer your last question first, then your other questions."

My servant shuffled through the papers for the ones with the laws.

I shook my head for him to be still and spoke from memory.

First: Anyone who murders will be executed.

Second: Anyone who commits violence that causes injury to another will repay double the income lost due to the injury. If the injury is permanent, then the accused must make a monthly stipend to the injured for a year. If the injury is to a mother, they will pay for a servant to aid her in her duties until she has healed or a year's time, whichever comes first.

Third: Anyone who steals from or defrauds another will repay double the amount lost.

Fourth: Anyone who causes loss of a neighbor's property—be it land, animal or building—through their own negligence, will work to repair or repay the loss in full.

Fifth: Any man who forces himself upon a woman will pay her a dowry price.

There were several gasps at this.

Sixth: A slanderer will go from door to door proclaiming his falsehood and the good name of the one slandered.

Seventh: None will be restricted from learning to read or furthering their skill or education, based on their own willingness to put in the work outside of their duties. Schools will be provided and funded by the crown for any who desire to learn.

Eighth: A servant or a serf is not a slave. A servant or serf by result of debt, will be given a fair income—decided by a judge and based on their service—to repay the debt, and is free to go once the debt is paid. An un-indebted servant or serf will also be given a fair income, based on their area of service, and may leave the service of his master and find labor elsewhere. Children of servants or serfs have a choice to take up work for their parents' master and are not responsible for their parents' debt.

Protests erupted around the room.

I pressed on, raising my voice above the clamor.

Ninth: Apprentices are bound to serve and learn the craft of their master for the agreed years. If one leaves before his bound time is up, he may set up his own trade, but he must repay his master for the time and skill given him.

Tenth: A master is free to send away any serf, servant or apprentice, without needing to prove cause, but he will provide three days' worth of coin so they may eat while they find new work.

Grumbling rolled through the room. I expected that.

The laws apply to all; man or woman, commoner or king.

The rumble grew to a thunder of protests. Some jumped up to leave. I'd had the doors barred so they'd hear me out. It could come back to haunt me, but I needed them to be here to the end, even if they hated me for it. After long moments and many door-guards' urgings to sit down and listen, the room settled.

"I understand you want a voice on which of these become laws. I will pass none into law without the royal council's approval, of which about fifty of you are part. And there will be no meeting about it until after this war is over. Before I meet with the royal council on these laws, I will call all the nobles together again to have a voice in a meeting similar to this one. For now, let me finish, and move onto things pertaining to the immediate protection of our land."

The room fell to a listening silence.

All who desire justice to be brought against another will take his case before a judge and jury made of half commoners and half nobles. The accused is presumed innocent unless a majority of the jury finds him guilty.

A relieved sigh came from one feathered dandy. How many of the proposed laws had he broken? And did he think he could get away with it in a court of that jury? It was less likely at first that anyone would be convicted with the divided jury. Over time, it would lead to more equal justice.

Lastly: Any who is proven to give false testimony in court will be branded on the right hand to warn others of his deceit.

The nobles were in enough shock they didn't respond much to this last one.

It was time to answer Sir Eemeli's other questions. "You asked: who will rule, and what will hold him to these laws? I don't know how much longer I will live. My physician says maybe a year. I don't know when King Halavant will return. If he doesn't and I die, neither of us have an heir. I believe the time of the kings is passed. It is time for a leader who is chosen by the people and may be removed by the people, both noble and commoner, a leader responsible to the people and held to the laws approved by the people."

I licked my dry lips. I'd been speaking more and longer than I'd ever done before. A jug of water sat to my left. My servant poured me a drink and held it to my lips.

I was so helpless I couldn't lift a cup to drink. I could only speak. They appeared to be listening. "To start, we need to be united. That is what I am attempting to do with laws that apply to all. Lansimetsa's strength is in its people, and we come from many lands. We are giant-blooded, Truvian, Kishkarish, and even Carani. We are the many parts of a great whole and each bring strength, wisdom, courage and beauty. We are one, and if we cannot be one, we will fall. I hope for a future where we all treat each other with respect, whether servant or lord, no matter their heritage—but forgive me, I wander."

Sir Eemeli chuckled dryly.

"Egvar or Pulska will attack soon. We need those with military experience to form the rest of the people into companies of hundreds. We need others to manage the logistics of feeding a city under siege. We need entertainment to keep the evils of cramped boredom at bay. You will work side by side with those you've only seen as animals to carry out your wishes. For us to win against the gathering forces against us, we must communicate and plan and work together. Let us preserve the liberty of our people and your children. Let us make it a land they will praise your names for."

Silence.

I mustered as much sincerity as I could. I wanted them to work with me, even if they were getting away with too much power. "Who is with me?"

Silence.

Then the young man who'd called me a true king stood and doffed his cap. "Aye. I'm with you to the end. And we still need kings. We need you."

A murmur of agreement rippled through the room and grew until a third of the men stood and vowed their allegiance. The rest wore a mixture of expressions of shock, thoughtfulness and anger. Some of them would flee Fairhaven to join Egvar, but it was better they left than stayed to cause havoc within our city walls.

I closed my eyes, bone weary. *I've done what You've asked. Please, tell me where Katrin is.*

A knock carried through the council chamber.

The door-guard waited for my nod, then answered.

A messenger entered, bearing the queen's crest emblazoned on his chest. He carried a small package.

Please God, this can't be the answer. "Let him approach."

The messenger sneered from the base of the throne, even though two guards had spear points inches from his chest. "A message and a present from her highness, the Queen of Lansimetsa, to the Shadow Demon tyrant." His voice carried through the room with the clarity of a herald. "Behold," he unwrapped the package and pulled from it long locks of curling red hair, then a blood stained handkerchief.

No! You promised you'd show me where she was. Not her death!

The messenger's sneer widened. "The Queen offers a trade. A kingdom for a maiden. You've often said you don't want the kingdom, and the maiden loves you. The Queen will even send you to your desert lands where you'll never bear the ill-suited burden of ruling. You could live your last year in peace. She offers greater leniency than you showed her."

She'd never keep her promise. But Katrin could still be alive. What could I say to keep her living? "Give me a day to consider."

The messenger shook his head. "You must make your decision this hour, or your precious Katrin will begin to lose bits of her lovely body, starting with her fingers."

An image of my friend's foreshortened fingers blazed before my eyes. He was one of many the queen used that tactic on. But I couldn't hand over the kingdom to her, nor could I let Katrin lose her life to slow torture. "Return in an hour, and I'll have my answer."

"I'll wait here for my answer and depending on your hospitality I'll deliver it with haste."

I motioned to one guard. "Get him food and drink and a chair."

I closed my eyes and turned my thoughts heavenward. I had

no more anger, only pleading need. *Dear God, I need your help and guidance. I need your miracles.*

The peace of the last few days, that I'd oft rejected, returned. *Trust me, my child.*

What should I do? I asked.

What could you do, that is honorable?

I will not give the old queen the throne.

Then what?

I trembled. *I could give myself in exchange for Katrin.*

And who will rule, if you do?

You've taught me a way of judges and chosen leaders. I've recorded it. Galliard and Makkara are wise and would keep the people together. I bowed my head further. *So this is the answer. I will die now instead of in a year. But Katrin will live and Lansimetsa may grow into a land of freedom. Thank you for letting me be an instrument in your hands. Soon I will see you.*

I opened my eyes. "I have your answer."

The messenger looked up from his goblet of wine. "So quickly?"

"I offer my life in exchange for Katrin's. The former queen may try to take Fairhaven and Lansimetsa, but it is not mine to give. It belongs to the nobles, merchants, peasants, and even servants. They will decide who rules them. However, if one more hair of Katrin is harmed, I make my last royal order that the former queen be shot on sight. She is a murderess, and I was wrong to deny justice before."

The messenger blanched.

"Now go. I will be outside the main gate at dawn tomorrow."

The messenger scurried from the room.

As the door slammed behind him, one by one the nobles of the room stood, held their caps to their hearts, and bowed.

Makkara came from a seat nearest the throne. "My King, I

believe I speak for all here. We will work to create the kingdom you envisioned. Who will lead with you gone?"

I motioned Galliard forward. "I recommend General Galliard and Lord Makkara to lead while you defend against the coming attacks and create a new ruling, but when it comes time to choose a leader by the voice of the people, then it will be whoever you chose as a whole. I've recorded the many details to this new way of ruling."

Galliard leaned near me and whispered. "You can't go. We'll find another way. We need you here."

I shook my head. "My part is done. It is your turn."

57

KATRIN

Edge of the royal forest before Fairhaven, Lansimetsa
Mars 13th

Open land stretched between the trees where I stood and the city of Fairhaven. The last two days were a blur of cold, hunger, and exhaustion. Now it was the coldest part of the night, the hour before dawn. My hands turned blue, but at least I could see them.

That first night at the serf's cottage, when the man, woman and child slept, I pulled on the man's discarded wool over-tunic and boots. He wasn't using them while sick in bed. Then I wiped tears from the sleeping woman's cheeks. After I pulled back my emotions, I had a harder time arguing the rightness of my theft. But the boots protected my feet, though I stuffed them with leaves to keep them from sliding off my feet with each step, and the tunic lessened the chill. I'd send them ten times the repayment.

I didn't stay the night at the hut. I couldn't. This would be one of the first places Egvar would search. I ran through the fields to a densely wooded section, climbed one tree, crossed its branches to another tree and another until I was far from the first tree.

It worked. When hounds picked up my scent, they bayed at a distant tree while men searched with torches. I was far enough that I couldn't hear the men's voices, only see their flames. They eventually gave up and left me to the forest sounds and darkness —and cold.

For two days, I trudged across the thawing forest, scrambled up trees when the hounds' bays echoed on the winter wind, drank from icy streams, gnawed at frozen berries, and slept in snatches of shivering. Now Fairhaven lay an hour's run from the forest. Egvar could be watching the city.

I shed my emotions, entered the shadow-walk, and stepped out from the trees. The road would have the most scents of animals and other people. I jogged along it, too tired to sprint. The gates would be barred, but I could climb the wall. I wouldn't wait for the morning.

The wall loomed up in the darkness.

I fell forward, tumbling down a steep embankment and landing in a slush of partly frozen mud.

I'd forgotten. One defense was a ditch dug around the whole outer wall. Even if I climbed up the other side, I'd be blocked by sharpened pickets and then the stone wall, which now was smoothed with cement. Yosyph was thorough in his planning.

I scrambled back the way I'd fallen.

I'd wait at the gate until it opened. Calling for the guard to open would show Egvar where I was, if he watched.

I huddled in the corner of the gate archway, trying to keep away from the wind. I'd be more sheltered in the ditch, but I didn't know if I could make the climb out again.

The sky began to lighten.

I pulled my arms and legs inside the tunic. My legs cramped

from crouching with just my booted feet touching the ground. It was less cold than sitting.

A loud sliding resonated from the other side of the gate. The cross bracing? They were opening the gate. I wouldn't have to wait as long. Good.

The gate opened, and a block of soldiers marched through. They must have been on some practice maneuver. When the last row of them passed through the gate, I slipped inside as the gate closed.

I was inside the city but not necessarily safe. Egvar's men took me while in Fairhaven. I'd make my way to the palace before talking with anyone. I gathered my strength to run again.

Yosyph's deep voice rang out from the other side of the gate. "I've come to exchange my life for Lady Katrin's."

"Yosyph," I yelled. "I'm in the city."

"Katrin?"

Cries of pain shattered the morning's stillness.

Another voice commanded. "Protect the Yorel! Open the gate!"

The gate swung open and the block of soldiers double-time marched through. The end of their block was a ragged, gapping line of staggering men. Arrows followed them through the gate and rattled against the street when they didn't hit flesh.

The gate clanged shut.

Yosyph commanded, "Let Lady Katrin through."

"They can't see me. I'm in the shadow state."

"Of course you are." His voice was weary. "Are you hurt? Can you come to me?"

"I'm not hurt, and I can, if the soldiers will part."

They parted slightly.

I slipped sideways between them.

Yosyph sat in his wheeled chair. Soldiers held shields around him, but parted enough for me to see his face.

I reached through the shields and touched his cheek.

He crumpled into sobs.

I'd only seen him cry twice before, and never like this. "Yosyph. I'm unhurt." I dampened my fingers with the tears that ran down his cheeks and pulled back my emotions.

The soldiers startled back, far enough for me to plant myself in Yosyph's lap.

I kissed him. I didn't care who saw.

"Katrin," Yosyph said through his tears. "You're the most beautiful sight I've ever beheld."

I laughed. "You're no good at flattery. A truer statement would be the most mud-covered, leaf-haired forest monster you've ever beheld."

A soldier coughed. "Honored Yorel, we should get you back to the palace. The barrage of arrows means they have an army hidden nearby."

"Yes." Yosyph bowed his head. "The battle will start soon. And God has preserved my life again. I don't know for what purpose."

I stroked his cheek. "Because they need you. And even if they didn't, I do."

58

HALAVANT

A DARK LINE of land grew into a stony beach, backed by a forest and speckled with small stone houses plus a few fishing boats. It looked like Lansimetsa. Even if it wasn't, maybe the inhabitants could sail us the rest of the way. Our small boat shuddered as it rolled over the last of the surf into the smaller beach waves. Elise gripped my arm and gave me a tight smile. Our boat scraped the sandy bottom. After twelve days on the ocean, we'd made it.

An old woman came to the door of her hut as our two Carani friends pulled the boat up on the beach. Her hand flew to her mouth. She darted back into her hut and slammed the door.

I suppose we were a sight. We were a bunch of foreigners washed up on the beach. Even Elise wore two village wraps over her travel-worn dress.

I gave Elise an arm from the boat, then followed her. "*Mido, Montu, I'll speak with the old woman.*"

Montu nodded towards the forest. *"I'll get us fresh meat. You've not eaten well enough, Moswen."*

"I've eaten better than you."

"We're made for the hardship. But you are always too pale. Like my third child."

I laughed. *"I was born this color. Though the sun has darkened me almost to match you."*

He shrugged and grabbed a spear from the boat. He jogged away while Mido started gathering driftwood for a fire.

Meat and a warm meal would be a luxury—raw fish got old fast. Or maybe the old woman would invite us to dine with her. Maybe.

I put my arm around Elise's shoulder. "Shall we go see if this is our homeland?"

"I hope it is."

I rapped on the door with the side of my braced hands.

A scuffling came from the other side.

"Old woman!" I called through the door.

Silence.

"Is this Lansimetsa?"

Silence.

I rapped on the door again.

"No, and go away." She had the distinctive burr of the coastal Lansimetsians.

We were home. "The Carani are coming, and we must warn the Regent Yosyph."

A bark of laughter. "The Carani are always coming. Go play your pranks elsewhere. War is already here."

War already here? Which noble? Had assassins killed Yosyph? Were we too late?

Elise wrapped her arms around my waist and squeezed. She didn't add her spoken worries on top of mine or try to comfort me with empty words.

I pounded on the door. "Old Woman! This is no prank. We escaped the Carani less than two weeks ago. They are sailing here and may arrive in a week or less. I am King Halavant."

The door opened a crack, and the woman studied me. "So you have returned, and your hands are still broken." She opened the door the rest of the way and hobbled out to a stool. She motioned with her cane to the empty beach and quiet houses. "You should have never left. The land fell apart. The people have gathered to the capital city or a noble's army to reinstate the old queen. All the men of my village left with their families. I am too old to go, and what army will care about one fishing village hag?"

"Is the Yorel still alive?"

"They say he is dying of the *King's Death*, but when the messengers came to warn us to flee to the capital city, he still lived."

A tremor ran down my arms and back. We weren't too late, yet. We had to hurry. "Where can we get horses?"

Her barking laugh turned into a coughing fit. When she'd caught her breath, she shook her head. "Horses? You couldn't find a horse for a king's ransom. So said the messengers when they warned us to go to Fairhaven. Take only what you can carry on your back, said they. And I spat at their feet. I won't go toddling through the countryside with only a cane to support me. I'd first cast off in one of those boats and try my luck for the Truvian islands."

So we'd run the distance. "We will trade for food and be on our way. Do you have traveler's bread or dried fish?"

She tightened her lips and stared out to the sea.

Elise patted the woman's knee. "I could make a rub that will ease the pain in your legs."

The woman's eyebrows shot up. "That would be a mercy."

I left Elise to find the proper ingredients with the woman and went back to prepare our departure with Mido.

Mido had a fire started and was in the middle of setting up canvas shelters.

"Mido, we'll not sleep here tonight."

He smiled. *"The old woman will give us shelter and sleeping mats?"*

"No, we must race to my brother. War stands between him and us."

His smile fell a moment, then he shrugged. *"The forest will be softer to sleep on than these pebbles. I'll call Montu. He can hunt on the way."* He lifted a curved animal horn to his lips and blew a low note.

I crouched by the fire as Mido packed supplies into bundles.

He checked the four sealed gourds of the duri, then nestled them into a four-pocketed bag. He laid a spear and a bundle of rope beside the duri bag.

"Rope?" I asked.

"For the enemies we don't kill."

I shuddered. He'd grown up the warrior. I'd only pretended at it until I fell into war last autumn.

He lay out our leather water pouches, checking the seams. Beside one water pouch, he laid a newly made sling. He'd woven it for Elise after he'd heard our tales of her sling saving my life. Our twelve days at sea were filled with our stories and theirs. It helped turn the time from worries. Elise kept at my side, laughing at my childish humor, being a quiet comfort when I couldn't joke, and occasionally, we stole a kiss when we thought Mido and Montu weren't looking. Elise was still shy about that.

Montu entered the beach bent under the weight of a wild pig. *"Mido, why did you call me? You almost scared away our meal."*

My stomach rumbled at the sight of the pig. *"We must leave today. How long will it take to roast the pig?"*

"*This is a pik? It is a heavy creature, and not fast. If this is the animal of your land, we'll grow fat on my hunting.*" He tested the weight of the creature. "*If we cut it into pieces and build many fires in the stones, we could roast it in an hour.*"

"*Good. We'll carry the meat with us and not hunt unless we must. We will run many days.*"

Montu laid the pig where the waves lapped at the pebble beach and began to gut it, throwing the offals into the water. "*Mido and I can run many weeks. But can you and E-ise?*"

"*We will. We must.*"

Montu glanced up from his work. "*Is it your brother?*"

I nodded.

He glanced at the sky. "*We still have half-a-day of light. Sleep while the pik roasts, and then we will find your brother.*"

Rest? How? Not on the pebble beach with the scent of slow-roasting pig. When I lay down on a piece of canvas with another rolled up under my head, my body remembered what it was to sleep stretched out and on an unmoving bed.

~

WE JOGGED along a road through the forest. The ground rose in a steep slope on one side and fell away on the other. We'd not met anyone since we bid the old woman farewell two days before, though we'd passed two empty towns. She'd sent us with traveler's bread, dried fish, and to the joy of Elise, a small supply of herbs. We left her with the pig meat we couldn't carry and the ointment Elise made for her.

As much as I hated it, a small swallow of the duri gave me energy to run as long as Montu and Mido. Elise refused it, on grounds it should be saved for Yosyph and me. I think she couldn't stomach the smell. Montu and Mido also refused to drink it, for the same reasons Elise gave.

Elise held her side, and her face pinched as we jogged.

I took a ragged breath. "I need to rest for a moment."

Elise put out a hand to steady me.

I wrapped my arm around her shoulder and held her while her breathing evened out.

She looked up into my face, and I grinned.

"Faker," she whispered.

"You wouldn't ask for a break."

"We must hurry."

"We'd go much slower if you passed out and I had to carry you."

She smiled and rested her head on my shoulder. "Only for a moment." She lifted her head and looked about. "There are some winter bush cherries. They would round out our diet and help us keep our strength."

"You rest. Mido and Montu can get them."

She shook her head. "No. A vine of bitter berry wraps itself in with the bush cherries. I don't want them mixed in the picking."

"You know your plants. At least sit while picking."

She slid down the embankment and picked red fruit from waist-high bushes.

I wanted to follow her, but it would mean Mido and Montu pushing me back up the slope to the road, and I couldn't pick anything. I sat down at the edge and watched. She picked through the berries and filled the pouch at her side. Her long braid of black hair swayed with her movement.

Montu scouted ahead while Mido got me water.

A shaft of sunlight cut through the branches. I closed my eyes and lifted my face.

Birds flavored the air with twittering and the occasional branch snapped with animal movements. A distant storm rumbled. We'd want our tarp covers that night. Rapid footsteps pattered along the road.

Montu ran towards us and motioned us off the road. He grabbed one of my arms, while Mido grabbed the other. They jumped over the edge and scrambled down the slope, towing me along with them. I'd have managed better if I'd slid down on my rump.

Elise jumped to the side as we barreled into the bushes.

The four of us burrowed under the bushes and lay still. Elise gripped my arm, and the pulse in her palm beat against me.

The distant sound of thunder grew into the pounding of horses and rattle of armor.

They stopped a short distance past where we'd fled the road.

"Where is he?" a gravelly voice asked.

A higher toned voice with its own hint of arrogance replied, "I'll find him."

"Don't bother. It's just one man. The towns and villages are empty. Our *recruits* won't be much good if we don't get them back to Pulska before our supplies run out. And I'm not scrimping on my rations to fill their bellies."

"The next village is just half-a-day more."

"And that is another full day we must keep this rabble fed. No, I don't care if we are twenty men short of our quota. We're going back now."

"It's your neck," the nasal-voiced man said.

"I'm brother-in-law to Egvar's sister. Pulska won't touch me. Just who do you think is leading this? Pulska is a fat coward, and the old queen is crazy."

"Yet Lord Egvar put you under your *younger* brother, and him under Duke Pulska's command. And they all obey the Queen. She'll have your tongue for suggesting otherwise."

"Not if she doesn't hear."

The slither of metal drawn from scabbards was followed

with a clash of steel on steel. Grunts, clashes and insults ended with the galloping thud of another horse.

"Stop!" This voice silenced the fight. "Brother, why do you fight our best scout?"

Silence and a scuffing. Was one of them shuffling his feet? I'd love to see the faces of the two men—abashed and shaking before this voice of command.

The gravelly-voiced one replied, "We couldn't find the man our scout claimed to have spotted."

The higher-voiced one cut in, "I can still find him. You're just lazy."

"Enough!" This must be the younger brother who commanded them. "We have a week's journey back and only rations for three days. The towns are stripped empty. We'll return on half rations with the fighters we've already gathered."

"See," scoffed the gravelly-voiced one.

A slap of skin on skin silenced his mocking.

The high-voiced one laughed. And another slap, followed by a whimper.

Oh, what I'd give to see the two reprimanded. Too bad the commander was on Egvar's side.

The thumping of trotting horses and rattle of armor died away in the distance, the direction we were heading. They had prisoners they'd compel to fight on Egvar's side. Probably as the front lines, forced forward by the spears of men loyal to Egvar. A horrible tactic used to bolster the strength of our army throughout our history.

Elise let out a breath. "Oh, those poor people."

"I could sneak into their camp tonight and free them."

She shook her head. "No, but maybe Montu could. At least cut their bonds so they have a chance of escape."

Montu grinned when we explained the situation.

~

WE HID outside an encampment of several hundred prisoners, strung out in five lines, either lying on the ground or crouched in a ball. Firelight flickered off the rope running from man to man. Most of their captors slept in thick blankets near fires. Hobbled horses grazed or slept to the north of the camp. The few sentries paced the perimeter, glancing from time to time back to the fires and ruining their night vision. Even I could have freed the prisoners.

Montu slipped forward without a sound, a hunter tracking his prey. His skin and clothes faded into the night. He appeared at the end of one line of prisoners and clamped one dark hand over the prisoner's mouth. Did he remember the words we'd taught him? *Be still. I free you. Don't move until I yell.*

I should have gone to speak to them.

The prisoner stayed silent even after Montu moved to the next one.

Did Montu leave a knife with him? We had only three to give to the prisoners, but with them, they could surprise their captors and gain their weapons.

Montu moved down the line like a shadow.

The prisoners stayed still and silent.

He finished one line and started on a second, and still the sentries didn't notice him.

This would work.

He slipped behind a small man who rocked back and forth.

The man's head jerked.

Montu clamped his hand over the man's mouth.

Please let the man be silent.

Montu moved on to the next man.

The man he'd just freed leaped forward and barreled headlong away from the camp.

A sentry cut him down, then bellowed alarm.

That was enough of a yell for the other prisoners. Those freed ran, some for swords laying next to blanket-wrapped captors and others for the woods. The captors woke groggily, but the prisoners weren't warriors. Even of those who grabbed swords, few swung them with any confidence.

Those not freed tried to run, pulling each other into a tumbling knot.

Montu moved into a knot of prisoners, slashing at the ropes with his serrated knife.

"*Montu, get out of there!*" I yelled as I ran towards him.

Either he couldn't hear me, or he didn't want to.

A sentry charged him with a spear.

I kicked the sentry in the back. A crack rang between my steel-toed boot and him.

Montu glanced up and nodded as he slashed another rope.

Something whistled by me, and a man fell with a grunt. Elise and her sling!

I chopped my braced hand into the shoulder of a groggy swordsman.

He dropped the sword.

A man in a farmer smock snatched it up, then bellowed as he swung it in a practiced arc over his head.

Mido tackled me, and we rolled to the ground as a spear flew through the spot I'd been in.

Mido said something, but it was buried under the bellows, clashes and screams.

"*What!*" I yelled back.

"*Horses!*" he yelled.

I swiped my legs at the feet of a soldier as he swung his blade at Mido.

His sword half-buried itself in the dirt at my side.

Mido pulled me to my feet, then drew out a sling like Elise's. He dropped one man between us and the horses.

Elise's scream cut through the mayhem. She stood with her back to a tree. An arrow stuck from her leg. She slung another stone.

Where was the archer? I spun about, kicking a space clear.

By the only tent, a man drew his bow and shot. The arrow caught Montu in the back.

I ran for the archer as he drew again and aimed for me. I rolled to the ground sideways. The arrow ruffled my hair. I rolled to my feet, running for him.

He reached behind for another arrow and fell backwards, two stones imprinted on his face.

～

THE PRISONERS BECOMING the captors and the dead surrounded us.

I kneeled next to Montu's body. If I had hands that worked, I could help Elise tend the other wounded or bind the cowards who killed my cousin. I raised my voice in the trilling mourning cry of my Carani kin.

Mido matched it across the clearing where he bound men.

Our voices rose in discordant grief.

"Quiet!" cried one freed prisoner. "Others might hear you, and we'll be captured again."

I rose to my feet. Montu gave his life for this coward! I'd teach him to show respect!

Elise laid her hand on my shoulder. "Halavant."

"I will mourn Montu!"

She brushed her hand across my cheek; it came away wet. She raised her voice in the trill beside me.

I joined in. When my tongue grew numb with movement

and my voice cracked in my throat, I sank to my knees next to Montu. "*My cousin and friend, may your golden goddess and your Moswen and whatever other gods there are welcome you into their family for your sacrifice.*"

A freed prisoner in a baker's apron bowed himself before me. "King Halavant."

I glared at him.

He flinched and lowered his gaze. "The captain is awake."

"Good."

The archer who'd killed Montu lay bound, his head bandaged. His nose was bent sideways, and blood crusted his face. He raised his eyebrows, then flinched at the movement.

I stood over him. "Where were you taking these prisoners? Where are the traitor nobles gathered?"

"The traitor shadow demon dwells in the palace, and the traitor prince stands before me."

"I'll not bandy words. You killed a man much better than you, and you will pay for his life with yours."

"Then why should I speak?"

"Because the war that is started between the traitors and the crown will soon be dwarfed by the war coming from across the sea. The Carani will attack. Then it won't matter if my mother is queen or I am king. If we are fighting each other, we will all die."

The man scoffed. "Carani attack? That is what you used last time when you drew away the queen's armies and overthrew her. You have the intelligence of a donkey to think you could fool us twice."

They wouldn't believe me. Even with Mido and — I swallowed. Even with Mido beside me why would they believe another tale of Carani attack? My anger drained away. We had to get to the palace. We had to stop the war amongst our people and prepare them to fight the Carani. If they'd believe me.

I turned away from the captain and to the farmer who'd

shown courage and skill in the fight. "Pick ten men to ride to the palace with me. We leave in the hour."

The chosen men packed the horses with supplies. We'd leave most of the food with the freed prisoners. They'd not eaten well since capture. And if it was only a week's journey to where Egvar camped by a jogging line of prisoners, then by horse, we might make it to the palace soon.

Elise limped over to me. Her leg bandage bloomed with red. "I'm coming, too."

"No. I've asked for a company of men to take you to safety."

She set her mouth in a firm line. "I'm coming, too."

"Elise." I whispered her name. "I didn't think I'd love again, but I do. You want me to take you into the middle of a battle and likely lose you?"

"I'll be safer with you than caught between the capitol and the Carani."

I snorted. Why must she be right?

She kissed my cheek. "I'll be ready as soon as I rebind my leg."

Mido bent over Montu's body, painting vines and flowers on his face and hands with a thin mud.

I kneeled beside him. *"Mido, I leave in an hour to find my brother and try to stop a war. You've done enough. Take Montu's spear and go home to his family. Please take care of them."*

Mido looked up with reddened eyes. *"I'm coming with you. I promised my chief to watch over you. Let me bury my brother and help save yours."*

I nodded around the lump in my throat. One more duty before we left. I called over the farmer, now the captain of my new royal guard. "We'll need all the men who are still able to join us at the palace as soon as they can. We don't have a way to keep the prisoners along the way."

The farmer blanched.

"We won't kill them. Just deprive them of weapons, horses, shoes and supplies. However," I glanced at the bandaged captain, "he's too dangerous. He's a leader, and he'll form more men against us."

The farmer nodded. "I'll dispatch him."

A bound man called out with a gravelly voice, "King Halavant. Have mercy on the captain. He's a good man and my brother."

"He killed a good man and almost killed El—a woman."

"So have many of us. This is war."

The captain deserved to die. He was too dangerous to let free, and we had to hurry. Yet—if I killed him, how was I any different from my mother?

I bowed my head. I'd tie him to a horse and drag the horse along with us rather than that.

"I'll spare your brother's life. But you must swear to not follow us."

"Thank you, sire."

There'd been enough death, and more would come. But not today.

59

ELISE

My leg ached from two days of hard riding. The muscles of my calf knotted around the arrow wound. Halavant wanted me to ride with him or another of his company so I could sit sidesaddle, but two to a horse slowed our pace. So I bit leather and hid my grimaces behind my mess of hair as it fell loose from its braid.

Our scout galloped back to us. "An army lays siege outside Fairhaven. There is no way in."

It was the answer I'd expected. I'd spent the last two days figuring how we'd get past an army into the capitol. One idea seemed less foolhardy than the rest. "Halavant?"

He looked up from a quiet counsel with the scout.

"We have one of their captains. A valuable one, related to Egvar—even if it is only his sister's brother-in-law."

Halavant knit his brows together.

"What if we offer a trade? We trade the captain for our safe passage to the city."

Halavant nodded and moved his horse nearer to mine. "It could work if I weren't king. But he wouldn't trade his own mother for the *traitor king's* safe passage back into Fairhaven."

"He need not know. Someone else can take the message to Egvar. He can say Egvar's captain tried to take our village, and we fought back. Most of our village died, as did many of the captain's men. The rest fled. We found the captain among the dead, and we only want to be allowed to join the other refugees in Fairhaven."

"Even if Egvar agreed to the trade, the captain will tell Egvar who we are before we reach the city wall."

"I'll drug him so he can't speak for a while."

Halavant smiled grimly. "It's good you are on our side."

～

WE RODE north through the parted army.

Our farmer-captain sat astride his horse with the soon-to-be ransomed captain in front of him, holding a knife near the captain's throat. He guided his horse with his knees.

Halavant had removed his hand braces and darkened his hair and skin to almost the tones of Mido's. He wore ragged peasant clothing, the outer layer of another freed prisoner. He looked the refugee.

We all did. Rubbing dirt on our faces and clothes did little to change our already grubby and worn appearance.

No one moved to stop us, though many hands lay on their hilts and at their bows.

We rode beyond the army into the no-man's-land between them and Fairhaven's wall.

Soldiers stood atop the wall. Sunlight glinted off their helmets and shields.

Halfway between the army and the wall, we stopped. We were in arrow's reach of both sides.

I swallowed. Would Egvar keep his promise? Would those along the wall allow us to enter?

If we went further to Fairhaven without releasing the captain, then Egvar had promised to shoot us. That promise he would keep.

Halavant turned to our farmer-captain. "Let him go."

The farmer pulled the knife away from the captain's throat. "Get back to the devil whence you came."

The captain slid from the horse, gave Halavant a haughty look, then stumbled drunkenly away from us back towards Egvar's army.

"Now!" Halavant called.

We all dug our heels into our horses and spurred them into a flat run for the city.

A minute later, when we'd pulled far from the stumbling captain, arrows rained down from behind us.

One struck my back and bounced off the thick bark I'd layered under my dress.

My horse reared, throwing me off backwards. An arrow stuck from his flank.

I lay, gasping breath, until a silhouetted figure pulled me onto his horse.

Halavant rode behind him, putting himself between me and the arrows.

Then we were beyond the range of the arrows and almost to the gate.

"Open!" commanded Halavant. "Your king has returned."

The gates remained shut. I turned. Egvar's mounted archers

loped across the field behind us, and arrows began to fall close again

"Please! Open!" I cried.

A voice called, "It's a woman. Open the porter's gate."

Another voice called. "Take down the enemy."

A small gate, too short for a man on a horse, swung open. Arrows flew overhead against Egvar's archers.

We slid off our horses and ran through the gate and into the safety of Fairhaven. Three of our men were already there. Mido, Halavant, and six others followed. We'd lost our farmer-captain.

～

KATRIN MET us at the palace gate. She ran and wrapped Halavant in a hug. "You're back!"

I stumbled back a step. Why did my fists tighten?

She released him, only to pull me into her embrace. "Elise! I'm so happy you're back, too." She whispered in my ear. "Did you find the cure?"

"Yes."

She buried her face in my shoulder and squeezed me tighter. "Thank you. Oh, thank you."

"How is he?"

She sniffled and released me from her embrace. Her face was covered in my grime. Her smile trembled. "The physician says he has a year. But you found the cure, so he'll get better." She looked about at the rest of our company. Her gaze stopped on Mido.

Halavant clapped Mido on the back. "Katrin, this is my cousin, Mido. He has the cure for the slow wasting—though Yosyph won't like it."

I limped over to stand by Halavant. "He won't complain like you do."

He placed his arm about my shoulders, "My sweet Elise, he never complains."

Katrin lifted her eyebrows. "I see you've found your heart again. Come. We must take it to him now."

"Just a moment," Halavant said. "Elise is hurt, as are some of our men. Yosyph will last an hour longer while their injuries are tended to."

"And yours." I touched his hip. It hadn't fully healed in the weeks since he'd been injured fighting Nkosi.

～

IT WAS many hours before I went to Yosyph, after two changes of bath water, a lightening of my skin to its normal Truvian caramel, and my leg wound getting scrubbed out like a dirty pot. Salve eased the ache of my leg and the bruising from ship tumbles, saddle sores, and falling from my horse. All I wanted was sleep.

A knock on my door woke me. I blinked and stretched. "Yes?"

Katrin spoke on the other side. "Elise?"

I yawned. Halavant and Mido were probably by Yosyph's side, not sleeping away the day.

Katrin stepped back as I opened the door, her hand poised to knock again.

I'd be anxious, too, if Halavant were in Yosyph's position. I smiled an apology for making her wait.

She returned the smile. "Thank you. Halavant and his cousin are with Yosyph, but they said you should be the one to administer the cure." She glanced sideways as I limped beside her. "I'm happy for you and Halavant."

"I'm not... We're not..."

Her laugh caught in her throat. "He looks at you like he once looked at me, but with more depth. He'll marry you."

"I'm sorry."

"Don't be. I love Yosyph. Even if you can't save his life."

"Has it progressed that much?"

"You'll see."

We entered a softly lit room. Yosyph lay a pale shadow of himself on a bed. His dark hair and tattoo lay in sharp contrast with his grayish skin. Halavant sat at the edge of the bed and talked quietly with him. Mido stood against the wall, near a chair with wheels.

A man in a physician's coat in royal servant colors ushered me over to him. "His royal highness explained you've brought a drink that helps strengthen those of the king's bloodline. He believes it will help reverse the slow wasting. How much do we use? We must get the dosage correct. Too much may overwhelm his weak system. Too little—he doesn't have much time left. He's pushed himself more than even a healthy man should, especially since Lady Katrin was captured at the start of the siege. He says his god sustains him, and some divine force seems at work, but it isn't saving him. He's not left his bed for two days. I thought he had a year remaining. Now I wonder if he has a week."

I'd rather start with too little. The healer woman had shown me a small shell, about the size of a tablespoon, when she told me the dose for illness. "We'll start with a teaspoon portion. Mido, the duri."

Mido handed me one of the duri gourds.

I held my breath and pulled out the wax and wood plug.

The room rippled with a collective gasp at the scent, followed with the gag reflex. I should have warned them.

Katrin coughed. "It's gone rancid." Her face crumpled, hope snuffed from it.

I shook my head. "It always smells this way. It will help him, though the scent is enough to kill."

Halavant breathed through his mouth. "I've had it too many times myself and am still alive, and stronger for it."

Yosyph closed his eyes for a long moment. Had he fallen asleep? He looked weak enough to slip unconscious. Then he spoke, his voice stronger than I expected. "I will take it."

I filled a teaspoon with the liquid, then pinched Yosyph's nose. "Swallow quickly." I poured the duri into his mouth.

He retched. The duri came up with a watery bile.

Katrin shoved me aside and held up his head so he could breathe. She wiped the bile away from his mouth. "Yosyph. Yosyph."

He took a few shaky breaths. "Again."

Maybe I could mask it with another strong flavor. They'd never done that for Halavant, and the healer woman told me it made it less effective. Less effective would be more beneficial than none at all. Which flavor? I couldn't keep testing it on Yosyph while he grew weaker with each dose rejected.

"I need wild honey, mint tea, spicy broth, and..." I searched for another strong flavor that might work in a liquid form that Yosyph could take, "a mustard paste."

Servants scurried out for the ingredients.

Halavant caught on the fastest. "I wish you'd thought of that for me."

"You weren't dying." I mixed a tiny part of duri with a large dose of honey, then tasted it. *If bees built their hive in a carcass— How did Halavant or any of his kin take this?*

The mint tea was worse.

The spicy broth helped, or I was getting used to it.

Then the mustard. Yes. It hid the flavor and texture more than the rest.

I mixed one part duri with two parts mustard. He'd only get

a quarter a teaspoon of duri, but if he could keep it down, then I'd give him another dose, as much as he could keep. "I'm ready."

Katrin piled pillows behind Yosyph and held him steady.

Yosyph swallowed, cringed, turned greenish, and kept it down.

I prepared another spoonful.

Yosyph shook his head. "I must drink something before I take more."

The hour passed with Yosyph taking mustard and duri doses between broth and teas. By the end, he sweated with nausea. Altogether, he'd only taken half of what the healer woman said should be given in illness. Yosyph didn't look like he could take another dose.

He slipped into a fitful sleep.

The physician excused himself to catch a few hours of rest. His face sagged with exhaustion.

Katrin slipped her hand into mine. "Will you watch with me?"

I just wanted to sleep. "Yes."

She squeezed my hand.

Halavant came to my other side. "I'll watch, too. Make sure he doesn't slip away on some fool hardy heroics when the duri heals him."

"Exactly." Katrin laughed, though her eyes shone with wetness.

Servants brought in padded chairs.

I sank into one and closed my eyes. My leg throbbed, and my head more so. I'd never take duri again. But let it be strong enough to reverse the effects of the slow wasting, or at least halt it. Please.

SOMEONE SHOOK my shoulder and whispered. "Elise, he's doing better!"

"Good," I mumbled. "Tell me if he's not, and I'll come help."

Katrin's excited whisper didn't stop. "Halavant, wake up, he's doing better!"

Yosyph's weak chuckle came from across the room. "Katrin, they are trying to sleep. Let's enjoy the privacy while we can."

"Yosyph, my Yosyph."

The duri worked. Good. I slipped back into sleep.

～

A NEW DAY brought clarity on Yosyph's condition. He'd lost all movement in his legs and forearms, but he had energy to sit up, which he hadn't the evening before. The duri had helped, and with time, it should help more.

Katrin was all over the room, tending to Yosyph, dancing about from person to person thanking us until I grew weary of her voice.

Mido said something to Halavant, and he burst into laughter.

"What?" I asked.

"He says the red-haired girl moves more than a fire and makes more noise than a long-tailed howler."

Katrin paused. "What is a long-tailed howler?"

Halavant grinned. "A noisy cat-like creature that swings from the trees and likes to throw things at people. Nothing like you."

Yosyph chuckled. "Oh, she can throw a knife well enough."

Katrin frowned. "I sure hope I'm prettier than a tree-swinging cat."

Yosyph straighten his face to a solemn thoughtfulness. "I don't know. I've never seen a long-tailed howler."

Katrin glared at Yosyph then burst into laughter.

Halavant sidled up to me, wrapped his arm around my

shoulders, and whispered. "She climbs a tree as well as one, too. You should have seen her as a child."

I nudged him with my shoulder. "Be kind."

"I am," he protested, then kissed me on the cheek.

I blushed.

We were a sight. Two couples making silly words and actions in the middle of a war. Time had paused in the joy of Yosyph's improvement, but it wouldn't have paused outside these walls. "Halavant, did you tell them yet of the Carani?"

Yosyph answered. "He has. We spoke with Galliard before you woke."

I stopped mixing duri and mustard. "What will you do?"

"Galliard is preparing a message to be sent to the siege armies, warning them of the Carani and inviting any who will lay down their arms to join us in the safety of Fairhaven. Though they will be imprisoned until this war is over, or until the Carani attack and they are willing to take up arms in defense from them."

"Do you think they will listen?"

Yosyph looked down. "No. But I must try."

And I'd do all I could to heal him, so he could keep leading. We needed a leader like him. I finished mixing a dose of duri mustard. "It's time."

60

YOSYPH

I sat in a chair atop the outer wall of Lansimetsa. Guards shielded my front, back and sides, leaving just enough room between man-height shields for me to see the distant tents of Egvar's army. He claimed it to be the queen's, but unless she'd regained her sanity, he was the power behind the gathered men. If they'd only listen to the warning. Otherwise, they'd be caught between the Carani and our wall, and many would die.

It had been little more than a day since Halavant and Elise gave me the cure for slow wasting. It was too foul to be mistaken for a poison. My hands lay in my lap. I twitched a finger. A small movement. One that took full concentration, but still a movement.

Thank you, God, for this miracle of movement and giving me more days to serve my people. I know you won't force any man to your will, but, please, send some way of escape for those who have no choice in being part of Egvar's army.

Black clouds glowered along the southern horizon. A wind whipped against the shields. A gust pushed one guard back a step.

Katrin touched my shoulder. "Yosyph, we should go. They've been warned. Those who listen will come."

If they are allowed. *Please help them.*

The wind stiffened, and my guards grunted with the effort to keep the shields around me.

I nodded. "Return me to the palace."

Our carriage rocked with the wind as we wound our way back through the city. Tiles tumbled from a shop roof and smashed to the ground, spooking our horses.

Katrin gripped my arm as the coachman calmed the horses. "I don't like this wind."

"It will be worse at sea. I remember the pirate captain tying my mother and me to the mast so we didn't wash overboard."

"I'd thank him for it."

"He did it so he wouldn't lose two valuable slaves, not out of any love for us. Though, you are right. Even then, God preserved my life."

"Even th—" She ended her word in a squeak as the carriage tilted sideways then righted itself.

The wind grew to a roar.

The carriage stopped, and a soldier pushed the door open, bracing himself. "The wind is too strong. It will tip over the carriage with the next gust. We must take shelter until this blows over."

Debris-filled air obscured the buildings. "Where are we?"

"Near a market square in the commoner's part of Fairhaven. The tavern looks the most sturdy built. Stay here while we make sure it's safe."

Katrin squeaked again as the carriage jerked forward, rocking side to side, until we stopped in an alley. The wind howled around us but the carriage stopped rocking. Long minutes passed to the screaming music of the wind.

Then hail poured down, rattling against the carriage roof.

The horses screamed, and the coachman bellowed curses.

"Get out," the coachman yelled. "Can't control the horses."

Katrin pushed the carriage door as a guard pulled from the outside. The wind caught it and ripped it from the hinges. The guard reached in, grabbed me under the arms, and pulled me out. Hail beat against shields held over my head. Two more guards strained to keep them there.

Katrin jumped from the carriage as the horses bolted.

The coachman jumped from his perch and rolled into the semi-shelter of the wall.

"Safe or not, we're taking you in," yelled the guard holding my arms.

They carried me through the alley entrance into the building. A long marble bar ran along one wall. I'd polished the bar many times in my youth. The room was once packed with enough round tables I had to turn sideways to get between them when the tavern was busy. Firewood scavengers had long since picked the room clean in search of fuel. Instead of tables and chairs, blankets, sacking, and bags lay in piles around the room.

"Yosyph, what is it?" Katrin caressed my face.

"Old memories."

The head of my guards rushed forward. "Are you hurt?"

"No."

"I apologize for taking so long. We've emptied the refugees staying here into neighboring buildings. You are safe."

What of the people forced into the storm to make a *safe* place for me? Even if it was into another packed building. "You will make sure the families moved get extra grain for their sacrifice."

"Yes, Honored Yorel. There are no chairs. We'll have a bed made up for you soon, though not of these lice-ridden rags."

My guards set about removing their outer coats and creating a softened spot with them, then laid me on it.

Katrin kneeled next to me. "Yosyph, what old memories?"

"This was the tavern of the man who adopted me."

She looked about. "Where is he now?"

"After we overthrew the queen, I sent him and his son to the desert to live with my kin. I didn't want them hurt by those who hate me."

She looked around at the empty tavern. "I'm glad for their sake they are not here."

A guard crammed rags into the shuttered windows. "It's a demon wind." He glanced at Katrin. "Beg pardon, lady, for the language. But it is."

~

RAIN FOLLOWED THE HAIL, and the wind never let up. Day passed into a howling night and back into darkened day. The storm eased, and slanted sunlight cut from the west. It was evening, a day and a half after the storm started.

The captain of my guards bowed to me. "I'm sending a rider to get a new carriage. We'll have you back to the palace by tonight."

Katrin caressed my hands.

I couldn't feel her touch again and I'd lost the little movement I'd gained. "Send other riders out to see how our soldiers on the outer defenses are faring. And organize replacement men for them."

"Yes, Honored Yorel."

Katrin held out a spoon full of grain porridge.

We were eating from the stores left by those people the soldiers had forced from the tavern. "Send over the grain to those you removed from here. They will be wanting for it."

Katrin tsked. "You talk too much when you give orders, and then you are all too silent when you have no one to order around."

I chuckled. Through the storm, she teased out spoken memories of my youth I'd not thought on in a long time.

Katrin fed me half a bowl of porridge before she asked her next question. "In one of your stories, you said you sometimes had to scare off unsavory men from the barmaids. How did you do it?"

"My favorite time was my friend Jack's doing. He liked one barmaid enough to marry her the following year. Anna had worked at the tavern about a month when a man entered wearing clothing as clashing as a street performer. Every time Anna walked by him, he pinched her. Finally, she ducked into the kitchen and told father she couldn't serve that man. Jack said, *Yosyph and I'll serve him,* then pulled me into the alley. *Do you still have the snake?* I pulled a large garden snake from an empty barrel. We entered, him with a bottle to replenish the pinching man's mug, and me with a cloth to wipe down tables, and a snake tucked into my tunic. As I passed by his table, I dropped the snake down the back of his shirt. He shot from his chair, clawing at his shirt and screaming like a woman. We never saw him again."

"A snake for a snake." Katrin laughed.

Some guards chuckled, then set about their duties as if they hadn't stopped to listen. Was it good for them to see this side of me?

Horse hooves pounded to a stop outside the tavern. A soldier burst through the door, bringing with him a man covered in scratches and with hair full of twigs. "Hundreds of men with women and children deserted from the enemy's camp. What do you want done with them?"

"Is this one of them?" I asked.

"Yes. He led them to our walls."

The man stood a little taller.

"Tell me what happened? And please, sit down so I can see you better."

He sat halfway across the room. It was as close as the soldier would let him. "Are you the Shadow Demon?"

"Some call me that."

"I thought you'd look something not human."

"Egvar would have you think so. I am human, with all its frailties. How did you bring the people to our walls?"

He studied me a moment longer before answering. "When the storm hit, our tents whipped away. Then the hail beat down. We ran for the woods, and there was nothing our task masters could do about it, for they were also huddling in whatever shelter they could find. The hail went on for an eternity. My skin will be bruised for weeks. It finally changed to rain, and the wind never stopped. I gathered as many as I could, and we decided if we were ever to escape, now was the time. We fought against the wind and rain until we reached your walls. I think it took all night, though it was hard to tell when day came. We almost froze at the gate before someone heard our shouts and pounding. Finally, one let us in. We've been sheltering in the barracks with the soldiers. We owe our lives to them."

That is why we had the storm. *Thank you, God. I asked for a way for them to escape, and you rained it down from the heavens.*

I turned to the guard who'd brought him in. "Get them food, clothes, and tents. And medical care for those who need it."

"What if there is a traitor amongst them?"

"There are just as many already in Fairhaven. Halavant and I will keep our guards about us. Encamp any of the new refugees away from the outer wall, so any traitors cannot weaken our defenses."

61

YOSYPH

PALACE, Fairhaven, Lansimetsa
Mars 30th

WITH FAIRHAVEN UNDER SIEGE, we couldn't watch the coastline for the approaching Carani, or even the roads. Five days had passed since the storm.

Halavant and I studied the reports.

The enemy army dug trenches just out of arrow reach across the three roads that led to the city. Then they extended the trenches to connect from road to road. Those were completed yesterday. The morning sun rose to show a second row of trenches started, a nighttime work. These were within arrow reach. The workers continued to dig away under the cover of shields.

Our soldiers' arrows did little to stop the work. When an arrow made its way through a space between shields, they dragged the injured man back to other trenches, and someone else took up his work.

Halavant pushed aside one report, and it fluttered to the

floor. Before a servant could pick it up, I leaned over from my chair, forced my fingers to remember how to pinch, and returned the paper to the desktop.

Halavant clapped the table with his braced hand, scattering more papers. "You'll be up and walking in a week. Then we'll walk the walls together to see what all these papers try to tell us."

"Perhaps." I let the servant gather the other papers.

He placed one in front of me.

Numbers on grain and people. "They can't plan to hold a siege sufficiently long to starve us out. We have supplies of grain gathered to keep all in our city fed for many months, thanks to Makkara's letters to the noblemen. So they'll attack. Will it happen before the Carani get here?"

Halavant's brow pinched. "If we can get a spy past the siege army with messenger pigeons, he could give us some warning. Maybe Katrin—"

"No." My fingers tensed almost into a fist but couldn't form the rest of the way. The tension shivered up my arms instead.

"But she said she'd learned to shadow-walk, and she's good at it. She'd be safe in the shadow-walk."

"Not her. Never again."

Halavant studied me. "What happened?"

"You may ask her. I'll not relive it in words."

He raised his brows, then shrugged. "She wouldn't be able to understand the Carani. Mido would be a better choice. He's a hunter and a warrior. He'll know how to go quietly. And if he can get close enough, he can hear some of their plans."

"Yes, that is wise."

"Occasionally, I am wise." Halavant rested his elbows on the table and brought his braced hands together. "And so I can grow more so, tell me about these laws and changes you've introduced."

"Do you have several days?"

"We are waiting for one army to attack from outside our walls and another from across the sea. Might as well fill that wait with learning, when we aren't attending to our other duties."

"Such as getting Mido briefed on his spying assignment, if he'll accept."

Halavant grimaced. "He'd accept walking into a barrage of arrows if I asked him. He and his village think I'm related to their god—you, too, since you are my brother. It is good to be back where people just see me as their king, one they can obey or overthrow as they think best."

I snorted. "It's good to have you back. We'll get him sent out first, and then I'll start teaching you what I've learned."

"Fair enough. Though I'll probably not agree with everything you are trying to do."

"No one does. I don't even agree with it all—yet my God has directed me to set it up this way."

~

Elise and Katrin entered the room, followed by servants bearing trays of food. My stomach grumbled at the scent. I still took a daily dose of the foul duri, but now in a large single serving, undiluted. I'd have to take it and wait half an hour before eating to get its full effect. At least after half an hour, most of the duri taste had died away and I could enjoy the food.

Halavant sat across from me with the dazed look he'd worn since I'd started teaching him.

I'd taught him what my God had taught me about universal freedoms, ruling by the people's voice, educational opportunities for all so they could make wise choices for their nation, and laws applied equally to all no matter their class.

Elise brushed her hand along Halavant's shoulders as she sat beside him. "What did Yosyph tell you today?"

Halavant blinked, then leaned his cheek into her hand. "I don't understand his god. Even though he is powerful enough to create the storm that battered us last week, he doesn't heal Yosyph. He should. Yosyph is doing everything his god asks him to do."

Katrin gripped my hand tighter. She'd asked that question more times than the others.

I'd asked, too. I was starting to understand why. "He is. You brought back the duri. I am healing."

Halavant's face twisted. "Why? Why send us off to get it and almost die? Why let you suffer? Why not just heal you?"

"There were certain things I learned that I'd been too stuck in my ways to learn otherwise. I needed to be humbled, and the slow wasting humbled me."

His brow pinched. "You serve a cruel god."

"Halavant, I'd never choose to suffer this way, but much good has come from it. The nobles are changing because I'm working with them openly, instead of sneaking around trying to change things from the shadow. I was on a path to destroy our people."

Katrin squeezed my hand so hard I winced. "Yosyph, you risked your life for them many times. You've never done anything to hurt this people."

"Yes, I have. I needed the slow wasting. I needed something to stop me so I'd listen. It's a blessing."

Halavant shook his head. "May your god never bless me like he's blessed you."

Elise opened the duri, and the stench filled the room.

I braced myself for the substance. "And may you never need that blessing, my brother."

62

KATRIN

In the twelve days since Yosyph started taking the duri, he'd grown strong enough I didn't fear his death. But war sat outside, and Yosyph's god would again claim his attention, even at risk of his life.

Elise sat next to Halavant and leaned her cheek on his shoulder.

I nestled as close to Yosyph as the wheels on his chair between us allowed and ran my fingers through the hair at the back of his neck. "Yosyph?"

"Hmm."

"Will you take me back to the desert after we are married?"

"When Halavant doesn't need me, yes."

Halavant laughed. "That will never happen. You better honeymoon there. I can hold on without your guidance that long, though you'll have to come back for the duri."

Yosyph quirked up a corner of his mouth. "Katrin and I should move to the Carani village. Then I'll get the fresh duri—it has to be better than the fermented slime."

"No, you don't." Panic tinged Halavant's voice. "You convinced the nobles to try a crazy new type of government and you can't leave me with the mess of making it a working reality. And no, just because I'm the king, I can't make things go back the way they were. The nobles are speaking in approving tones of your proposed changes, at least some of them. They'll never let me take back the power once reserved for the kings."

I squeezed Yosyph's hand. "See, your words are making a difference." He'd been concerned that despite all he'd done and said, they'd fall into anarchy or tyranny—the two extremes he wanted to avoid. "But tonight, let's not worry about the nobles, or a new government, or the war. You two promised Elise and me an evening of singing. I know Elise can sing prettily. And Halavant did when he was a child—high enough to match my voice."

Halavant turned bright red.

"Yosyph can ground us in low notes."

"I only hum," he said.

"Then you can drone bass, like a mountain bagpipe. Elise, which song—*Morning Rose* or *Dancing on the Dock*?"

Elise hummed a measure of each. "*Dancing on the Dock*, as long as you and Yosyph will sing and I can dance with Halavant."

"Perfect."

Halavant stood and offered his arm to Elise.

I wheeled Yosyph's chair next to mine against one wall while servants cleared the furniture from the center of the room.

Yosyph hummed the starting note. He knew how to sing. He'd sung *Dancing on the Dock* when we danced in the New Year, just the two of us, in the empty council room. Everyone else was at a ball, but he'd pulled me aside to the quiet, and surrounded me with his voice and his arms. It was the night he first kissed me. Before the slow wasting.

Now he hummed it. I added words on top.

The sea washes below our feet.
The moon lights your face.
The warped boards of the dock
Drum deeply to our steps.

Halavant stepped, mirroring Elise back and forward.

Elise laid her hands on his forearms, her dress swishing around his legs.

Then he spun her out so her skirts belled and her long braid whipped.

Come! Dance! Fill the air,
With the rhythm of our feet.
Leap, spin, away and back.
Held closely in my arms.

He lifted and spun her in a full circle, then pulled her in close so her back was against his chest. He leaned his cheek against hers for a moment before spinning her out to face him.

The sea pulses like my blood for you,
The moon's but a shadow of your light.
The warped boards of the dock
Drum deeply to our hearts.

They danced as one, as I'd once danced with Yosyph. My voice caught, and I faltered.

Yosyph picked up the words, his deep voice filling the room as he looked into my face.

Come! Dance! Fill the air,
With the rhythm of our feet.
Leap, spin, away and back.
Hold—

The door burst open. Galliard entered, and behind him limped Mido, aided by two guards.

Mido looked like he'd crawled through a bramble patch. Scratches and bruises marred his face and arms. His hair was cropped short. His clothes were different from what he'd worn before—a muddied sleeveless tunic and once-white calf-length pants. He burst into a rapid string of foreign words.

Halavant held up a hand, and Mido slowed.

What had happened?

Yosyph put his arm around my shoulders and held me.

Finally, Mido stopped talking.

Halavant asked a few questions, listened to the answers, then sank to a chair. "The Carani are here. Mido stole some clothes, mixed in with the common soldiers, and listened to their gossip. His low-lander accent gave him away, and he is lucky to have escaped by a tumble down a rocky ravine into a brambled bottom."

"What did he learn?" Yosyph asked.

"They sat a day's distance away when he left, but they'll have marched while he ran. They've spied out the siege army and our city. They plan to destroy the outer army and then take Fairhaven. They have almost twice as many as Egvar, even though they lost half their ships in a storm." Halavant glanced at Yosyph.

Yosyph's god had more than one purpose in that storm.

Couldn't he have sunk all their ships? Still, half was good. Half was a blessing. I signed, *thank providence,* as Yosyph taught me in the desert.

"Anything else?" Yosyph asked.

Halavant frowned. "The king of the Carani leads them. Thabit also leads."

"Oh, not Thabit." Elise murmured.

"Who is he?"

Halavant frowned deeper. "He was both friend and betrayer. He showed mercy to us many times in our imprisonment. He also had spied out our land. He knows our language, though I didn't know until too late. He listened to my unguarded conversations with Elise and Gaven. He told the Carani king who I was and counseled him to attack our land."

Yosyph closed his eyes. His brows furrowed. When he opened his eyes, his face set in determined lines. "We'll help them."

"What!" My voice overlapped with Halavant's.

"We'll help our people outside the walls defend against the Carani."

"Egvar is trying to conquer us," I protested. "He's tried to kill both of us. He's a murderer. He's—"

"He's one person, as is the queen, and Duke Pulska. There are nearly eight thousand others out there that listened to their lies but are not them."

"If we send out our soldiers, won't they be killed by Egvar's?"

Yosyph sighed, his eyes deep set with sorrow. "We'll wait until the Carani attack. Then we'll help them. Many will die, but less so than otherwise."

Halavant nodded. "We'll send our soldiers in from the sides so the Carani must turn and protect their flanks. Galliard, get the other officers and draw out plans of attack. I want every company of men ready to march by tomorrow morning."

I didn't agree. "What about defending Fairhaven and the people sheltering in it?"

Yosyph straightened in his chair "We'll keep half of the soldiers to hold the defenses. We'll arm the youth to fight. Women and children can gather stones to cast down from the walls. We'll send out messenger birds with the companies so they can send news back to the city. Why didn't Mido use his messenger birds?"

Halavant asked Mido and laughed grimly at the response. "He said the birds were too noisy for sneaking around. He ate them the first night. I'll remember not to send birds with a spy again, at least not with Mido."

～

I STOOD behind Yosyph as he watched the distant armies from Fairhaven's wall. Halavant stood next to him. A dark, unending line marched northward. Egvar's army formed in eight lines to meet them, now turned sideways to us. Each line was four men deep and several hundred wide. If Halavant was a bloodthirsty king, he could have ordered arrows to rain down on the edge within reach.

Halavant leaned forward. "We should send our men out now, before the Carani reach Egvar's lines."

Yosyph's shoulders rounded as if he bore a great weight. "Not yet."

"When?"

"When the first line of Egvar's army crumples."

The Carani line stopped more than an arrow's shot distance from Egvar's army and spread out on the fields, forming square companies of men, maybe ten by ten. Each company had a space between it and the next square of men. Captains on horses trotted up and down between squares, each bearing a different-colored flag. The dark line of men kept spreading out into squares until they checkered the whole land southward. In the center at the back, a red-and-black-striped banner fluttered over a larger square of men. There were seven squares across the front and twenty going back. If each square held a hundred, it was fourteen thousand men against eight thousand. Fourteen thousand that moved with exactness. I swallowed at the lump lodged in my throat.

A distant trumpet call echoed over the fields. The horsemen waved their flags, and the front squares of men jogged forward.

The first square battered into Egvar's front line in a silence created by distance. The line crumpled like thin armor under a mace. Another, and another, and another square battered into the line. I gasped for breath as the last of the seven broke through.

"Now!" shouted Halavant.

A shrill flute trilled, and our cavalry galloped away from the shelter of our city walls. They streamed across the plain. Behind them marched our soldiers.

Egvar's first line fell back to the second. Combined, they hacked away at the edges of the Carani squares. The white of the Carani-uniformed men mixed in with the browns and colors of the Lansimetsians. The squares dissolved. The rest of the Carani held back, letting the seven companies in the front fight and fall under Egvar's front two lines of about two thousand.

The numbers came unbidden to my head, born of my years being a scribe for my merchant father. Yet these were not rugs or jewelry, but people with families.

Egvar's men fell, too. The brown of the field turned multicolored with motionless forms.

So many lives snuffed out. I blinked away the tears that blurred the battle.

Our cavalry reached the lines. Half of them bored into the remnants of the attacking Carani companies. The other half set themselves between Egvar's lines and the Carani in five wedges. Our soldiers marched across the field in sluggish motion. Still too far.

"Yosyph, I can't watch."

He looked up at me. Tears streamed down his cheeks. "Go. This is not your burden to bear."

But it was. I'd remember this in my dreams, even if I lived to be a grandmother. Unless I did something, it would eat away at me like acid.

I descended the wall. My bay stood, her reins wrapped around a hook on the inside wall. I unlooped her reins and mounted.

The gate still stood open. The distant marching of our troops rumbled. They marched to their deaths, to help defend those who would have killed us. All had families whom the Carani would massacre if the soldiers didn't fend them off.

I pulled my horse's head around and galloped through the gate.

"Katrin, no!" Yosyph's voice reached out for me. "Get her! Bring her back!"

Hooves pounded behind me. The rain-sodden field sucked at my horse's hooves, and mud flicked across my face. I leaned closer to her neck and wiped a sleeve across my eyes, clearing them of mud, and spat out a clump. Damp horse mingled with the gritty scent of soil.

"Lady Katrin," a man shouted behind me. "The battle is no place for you. Turn back!"

I glanced over my shoulder. Ten mud-splattered soldiers whipped their war horses. But I was lighter than the armor-clad men, and my horse was bred for speed, not strength.

I squeezed my knees tighter. My bay stretched her neck and lay back her ears. The galloping thud of hooves behind faded, replaced by the growing clash of swords, spears, and battle shouts. The *thump-schlook* of her hooves carried me ever closer. The startled faces of our marching soldiers blurred as we sped past them. Ahead, the battle lay in a messy line, the clash of men an ever-shifting horizon of death. A Carani, his white tunic splattered with brown and red, thrust his spear into a sword-bearing noble. A farmer fended off another spear with a rake.

I galloped towards the backmost dense squares of Carani, the ones who held back from the battle. Carani turned as I drew closer, black rows of hair making striped helmets over impassive faces—they could have been masks for all the emotion they showed. One raised a bow. An arrow whistled, snagging in my skirt and jerking me sideways. My bay screamed and stumbled, then regained her feet. I clung, gripping with knees and arms as her body jerked under me. Another arrow lodged in her shoulder, bobbing up and down with her limping steps.

The Carani closed in around me.

I pushed my emotions to my skin. Anger burned over fear. Sorrow swam under remorse that I'd not be with Yosyph. Love, joy and hope clung and urged me to turn back.

Two hands grabbed me from my horse, slinging me to the muddied ground.

I melted into a half-shadow, holding onto a portion of my emotions, including hope, indignation and feelings of justice as a shield to what would come. My skin turned translucent and the muddied ground showed through my ghostly hands.

The soldier let go, and what was surely a string of curses filled the surrounding air.

I pushed to standing. "Take me to your king."

They couldn't understand my words, but shouldn't they want

to capture me? The men didn't move. Their impassive faces had shifted to horror.

I'd have to go there without their help. I trod toward the striped black and red flag. They parted around me. Whispered curses carried before me until it seemed the ocean surf had taken its voices to land. Over top scraped the screams of the injured and dying.

I broke into a jog.

Ahead, the red-and-black-striped flag whipped in the spring wind, its fabric snapping.

I pushed my jog into a run, my dress heavy with mud.

A large man sat astride his horse. His clothes were white, like all the rest of the army, and embroidered with geometric designs along the cuffs, hem, and collar. His hair lay in rows of black braids tight against his head. A necklace of precious stones sat around his neck instead of a crown on his head.

He reined his horse backward several steps as I approached. Twenty men stepped between him and me, though none tried to touch me.

I placed my hands on my hips and stared at him. Justice and indignation boiled along my skin. "You will stop this war now!"

He yelled something, and a man ran.

The king returned my stare with a sneer, but the corner of his eye twitched as we waited.

The man returned with a tall, white-haired man, whose bare arms bore small rounded scars from wrist to shoulder. This was Thabit, by Elise's description. The king wanted someone to translate. Good. I had much to say.

Thabit's eyes widened as he stepped to face me, though his mouth stayed firm.

I pointed my finger at him. "Thabit. You will tell your king to stop this war and leave our nation."

He flinched when I said his name. "You must be a shadow

demon, though I'd only heard of one in the land, and he was described as a tall shadow of a man."

"There are many, though I am not one of them. I am a fiery angel from this land's god. If you do not leave this land, my god will strike you with a worse storm than plagued you at sea." Maybe he would, though he might just as well strike me down for lying. Yosyph said that his god didn't often directly interfere but directed men and women to act. I was acting.

Thabit spoke with the king while keeping his eyes on me. The king glowered, then bellowed and a man darted forward.

No, you don't. I flipped a knife from my belt. It spun through the air and sank into his calf. He cried out, clutching his leg.

Thabit stepped forward, then froze as I drew a second knife. "My king is making you prisoner."

"Do you think he can hold an angel prisoner?"

Thabit whitened.

"If any of his men or their weapons touch my skin, my god will kill him." The lies flowed over my tongue. I'd say anything needed to get them to leave. Yosyph's god could do with me what he would for my falsehoods about him.

Thabit spoke and the king turned purple.

A clash of weapons and the grunts of men drew closer. The king motioned to his soldiers, and a third drew away. Had the soldiers Yosyph sent to bring me back fought their way to this point? I didn't turn. I had to keep my pretense of power.

"Lady Katrin!" A voice bellowed behind me, "Run! We'll—" his words ended in a grunt. I gasped against the band that tightened around my chest. I should have shed remorse. The clashing of weapons soon silenced.

Two Carani soldiers dragged a Lansimetsian soldier by the feet into the space between the Carani king and me. The man bore the falcon of the royal guard emblazoned across his blue surcoat. Dark dampness spread under the left wing. I stared at his chest, not daring to lift my eyes to his face. He moaned and my eyes darted upward. It was Hoft—the giant-blooded always loyal guard to both Halavant and Yosyph.

The band of remorse tightened further, and my legs wobbled. I pushed at the emotion, trying to get it to the surface and wash it away before it could cripple my ability to convince the Carani king. It clung around my lungs.

The king chuckled and spoke again, his voice dropping from a yell to a purr.

Thabit nodded. "My king will have mercy on this man, but you must not interfere in our war. Your god won't mind if this land's people has a new king, when your old one does not stop war between his own people."

Hoft met my gaze with acceptance, though his body flinched with pain. Why did he come after me? Why did any of them? But if I left now to save his life, then so many more would die. I gritted my teeth. I should have shed remorse. "Kill him if you must. You've already killed many others. But stop the war now."

"Why do you care?" Thabit asked.

"Because," I cried, letting justice swell my words, "the god of Lansimetsa will not have his land stained further in blood. I am his fiery angel. I will not change his message."

Thabit conversed with the king, then spread his hands to motion over the battle. "If your god wants the battle to end, then tell your king to surrender and the death will stop."

"It won't. We know how you treat your prisoners and your slaves. He will destroy you on the sea before he allows you to take his people to your lands. His storms on your way here were but a warning. Do you want to leave your own land leaderless and without an army? What will happen to your great city and mountain garden?"

Thabit translated and the Carani king jerked his head up, his purpled face turning white. He kicked his horse, and it lunged toward me. My knife left my fingers and buried itself in his shoulder.

Carani converged, yelling in a high-pitched, trilling anger, grasping my dress, though none touched my skin. I slashed with my last two knives, one in each hand. Where I met skin, a hand released and another grasped. I stumbled as they pushed and jerked me backward, away from the king. They'd heard my translated threat that any who touched my skin, even with a weapon, would die. But how long would that fear keep them?

A bellow rose behind their mass, and three men toppled over as Hoft barreled through them. He grasped another Carani, pulled the sword from his hand, and tossed the man over his shoulder. The Carani turned their weapons on him. He parried and thrust and swept them aside until he stood beside me. He towered over the Carani, an injured elk amongst hunting dogs, stinking of blood and radiating danger.

"Why are you helping me?" I slashed a Carani's arm as he grabbed my dress. "I told the king he could kill you."

Hoft parried a spear thrust, then spun to deflect a sword before it pierced his already bleeding side. "Because you may still stop this war. Go. Do what you must."

I ran through the space he'd created. As I ran, I shed the last of my emotions. Even remorse dislodged and washed away. My arms and skirt no longer swung into view with each stride. Coldness surrounded and suffused me.

The Carani king lay on the ground while a man wrapped his shoulder. I dropped to my knees at his side and pressed a knife against his throat. His eyes widened until white showed around the whole dark centers, and he made a gurgling sound. Flowery perfume turned rancid with fear.

I could kill him. An image flashed before my eyes: a shattered water jug and Farid's lesson on the chaos that followed when a leader is killed. No, I had to convince him to agree to peace.

Thabit ran to the king's side.

"Thabit." My voice came out level and dispassionate. "Your king forfeits his life for attacking me. He may ransom it if he signs a peace treaty and promises never to return to our lands."

Thabit spoke. The king's eyes narrowed. He swept a hand towards his throat and I cut that hand with my other knife. Blood pooled where I notched his throat in the exchange.

"Don't cut him more," Thabit pled.

"Why?"

"Our people are millions. But they will be divided between the generals seeking power and then overrun by neighboring countries without their king. I'll convince him to sign the treaty."

"You have until the sun reaches the center of the sky."

He nodded. He spoke long with the king, his words firm, despite his subservient position.

The king finally spoke in short, shallow breathed words.

Thabit turned to us. "My king will withdraw his armies if you tell him the secret of turning into a shadow."

"There is no secret. Neither the abilities of shadow demon nor a fiery angel can be taught." Yosyph would have laughed to hear my words.

"Then the king demands a tribute of ten slaves sent each year, and he will leave your land forever."

"Never." The battle's cacophony had drawn further away. The Carani were pushing our people back. How many more had died while I spoke? Would I promise away lives for peace? Would those sold as slaves be more than those that had died or would die in the battle? Ten a year to maybe thousands dead in battle. But where would it stop? Ten years, forty—an agreement taking the freedom of men for generations until another war broke it? "Never. I'll kill the king and let your armies fall to anarchy."

The king shifted under my blade and grunted as the edge cut into his skin. Rage and frustration flashed over his face, replacing all remnants of fear. Perhaps he didn't believe I'd carry out my threat, or he'd rather die than back down. If I killed him, would it accomplish anything?

What could I give to convince him to order a retreat? What could Lansimetsa give? Understanding pushed forward. It wasn't my place to make those promises. "Thabit, tell the king that I am a messenger of Lansimetsa's god. But I do not speak for the people. He must counsel with the Lansimetsian king. Call a meeting to create a treaty."

If they sat down and discussed, the killing would stop and Yosyph would find some way to convince the Carani to leave without the slaves. He just needed the opportunity to talk.

The king slowly nodded. A few words later, a trumpet vibrated in two long sustained notes, one low and one high. As the second note died away, so did much of the battle. The shrill call of the flute ended the remaining clash of weapons, but not the cries of the wounded. Messengers ran to and from the Carani king. My knees ached from kneeling, and my knife-gripping hand trembled.

Finally, ten falcon-crested soldiers came and stood a respectful distance from the Carani king. The Carani soldiers formed a barrier but did not attack. A Lansi soldier stepped forward and stopped as a Carani pressed a spear to his chest. The Lansi soldier stood his ground. "A pavilion is set for the signing of the treaty. We will escort you there."

"And how will you assure his safety?" Thabit asked.

The Lansi soldier glanced at the prone king. "He'll be safer with us than with the shadow demon that holds a blade at his throat."

"I will go with the Carani king," I said.

The Lansi soldier jumped at my ghostly monotone, then bowed. "As you wish, Lady Katrin."

I let the king stand and kept my knife at his back and the other knife ready to fend off an attack. We marched past the fallen. Hoft lay face-up amongst them, his still hand gripping a sword. Empty coldness surrounded me, detaching me from the thought, *He died to give us a chance.*

I brought my gaze forward to the white pavilion set in the field between the armies and the city. Two flags fluttered in the front, one with the king's falcon and the other the red rose of Egvar. A Carani posted a red-and-black striped standard beside them.

Halavant stood surrounded by guards. His face was weary, grief-lined, and regal. He looked like the statue of his father. At a far corner of the pavilion sat a battle-stained Egvar, his head bandaged and his face pale. He leaned heavily on a rose-heralded soldier.

So the peace treaty was between all three. But where was Yosyph? Could Halavant handle the negotiations?

Halavant bowed to the Carani king, then his eyes shifted past him. "Lady Katrin. Thank you for your aid. You will release our guest."

"Wouldn't it be wiser that I continue to guard him?"

"No." He didn't speak as a proud and foolish boy or a hurt and forlorn young man. He spoke as king—with power and conviction.

"Yes, my liege." I released the Carani king and stood a few feet behind him. I still had my two knives and I could stop him if needed.

Halavant motioned to a stool. "Please, be seated."

The Carani king glanced around, his eyes lingering on Halavant's guards, then lowered himself to the stool.

Halavant remained standing. "I'm not a diplomat. But neither are you. Let us speak plainly. You attacked because you believed us too weak to withstand you. You've learned we have more defenses than just our army. Will you continue this war?"

The Carani king lowered his brows at Thabit's translation, then jerked his head in a sharp nod and spoke in rapid Carani.

The corners of Halavant's mouth turned down, and he answered the king in the Carani language.

As they conversed, the Carani king's face shifted from contempt to surprise. A begrudging smile spread across his face.

Halavant didn't smile back. His face became more grim as he turned to Egvar. "You are a traitor to the crown and sought to destroy your own people. By law you should hang."

Egvar blanched till his face matched the white bandage around his head.

Halavant was only a shade less white, though he held his regal presence. "Or you can choose to go as a slave to the Carani. I offer this choice to all who are convicted of crimes worthy of death."

Egvar grasped the seat of his stool. "This is a peace treaty, not a trial!"

Halavant nodded, his face grave. "True. You may continue to fight. The Carani king has promised peace with us, but not with you. I will withdraw and I offer the choice to all who would defect from your army to come to the safety of the city, and only the leaders will bear punishment. Those remaining loyal to you will stand against the entire Carani army. Any who survive will go as slaves to their lands."

He paused for Thabit to finish translating. "Or, if you surrender, the Carani king has agreed to sign a peace treaty to leave now and take all of our traitors who choose not to die the traitor's death. So what will you choose—continue the fight and die, surrender and go as a slave to the Carani lands, or surrender and await execution?"

Egvar closed his eyes. His jaw bulged. "You warned us about the Carani. You sent men to defend us. I thought you were too soft to be king. But I was wrong. You are stronger than the queen and—had I known—I would have followed you." His shoulders rolled forward, the broken slump of the defeated in response to an unexpected opponent. "I will surrender and go to Carani as a slave."

Halavant motioned a scribe forward. "May you serve the Carani king better than you served me."

$$\sim$$

THE SUN LAY near the western horizon when the three men signed the treaty. Halavant signed last, a pen strapped to his braced hand and the resulting signature large and shaky. He then lifted a gold chain from around his neck, his seal ring hanging at the end. The scribe dropped melted wax onto the treaty, and Halavant pressed the band of the ring between his two braces and sealed the wax. Egvar sealed his with a rose ring. The Carani king held out his hand and, after one of Halavant's guards pricked his thumb, he sealed the peace treaty with a red thumbprint.

Soldiers marched away to imprison the leaders of Egvar's army. Messengers spread the news of peace. Cheers rose in place of battle cries. And Halavant stood looking over the distant battlefield, his face grim and his lips tight. When the Carani king and Egvar had both left, the first with his soldiers and the second in bonds, Halavant's shoulders shook.

I came to stand next to him. "My liege."

"Don't come out of the shadow yet." His voice cracked. "I

would have you someplace where you can rest when you face the emotions of today. Come, let us return."

He was silent as we rode back to the city, his guards surrounding us, while my thoughts filled with questions. "Halavant, where did you come up with those ideas for the peace treaty?"

He snorted. "They weren't my ideas. Lord Makkara suggested we leave Egvar's men to the Carani if he refused to surrender, first allowing all who would defect to come safely to our city. Yosyph suggested offering the Carani king those lives already forfeit for treason. I didn't like either idea, but it stopped the killing and bought us peace."

"Why didn't Yosyph or Makkara come?"

"I'm the king. I needed to show a strong front without leaning on others, or neither the Carani king nor Egvar would have listened. Besides, I was the only one who spoke Carani, and I needed to speak with the Carani king privately before speaking with Egvar."

"I see."

Halavant snorted again. "Sometimes I wish I could go into that emotionless state and just think without feeling. Maybe I'd see too."

"No, Halavant," I said, the empty cold sitting in my core. "You're a better king for feeling alongside thinking."

∼

YOSYPH HELD me as if he'd never let me go. The arms of his wheeled chair dug into my legs and back as I sat in his lap and buried my head in his shoulder. My entire body shook with the emotions that after hours of crying still couldn't find a resting place. Finally, words found their way past the sobs. "They followed me to their death."

Yosyph held me tighter. "Many followed my orders to their death."

"If I hadn't left, they'd—"

"They'd have fought in a battle that would have ended with their death or enslavement. We would have lost against the Carani if you hadn't gone. You did what needed to be done."

"Hoft."

Yosyph held me and let me cry.

63

HALAVANT

PALACE, Fairhaven, Lansimetsa
    Apri 8th

I WALKED ALONG THE TURRET. In the distance, a field was spread with rows of white stones, marking the week-old graves of thousands, both Lansimetsians and Carani. We'd not again grow wheat in that place of blood.

Who would care for the families of those dead and those taken prisoner to Carani?

It would have been much worse if not for Katrin's intervention and if Yosyph hadn't gathered all the people to the city. The Carani king promised he'd leave our city alone but would enslave any left outside of it a day after the signing of the treaty. And because of the gathering of the people, the only ones left outside the city were those who remained loyal to Egvar—or knew they'd be executed for treason—and they were now marching as slaves to sail to Carani.

I couldn't force the Carani to leave, only make it the most

appealing option. I hated that option, even though it meant that the most traitorous of the nobles were exiled from our land—including Lord Egvar and Duke Pulska.

Elise leaned her head on my shoulder. "Are you thinking about her?"

"Who?"

"Your mother."

My stomach soured. She was a prisoner again, awaiting trial. I wouldn't send her to Carani. I'd visit her sometime, but not yet.

Elise snuggled closer. "I was thinking about our wedding tonight."

I kissed the top of her head. "I'm sorry there won't be a celebration. No feast, no dance. Just the ceremony, and we'll be husband and wife."

She tilted her face up, and her eyes danced with tears. "It sounds perfect."

"Why are you so good to me? Most women would show their disappointment."

She laughed through her tears. "Even if it wasn't at the end of the war, I'd want it simple. I just want you and my family there. I'm not marrying a feast or a dance. I'm marrying you."

I kissed her. Yosyph had almost lost Katrin. I'd not lose another day with Elise. Before that happiness, however, I had to face my nobles. I linked arms with Elise and descended the stairs.

* * *

The Grand Council hall was filled with hundreds of nobles, some of them bound, but all free to speak. One section contained the many newly noble. We met to see if peace was possible.

Yosyph sat next to me, his face lost in thought.

Katrin stood to his left, and Yosyph held her hand. He'd not let her out of his sight since she'd returned from the battle. I thought he'd have bound her to him with chain if he could. In a way, he was. They'd set a wedding date for two weeks. She glowed with happiness, though under-toned with sadness.

Elise sat at my right, regal in her purple gown.

Who would speak, Yosyph or I?

He was older.

I was raised a prince.

He'd led the way to change our kingdom.

I was still king. I would speak.

"My people. Today I seek peace. I seek to destroy my enemies by making them my friends. Let us set aside our pride and misunderstandings. Let us bind up wounds. To those who've fought against me, I offer reconciliation. If you swear an oath to never take up the sword against your nation, then you may return to your lands. For all who fought, I plead with you, be brothers again. Let us forgive."

A murmur ran through those gathered.

I continued. "Today we start a new way of rule. I appoint Yosyph as ruler-judge over our people. He will establish laws with you and hold all to the same laws. I will remain king, but with much less authority. The power will now be with you. In five years' time, you may choose another ruler-judge. And so law will rule our people."

Elise reached over and caressed my fingers between the bracing.

I nodded to Yosyph.

He pushed himself to standing, bracing his arms against his chair to hold his weight where his legs still couldn't. "I promise I will carefully consider all your concerns and suggestions. I will work beside you, openly and fully. I'll never shadow-walk again. I offer my life to serve you."

"As you always have." Katrin's whispered words carried only enough for us to hear.

Yosyph sank back to his chair. Sweat stood on his forehead.

Lord Makkara, now Chamberlain Makkara, stepped forward at the foot of our dais. "All will now cast their vote whether to accept Yosyph, eldest son of King Luukas and Yorel of the people, as ruler-judge over Lansimetsa."

The process had been explained previously to my speaking. Locked boxes, each with a slit in the top, were passed down the rows. Each man placed a slip of paper in it, even those who'd fought against us. Yosyph insisted they, too, have a voice, or they'd rebel again. I tapped my foot as the boxes slowly made their way down the rows of hundreds of nobles. *Why must I wait for them to decide what I knew was best for them? I was king, they should do what I ordered. No, I wasn't. I'd given that power up moments before.*

Elise placed her foot next to mine and covered it with her dress, then joined her foot to mine in the bouncing impatience.

An hour passed, then two. Some stared long at the box before folding a paper and slipping it in.

Then the count. Makkara was still the most trusted by all the nobles and read off the papers, while three other men watch over his shoulder and two men made tally marks in chalk on a large, black-painted wall. One side for yes, Yosyph be the ruler-judge, the other side for no. Though if the no's won out, would they let me take back the power of the king?

The tallies grew on both sides, always more yeses, though sometimes not by much.

My foot beat the floor faster as the board grew white with marks.

Makkara read. "Yes, no, yes, absolutely not, yes, no, no, no, no..." That box must have come from amongst those in bonds. The no's stretched on, with an occasional yes. I should have been happy some wanted him as a leader, even after fighting against him, but all of them should have wanted him. We'd helped them against the Carani. Some would never be satisfied, blaming us for holding back as long as we had.

The chalked marks under the no's grew to outnumber the yeses.

Katrin stood muttering, "Thankless ingrates, fools..."

"Katrin." Yosyph pulled her to sit in the chair beside him. "Be still. He is watching over us. And no matter what the people decide, we can trust Him."

Oh, to have that faith.

Makkara opened a new box and started reading. The yeses predominated. Soon the board stood more heavily on the yes side. We'd made it through the thankless ingrates section. I let out a breath.

When the last box was opened and the last paper read, the board stood in favor of Yosyph as ruler-judge.

"Thank you." Yosyph's eyes were heavenward, and his fingers flickered in a prayer.

"They did it!" Katrin squealed. Her voice bounced around the room.

Chamberlain Makkara glanced up at her with a raised eyebrow.

"They actually did it," she whispered, then kissed Yosyph soundly on the lips.

A scattered roar, approval and otherwise, rose from the nobles.

Chamberlain Makkara cleared his throat. "The vote has been counted. Six hundred forty-nine in favor of Yosyph as ruler-judge. Three hundred seventy-six in opposition. All rise and honor the new ruler-judge, Yosyph, son of King Luukas, and Yorel of the people."

The men rose. A cheer started in one section and spread until the whole room reverberated with voices. Even some bound nobles took up the noise. Those who did not shared a mix of nervous, angry, and conniving looks. This vote did not solve everything, just started us on the path.

64

ELISE

Mama tucked the last daffodil into my crown of black hair. The blossoms' spicy scent competed with the bitter tang of herbs and medicinal alcohol. I smoothed the skirt of my white linen dress and ran my fingers over the embroidered hollyhocks and lilies.

Papa moaned in his bed beside us. Bandages swathed his whole torso where a spear had entered his side and exited his back. By an act of providence, it missed his organs. Mama sewed the torn muscles and packed everything with herbs to kill infection. Papa had slipped in and out of fever for days. Yesterday, he woke long enough for Halavant to ask his permission and Papa to tell us to marry before he died.

I bit my lip to hold back tears. Halavant didn't need a red-eyed bride. "Papa." I leaned over and kissed his feverish brow. "Halavant will be here soon. We'll be married like you asked us."

His eyes fluttered open. He reached up and touched my face.

406

"My sweet daughter. Be joyful." His hand dropped, and his eyes closed again into a fevered sleep.

Mama wrapped her arm around my shoulders. "He's strong. He'll heal." She sniffed and dabbed my wet cheeks with her already damp handkerchief.

After a gentle knock the door opened. A guard pushed Yosyph in his wheeled chair, followed by Katrin and Mido. Then Halavant entered, and I gripped Mama's hand tighter. His green eyes, brightened by a green surcoat, widened and his mouth opened in an O. "Elise, you are—you look—" He bowed. "I am honored to be in the presence of such a beautiful goddess."

My face burned hot enough to scorch away tears sitting on my cheeks and in my heart.

He grinned and came to my side. "Are you ready?"

I looked around the room. Mido and Katrin stood along the wall with my six siblings. Mama stood next to where Papa lay. Yosyph sat solemnly in front of us. We were all here. I nodded. "I'm ready for joy."

"You already are joy," he whispered back. We turned to face Yosyph.

Yosyph's fingers flickered in some sort of prayer, his eyes heavenward, then he turned a piercing gaze on Halavant. "My brother, do you take Elise, with all her strengths and faults, as your wife, to love, honor, and protect, even above your own life?"

Halavant pressed his shoulder closer to mine. "Yes. Always. Though she has no faults."

Yosyph turned his gaze to me. I shivered under the intensity. He softened it with a slight smile that reached his eyes more than his mouth. "Elise, do you take Halavant as your husband, with all his strengths and faults, to love, honor, and protect, even above your own life?"

I glanced up at Halavant. I'd love, honor and, if needed, protect my Halavant. Even as he'd protected me often in the last few months. And as for his weakness, they were part of what I loved about him. What some called levity, I found as brightness in a world already too dark.

Halavant's face crinkled with concern.

I'd waited too long in my response. "Yes," I said, "always and forever."

Halavant whooped and bent down to kiss me.

"A moment," Yosyph interrupted.

Halavant paused, his lips inches from mine.

Katrin brought forward two silver goblets filled with clear water. She handed one to me. Halavant clasped the other between his two braced hands.

Yosyph flicked his fingers in prayer again, then motioned to the water. "May your marriage be like this water. May you love with purity, clearly communicate, and bring each other daily renewal and refreshment from the trials of life."

A deep and quiet voice intoned, "Amen." Papa lay with his eyes open and a peaceful smile on his face.

"Papa!" I ran to his side, dragging Halavant with me. My goblet sloshed, and Halavant's spilled down his front, darkening his green surcoat.

Halavant set his goblet on the bedside table amongst teas and tinctures and kneeled next to my papa. "Father, I'm happy you are awake for our marriage. I promise you to take care of her, bring her joy, and do all I can for her."

Papa's smile broadened. "I know you will. I once hoped to adopt you as a son, when I didn't know you were a king. And now, you are my son." He turned his smile to me. "Elise, I couldn't be happier for you." He nodded to the goblets. "I didn't mean to interrupt the ceremony. Please, drink."

We drank and were enveloped in cheering hugs from my six siblings.

My littlest brother climbed onto Halavant's back, "You're my brother now. That means we can play *Frogs and Toads* every day."

"Daffyd," I pulled him off of Halavant. "He'll be too busy for children's games."

Daffyd's face fell.

Halavant wrapped one of his arms around my shoulder, pulling me close, and the other around Daffyd. "I'll play it with you when your sister is too busy for me."

I kissed Halavant on the nose. "I'll never be too busy for you."

65

ELISE

PALACE, Fairhaven, Lansimetsa
  Aprí 16th

I WORE A LONG, linen dress with pockets to hold bandages and ointments. It was much more practical than the one I'd worn to the counsel. And I needed practical. A long line of wounded filled the barracks. In the two weeks since the battle, those who would die, had, and those who would live, hung on. Now to keep them well enough to finish healing.

Mother worked beside me. How I'd missed her practiced hand and gentle guidance.

We came to the beds we saved for last, because we couldn't tear ourselves away once there. Father lay in one, and Galliard in the other.

I dipped my hands into a soapy bucket of hot water, rinsed them and dried them. I would not spread infection from wound to wound, though my hands looked as rough as a washer-woman's.

Father lay on his cot, his abdomen white with bandages. "Good afternoon, my love. I've been waiting all day for you."

Mother blushed and busied her hands unwrapping his bandages. His fever broke five days before, and he'd demanded to be moved from the palace to the barracks where the rest of his wounded company lay. He must have known if we were tending him amongst the other wounded, we'd help them, too.

Galliard moved to the barracks, too, with the quip, "I'll get better care from you two than from any stuffy physician."

Mother pulled bloodied packets of herbs from Father's spear wound. The redness of infection had faded. I blinked at tears. Many had lost father, husband, or brother in this war. I hadn't.

"Now, Elise," Galliard patted my hand. "No need to cry. Married life isn't that bad, is it?"

I laughed through my tears.

"That's better. You tell me if that young scoundrel isn't good to you, and I'll give him a drumming he'll never forget."

"He's good to me. Too good."

"Can't be. I've known you since you were waist high. No one is too good for you."

I pulled the blanket away from Galliard's left leg. Splints held his bones in place. He'd led the cavalry against the Carani. His horse saved his life when it took a spear meant for Galliard and then fell on him. The fall broke his leg, but the Carani didn't spare time to kill a fallen and crushed man.

I checked the wrapping to make sure it wasn't too tight or had shifted.

Galliard grimaced with such faces, he'd make the street performers jealous of his skill.

"Is that where Halavant learned his faces from?"

"Not at all. I learned it from him."

"You do a better job than him."

"Is that so?" Halavant's voice, right behind me, made me jump.

I turned and wrapped my arms around him. "Hm-hmm."

He tilted my face up, and I expected a kiss. Instead, he wore the most grotesque grimace.

I yelped, and he laughed. Galliard joined in.

I glared at Halavant. "Galliard, you can give him that drumming."

Galliard waved Halavant over. "Come here, my boy. Your wife says you deserve punishment for your face, though I must wonder that any wife would be so cruel to condemn her husband for something he was born with."

Halavant kneeled next to Galliard. "I'll take my punishment to please my wife."

Galliard cuffed him gently on the shoulder. "Now, let that be a lesson to you. Never let your wife see your face again."

Tears of laughter rolled down my cheeks. "Halavant, may I bring you as much brightness as you bring me."

He jumped up and pulled me into an embrace. "You already do."

∼

MOTHER SAT on an empty cot next to Father. "Elise, you'll rest better by your husband. As I will by mine."

Halavant nodded. "Your mother is always wise." He offered me his arm and led me into the spring evening. We walked through the gardens.

I stopped and looked up into his face. "Halavant?"

He bent forward, this time for a kiss. After that sweetness, he asked, "What is it, Elise? You have something on your mind."

"We need more healers. Many of those who help don't even

know enough to wash their hands between tending patients. A few know home remedies, but half of what they know hurts more than it helps. Yosyph promised schools. We need a school for healers. If we can get Gaven back, he could teach, and so could my mother."

"It's a wonderful idea. And you would be a wonderful teacher."

"Me? I mean, thank you. You could teach the Carani language. If we're to keep up trade with our Carani kin for duri, we will need sea captains and others who can speak with them —unless you plan to go back every year for a new supply."

Halavant blanched. "As much as I love my Carani cousins, I never want to leave Lansimetsa again."

"That settles it. We'll help found an academy of medicine and languages, maybe a little Lausatök. You could also teach history. You are always quoting what you learned in the studies you claimed to have slept through."

He gripped a tulip between his braced hands, broke it off and slipped it into one of my dress pockets. "I learn while I sleep. Like I've learned you shiver when you have bad dreams. And you'll sneak out to the balcony to calm down, though it is much colder out there than next to me."

"I need the freedom from walls. I miss the open space of my father's farm."

"Then we'll establish the academy out of Fairhaven, in an open place with many fields and orchards around."

I leaned against him. "Thank you. You are truly king to me."

"You're the only person I want to be king to, my queen." He held me close. His breath brushed against my cheek.

I wanted to make him laugh. Every time I tried to be witty it fell flat, though he didn't seem to mind. I played with words in my head, then rushed them out before I could step back. "You'll

413

rule over the academy, orchards, and fields. And I'll keep you out of mischief."

He whispered in my ear. "Not so. I'll bring you with me in mischief."

"I'll gladly come along."

66

YOSYPH

Palace, Fairhaven, Lansimetsa
  Maí 10th

I sat in the library at a long, oval table. Sunlight streamed through tall windows, and dust motes danced between the bookcases. Around the table sat twelve other men—the prince-judges of Lansimetsa.

It took a month for the nobles to choose the prince-judges. And each of the twelve would choose the local judges, when they'd been trained in what that meant.

Today was the first of such training.

I rapped the table with a short stick.

The conversation fell to silence.

"In order to judge this people justly, you must know the history of our land. You must learn the customs of its many people. You must study what motivates people and what destroys trust. The law applies to all equally, but understanding where a person's actions come from will allow you to show mercy and help them change, even with the required consequences."

A few of the men nodded. All of them were older than me, one of them almost four times my age. Though I was elected their leader and teacher, I'd have to work to retain their respect.

I motioned for a servant to hand out stacks of books, a different one per judge. "You will study these, write your observations and your questions, and then report at our meeting next week."

A man in a quilted doublet, with a pock-marked face carefully covered with face powder, scowled. "I had my fill of studies as a child. I'll not start again."

"Then you will relinquish your right as prince-judge and another will replace you. None will have any voice in judging laws and people until they've studied all these books."

The youngest amongst the prince-judges spoke up. "Why can't you just tell us what to do, since your god tells you everything already?"

"That would negate the reason to have you as judges. If I were to tell you how to judge every case, only a few them would be resolved because of the limited hours in a day. You will teach your under-judges the same as I'm teaching you. And I hope you will have them go through a similar study. My God doesn't tell me everything to do. He guides me in where to study, but He expects me to study and learn, just as I ask of you."

"Impossible!" said the pock-faced noble. "Even one of these tomes is enough to give us headaches. And you expect us to read them all? You just seek to keep the power to yourself, while making the appearance of giving us power."

"I've read and studied each of these, and I will continue to study. I do not require you to read all I've read, only which I find most beneficial to your role as judges. Though, if you desire, I'll send you a list of all I've read, if you feel I'm keeping the best books from you."

The oldest on the council raised his gnarled hand. "I apologize for my discourtesy in questioning your methods. Who will judge the people until we are allowed to?"

"I'll be busy for the next couple of months." That was only a breath of the truth; I'd never been busier since the time they'd appointed me ruler-judge. "And many must wait for you. I hope you will be quick in your studies. Once you've completed these, you will be given the power to which you are appointed. Those who finish first and show their mastery of this knowledge will have the first choice of which province they judge over."

I let the statement sink in. I didn't choose these men, and I didn't trust them yet, but hopefully, with knowledge, they'd become wiser men. The old one seemed open enough, or just diplomatic. Those who had yet to speak were at least thinking about it. Though I needed them to speak, even if they opposed me.

When they shifted in their seats, I continued. "I have started a school for others who would learn to be judges. They are reading the same material as I've assigned you. Some of them have been in study for a month already, ever since I was appointed ruler-judge. If any of you decide you would rather not take on the weight of this duty, they will be ready to step into your place. And if you choose to stay, they will be ready to work under you and take on the weight of your province. I recommend getting to know them and working beside them. They can help you in your studies. That is all for today. Next week, we will have much to discuss, depending on what you've learned."

The oldest prince-judge blew out his cheeks. "I guess I'll not be attending any concerts or plays for a while." He gathered up his volume and hobbled from the room.

The others slowly followed.

The pock-faced one came up to me. "I don't know if I'll make it through the trial you've set for me. But I'll give it a running go."

I bowed my head to him. "That is all I ask."

~

KATRIN WAITED for me outside the library. "When they left, they looked as excited as rain-soaked cats. What did you tell them?"

"That they must work to be judges."

"Ah—asking a noble to work. They'll be different men when you are done with them."

"As will I."

"I want you to stay the same. You're perfect."

I snorted.

She ran her fingers through my hair. "Do you think the messenger has reached the Kishkarish land yet? I don't want to wait another day to get married, but your foster father should be here. And Naven."

Yes, Naven should be there. He was the real father to Katrin, though not in blood. "We'll get married the day they arrive."

"How will we survive the long days until then?"

"By working, studying, and teaching. How is it going teaching the messenger corp knife throwing?"

"They are the sloppiest, most ill-aimed group of young men I've ever met."

"It doesn't help that their teacher is a distracting beauty."

"Then I'll put on a gray sack dress and cover my hair in a floppy hat."

I pulled her into my lap and motioned for the servant to push us both down the hall. "It won't help. You could stain your face and chop off your hair, and you'd still be beautiful."

"Yosyph, you're sweet, but no good as a poet."

"I'll try again. Your beauty shines through any disguise, even the shadow-walk. You are my fiery angel, and heaven-sent."

She tucked her feet on my lap and leaned her head onto my shoulder. "This will be the longest month in my life. You certain we can't get married before they get here?"

"We don't have to wait. I'll call Halavant now."

She shook her head and snuggled closer. "No. We should wait. But I must keep busy. What other classes could I teach?"

I wrapped my arms around her. "You could join the classes for becoming a judge. You'll not have a spare moment to think outside of it."

"Only if you are teaching."

67

KATRIN

Royal forest, Fairhaven, Lansimetsa
Júní 23rd

Yosyph stood beside me. He wore leg braces under his desert wedding robes and balanced against a cane.

I held his other hand. Warm and trembling. His or mine?

We faced Halavant.

The evening sun stretched through the forest trees to light the pond and the spring flowers, casting our shadows forward towards Halavant; Yosyph's tall and straight, mine not up to his shoulder. The sun through my hair tinged my shadow red. He'd wanted my hair loose with the sun shining through it. Was he stealing glances at me, as I was at him?

He wore a white robe with silver filigree at the cuffs and hem. I wore a matching robe, though my cuffs were stitched in gold.

Farid brought the robes. They were the ones he'd saved from his youth for his own longed-for wedding to Yosyph's mother, Tanyeshna. Yosyph's fit perfectly. Mine needed the waist folded over to take in the length. Yosyph's mother would have been regal in it. Farid didn't reveal what he felt, but I think he fought tears by the slight twitch of his eye.

Yosyph's hair curled around his ears, and his beard was trimmed back to a goatee. His left hand balanced on the cane and showed the tattoo marking his journey through the king's trial. Now he was the ruler-judge of Lansmetsia. More important was his right hand gripping mine. Those hands we'd bind together with ribbons, showing our promises to each other.

Halavant shifted, scuffing the pebbled shore of the pond. He grinned like he had so often when we were children together. "Have all gathered who would witness this event?" His formal words didn't fit his face.

Yes, though we'd waited almost three months for the rest of our family to arrive.

To our side sat Yosyph's foster-father and brother, Hadron and Timothy. The young man watched us with wide eyes, while his father dabbed at his eyes with an already wet handkerchief. Next to them sat Yosyph's childhood friend, Jack, his torture-shortened fingers entwined with his wife's slender ones. Their children poked at each other in the next three seats.

Naven smiled as I caught his eyes. He'd protected me so often when I was a child and taught me to protect myself—the father I'd always needed. Farid let a ghost of a smile pass over his still face. He taught Yosyph to shadow-walk and, more importantly, to hear his god. Our lives would never be the same because of Farid's lessons. Only Qadir hadn't come. Said he couldn't leave the king's gate. I think Yosyph was relieved. I'd set my heart on having Qadir tattoo our marriage bracelets, like the Kishkarish do.

Behind them sat Galliard, Elise, and her whole family, who'd opened their hearts to me. With them sat the physician who'd saved Yosyph's life many times. Maggie, no longer my maid but always my faithful friend, beamed with a smile too big for her small face. Chamberlain Makkara was the only noble. An empty chair sat beside him in memory of Hoft and his sacrifice. A few guards, including the dog-jowled one, filled the last row of chairs. That was it. These were the people who mattered. Anyone else could celebrate in the streets if they so desired.

Halavant stepped towards us. "We've gathered to witness the binding of two lives in one. Do you Yosyph, son of King Luukas and Tanyeshna of the Kishkarish, promise to bind your life, heart, and soul to Katrin?"

"Forever, in this life and the next." His words rolled over me like deep thunder.

Halavant looked to me. "Do you Katrin, daughter of Lady Susanne of Conborner, promise to bind your life, heart, and soul to Yosyph?"

"Yes, now and always, for as long as my soul exists."

Yosyph trembled.

Halavant held up a ribbon, woven with light and dark for the joys and sorrows of life, transparent silk threads representing our time in the shadow-walk, and gold for the richness of our new life together. "Elise, if you will?"

She tied the ribbon around our wrists, then leaned forward and kissed us each on the cheek. "Not for luck, for you have guidance much more than luck provides, but for joy and happiness." Then she stepped back and raised her voice in a trill that frightened the birds from the tree. Halavant joined in. I didn't care what strange Carani tradition they brought back; I was wedded to Yosyph.

"Katrin," Yosyph whispered. "Forgive me. I must sit."

"Of course you must." I helped him over to the chair, waving aside Halavant, Elise and the guards who'd jumped forward. He was my husband; I would help him many times like this. Once he'd settled in his chair, I settled myself in his lap. "You make a most comfortable seat. I shall sit here the rest of the evening."

"Can't be comfortable with my leg braces digging into you."

"We'll remedy that. Everyone turn around. I'm going to remove his leg braces, and he is shy about showing his legs."

"Katrin, not here, in front of everyone."

"That's why I told them to turn around."

Galliard laughed. "You heard the fiery angel. Turn around."

Chuckles mixed with the rustle of movement.

Yosyph's legs had shrunken over the months of slow wasting, something not even the duri changed. I unbuckled the braces and rearranged his robes. Later, I'd rub them with ointments. So much I could do now. So much I couldn't before.

Our friends filed by to give us hugs and best wishes. My tears mixed with theirs. My cheeks hurt from smiling.

Farid bowed to Yosyph. "You've grown strong in God. If you continue on this path, future generations of Lansimetsians will praise your name as the Kishkarish praise the name of the great sage Akram." He then bowed equally low to me. "You've done what never was done before in our history and learned to *qwaalaar* when you had no born skill to do so. Your courage and love for Yosyph will be a support to him through the years. May you learn to patiently council with him, and your lives will be full of joy."

I nodded. I would try. Patience wasn't my talent. But I would try.

Farid moved on, and Naven embraced the two of us in his long arms. "Yosyph, I'd hoped since we first met you would marry my Tinder Flower."

Hadron, Yosyph's foster-father, patted Yosyph on the back. "This is good. Very good."

Timothy pushed up next to him. "Does this mean I'll be an uncle? Soon, right?"

Yosyph blushed.

I caught Timothy's hand in mine. "Yes, soon as we can."

Halavant came last. He bent over and kissed me on the cheek. "May you have all the joy this world and heaven can bestow." He reached behind me and caught Yosyph in a fierce hug. "My brother, I am happy for you."

And so each friend who'd become family shared in our joy, then moved to the banquet table set up on the other side of the pond. It was a kindness. We were alone as much as we could be away from the safety of the palace, with guards always watching over us.

Yosyph kissed me. "For joy and happiness."

"And for love."

Yosyph sang, his voice as deep as the ocean and rich as a king's ransom.

The sea washes below our feet.
The moon lights your face.
The warped boards of the dock
Drum deeply to our steps.

I stood and spun around him, swishing my desert robes, passing my hands over his shoulders, down his arm and back to his hands. He clutched my hands and sang deeper yet.

Come! Dance! Fill the air,
With the rhythm of our feet.
Leap, spin, away and back.
Held closely in my arms.

He spun me out and pulled me back. I settled into his lap. His arms enfolded me, and his voice washed around me.

The sea pulses like my blood for you,
The moon's but a shadow of your light.
The warped boards of the dock
Drum deeply to our hearts.

I cried, burying my face in his neck. Then I added my quavering voice to his strong.

Come! Dance! Fill the air,
With the rhythm of our feet.
Leap, spin, away and back.
Held closely in my arms.

68

HALAVANT

Manor outside of Fairhaven, Lansimetsa
   Júní 26th

I DIPPED the quill strapped to my hand brace and wrote in large wobbly letters along the blank front page of the Tome: Judges of Lansimetsa

Yosyph, 1ˢᵗ Ruler-Judge of Lansimetsa
Born: 319ᵗʰ year of Lansimetsa's rising from the sea and the 1035ᵗʰ year
of the Kishkarish peace.
Ordained: 338ᵗʰ year. Established the rule of law and of the people.
Married: 338ᵗʰ year. To Lady Katrin of Conborner
Died:

I left it blank. My brother would live to a good old age, as would I.

Elise wrapped her arms around my shoulders. The just-rounding of her belly pressed against my back.

I kissed her hand. "Come, my love. Tomorrow, we'll face our

first day teaching at the academy. And I trust it will be interesting. But tonight, and every night, I am yours."

We unlatched the window and stepped onto the balcony of the manor where a pile of quilts and pillows lay in the warm summer night. Lansimetsa stretched before us, and beyond that Carani. And beside me stood my entire world.

69

EPILOGUE: FIVE YEARS LATER

Letter from Yosyph to Halavant
  Lansimetsa to Carani
  Mars 23rd

Halavant,

The people voted and I'm still ruler-judge. They'll not let me rest.

The voting process was interesting. Everyone, noble and commoner, voted. Instead of a thousand votes, we collected a hundred thousand from all over the land. Once the people had a choice, they didn't sit quietly. It was a confusion of arguments and persuasion. Some raised their voices for me, some for restoring to the rule of a king, and some to overthrow the noble class. If ever I thought we'd fall into anarchy, it was these past few months. When all the votes were gathered, I remained ruler-judge. Most of the prince-judges retained their positions. They've grown to be good and just men.

Do not search long for other cures for my legs. Your wife works wonders, and we could use her skill back in this land.

Though Gaven has returned and his mind and tongue are sharp again, he's frail. Besides, the duri keeps me well. The blacksmith who modified your hand braces so you can grasp also improved my chair so I can wheel around without the help of a servant.

There is another reason I hope you will return soon. Katrin sits in the other room rocking our new baby. We've named him Halavant, as you've already taken our father's name for your son, and I hear my name all too often in my duties. He has our green eyes, Katrin's red hair, and skin as dark as mine.

I must go. Kate wants to play. And, like her mother, she is vivacious and a joy.

I am truly blessed.

May God bless you.

Yosyph

~

IF YOU LIKED *The King's Shadow,* please leave a favorable review, even if it is just a sentence. And please, share with a friend. I created the book, but the story lives through readers like you.

KEEP READING for *Food for Thought* questions.

BOOKS BY M.L. FARB

THE KING TRIALS
The King's Trial (also an audiobook)
The King's Shadow

HEARTH AND BARD TALES
Vasilisa
Fourth Sister
Heartless Hette

HEARTH AND BARD SHORT STORIES
Flight: A Vasilisa Novelette
Birth: A Fourth Sister Novelette
Gift: A Heartless Hette Novelette

FREE SHORT STORY
East of Apollo's Palace

FAMILY AND HUMOR
When I Was a Pie: and Other Slices of Family Life

FOOD FOR THOUGHT

If you had to choose between losing the use of your hands or your legs, what would you choose and how would you have to adapt?

What trials in your life have made you stronger or even made you who you are?

Should a leader ever force their will if they feel it is for the good of the people? Why or why not? If so, when?

Research highlight:

Duri is based on an actual fruit call durian. Its scent is described by some as, "civet, sewage, stale vomit, skunk spray and used surgical swabs."
https://en.wikipedia.org/wiki/Durian#Flavour_and_odour

The upper-land Carani people were based on ancient Assyria. What they did to captives is nightmare inducing. I kept my Carani comparatively mild.

The Carani capital city had hints to the *Hanging Gardens of Babalon*.

The kingdom Lansimetsa has elements of Scandinavia.

- Lansimetsa: Based on Finnish for West Forest (länsi = west and metsä = forest)
- Lausatök: a confusing combination of kicks, open palm strikes, choke holds, and throws. Viking wrestling.
- Dances in Norway: ganger, springar, lausdan, and samdan (see chapter 30)

ACKNOWLEDGEMENTS

Thank you, to my Heavenly Father who blessed me through every step of writing and publishing, and all other areas of my life.

Thank you, to my husband, Jesse, for playing with our children in the evenings so I could write, supporting me in many author events, and being a voice of reason and balance when I felt overwhelmed. You are my hero and best friend.

Thank you, to my six children for begging for stories, putting up with sometimes burnt dinners, and cheering me on. You fill my life with joy.

Thank you, to my beta readers Kimberly King, Melva Gifford, and Morgan Muir for pointing out plot holes and encouraging me to get it right.

Thank you, to my editor, Martha Rasmussen, for finding all the little things that make the difference between a good story and a well-told one.

Thank you, to my cover artist, Rachael Wilkinson. You continue to create beauty wherever you go.

Special thanks to:

- Tori Gollihugh, my angel of a critique partner.
- Rebecca Lamoreaux for saving Katrin.

ABOUT THE AUTHOR

Ever since I climbed up to the rafters of our barn at age four, I've lived high adventure: scuba diving, mud football with my brothers, rappelling, and even riding a retired racehorse at full gallop— bareback. I love the thrill and joy.

Stories give me a similar thrill and joy. I love living through the eyes and heart of a hero who faces his internal demons and the heroine who fights her way free instead of waiting to be saved.

I create adventures, fantasy, fairy tale retellings, and poetry. I live a joyful adventure with my husband and six children. I am a Christian and I love my Savior.

You can contact me at:
mlfarb.author@gmail.com
mlfarbauthor.com
twitter.com/farbml
facebook.com/mlfarbauthor

Made in the USA
Middletown, DE
24 January 2022